QUEEN OF OAK

A Novel of Boudica

MELANIE KARSAK

Clockpunk Press

QUEEN OF OAK: A NOVEL OF BOUDICA
THE CELTIC REBELS SERIES, BOOK 1
Copyright © 2021 Clockpunk Press

Editing by Becky Stephens Editing
Proofreading by Contagious Edits
Cover Art by Damonza

❀ Created with Vellum

For my family…

• MELANIE KARSAK •

QUEEN
• OF •
OAK

• A NOVEL OF BOUDICA •

ISLE OF SKYE

CALEDONIAN CONFEDERACY

BRIGANTES

VOTADINI

PARISII

ÉIRE

SENTAII

MONA

DECEANGLI

CORITANI

NORTHERN ICENI

GREATER ICENI

ORDOVICES

CORNOVII

DEMETAE

SILURES

CATUVELLAUNI

LINDINANTIA

DOBUNNI

ATREBATES

CANTIACI

DUROTRIGES

BELGAE

REGNENSES

CORNOVII

DUMNONII

MAP OF THE CELTIC TRIBES A.D. 42

GLOSSARY

THE NORTHERN ICENI

OAK THRONE
Aesunos, King of the Northern Iceni
Albie, kitchen boy
Balfor, housecarl of Oak Throne
Belenus, druid adviser of the King of the Northern Iceni
Boudica, second daughter of Aesunos
Bran, second son of Aesunos
Brenna, first daughter of Aesunos
Cai, leader of Bran's warriors
Can, brother of Saenuvax
Caturix, eldest son of Aesunos, ruler of Stonea
Children from Oak Throne: Eiwyn, Phelan, and Birgit
Cidna and Nini, cook in Oak Throne and her dog
Conneach, jewel crafter in Oak Throne
Davin, one of Bran's men

Damara, deceased wife of Aesunos

Druda, Boudica's horse

Ector, chief guard of Oak Throne

Egan, father of Aesunos and Saenunos

Foster, Bran's horse

Kennocha, widow in Oak Throne

Moritasgus, stablemaster in Oak Throne

Riona, Brenna and Boudica's maid

Riv, Brenna's horse

Saenunos, brother of Aesunos, chieftain of Holk Fort

Saenuvax, grandfather of Aesunos and Saenunos

Tadhg, stableboy in Oak Throne

Ula, seer in Oak Throne

Varris, warrior of Oak Throne

Ystradwel and Arddun, mother and daughter, helpers to Cidna

Frog's Hollow, village in the territory of the Northern Iceni

Cien, sister of Lynet

Children from Frog's Hollow: Tristan, Henna, Aiden, Kenrick, Aife, Connel, Glyn, and Glenndyn

Gaheris, son of Rolan

Gwyn, deceased sister of Gaheris

Lynet, wife of Rolan and mother of Gaheris

Mavis, Gaheris's hawk

Morfran, Gaheris's raven

Rolan, chieftain of Frog's Hollow

Villagers from Frog's Hollow: Egan, Becan, Turi, Oran, Guennola, Kentigern

The Grove of Andraste

Dôn, High Priestess of the Grove of Andraste
Priestesses of the Grove: Bec, Grainne, Tatha

STONEA, A FORT IN THE LAND OF THE NORTHERN ICENI
Brigthwyna, cook in Stonea
Einion, druid of Stonea
Innis, a stableboy in Stonea

THE GREATER ICENI

VENTA

Ansgar, chief druid of the Greater Iceni
Antedios, ancient king of the Greater Iceni
Ardra, novice druid of the Greater Iceni
Artur, son of Esu
Betha, Ronat, and Pellas, kitchen staff in Venta
Prasutagus, son of King Antedios
Elidir, messenger of the Greater Iceni
Enid, deceased mother of Prasutagus
Esu, deceased first wife of Prasutagus
Galvyn, Prasutagus's housecarl
Ginerva, mother of Esu
Nella, servant in the house of Prasutagus
Raven, Prasutagus's horse

THE ATREBATES

Defeated tribe under Catuvellauni rule
Verica, exiled king of the Atrebates

CHAPTER 1

Blobs of sunlight shimmered down through the canopy of green leaves overhead. I closed my eyes, swaying in my saddle as Druda made his way down the familiar path. Overhead, a dove cooed. The thick blanket of leaves offered much-needed shade from the summer sun. Exhaling deeply, I undid the lace at the top of my jerkin to breathe a little easier. At the end of the road, the forest opened to the village.

Almost there.

The loamy scent of the forest floor, covered by a thick bank of ferns and heated by the morning sun, perfumed the air. The fern fronds twitched, catching Druda's attention. I pulled the horse to a stop.

"A hare," I whispered, reaching for the bow on my back. I grabbed it slowly then pulled an arrow from the quiver. I nocked it then waited.

The ferns shuddered again.

I took aim.

But then...nothing.

Henna laughed. "You *never* remember, Princess."

"I know. I'm so terribly disappointed in myself. Ula, the wisewoman in Oak Throne, tells me I have mud between my ears," I said with a chuckle. "All right. Now, let me see…"

They grinned with anticipation.

"Mustardseed," I said, pointing to Aiden, a boy in the group.

My misnaming set off a peal of laughter.

"And Bluebell," I dubbed Henna in a matter-of-fact tone.

"No, Princess," she said with a laugh.

"No? Well, surely, I remember everyone else correctly. There's Moth, Cobweb, Peaseblossom, Toad, and Puck."

"No, Boudica. No!" Henna cried. All of the children were laughing so hard, two of them fell to the ground.

Lynet, the chieftain's wife, appeared from within one of the houses. She wiped her hands on her apron as she approached us, smiling at me.

I gave her a knowing wink.

I turned to little Tristan, a boy of five who was born without the ability to speak. He grinned at me.

I pointed to the others then shrugged, as if confused by their wild laughs.

He smiled.

Kissing the boy on the head, I pulled him close.

"Have I gotten them all wrong again?" I asked the children.

"Yes, Boudica. Yes, you have!" Henna said.

"Oh, dear. But he is Tristan, right?" I asked, gesturing to the child who beamed a smile up at me.

"Yes! That's right. But what about us?" Henna asked.

"Well, as I said, you are Mustardseed, Bluebell—"

"No, Boudica. No," Henna said with a laugh. "I'm Henna,

and we are Aiden, Kenrick, Aife, Connel, Glyn, and Glenn-dyn," she clarified, pointing to each child.

"Just as I said!" I protested.

At that, they all groaned then laughed heartily once more.

I sighed. "Well, I'll try again next time. It's regrettable, though. I brought some honey treats from Oak Throne, but Cidna, our cook, said I should give them to no one but Mustardseed, Bluebell—"

"Wait, I *am* Bluebell," Henna protested.

"And I am Mustardseed," little Aiden said, the others chiming in after him, giving their false names.

"Ah, you see, I remembered correctly after all. I knew I was right. Very well, then," I said, handing the sweets to the children.

"What do we say to the princess?" Lynet asked.

"Thank you, Princess Boudica," Aiden called.

"May the Great Mother bless you," Henna added, her mouth full, honey juice dripping from the corners.

"Thank you," the others called.

"Now be off with you all," Lynet told them.

Happy with their wins, the children ran back into the village.

I turned to Tristan, handing him the largest piece. He kissed me on the cheek and ran to join the others.

"Thank you for thinking of them, Boudica. Tristan just got over the collywobbles. That should set his stomach straight," Lynet said.

"I'm sorry to hear it. Are the others well?" I asked.

She nodded. "A touch of sickness went through all of Frog's Hollow. I have everyone drinking mint and lemon balm tonics. They're all on the mend now."

"I'm glad to hear it. Please remember, you can always send to Oak Throne if you need anything."

"Thank you." Lynet paused a long moment, studying my face. She smiled softly at me. "He's loading the last of the stones with the other men," she said, gesturing to the other side of the village.

"Sounds like he needs a rescue."

Lynet smiled then stepped toward me, setting her hand on my cheek. "May the Great Mother bless you, Boudica."

"And you, Lynet."

Leading Druda, I made my way down the narrow paths of the forest village until I reached the quarry. Two wagons sat above the deep pit. One was already laden with stones; the second wagon was nearly full. Within the quarry, a dozen more men worked removing the large, flat rocks.

Catching sight of Gaheris, Druda whinnied softly.

Becan, one of the young men in Frog's Hollow, who had been stationed at the wagons, looked up. With a grin, he whistled to Gaheris.

"There's a red-headed faerie queen and her dapple-grey watching us. Look sharp, men."

Gaheris, carrying one end of a heavy stone, his father, Rolan, the other, looked in our direction.

A wide grin spread across his face, but he turned back to his work, moving carefully as he handed off the stone to another pair. Once they were done, Gaheris and Rolan made their way to me.

Both of the men were covered in dust. Gaheris's long, brown hair was powdered grey. His hands, arms, and clothes were coated in dust and dirt. Rolan looked the same.

"Princess," Rolan said, inclining his head to me.

"Merry met, Chieftain."

"Almost done here. We'll be bringing the wagons over to your father tomorrow."

"I'm sure he'll be pleased."

Rolan chuckled, then looked from me to Gaheris. "Although, I suppose you aren't here about the stones."

I grinned. "Haven't you heard? I'm a faerie queen. I'm here to kidnap your son," I said, but my gaze drifted to the crew hard at work. "But it seems there is much work to be done. I can help Lynet in the village instead."

"We got behind with some of the men getting sick," Rolan told me, then turned to Gaheris. "But we have enough help here to have the work finished by nightfall. Why don't you go on," Rolan told his son.

Gaheris paused. "Are you sure, Father?"

Rolan nodded. "But go wash up first. You're a mess, Son."

Gaheris chuckled. "Thank you, Father," he told Rolan, then turned to me. "Come on. I want to show you something."

I nodded to him, then turned to Rolan once more. "Thank you for your hard work, Rolan," I said, looking behind him. "It's a difficult job."

"Nothing worth doing is ever easy, Princess," Rolan said, inclining his head to me, then turned and headed back into the quarry as Gaheris and I turned toward the village.

"Hey, where's Gaheris going?" Becan called. I heard the mirth in his voice.

"With Boudica," Rolan answered.

"Oh, I see. Just like that, he's able to sneak out of work," Becan replied with a good-natured laugh.

"Well, the next time you get a king's daughter to fall in love with you, you're free to go when you like," Rolan replied, making the crew laugh.

7

"It's a good thing Mavis didn't see him first," I said, referring to Gaheris's hawk. "What is it?"

"A raven. He's doing well," Gaheris said, smiling softly as he stroked the little bird's head. "I think he'll make it."

I reached out to gently touch the curious little creature. "Soft little ball of fluff."

"They're clever birds. They're as smart as dogs and will work with you if you can win their loyalty."

"You'll need to think of a name for him."

"*You* name him."

"Me?"

Gaheris nodded.

"Hmm. Let's call him Morfran."

"Morfran?"

"It means 'sea raven.' And it's one of the names of the son of the goddess Cerridwen."

Gaheris nodded. "It's a good name. Hold out your hands," he told me.

Making my hands into a cup, I held perfectly still as Gaheris set the tiny creature into my palm.

"Hello, Morfran," I said, then grinned at Gaheris. "Could be fey, you know."

"It had occurred to me."

"What do you say, Morfran? Are you some fey thing left to trick Gaheris and me?"

The baby bird gave me a tiny chirp.

I giggled.

"Shall I take him back so we can go on?" Gaheris asked.

I nodded, then gently returned the raven to Gaheris, who took him inside.

I returned to Druda, leading him away from the goats. He huffed at me with annoyance.

"Poor you. I won't let you play with the goats all day. Such a terrible life."

When Gaheris returned, he went to retrieve Mountain, his sorrel.

Mountain knickered when he saw Druda.

"Seems our boys are ready. You?" Gaheris asked.

I nodded, then mounted, Gaheris doing the same. Once he was ahorse, he whistled. Then, from overhead, came the reply call of a hawk. I looked up, catching sight of Mavis soaring above the trees.

"Let's go," Gaheris said with a grin, then clicked to Mountain.

We set off for the sea.

IT WAS A SHORT RIDE FROM FROG'S HOLLOW TO THE SEASHORE. The village, hidden in the forest, was ideally situated to enjoy the best of all worlds. The River Mun offered mussels and fish, while the forest offered protection from the sea and a bounty of animal life. The ocean provided more: fish, oysters, birds, and a perfect escape for people who were forbidden to be together—at least, from my father's point of view.

Gaheris and I traveled to our camping spot near a thicket of trees. We watered the horses then tied them loosely, both of them dozing in a shady spot out of the summer sun.

"You ready?" Gaheris asked with a grin.

I checked the beach to make sure we were alone, then nodded.

Gaheris pulled off his boots, trousers, jerkin, and tunic, and with a whoop, rushed toward the water in only his breeches.

Stripping down to my undergarments, I rushed after him.

The sunlight danced across the top of the blue waves, making it sparkle like a thousand fairies danced on the surface. I raced after Gaheris, splashing as I went, then fell backward into the water. My body bobbed and swayed as I floated on the surface. The bright sunlight shimmered down on my face. I squeezed my eyes closed.

I could feel the water swirl as Gaheris approached. He was trying to be sneaky, but I caught the faint sound of his breaths.

I grinned, pretending to be oblivious. I wanted Gaheris to feel triumphant.

But then...nothing.

I opened my eyes, trying to see him in the periphery.

"Gaheris?" I called. "Where did you—"

But no sooner had I spoken when I felt someone grab my waist from underneath the waves.

I yelped then buckled, losing my buoyancy. My head went under for just a moment as I sought to right myself. I squirmed and kicked lightly, breaking the surface of the water once more. Laughing, I wiped the water from my eyes.

"Gaheris," I said with a laugh.

"I have you now, selkie. Sing for me," Gaheris said, lifting me from the water.

"As you command!" I said with a laugh, then began singing in my best-worst singing voice.

"Ah, may the Forest Lord protect me. My ears. Torture me no more," he replied with a laugh.

Still singing louder, throwing in a "you have to stop me," as I continued belting out a random array of notes that sent a small flock of seagulls on the beach nearby squawking away.

Disturbed from his nap, Druda whinnied at me.

Gaheris set his lips on mine, stopping my torturous song with

Ula huffed a laugh. "Of course. And does the king know you were that way?"

"What do you think?"

Ula chuckled then began breaking one of the mushrooms into pieces, adding the bits to her bowl of herbs.

"Ula, what is the greenwood warning of?" I asked.

Ula motioned for me to be silent. She closed her eyes and whispered in a low voice. When she opened them again, she tossed a handful of herbs and mushrooms into the center fire pit. They sizzled and sparked green. A cloud of pungent smoke filled the little space.

Ula raised her hands. "Sacred Mother. Forest Lord. I call upon you. By earth, air, water, and fire, I call. The earth is whispering. Something is coming. Show me," she said, then tossed the herbal concoction into the fire once more.

I suppressed a cough as the cloud billowed once more. But this time, I felt dizzy. I swayed.

Lifting a feather, Ula waved the smoke from the fire over the spiral she'd laid out on the ground, her hands dancing over the symbol. "Ancient Mother, show me..." Ula whispered. "Ancient Father, show me..."

I stared at the spiral. Then, after a moment, it seemed to me that it was moving, spinning.

Once more, Ula threw the herbs into the flames. Using her feather, she traced the spiral in the air. "By earth," she whispered, pausing above the moss. "By air," she said over a black feather. "By fire," she said, hovering over a small pot filled with orange embers. "And by water," she added, hovering over a clay cup filled with water. "Show me what is coming."

I swooned, my head feeling heavy.

"Show me..." she said, lifting a rattle and giving it a shake. She lifted her feather high into the air then let it spiral down.

The moment it touched the floor, a piercing cry shot through my head. I covered my ears with my hands. Strange images danced before my mind. An eagle soared above the water, the stars reflecting on the dark sea. Waves broke on the sand, the water tinged with blood. Then, I saw a red-haired man—horns growing from his head—standing beside a fire. A woman wielding twin swords, her face painted blue, a fox tail pinned in her blonde hair, let out a battle cry. Once more, the eagle screeched, the sound so loud I thought my skull might crack. Huffing heavily, I fell over.

Everything went black.

❦

I WOKE, I DIDN'T KNOW HOW LONG LATER, TO FIND ULA SITTING on the bench beside her table smoking her long pipe. She stared into the flames. She had propped me up against a sack of turnips. The scent of smoke still lingered in the air.

"Banshees be cursed," I said, holding my aching head. "What happened?"

Ula turned to me. "What did you see?"

I shook my head. "I don't know. A mess of things." The vision was already fading as I struggled to remember. "What did *you* see?"

"Nothing good," she said, turning back to the flames.

I followed her gaze. "Eagles," I said. "Their cries deafened me. And there were people I don't know. A man with red hair. A blonde-haired woman painted with woad. It doesn't make any sense."

"Of course not. You have the sight of a druid and the talent of a goat herd."

I frowned at her. "That is not my fault, and you know it."

"Belenus is as dry as last summer's apples. You should go to Dôn, like your mother," Ula said, referring to the high priestess of the Grove of Andraste where my mother once served as a priestess.

"Rolan will come tomorrow to ask for my hand for Gaheris."

"You should go to Dôn."

I sighed, then rose, my head swimming when I did so. "Where I need to go is the roundhouse. I was already late when I got back to Oak Throne. Now, I am twice as late, thanks to your mushroom smoke."

Ula puffed smoke from between her lips. "You are in the May of life, seeing yourself queen of Frog Hollow. But dark times are before us. You must make ready, or when you finally learn the meaning of what the gods have shown you, it will be too late."

"Now, that is very fatalistic," I told her with a wry grin, which made her smile.

"Boudica," she said, then shook her head. "It's no use. You're as stubborn as your uncle and the stupidest of Damara's children. Be off with you."

"You're welcome for the mushrooms."

"They were not from you. You were only the messenger."

"Really? And did the faerie people climb off Druda, scour the forest floor, get their hands dirty picking them, sweat in the summer sun, then lug the stinky things from the Wash and back to get them to you?"

Ula chuckled lightly. "Good night, Boudica."

"Good night," I replied, then paused at the door. I turned back to her. "Ula, I do not wish to be ignorant if the gods have something to say, but I don't understand the visions I saw. Do they... Do the gods want me to go to

Dôn?" I asked, my heartbeat quickening in fear of her reply.

Ula stared into the fire. She puffed her pipe then set it aside, blowing smoke from her lips. "The little people are whispering."

"I *will* marry Gaheris. But if the gods are speaking…"

"The gods demand nothing. It is the greenwood whispering, Boudica. They are another voice entirely and one you should learn to hear. Already, they call to you, but you are too thick to hear. If you do not heed them, then…"

"Then?"

Ula tilted her head as if to listen. For a moment, I saw strange, fleeting shadows around her. "Then they will send someone to help."

I grinned. "I like the sound of that."

Ula shook her pipe at me. "Beware of faerie gifts."

"Like the mushrooms?"

"Those came from *you*, remember?"

"Good night, Ula."

She waved for me to go on.

Feeling unsettled, I turned and went back outside, ducking under the talismans once more as I exited. Leading Druda by his reins, I turned toward our roundhouse. While Ula's cloud of smoke was gone, the weight of it still lingered in my mind and heart. And despite my words, I could not shake the sense of dread.

CHAPTER 4

After taking Druda back to the stables, I headed toward the entrance of the roundhouse. The guards nodded to me then stepped aside. Within, I followed the hallway to the main chamber at the center of the house. The smoke from the large, central firepit drifted upward toward the hole in the ceiling. Tall oak beams supported the massive thatched roof that covered our home. Deer antlers hung from the ornately carved beams. Images of the Forest Lord, animals, and winding oak limbs had been carved on the beams. Rich furs covered the stone floor.

My sister Brenna and the druid, Belenus, sat on the cushioned benches near the central fire. Brenna held her lyre. As she plucked the notes, Belenus nodded.

"Very good. Now this," the druid said, playing a melody on his own instrument.

Brenna followed suit, copying him.

I went to the table and poured myself a glass of wine, sitting down with a tired huff. Ula's mushroom smoke still had my head reeling.

A moment later, my brother Caturix appeared from the back, a sour look on his face.

"Where have you been all day?" he asked, joining me as he poured himself a glass.

"Riding."

Caturix was looking for a fight. I could see it in his eyes.

He frowned. "Your nose is sunburnt."

"It was sunny," I said with a shrug.

"You should be here learning the lyre, like Brenna. Your sister is learning how to be a proper lady. Instead, you are out in the forest every day like some damned wild thing."

"She's part dryad," Bran, my other brother, said as he entered the room. "She has to return to her tree each day, or her lifeforce will fade," he added, giving me a wink.

Bran helped himself to a round of bread, poured himself some ale, then sat down.

"Don't encourage her," Caturix said seriously. "Without Mother, Boudica has been left untamed. She's too free."

Bran shrugged. "She likes to ride. What of it? The goddess Epona inspires our sister. Who is to say there is anything wrong with it?"

Caturix frowned. "There is nothing wrong with riding. It's where she's going that poses the problem."

I glared at Caturix. "Why don't you concern yourself with your own affairs?" I said waspishly. "Isn't your upcoming marriage enough to keep you preoccupied?"

Caturix set his goblet down hard, letting it splash out. "Everything we do reflects on the family, Boudica. Everything. We are not free to just do what we want. Remember that," he said, then turned and left the hall.

I shook my head. Caturix was never easy to deal with. But, these days, he was a hundred times worse.

Bran dropped down into a chair. "Must be wedding nerves."

I raised an eyebrow at my brother.

We both laughed.

If there was anything Caturix was not, it was nervous. My elder brother *always* knew what was correct, what was best for the family. It seemed to me that Caturix didn't care who he was actually marrying—the girl made no difference to him. He was simply doing what was right, as he thought the rest of us should do. Bran and I were hopeless in his eyes. Brenna, in the least, had some redeeming qualities. Except for the fact that my sister would rather go to Mona to train as a bard than be wed to some random king.

I eyed Brenna. Our maid had woven her hair neatly. Half of her long, auburn tresses were lying perfectly curled on her chest. The rest of her curly locks were neatly braided and piled into a bun on top of her hair. She wore a pretty, plum-colored gown that was belted at the waist and bunched at the shoulders with ornate silver pins. I didn't remember my mother well, but Brenna was the very reflection of her from what I could remember.

Paying us no mind, Brenna kept her concentration on Belenus's instruction. The hall filled with the sweet sound of her lyre music.

My gaze shifted to Bran. Like Brenna, he had curly auburn locks. The long curls fell over his eyes, getting in the way as he scanned across the table for something else to eat. Only my hair took on the full sheen of fire red that lingered as mere highlights in Bran's and Brenna's locks. Caturix's hair was black, as our father's had been when he was young.

I sighed, then rose.

"Where are you going?" Bran asked.

"Caturix put me in a bad mood. I'm going outside."

"Don't let him unnerve you," Bran said, then lowered his voice. "How is Gaheris, anyway?"

I leaned closer to my brother. "When Rolan comes with the flagstones tomorrow, he will ask father's permission for Gaheris and me to wed."

"Shite," Bran said.

"Shite? What? Why?"

"If father agrees, they'll start looking for someone for me. By the way, have you seen Bec recently?" he asked, ripping off a hunk of bread and shoving it in his mouth.

Bec was one of the priestesses at the Grove of Andraste, the holy seat in the Northern Iceni lands. Led by the high priestess, Dôn, Bec and a small group of women lived and served at the grove, a sacred place dedicated to the Dark Lady. Our mother had been a priestess there before she and our father had wed. Quite by accident, Bec and my brother saw something in one another. Over these past two years, the attraction between them had grown into something more. I strongly suspected my brother loved the priestess but was afraid to admit it. It would take both Dôn and Father assenting to a match between them. His chances were more impossible than mine.

I shook my head. "I haven't been to the grove in many weeks."

"I was there today," Bran told me. "Dôn sent a boy to ask for some supplies. I took them over."

I cocked an eyebrow at my brother. "Indeed?"

Bran nodded thoughtfully. "In-deed," he said in a singsong. "With eyes as deep and dark as a river...Bec."

I leaned toward Bran. "Let us both pray that Brenna finds a

king. If we can wed her and Caturix well enough, Father may leave us alone."

"Father may, but Uncle will not," Bran said with a frown.

My expression soured, matching my brother's. Our uncle, Saenunos, was an ambitious creature. With no children of his own, he was far too interested in our fates. Determined the family stay in power, Saenunos would stop at nothing. His bullying often caused a rift between him and our father. And many times, I could see in Saenunos's eyes that he wished himself to be the king of the Northern Iceni.

"May the Morrigu eat Saenunos's ambitious heart," I said with a frown. "Now I'm twice as annoyed. Thank you, Brother."

Bran laughed. "Sorry."

Leaving him, I slipped through the back of the house into the kitchens. There, I was met by Nini, our cook's dog.

"Nini-Nini-Nini-Nini," I sang, ruffling the dog's ears. She danced around me happily.

"Boudica, why are you always underfoot? I'm in here sweating in the heat to get your supper on the table, and you're singing like a lark," Cidna, our cook, grumbled at me.

"Want me to bring you a cold ale?" I asked with a grin.

Cidna paused. "That would be a good way to make yourself useful."

Grinning, I headed to the back of the kitchens and into the dark storage area. It was significantly cooler there. I poured the cook the most enormous tankard I could find then went back into the kitchen, setting the mug on the end of her counter.

"Here you are, m'lady," I said, bowing to her.

Cidna laughed. Wiping the sweat off her brow with her arm, she lifted the tankard and drank, and drank, and drank. When she was done, she exhaled deeply.

"Now my eyes be crossed," she said with a loud laugh.

I chuckled. "That's what you get for drinking too fast. Best keep those crossed eyes on the supper. If you scald the cream, Caturix will complain."

"I serve food fit for a king's table, and I still hear Caturix grumbling. I hope that princess of his has better cooks than me."

"I'll tell him you said so."

"You'd better not, or your brother will have my tongue."

I laughed. "I could never risk you, Cidna," I said, giving her a kiss on the cheek as I stole a hunk of cheese from the workbench.

"I saw that."

"Saw what?" I asked. "Come on, Nini. You'll get too fat sitting in the kitchen eating scraps all day. You need a run," I said, then headed toward the back door.

"An hour. No more, Boudica, or they'll send the whole house looking for you."

"That long? Bran's out there picking over what's on the table already."

"Oof," Cidna said in frustration. "He'll be full before the dinner is served."

"Bran is never full."

Cinda laughed. "Well, that's true."

I chuckled then slipped out the back door, Cidna's wiry-haired dog following behind me.

We exited out the back of the house, the chickens squawking loudly as Nini wandered by. The dog, however, knew her limits and left the creatures alone. We made our way into the fenced horse pasture. Grabbing a fallen stick, I tossed the branch for Nini to retrieve until the dog—who really spent far too much time eating scraps—had her fill of entertainment.

Taking her stick with her, she scampered back into the kitchens.

Chuckling, I made my way to the stables.

Druda spent a lot of time in the sun today. While I knew the stable hands would treat him well, I also knew he was likely to drink half his weight in water. Of course, no one knew I'd ridden to the coast, so they wouldn't be expecting him to be extra thirsty.

When I arrived, I found the stables quiet. I opened the door just a crack, slipped inside, then closed the door behind me. All the horses had been fed and put in their stalls. Several of the horses turned to look when I arrived. Bran's young gelding, Foster, knickered at me. I made my way down the line, giving all of them a pat until I reached Druda's stall. As I suspected, he was out of water.

"Glutton," I told him.

Grabbing two buckets, I slipped out the back door and went to the well. It took me a few hauls of water to finally finish filling both buckets. I brought them back inside, sliding into Druda's stall to pour water into his trough.

Setting the buckets aside, I grabbed a brush and began brushing the animal down.

At the front of the stable, I heard the door slide open.

I stilled a moment.

"There is no one here," I heard a masculine voice whisper. The sound was barely audible from where I was at the back of the stables.

A stall door creaked open and closed. I made out the sound of soft, murmuring voices, but I couldn't see or hear anyone clearly. Had some damned thief slipped into the barn? Setting the brush aside, I slowly pulled the knife I wore on my belt. I would slip out the back of the stables and raise the guard.

But then, I heard…

The sound of kisses and soft moans emanated from one of the stalls.

I bit my bottom lip, suppressing a giggle.

Not thieves.

Lovers.

Quietly slipping my knife back into its sheath, I moved as quickly as I could out of the stall. But Druda, reluctant to let me stop brushing him, huffed then knickered, bumping into me, causing me to knock down one of the buckets.

The sound of the lovers halted.

Moving as fast as I could, I dashed out the back door of the stall and slipped into the night, rushing to the well. I knelt down, hiding in the darkness. A moment later, the door opened a crack as someone looked outside.

"No one," a masculine voice replied. "Must have been the horses."

Then, realization washed over me.

Moving slowly, I looked around the side of one of the buckets sitting at the side of the well in time to see Caturix slide the stable door closed behind him.

CHAPTER 5

S tunned, I made my way slowly back to our roundhouse. Caturix had always been sullen and taken with moods, but his attitude had been sharper than ever these last few months. Now I knew why. He had a lover here at Oak Throne. No wonder he looked far more agitated than happy about his impending marriage. He already had someone else.

Why hadn't he said anything?

Why didn't he tell Father no?

Maybe the liaison wasn't serious, but if it was, the answer to why he kept it secret was clear. What use was it? No one in Oak Throne would be good enough for my brother, who would one day be king of the Northern Iceni. Any protest my brother may have made—though I knew he had made none— would have been useless. My father needed Caturix wed to someone important to cement our power.

My uncle, Saenunos, lived in perpetual fear that King Antedios of the Greater Iceni would come for our lands. While the Northern Iceni and the Greater Iceni had always kept an amicable relationship, Uncle Saenunos was convinced that King Antedios, and his son, Prasutagus, would turn on us at any moment.

It wasn't impossible.

The Catuvellauni tribe had done it to their neighbors. As their father had done to the Trinovantes, the current rulers of the Catuvellauni, Caratacus and Togodumnus, warred on the Atrebates. They had ousted the Atrebates' king, Verica, and taken over his lands. It was whispered that Verica had fled south to the Romans for protection. That was news that sent a shiver through every tribe. No one wanted Rome to return. No one wanted Rome to remember we existed.

Out of fear of such an incursion, my father had arranged Caturix's marriage to Princess Melusine of the Coritani, giving us a powerful ally to the north.

With everything at stake, there was nothing Caturix could have said. His fate was sealed, lover or no.

May the Great Mother protect me from my father or uncle finding such use for me.

I made my way back to the roundhouse. The dining hall was empty except for Belenus. Still lost in my thoughts, I sat down by the fire near him.

"Your thoughts are so loud, I can almost hear them," the druid told me with a soft laugh.

I looked up at him. "Belenus, how did my father come to marry my mother? She was only a priestess. Why did Grandfather ever permit it?"

"Your mother came from Mona to serve in the Grove of Andraste. She was no simple priestess. She was the daughter of our Arch Druidess. Your father did not wed her for political alliances; he wed her to tie himself more closely to my order, winning the support of the druids—and the gods."

"My grandmother was the Arch Druidess of Mona? How did I not know this?"

Belenus nodded. "Rian. That was her name. Alas, she is gone now."

"Then my parents didn't marry for love?"

Belenus paused. "There was affection between them, yes, or your mother would not have agreed to the marriage."

I paused. I'd known that my mother was a priestess at the Grove of Andraste, but I hadn't known she'd been born on Mona. Nor had I known she was the daughter of the Arch Druidess. I was only five when our mother, Damara, died. Out of all of us, only Caturix remembered her well, but he spoke little of her.

"Do I have a grandfather somewhere? Who was my mother's father?"

"Your mother was the child of the Beltane fires, the offspring of a greenwood marriage."

"Why did no one ever tell us she'd come from Mona?"

Belenus smiled, but more to himself than at me. "Perhaps, no one thought it mattered. Brenna has the stirrings of the bardic blood, but as the eldest daughter, it would be difficult for her to walk the green path. Neither of your brothers hear the call. As for you," he said, raising an eyebrow at me. "The gods whisper your name, Boudica, and the greenwood has hovered around you since you were a girl. In fact, your mother cast many spells upon you to protect you from the eyes of the Otherworld. But I think your heart is already given to a man, not the gods. Am I right?"

I stared at the druid. "I... Yes."

Belenus nodded slowly. "Then there is nothing more to be said. Perhaps you will have a child who will be called to the old ways."

A moment later, Cidna appeared carrying a large tray, one of the kitchen boys following behind her.

"Here we are," she told us. "No scalded cream," she added, tossing me a wink. "Set down your trays, Albie, then go see that the king is told that dinner is served."

"Yes, Cidna," the little boy said, working quickly. He finished his work then shot off to fetch Father.

I rose, setting my hand on Belenus's shoulder. "Thank you for telling me."

Belenus patted my hand. "You have your mother's spirit, Boudica. You always have. Your father is wrong not to speak more of Damara. Your mother was very special."

"Thank you, Belenus. I'll fetch Brenna," I said, then left the main chamber, winding down the hall to the room I shared with my sister.

Our small chamber had two beds, a wardrobe for our things, two benches, and some other small trinkets my sister and I had accumulated. Within, I found Brenna placing her lyre back into its case.

"The evening meal is ready. Where's Bran?" I asked.

"Father sent him on an errand."

Brenna eyed my expression. "What is it?"

"Did you know our mother was the daughter of the Arch Druidess of Mona?"

"Where did you hear this?"

"Belenus."

Brenna looked back at her lyre case. "Belenus always said my talent for music comes from Mother. I never really thought about Mother's family. I just assumed…"

"She was a foundling? An orphan?"

Brenna nodded. "Yes."

"As did I."

"I suppose it makes no difference now."

"How can you say that?"

"What does it matter? She is a ghost to us, and her influence here is no stronger than a light breeze. We are our father's children. We will do and go where our father wishes."

"But we have the blood of druids in our veins. Brenna, it's no wonder you are so skilled with the lyre. Tell Father you want to go to Mona to train with the bards."

She laughed then shook her head. "What's the use of creating conflict?"

"Brenna," I said with irritation.

"Mother is dead. Who she was doesn't matter. Father will decide our fates."

"I can't accept that. Maybe if you reminded Father that Mother was born on Mona, he would listen about sending you to the bards."

"I will wed for the good of the tribe. You know that. As will Caturix, and Bran, and you. We serve the tribe first, before ourselves. How many times have you heard father say that? Our duty is to the tribe; our own will comes second."

"Ugh," I said, throwing up my hands. "You and Caturix sound the same. We have our own hearts and minds. Those count too."

"No. First, we are Northern Iceni."

"You sound like Father."

"That is exactly my point."

"My head hurts," I told my sister. In one day, I had learned Gaheris would ask for my hand, Ula had filled my nose with mushroom smoke, I'd discovered Caturix had a lover, and I found out that my grandmother had been an Arch Druidess, not that anyone seemed to care.

"It will hurt worse if Cidna discovers we let the meat get

cold," Brenna told me. "Don't let this news trouble you, Boudica," Brenna said, setting her hand on my shoulder. "I love what few memories I have of our mother, but who she was makes no difference in our lives anymore. Besides, you have your own life and future ahead of you."

"Yes."

My sister smiled at me. "Gaheris has the sweetest heart and loves you dearly. I confess, I'm jealous."

"Maybe you should beat up a chieftain's son and force him to love you too."

Brenna chuckled. "Even Father laughed that day."

"Well, Gaheris should not have insulted my horse."

"I suspect he learned his lesson. You were what, eight years old?"

I nodded.

Brenna smiled. "Some loves are meant to be. As for the rest of us… I can only hope my husband will not be too old or too ugly."

I laughed, but she was right. "Pray to the Great Mother. She will listen to you. After all, you are the granddaughter of the Arch Druidess of Mona."

"For all the good it has ever done me," Brenna replied. "Come on," she said, taking my hand and leading me from the room. "Who knows," Brenna added as we went. "Perhaps someone will come to Stonea and catch my eye."

"Be sure to beat him senseless."

"Oh, Boudica," Brenna replied, then laughed.

CHAPTER 6

When we entered the dining hall, we found Aesunos, Bran, and Caturix already gathered.

I eyed my father over. His long, silver-and-black hair had been neatly groomed, and his emerald-green robes were tidy, but he did not look well. He had dark rings under his ice-blue eyes, and he looked pale. He narrowed his gaze at Brenna and me, his brow scrunching. With a wave of his hand, he motioned for Brenna and me to sit. "We waited for you."

"Our apologies, Father," Brenna said, taking a seat beside Caturix.

Caturix frowned at me but gave no warning glance to Brenna. Of course he would assume it was my fault we were late.

"Caturix, have you seen to everything I asked?" Father asked sharply, motioning for the servants to fill his plate.

"Yes, Father. All will be ready in time."

Scowling, Father poured himself a goblet of wine. "Saenunos sent word. He will leave King's Lynn and meet us in Stonea."

No one said anything. None of us looked forward to spending any extra time in Saenunos's presence. His constant sniping and war-mongering grew weary. Half the time, he and Father quarreled. The last time we had been together at King's Lynn, the argument had grown so heated that father packed us all up and left.

Seeking to turn the conversation, my sister asked, "Shall Boudica and I arrange a bridal gift for Princess Melusine?"

When Father didn't answer, Belenus said, "It is common for the women of one family to welcome the other with a gift. The princess's mother is dead, and she has no female relatives. I am sure the gesture will be appreciated."

Brenna nodded. "Very well. We will see to it tomorrow."

"How long will we stay in Stonea?" Bran asked.

"I shall see Caturix and Melusine settled there," Father said. "And I will make sure the construction is coming along as I have dictated."

So, weeks.

Bran frowned but said nothing.

Stonea Fort sat to the west where our lands met those of the Catuvellauni tribe. Situated deep in the misty fens, Stonea had once been ruled by my grandfather's brother. After his death, the fortress had fallen into disrepair. Since the spring, men had gone between Oak Throne and Stonea seeing to the renovations.

"Rolan will be here tomorrow to deliver the flagstones," Father told Caturix. "I trust you've made the other purchases needed."

"Yes, Father."

"Good," my father replied stiffly then turned back to his meal.

I eyed my father for a long moment. They said my father used to be the mirthful sort. I had fleeting memories of him from when I was a girl, his tangle of long, black hair falling over me as he tickled me until I screamed with laughter. In my mind, I saw him happy, smiling. But those were old memories. Now, everything was transactional. The man from those recollections was gone, as intangible as my mother. We were all something to be traded. I could only hope my worth as a second daughter measured to the value of a chieftain's son. Aesunos had never encouraged the relationship between Gaheris and me. He had forbidden me from riding to Frog's Hollow to visit Gaheris. It was not anything Gaheris had done wrong. It was more a matter of who else might be out there for me. If my uncle and father could find a more strategic match, then my lifelong love for Gaheris meant nothing.

What my father didn't understand was that I would marry no one but Gaheris. I would leave before suffering a fate I hadn't chosen. Lynet's tribe lived far to the north. There, Gaheris and I could make our way by the sweat of our brows.

I only hoped it didn't come to that. It would hurt me too much to leave my siblings—even Caturix.

We ate the rest of the meal in silence.

As soon as he was finished, Father rose. "There is much work to be done tomorrow. Boudica, no more riding the whole day long. You are not Epona herself. Understood?"

"Yes, Father," I said dutifully, mindful not to make trouble knowing Rolan would come tomorrow.

"Belenus," my father said, waving for the druid to follow him.

Leaving what was left of his meal aside, the druid rose, following my father.

As he walked away, I noticed that Father was limping.

"His leg is bothering him today," Brenna whispered to us. "That's why he is in such a foul mood. He barely left his meeting room the whole day."

"Easy enough to spout orders from there. He had me chasing all manner of things today. I even had to send some men to Venta to get what he wanted," Caturix added, referring to the capital city of the Greater Iceni.

"Seems like he's building Stonea to suit himself," Bran said. "Don't be surprised, Brother, if he tries to take your fort."

Caturix huffed a laugh. "You will not be rid of him that easily. When we went to Stonea in the spring, Father was furious when he saw the condition of the fort. When he discovered the villagers had been keeping pigs in the hall, old Arturus almost lost his head," Caturix said, referring to the chieftain who had been in charge of Stonea.

"How nice for the pigs," I quipped.

"Nice for the pigs, but not nice for Arturus and his family. Father banished them from Stonea and put another man in charge," Caturix said.

Brenna set her hand on Caturix's arm. "Everything is well in hand now. Don't worry, Brother. No doubt, you and Melusine will have your new home ready in no time."

"Just in time for your neighbors to stir up trouble," Bran said.

Caturix nodded. Seating Caturix in Stonea on the Catuvellauni border was intended to remind the ruling Catuvellauni brothers, Caratacus and Togodumnus, that the Northern Iceni were not to be trifled with. Much would depend on my brother's ability to keep good relations with the pair—if it was possible. At least for now, the brothers seemed mainly concerned with subduing the Atrebates.

Caturix frowned. "If there is one good thing about Stonea, it's that no one can find it in the mist. You can't attack a fort you can't find."

"All the same, you will have to make nice with Caratacus and Togodumnus," Bran said.

"When did you become a politician?" Caturix asked, irritation in his voice.

"You're right. I cannot think of a task less suited for me," Bran replied with a laugh.

Caturix scowled. "You and Boudica are one in the same, too wild and free for your own good. Your days of roaming around the countryside free to do as you like will soon come to a close."

Bran rolled his eyes at Caturix.

"The turmoil with the Catuvellauni aside, I think it sounds romantic," Brenna said sweetly, redirecting the conversation. "You and Melusine will be alone, free to enjoy your time with one another in your misty land where you'll begin your new life."

"Romantic," Caturix said stiffly. "That is a fool's daydream." Grabbing a jug of wine, Caturix rose and left the dining hall.

Brenna looked down at her plate. Unshed tears welled in her eyes.

"Father is not the only one who is waspish today," Bran said.

"Ignore him," I told my sister.

Brenna nodded sadly then asked, "Does he not wish to marry the princess? I don't understand. She sounds lovely."

Bran shrugged. "Aesunos and Saenunos made the arrangement. Caturix had no say."

"But Belenus speaks so well of Melusine," Brenna said.

"Belenus is old. Every young woman is a charming beauty to him," Bran said with a laugh. "In reality, she may be as ugly as old Ula."

"Leave Ula out of this," I told Bran.

Bran chuckled.

"Perhaps Caturix hoped to wed for love," Brenna said.

Bran laughed. "I doubt that. Nothing ever lives up to Caturix's expectations, that's all."

Suddenly feeling uncomfortable with the knowledge of what I had seen, and very aware that Bran could read *any* secret on my face, I rose.

"I'm tired. I'll see you all tomorrow," I said.

"Oh, yes. I'm sure you've had a *very* tiring day," Bran goaded knowingly.

"What do you mean?" Brenna asked, looking from Bran to me. "Where did you go today?"

"Yes, Boudica. Where *did* you go today?" Bran chimed in, setting his chin on his hands, giving me a knowing grin.

"Riding."

"Riding where?" Brenna asked.

"Riding who?" Bran added.

"Bran!" Brenna scolded.

"I said good night," I told them again, giving Bran a scowl, then left.

I made my way down a side hall to the chamber I shared with my sister. There, I found Riona, our maid, readying the brazier for the night.

"Hot today, Princess, but the night air is already cooling," she told me. "I have your things laid out for tomorrow."

I looked to see a pair of riding breeches and a fresh tunic sitting on a bench nearby.

"Would you mind setting out the lavender-colored gown instead?" I asked, going to the basin to wash my face.

"Of course. And *why* do you want your best gown?"

"Just…because."

"Oh, Boudica. I know well enough when you are up to something."

"Who? Me?"

Riona laughed. "Yes. You. Now, come to think of it, I did hear the king say that Rolan was coming tomorrow. You suppose that good-looking son of his will be with him?"

"I wouldn't know a thing about it."

"Liar."

I laughed.

Riona shook out the pale purple dress and laid it longways to get out the wrinkles. "I'll be back in the morning to fix your hair. Suppose I should see if we can find some flowers hereabouts to weave in that wild mane of yours?"

"Wouldn't hurt to spruce things up a bit."

Riona laughed. "Ah, Boudica. I'll pray to the Great Mother that she brings you what you want."

"How do you know what I want?" I asked her teasingly.

"I was a young woman once too," Riona replied with a laugh. "I remember very well what young women want. Good night, Princess."

I followed her to the door, waving goodbye.

I was about to turn back when the door to the chamber across from mine opened to reveal Caturix.

I frowned at him. "You hurt Brenna's feelings."

"And?"

Frustrated, I glared at him.

He sighed heavily. "I'll make amends."

"Good," I said then turned to go back inside. After a moment, I paused, looking back at my brother. But what could I say? I knew Caturix well enough to know that he would be furious if he knew I had discovered his secret. "We all wish you happiness, Brother," I finally told him. "I hope you know that."

Caturix met and held my gaze. After a moment, he huffed, then turned and closed the door behind him.

Sighing, I went back inside. Changing from my riding clothes, I made ready for bed then slid under my covers.

When I closed my eyes, I could still feel the warmth of the sun on my face and the taste of Gaheris's lips. I centered my thoughts on him, drowning out the noise about everything else. In the end, my own life was waiting for me. I'd soon be Gaheris's queen of oak. Nothing else in the world truly mattered.

CHAPTER 7

I woke the following day to the sound of Brenna humming as she got dressed. When she realized I was awake, she sat down on the end of my bed.

"Does the fact that Rolan is coming today have anything to do with why your best dress laid out?" she asked.

"I was in Frog's Hollow yesterday. Rolan will speak with Father when he comes today."

Brenna's eyebrows arched in surprise, her hazel eyes, a match of my own, twinkling. "Boudica! What good news."

"I suppose that depends on what Aesunos answers."

"He will say yes," Brenna said with a nod. "Father is practical...too practical at times. But his practicality will serve you. Rolan is the most important chieftain in our lands and controls the biggest village aside from Oak Throne. Having you wed to Gaheris will secure our hold there. For that reason alone, he cannot say no."

I smiled lightly. "I hope you are right."

Brenna pushed a strand of my red hair behind my ear. "I am glad for you, Sister. Now, get up. Riona will be here soon,"

Brenna said, jabbing me with her sharp fingers. "Two weddings," she said, then rose, lifting the gown and giving it a shake. "That is a good thing."

"Let's not get ahead of ourselves."

"We'll see."

"Brenna, is there anyone in Oak Throne who…" I began to ask, but I already knew the answer. Brenna was not like me. She would not put her heart where she was not permitted.

"No," my sister said, then set down the dress. "What good would it do me? Already, my heart pines for Mona. I don't need two things to mourn."

A moment later, there was a knock on the door.

"Boudica? Brenna?"

It was Riona.

The maid entered, a clutch of purple and blue flowers in her hands. She grinned at me. "All right, let me at you."

⚓︎

BY THE TIME THE MORNING MEAL WAS READY, RIONA AND BRENNA had me looking as bright as a May Queen. My long, wild red locks were properly untangled, braided, and adorned with flowers. Brenna and I joined the others in the dining hall.

When Bran saw me, he opened his mouth to say something, but I gave him a warning look, silencing him.

Caturix, lost in his thoughts, said nothing.

"Good morning, Father," I said, settling in beside him.

My father gave me a passing glance. "You look very fine this morning, Boudica."

"Thank you."

"Father," Brenna said, giving our father a kiss on the cheek.

"Brenna," he said, patting her hand absently. "Caturix,

when you're done, go down to the river and make sure Liam has the boats out. He's been lingering half the morning these days," Father said sharply.

"Yes, Father," Caturix replied.

"I want those horses ready to go first thing tomorrow morning, Bran. Go to the stables and see it's arranged."

"I spoke to Moritasgus yesterday," Bran said, referring to our stablemaster. Moritasgus was more than competent, but Aesunos seemed particularly irksome today. I suddenly started to worry. Perhaps this wasn't the best day for Rolan's inquiry.

"Talk to him again," Father replied tartly.

A moment later, Balfor, our housecarl, appeared. "Your Highness," he said, bowing.

"What is it?"

"Rolan and the men from Frog's Hollow are here with the stones."

"Good. At least someone knows how to get up before the sun and work hard. Caturix," he said, motioning sharply for my eldest brother to follow him. Together, the pair of them made their way outside.

Father was limping again.

"Come on," Brenna said, tugging my arm. "We'll go together. That way, he will not wonder."

Brenna and I rose, following Father and Caturix.

"Bran," Brenna hissed sharply.

Bran, whose cheeks were stuffed with food, looked up. "What?"

"Are you joking? Come on."

Clapping off his hands, Bran joined us.

When we stepped outside the great roundhouse, I spotted two wagons. Rolan, Gaheris, and half a dozen men from Frog's

Hollow waited.

Gaheris was dressed nicely, wearing his leather jerkin and a heather-grey tunic, his long, chestnut-brown hair neatly combed. His father was also more finely dressed than usual, wearing his multi-colored cape pinned at the shoulder.

"Well met, King Aesunos," Rolan said, bowing.

Gaheris followed his father's lead.

Brenna, Bran, and I joined our father, who gave us a passing glance.

"Two loads, My King," Rolan said, turning back to the wagons. "We paid attention to color and shape as best we could.

Aesunos went to the wagons to examine the stones.

"The river was reluctant to give them to us. Kept flooding. But we made our prayers to Lady Mun, and the waters calmed," Rolan told him.

Father smiled for the first time this morning. "Very good. Very well done, Rolan. What say you, Caturix?"

"No finer stones. Thank you, Rolan," my elder brother said.

Father's gaze drifted to Gaheris. "Help your father?"

Gaheris nodded to Father. "Yes, King Aesunos."

"He's a hard worker, Your Highness. Good with our animals and on the hunt. He will make a fine chieftain one day... when I am gone."

"Well, we shall not rush that. Caturix will see to your payment," Father told Rolan, then turned to the men gathered there. "I thank you all for your hard work."

A series of thanks and other pleasantries were returned in kind.

Father nodded to the men of Frog's Hollow, then turned back to Rolan. "Come inside, Rolan. You have something more to say, I think." His gaze shifted from Gaheris to me. He *had* noticed.

"I do, Your Highness, if you have the time," Rolan said.

Father laughed lightly. "No father ever has the time for what you want to ask, Rolan. Have you any daughters?"

"Yes. Well, no, Your Highness. We did, but she died quite young. Gwyn…"

"Ah, yes. I remember now. I am sorry for it. Come," he told Rolan, then turned to Bran. "Go find Belenus. Tell him to join us in my meeting chamber. Brenna, see to Rolan's men. Make sure they have ale and something to eat before they head back."

"Of course, Father," Brenna told him, then turned to the men of Frog's Hollow. "Take your rest, gentleman. I shall return with refreshments," she said, then went back into the roundhouse.

Father and Rolan departed. Bran rushed across the fort to the druid Belenus's house.

Looking nervous, Gaheris joined me.

"Shall we just run away now? In case it doesn't go well?" I asked Gaheris.

"I'm just glad your father liked the stones," Gaheris said, his gaze turning to Father's wake. "He is an honorable king. I have the greatest of respect for him," he said, then caught my fingers. "And love for his daughter."

Gripping Gaheris's hand, I led him away from the others to the great holly oak that grew at the center of our village.

"The throne of oak," I said, setting my hand on the tree. "Belenus says it was planted by the first druid who served here, the first adviser to the Northern Iceni." I looked up into the limbs of the tree. "Ancient oak, Father of the Forest, give Gaheris and me your blessings," I whispered.

Gaheris set his hand on mine.

"Cernunnos, Forest Lord, hear us," he added.

I looked up into the shimmering green leaves. Blobs of golden sunlight gleamed down on my face.

"Boudica.

"Daughter of kings.

"One day, you will be the oak queen."

I swayed a little, feeling dizzy.

"Are you all right?" Gaheris asked.

I nodded.

"Don't worry," Gaheris said, touching my chin. "The gods are with us. All will be well, Boudica."

A SHORT TIME LATER, BALFOR APPEARED AT THE DOOR OF THE roundhouse.

"Boudica, Gaheris, the king requests your presence," he called.

To my great relief, I heard Rolan's laughter emanating from the hall. My gaze flicked to Gaheris, who exhaled deeply.

I entered the dining hall to find Belenus, Father, and Rolan drinking wine as they talked. Caturix and Brenna were missing. Bran, however, grinned knowingly at me.

When we entered, my father turned. He met my gaze briefly, giving me a slight smile, then turned to Gaheris.

"So, Gaheris. Your father tells me you wish to marry my wild daughter. Are you certain you can match Boudica's willfulness? She will not be an obedient wife, but I believe she will be a loyal one."

"I would have her no other way, Your Highness," Gaheris said.

My father nodded approvingly then turned to me. "Belenus and I have consulted, and I have consented to Rolan's request."

"Father," I said, exhaling heavily. "Thank you."

"Gaheris will be a fine chieftain one day. I am pleased to give my permission for you to wed. You have always been good with the people, Boudica. I trust that you will show the people of Frog's Hollow the same care you have shown those in Oak Throne. You will have many duties as the wife of a chieftain, caring for your people and ensuring the prosperity of the Northern Iceni. Do you understand?"

In other words, our family—particularly mine and Gaheris's children—would lord over Frog's Hollow, making it the next Oak Throne, King's Lynn, or Stonea. Father had not agreed to this marriage due to any consideration of my and Gaheris's love. This was deliberate, a plan for the future. Frog's Hollow would one day be another stronghold, strategically set on the River Mun close to the sea. I tried not to let my frustration at realizing my father's plan show. Instead, I forced myself only to focus on my gratitude. I thanked the gods for placing my heart in a tactically convenient place.

"Yes, Father," I replied as sweetly as I could.

"Your Highness," Gaheris said, bowing deeply. "You have given me my heart."

Father, not one for sentiment, nodded. "Such is the passion of the young," he told Rolan.

Rolan smiled at Gaheris. "He has always been a boy with much heart. And he's loved Boudica for as long as I can remember. We are honored to have your consent."

Father nodded. "Very well. First, I must settle Caturix in Stonea. You and your men will go to the sea to bring in the pilchards soon, am I right?"

Rolan nodded. "We leave tonight, Your Highness. The old men in the village say it's nearly time. We've had people at the shore watching. The pilchard schools should come close to shore by the full moon."

"I wish you a good catch."

"Thank you, Your Highness."

"Very good, Rolan. When we return from Stonea, you will be fat on fish, and I will be leaner one child. We'll wed Gaheris and Boudica at Lughnasadh, if that pleases the gods," he said, turning to Belenus.

The old druid nodded.

Rolan smiled. "That is excellent news. My wife, Lynet, is very fond of Boudica. We'll be glad to have her help this winter. And that should give us enough time to have their house built as well. Gaheris has already been making plans. You are welcome to come see when you return. We should have the house ready by Lughnasadh."

Father nodded absently. It was apparent to those of us who knew him that with the bargain settled, he'd already lost interest in the conversation. The arrangement was made. He had no interest in the details. "Yes. Very well. Now, we have much to do today. If you don't mind…" Father said, motioning for us to adjourn outside.

"Oh. Certainly," Rolan said, setting down his wine goblet. "I'm sure you have many preparations to make."

Father gave him a forced smile then motioned for us to exit.

Gaheris and I went ahead. Neither of us dared look at one another.

Outside, Brenna waited with the men of Frog's Hollow, pouring ale in their cups. Cidna had already made the rounds with a basket full of bread. She was chatting with one of the older men of their company, laughing, her hand on the man's arm—was she flirting? Nini danced around the strangers, begging—successfully—for scraps.

Brenna, Cidna, and the men of Frog's Hollow turned to us, all of them with anticipation on their faces.

"It seems I am the last to know this request was coming today," Father said then turned to Gaheris. "Go on, Gaheris, you tell them..." he said, gesturing to the crowd.

"Your Highness?" Gaheris asked, demurring out of caution.

Father motioned for him to go on.

Grinning, Gaheris turned to the crowd. "We shall have a wedding at Lughnasadh!"

At that, everyone cheered.

Caturix, who was pulling a tarp over one of the wagons, turned and looked back. A wash of emotions—from jealousy to anger—swept over his face. He turned back to his work.

Brenna and Bran joined us.

"Oh, Boudica. I'm so happy for you," Brenna gushed, pulling me close.

Bran laughed, then slapped Gaheris on the shoulder playfully. "Soon to be my brother, eh? Good. You and I will hunt together. We'll leave Boudica at home pining for you."

Father, looking uncomfortable with the displays of emotion, nodded curtly. "Very well. Now, I have matters that need my attention," he told Rolan.

"Of course, Your Highness. We wish you a safe journey to Stonea."

Father nodded to him then turned back toward the hall, motioning for Belenus to accompany him.

Once my father was gone, Gaheris turned and planted a kiss on my lips, causing everyone to cheer. When he finally pulled back, he whispered, "You see, Boudica. All will be as we wish. The gods are with us."

"May the Great Mother and Forest Lord be praised."

Gaheris kissed me on my forehead. "I love you," he whispered.

"I love you too," I replied.

"All right, Frog's Hollow. Let's revel in this joyful news and return home and spread the cheer," Rolan called to the others who rooted loudly. Rolan turned to me. "We shall see you soon, Boudica. Lynet will be so pleased. She is already making plans for the two of you to make lavender ale this autumn," he said with a laugh.

"I look forward to that."

Rolan waved to the others, and the men prepared for departure. I walked with Gaheris as he returned to Mountain. I patted the horse gently on the nose. "Hello, old friend. Druda will be jealous if he sees you."

"Too late. They already exchanged whinnies. Druda must have caught wind of him."

I chuckled. "Such dear friends."

Gaheris smiled at me. "On the off chance your father agreed, I have something for you," he said, reaching into his pocket. "Close your eyes."

"Why?" I asked teasingly.

"Because it's a surprise."

"The last time you convinced me to close my eyes for a *surprise*, you dropped a frog down the front of my dress. And I thought you were going to kiss me."

Gaheris laughed. "I wanted to, but I was too shy."

"So you thought a frog would make up for it?"

"Funny you should say that," he said with a chuckle, then

placed something around my neck. "All right. Now you can look."

I looked down to find a silver pendant in the shape of a frog hanging from my neck.

"Gaheris…" I whispered.

"You will be my wife, Boudica. My queen of oak and lady of Frog's Hollow. This little fellow," he said, lifting the frog pendant, "will watch over you until Lughnasadh."

"Thank you."

Gaheris leaned in and kissed me. "I love you."

"I love you too."

Behind us, Rolan whistled to the men of Frog's Hollow who prepared to ride out.

Gaheris gave me one last kiss, then slipped onto Mountain.

I reached up and took his hand. "Be safe. May the Forest Lord watch over you."

"And the Great Mother watch over you," he said, then plucked one of the purple flowers from my hair. He gave it a whiff then stuck it into his pocket.

Smiling, I let him go then stepped back.

Rolan motioned to his men then gave me a wave. "We shall see you soon, Boudica."

"May the Great Mother bring you a bountiful catch!"

Rolan smiled and inclined his head to me.

I waved to Gaheris once more as he and Mountain rode toward the gates of Oak Throne.

Bran and Brenna joined me.

"Strange that Father didn't ask them to stay to feast," Brenna said, turning to Bran. "Isn't it common for families to break bread and celebrate such an occasion?"

"Father is thinking only of Stonea. Boudica's engagement

only adds mortar to an already-firm foundation. Caturix is the one building new watchtowers."

"Are you likening me to clay?" I asked my brother.

With a grin, he shrugged.

"That may be, but still," Brenna said with a frown. "It was rude. Rolan was surprised by Father's breach of etiquette. I saw it in his eyes. Rolan is Father's most important chieftain. He should have been shown more respect. Why didn't Belenus say something?"

My sister was right. I hoped Rolan had not been offended by my father's handling of what was typically seen as the merging of two families.

"When has Belenus ever disagreed with Father?" Bran replied.

"That's true," Brenna agreed.

"I'm going to..." I said, motioning toward the ramparts, then I left my brother and sister. It didn't matter how rude Father had been. The agreement was made. Nothing could stand in our way now. I hurried to the wall that surrounded the fort. Rushing up the steps, I made my way to the spot on the wall where I could spy the party riding back to Frog's Hollow.

Rolan rode at the front of the party, Gaheris right behind him. I watched my love as he turned down the path toward the forest.

Gaheris, who must have felt my eyes on him, twisted in his saddle. Catching sight of me, he waved.

I returned the gesture.

Great Mother, thank you. Thank you for bringing my love to me.

Gaheris turned in his saddle once more and rode into the woods. Soon, the party was gone, like the forest had swallowed them whole.

CHAPTER 8

I spent the rest of the day feeling like my heart might burst. My father made no further mention of the arrangement. Caturix was nowhere to be seen. Bran was busy running what seemed like an endless list of errands for Father. Brenna seemed to be the only one who noticed my whole world had just shifted.

"Come on," Brenna told me. "Let's go to the market together and find something for Melusine. What a happy day," she said, then paused, looking at the necklace Gaheris had given me. "I can see the future. You will have a pack of grubby children and a dozen animals in your house."

"You say that like it's a bad thing."

Brenna laughed. "Not at all. I'm so happy for you. Let's go."

The marketplace was busy. The sounds of ringing hammers and the smell of freshly baked bread filled the air. Vendors sold everything from leather goods to chickens to clay pots. Due to Oak Throne's location on the river, an array of new goods came in almost daily. We would even get some traders from across the Channel who sold rich fabrics, oils, and exotic spices. Cidna and Ula often raced to buy the strange herbs.

As we made our way down the thoroughfare, the children of Oak Throne rushed toward us. From the looks of their wet pant legs and hems of their dresses, they'd been at the river.

"Boudica!" Eiwyn, the eldest of the group, called to me. She had a wild tangle of dark hair that never stayed in its braid no matter how much her mother tried. "Boudica! Wait! Wait for us!"

I grinned at Brenna then paused.

Six children, three girls and three boys, joined us. All of them breathless, they struggled to catch their breaths.

"We were hunting tadpoles when we heard the news that you will marry Gaheris of Frog's Hollow! Is it true?" Eiwyn asked.

"It is."

At that, the children let out an excited whoop, all of them dancing in circles. "Will you have the wedding here?" Eiwyn asked. "Oh, please do."

"And a big feast?" Phelan, the eldest boy, chimed in.

"And a cake!" little Birgit asked.

"And music?" Eiwyn added.

"Yes to all of it. Maybe my sister will play her lyre," I said, turning to Brenna.

Brenna chuckled. "Such merrymakers you all are!"

"Princess Brenna," Eiwyn said, curtsying in her bare and muddy feet.

"Princess," the others added, giving Brenna formal bows and curtsies.

Brenna smiled at them.

Her politeness spent, Eiwyn turned back to me. "Promise

us you will have a big cake and that we can all eat some," she said, tugging on my arm, leaving a smear of dirt behind.

"I'll have to convince Cidna to make it."

"You can persuade her. I'm sure of it. Now, promise it!"

I laughed. "All right. I promise."

"When will you have the wedding?" Phelan asked.

"Lughnasadh," I replied.

At that, the children let out a cheer again. "Come on. We must make a wedding gift for Boudica and Gaheris. We need to find something," Eiwyn said. "Back to the river!"

And with that, the gaggle of children departed.

"Children love you," Brenna said with a smile. "Everywhere you go, children and animals flock to you."

I laughed. "It takes one wild thing to know another."

Brenna chuckled, then the pair of us turned and went on our way, stopping at the stall of Conneach, the jewel crafter. Displayed on his table were all manner of silver pins, brooches, hairpins, and other fine pieces. Many were made with glass beads, pieces of shell, or pearls. A few had polished gemstones.

"Princesses," he said, inclining his head to us.

"Show us your best pieces, Conneach," Brenna said politely. "We will take a gift to Princess Melusine."

"Ah," Conneach said, nodding. "Then, none of these. Here," he told us, lifting a box. He opened it, removing several items wrapped in skins. He slowly opened each one. Hidden in the wraps were lovely necklaces. One piece featuring an oak tree—the symbol of the Northern Iceni—was made of spun gold and trimmed with teardrop-shaped pearls.

"What about this one?" I asked Brenna.

My sister gave a soft "hmmm" as she considered. It was then I realized that Brenna was playing. Obviously, that was the right gift for the princess. A symbol of our family made with metals from our lands and the pearls from the Wash. "And the price on this piece?" she asked Conneach.

He replied in a low tone so only Brenna could hear.

My sister's eyebrows arched. She turned to me. "Perhaps Caturix is right. Maybe we would be better off with a fine Northern Iceni horse."

I raised an eyebrow at her.

Conneach paused. "Well... I can reduce the cost by a fifth."

"A fourth."

"A fourth?"

Brenna smiled prettily at him, then nodded.

Conneach sighed. "Very well. By a fourth, Princess."

Brenna smiled. "Then we shall have it. I will send Balor with the payment if that is agreeable to you."

"Very good. Thank you, Princess," he said, wrapping up the piece.

As we waited, my eyes darted across the marketplace, catching sight of Ula as she dashed quickly through the crowd, basket in hand, on her way out of the fort.

"Here you are," Conneach said, handing the necklace to Brenna.

Brenna turned to me. "I'll take this back to the roundhouse. Coming?"

I shook my head. "I... I'll be back later," I said, gazing over my shoulder in the direction toward which Ula had disappeared.

Brenna frowned at me. "Keep in mind that you are wearing your best dress, and you are trying *not* to agitate Father."

I winked at my sister.

Shaking her head, Brenna turned and made her way back toward the roundhouse.

With a grin, I turned and followed Ula.

I passed through the outer gate and over the earthen bridge. Near the river, I spotted Ula. She was muttering to herself as she searched the ground, plucking flowers and putting them in her basket.

Turning from the road, I crossed the meadow to join her. The summer sun shone down on the grassy field between the fort and the river. The green space was adorned with wildflowers. Rock rose, levant, wild thyme, quaking grass, and cowslips covered the field. Blue butterflies danced from blossom to blossom.

"What are you hunting?" I called.

Ula turned and looked at me. "Boudica... Bah, always underfoot."

Shaking my head, I joined her. "Be nice. I just got engaged."

She turned and looked at me again, her sharp green eyes studying me. "Masterwort."

"Masterwort."

She lifted a flower from her basket. It had a long, thin stalk with a head of white flowers. "Masterwort. Go on. Make yourself useful and look," she told me, motioning toward the field. "And watch for poison hemlock. The good neighbors will trick you into mistaking it for masterwort. You can tell by the leaves. It's all in the leaves. The leaves. Look," she said, shaking the flower at me.

I dutifully studied the leaves. I wasn't sure if she'd meant to or not, but over the years, Ula had taught me quite a lot about herbs. She always had me helping her find this or that— she was right, I was always underfoot. "I see. I see," I told her.

"Good. Now, go on."

"And what does one do with masterwort?" I asked.

"Head thicker than a clump of dung," she muttered at me. "It's for healing."

"Are you sick?"

"Not me."

"Who is sick?"

"Elnish has a sore tooth," she said. But I could tell from the tone of her voice that she was lying.

I scanned the field, looking through the herbs, grasses, and flowers. A pair of blue butterflies danced in circles around me then fluttered off once more. "Found some," I called.

"Get the root, too," Ula replied.

I yanked the herb from the ground, cursing under my breath when the dirt soiled the hem of my dress. Brenna was going to chide me. And if she didn't, Riona surely would. "Who has a sore tooth?"

"Um...Elgin."

As I thought. "What do you do with masterwort? Make a salve? Dry it? Eat it? Grind it? Boil it? Burn—"

"You will kill me with questions. No wonder your father gave you to Frog's Hollow. You boil the roots and stem for healing."

"And the flowers?"

"You can boil the flowers too, but those are better for cooking."

"And the leaves?"

"Boil or dry them and burn them. The smoke is for visions."

"Like the mushrooms?"

She didn't answer.

"Ula?"

"I need more than that. Go check by the river."

With a chuckle, I headed toward the water. As I went, I

found two more specimens. Unrooting those and trying—but failing—to keep my dress clean, I made my way to the water's edge. There, I found a bunch of the flowers growing along with some wild basil. I plucked both, suddenly wishing I had a basket of my own. I was about to turn back with my haul when I heard the sound of someone singing nearby.

I paused.

My skin rose in gooseflesh. There was something about the sound that was... otherworldly.

Curiosity getting the better of me, I followed the sound around the bend in the river. There, I spotted a woman in a green gown. She had long, wheat-colored hair. She was sitting on a stone, washing her clothes in the river, as she sang—and cried.

Cold air blew across the river, sending a shiver down my spine.

The woman sang, but not in any language I knew.

She looked up at me.

Her eyes glimmered with sparkling golden light. I looked to the clothes in her hands. She was washing blood from the garment in her hand—a man's tunic. Tears streamed down her face.

A moment later, she wailed sorrowfully.

A lump formed in my throat, and tears welled in my eyes.

Ula appeared beside me. She stared from the woman to me then dug into her basket.

"Here. Chew this. Now," she said, trying to hand me a grubby piece of root.

I stared at it.

"Open your mouth, you stubborn girl," Ula said, forcing the dirty piece of root into my mouth before popping one into her own.

I winced as the bitter taste, paired with the grainy texture of the soil, filled my mouth.

"Chew," Ula said, slapping my cheek.

I did as she told me, the bitter taste so horrid that it made me squint my eyes closed, tears rolling down my cheeks.

When I opened my eyes once more, the woman was gone.

"Good," Ula said. "Good. Good. Now, spit it out."

I spat the root into the water then looked across the river to the rock where the woman had been working. The stone was wet, but there was no sign of her.

"Who was that?" I asked.

"The washer."

"The washer?"

Ula nodded. "She washes the clothes of those who will soon die. No good, lonely sidhe. She's nothing but a nuisance, wandering around crying and bringing bad news. Pay her no mind."

"But she... She is foretelling the future, isn't she?"

"So they say. But all men and women die, Boudica. She will have to wash night and day to keep up the pace."

I stared across the river.

"Masterwort," Ula said affirmatively. "None of them—the golden troupe, the good neighbors, the little people of the hollow hills, or the lonely sidhe—none of them like the herb. Sent her on her way, it did. Keep it in mind," she said, then sighed heavily. "The greenwood is always around you, Boudica. Be wary," she said, then took the flowers from my hand. "I didn't ask for basil."

"It's for Cidna."

Ula handed the basil back to me. "Then take it to her."

I nodded.

Ula set down her basket then took out one of the masterwort flowers. She tore off the head and leaves, giving me a small sprig of the stalk. "Keep it in your pocket on the road to and from Stonea. It will keep the eyes of the greenwood off of you."

I took the sprig. "Thank you, Ula."

"Bah," she said, then picked up her basket once more. "Always underfoot, drawing fey things. I'll be glad to be rid of you. You can go be a nuisance to the wisewoman of Frog's Hollow."

"There is no wisewoman in Frog's Hollow. Why don't you come with me?"

Ula just laughed. Picking up her basket, she laughed and laughed as she walked away.

CHAPTER 9

I spent the rest of my day with my mind waffling between the news that Gaheris and I would wed and dwelling on the vision of the woman Ula had called the washer. Even if she had been some fey creature, there was no telling what she was prophesizing. For all I knew, she was foretelling the death of old King Antedios, the ancient king of the Greater Iceni.

I returned to the hall, finding Brenna and Riona in my bedchamber packing up our things.

"I have you all set here, Princess," Riona told me.

"You're coming with us?" I asked.

"So the king tells me."

"Don't you want to come to Stonea?" Brenna asked her.

"That misty place, full of wisps and boggarts? No, thank you. But for the sake of you girls, I'm going."

"Because Father told you to," I said with a grin.

Riona winked at me, then said, "It is the talk of Oak Throne that you will soon be the wife of the future chieftain of Frog's Hollow."

"Is it? I hadn't heard."

Riona laughed. "We are all happy for you, Boudica. It's a fine match. The Great Mother saw to that. She is the one who keeps watch over maidens... even ones with stained hems. Boudica. That mud! Get that dress off so I can wash it."

I sighed heavily, then complied, changing into my tunic and breeches. As I did, I realized Riona was right. I owed the gods my thanks. I knew where I could go to be sure they heard it. Once I was redressed, I grabbed my bow and quiver from the corner.

"Best be back by the evening meal," Riona told me, a knowing sound in her voice.

I gave her a wink, then slipped out of the chamber, making my way to the kitchens where I found Cidna sitting with her feet propped up on a stool, a giant mug of ale in her hands.

"Boudica," she said, moving to rise. "I just stopped for a rest."

"Don't get up," I told her, dropping the bunch of basil I'd picked for her on the workbench. "A bit weepy now, but still a good batch."

Cidna nodded. "I thank you. Next time, bring it roots and all."

"You sound like Ula."

Cidna laughed. "You dog that old woman as much as you nag me. What do you want from old Ula?"

"The same thing I want from you."

"Which is?"

"To enjoy your mirthful company," I replied.

Cidna laughed. "When was Ula ever mirthful?"

I chuckled. "She did tell me that my mind was a dung heap this morning."

Cidna let out a loud laugh. "She's a sour old apple, that

one, but there isn't a person in Oak Throne who knows more than her. And she's wise enough to know to bring the roots and all."

I chuckled. "Maybe I won't make a good wisewoman, but hopefully, I will make a good chieftain's wife."

"Ah, yes! Congratulations are in order! I was so pleased the king said yes. Rolan is an honorable man, and that young son of his is very easy on the eyes."

"Cidna!"

"Isn't he, though?"

I laughed.

"At this rate, I'll only have King Aesunos and Belenus left to cook for. I'll look forward to that. Can't keep up with Bran's hunger," Cidna said, then took another large swig, polishing off the ale.

"Another?" I offered, holding out my hand to take the tankard from her.

"If I have another, I'll wobble about this place."

"All right. I'm off then," I said, giving Cidna a wave.

Disappearing out the back, I found Nini sleeping on the flagstones just outside. She was flipped upside down, a slight snore emanating from her. Skirting around the dog, I went to the stables. With everyone so busy, who would miss me if I went out for one short ride?

DRUDA AND I TROTTED OFF INTO THE COUNTRYSIDE. PART OF ME urged me to ride on to Frog's Hollow. While my father couldn't be bothered to celebrate my upcoming nuptials, at least there, I'd feel like I was part of something. But, instead, I turned Druda toward the forest.

Deep in the wilderness, amongst the ancient trees, was the Grove of Andraste. Like so many holy sites in our land, the ancient grove was dedicated long ago to the dark goddess. While my family often called to the Great Mother and the Horned Lord of the Forest, Andraste was forever on the edge of my prayers. She was a lady of dark things, omens, riddles, secret places, and knowings. I both honored and feared her. In times of darkness, she was the name I whispered. After all, my mother had once served her in her ancient grove. In a way, I'd always felt the eyes of the Dark Lady on me.

The air grew cooler as Druda and I disappeared amongst the trees, winding down a path that led deep into the forest. But even at this distance, I could see the ancient oaks that made up the shrine on the hill above the small village where the priestesses lived. We were nearly there when we passed a section of forest where bluebells blanketed the woodland floor. Overhead, I heard the caw of a raven. I could just make out the black-winged creature as it moved through the trees. It seemed to be following us.

A few moments later, I caught the light scent of woodsmoke. Druda and I wound through the trees and found ourselves approaching the sacred grove.

The Grove of Andraste was a tiny village all unto itself. Half a dozen stone roundhouses sat around a central firepit. There was a stable for horses and, beside it, a pen for the goats and hogs. A flock of chickens picked at seed outside. Tatha, one of the priestesses of the grove, was busy by the stables hammering. As usual, the pack of hounds that lived at the grove sounded the alarm at our arrival and came to greet us.

I dismounted, then waited to meet them.

"Look at you, vicious beasts. Andraste's hounds... What a

pack of kittens," I said, petting the massive dogs who wiggled around me.

"It's only because they like you. A stranger would be met less cordially," Tatha told me as she wiped her brow with her forearm. Tatha, her blonde hair pulled back in a tight braid, a leather band around her forehead, was dressed in the same deep blue, almost purple, gown worn by all the priestesses at the grove. A toolbelt hung from her belt.

"What are you building?" I asked.

"Rabbit hutch. Easier to keep and breed them than hunt them," she said with a light laugh.

"Boudica," a voice called.

I turned to see Bec emerge from one of the little houses. Bec's long, light brown hair danced in the breeze behind her as she crossed the square to meet me. She, too, wore the deep blue robes of a priestess. On her upper arm, she wore her familiar armband, which had a shape of a crescent moon upon it.

"Priestess," I said with a grin, inclining my head to her.

"Princess," she replied with a smirk.

Bec had come to the grove from a prominent farmstead in Northern Iceni lands. Both Bran and I had liked Bec instantly. And over time, a fondness between Bec and my brother had developed. While Tatha had been at the grove for as long as I remembered, Bec had slipped into the position of being the high priestess Dôn's chief aide, a position my mother once held—or so I was told.

I scanned the grove. "Where are the others?" I asked. Nine holy women served at the Grove of Andraste. As well, the priestesses cared for four orphaned girls. At the moment, the grove was empty except for Bec, Tatha, and the grove's less-than-intimidating hounds.

"Grainne has taken everyone blackberry picking," Tatha said. "They're trying to get the crop before the bears do."

"Dôn?"

Bec gestured to Dôn's small house. "Shall we?"

I raised and lowered my eyebrows.

Tatha chuckled. "I'll leave you to it then. I'm already dreaming of rabbit stew and fur slippers."

"You don't even have the thing built yet," Bec replied with a laugh.

"Don't ruin my dreams," Tatha replied with a chuckle. Pulling her hammer, she set off once more.

Bec eyed me closely as we approached Dôn's hut. "You have news, I think. I can see it sparkling in your eyes."

"I do, but I'll leave you to suffer in anticipation."

"That's just cruel. There's no gossip out here amongst the trees, and you know it."

"I never took you as one for gossip."

Bec winked at me.

When we reached the little house, Bec knocked on the door. "Mother? *Princess* Boudica is here."

"Come," a voice called from within.

Ducking under the eaves of the thatched roof, we entered. Dôn's small house had a firepit at the center, the smoke escaping through a hole at the top of the roof. At the far end of the room, there was a long table and chairs where the priest-esses gathered to eat. A cot had been built along the wall. Chests and cupboards filled the place. Baskets and bunches of drying herbs hung from the rafters overhead.

"Ancient Dôn," I said, bowing to the priestess who stood at her table working with a mortar and pestle. Dôn, the high priestess of the Grove of Andraste, had snow-white hair which she wore long and loose. Like the others, she wore a deep blueish-purple gown. Her face was deeply lined, the symbols of the gods tattooed thereon lightly faded.

"Ancient..." she murmured, then gave Bec a knowing look, making the priestess giggle. "It is good to see you, Boudica. It has been many weeks since you were last here."

"Yes. I'm sorry. Time got away from me."

"As it does to us all... Before you know it, people are calling you *ancient*," she said with a laugh.

"Boudica has news, but she wouldn't tell me," Bec told Dôn.

Dôn set her work aside and joined us. She eyed me over. "Love," she said matter-of-factly.

I nodded. "My father has agreed to let Gaheris and I wed. At Lughnasadh."

"That is wonderful news," Bec said happily.

Dôn nodded slowly. "Alas, we will never get Boudica here now. But the Dark Lady moves us all where she wants us."

"I came to give her my thanks."

Dôn nodded. "You are wise to do so. The Dark Lady has a keen interest in you, Boudica. For what purpose, I cannot say just yet, but you are Damara's daughter. Andraste moved your mother where she wanted her as well—for good or ill. Come," she said, then motioned for me to follow her back outside.

Grabbing the staff leaning beside her front door, Dôn led Bec and me away from the village. We made our way up the path to the circle of oak trees that sat above the village. The ancient stand of trees had many myths surrounding them. Some said they were planted there by the Seelie as a gift to the priestesses. Others said that the ancient goddess Andraste herself brought them from the shadow world in which she lived. Many believed the trees were once priestesses who chose to stand sentinel, watching over their sisters for all eternity. I didn't know the true story, but I knew that the oaks that grew in Andraste's shrine were as big around as six men and towered over any other trees in the forest.

Following the worn footpath, we finally came to the shrine at the hilltop, passing the menhir that stood like guardians at the entrance to the sacred grove. Dôn led Bec and me to the fire. She gestured for me to stand before the flames.

"Come. Give the Dark Lady your prayers. Close your eyes and still yourself, Boudica," Dôn whispered. "Your mind is too loud. Quiet your thoughts. Listen to the fire. Think only of the Dark Lady."

I did as she asked of me. The fire popped and cracked. I heard the flames flickering, the logs shifting. Dôn was right. My mind was loud. Thoughts twisted through my head— Gaheris, Caturix's wedding, Ula, the washer at the river, my mother…everything.

I exhaled slowly, deeply.

Then, I listened to the flames.

When my head calmed, I called out my prayer.

Andraste.

Dark Lady.

I come to your holy grove to thank you for your many gifts. Thank you for moving my father's heart. Thank you for bringing me to my love. I will wed Gaheris. I promise to honor you in my role as wife, mother, and one day, chieftain's wife.

Dark Lady.

Hear my prayers.

Overhead, a raven cawed, but I didn't open my eyes. The Dark Lady Andraste appeared in many forms, a raven one of them. Was she there? Had she been watching me?

"Boudica…

"Daughter of kings…

81

"What makes you think I did any of this for you?" a gravelly female voice asked in reply. And then she laughed while my entire vision lit up in flames.

I SWAYED, MY BALANCE SHIFTING. I ALMOST STUMBLED FORWARD when Bec caught my arm.

"Boudica," she said, grabbing me.

"Be still," Dôn said. "Drink this," she added, handing me a small flask.

I undid the cap then took a drink. To my surprise, the taste of alcohol burned my throat.

"What is that?" I asked, wheezing.

Dôn laughed. "Spirits… and not the fey kind."

Dôn motioned for Bec to take me to a stump nearby. I sat down, catching my breath once more.

"What happened?" Bec asked.

"I don't know. I heard a voice, and then I saw fire."

Bec and Dôn looked at one another.

"The Dark Lady always riddles. That is her way. But you have done what you came to do. She can be a hard mistress, but her gaze is long—to the future and the past. We must put our faith in her."

I looked at the trees overhead. The raven was gone.

"Bec, take Boudica back to the village. I will stay awhile."

Bec nodded, then offered me her arm.

"A wedding," Dôn said. "That will be a merry time. We will be your handmaidens, Boudica. Even *ancient* as I am," Dôn called with a laugh.

I smiled at her. "Thank you, Mother Dôn."

The old woman nodded to me, and Bec and I departed.

After a time, Bec said, "Fire?"

I nodded. "When I sent her my thanks, she said—"

"Tell me nothing. The Dark Lady does not like her words shared. Whatever message she had, it was for you alone."

"For me..." What had Andraste meant that none of these things I counted as blessings were for me? "She riddles."

"Yes."

"Why?"

"Only she knows. But when the pieces of her puzzles come together, you often chide yourself for your own stupidity at not understanding all along."

When Bec and I reached the bottom of the hill, Bec paused. "You leave for Stonea in the morning?"

I nodded.

"For how long?"

"A month or more."

Bec's eyes went to the forest, her gaze growing glossy. "That is a long time."

I smiled gently then set my hand on her arm. "Bran will miss you too. He already does."

Bec smiled lightly. "That impish creature," she said, then laughed. "Who can tell?"

"Me. Bran has spent his whole life worried about horses, and hunting, and fighting, and running, and eating... I don't think he ever noticed a woman before you."

Bec smiled gently. "Nor did I care for anything but getting to this place. All my life, I have heard the Dark Lady's whispers, but now, all I can think of is Bran."

I shook my head. "I don't know why. Half the time he's filthy, and he never stops eating."

Bec grinned, her mouth shifting sideways, evoking a dimple. "It's endearing."

"If you say so."

Bec sighed heavily, the sound coming from deep within her. "All will be as the gods wish. For better or worse."

"For better or worse."

I could only hope it was for better, because the Dark Lady's words had left me with a terrible sense of foreboding.

CHAPTER 10

After I said my goodbyes, I mounted Druda and rode back to Oak Throne. Hoping to ensure my flight had gone unnoticed, Druda and I made haste, getting to the fort before the gates closed at dusk.

Working my way to the stables, I tended to Druda myself, feeding and watering the horse, then returned to the hall. I followed the hallway to the dining hall at the center of the roundhouse, joining the others. Bran, Brenna, and Caturix were already there.

"Where were you?" Caturix asked waspishly.

"Be nice. She's newly engaged," Bran told our brother.

Not answering Caturix, I poured myself an ale. It had been a long ride, and Dôn's spirits had left a sharp, lingering taste of anise in my mouth.

Before Caturix could grumble at me more, Father arrived, gesturing for all of us to come eat.

"We will leave at dawn. I want you all ready. Brenna, make sure Riona has you and Boudica packed. We'll be bringing the ox wagons. Do you want to ride with them?"

"No, Father. I will ride Riv," Brenna said, referring to her horse.

"Good. That way, we won't have to wait. The oxen will be slower. Bran, tell your men to ride with the wagons. We will ride ahead."

"Yes, Father," Bran replied.

"Have those men gone ahead with the grain for the horses?" Father asked Caturix.

"Yes, Father."

Father nodded. "Very well," he said, then turned back to his food.

"Where is Belenus?" Brenna asked.

"Consulting the gods," Father replied between bites.

A strange silence fell over the table. What would have been a happy occasion—for both myself and Caturix—felt dull and lifeless. No doubt, in Frog's Hollow, Rolan had everyone in the square eating and drinking in cheer to our upcoming nuptials. Here, it felt like we had all just come from a funeral.

I pushed my food around my plate.

Caturix, apparently in the same mood as myself, set his plate aside. "I have some things to attend to, Father. If you don't mind…"

Father waved for him to go on.

Lifting my eyes from my plate, I looked at Bran. Even my younger brother looked tired and exasperated. Brenna, too, was lost in her thoughts.

I frowned. "May I be excused as well?" I asked, rising.

He nodded, then paused. "I hope you are happy, Boudica."

"I am, Father. Thank you." I stood there a moment, waiting —hoping—he would say something more, but he didn't.

Without another word, he turned back to his plate.

A swell of self-pity rose in my chest. So many times, I

wondered what it would have been like if my mother had lived. Would there have been more joy? More moments of cheer and gladness? What little I remembered of her, they were good memories. When I thought of my mother, I remembered her red hair and a smiling face, the sun shining on her. Now...

Mastering my feelings, I left the hall, slipping through the kitchen and back outside. I nearly tripped over Nini who was lying by the back door.

"Silly girl," I said, bending to pet her. "I nearly trampled you to death." Sitting on a bucket, I pet the dog and willed myself not to feel sorry for myself. After a time, I inhaled deeply, collecting myself. It made no difference how gruff and dismissive my father could be. In two months, Gaheris and I would be wed, and everything would be different.

Refocusing, I turned toward the stables. Brenna rarely rode her horse. The stable hands took good care of Riv, but I should look over Brenna's saddle just to make sure nothing needed a repair.

I made my way into the stable and went to the tack room. My mind busy as I mulled everything over, I didn't notice a lantern was already glowing within until I opened the door.

My shock paled in comparison to the look on Caturix's face as I found him there in the arms of Kennocha, a woman from the village. Kennocha, who was twice Caturix's age, lost her husband two winters back. There had been much gossip in the village when she turned up pregnant earlier this spring. I heard the women gossiping about who the father might be. Now, I knew.

"Boudica," Kennocha whispered.

Struck dumb, I simply turned around and started to walk away.

"Go after her," Kennocha told Caturix. "Caturix, go after her."

I had just reached the stable door when I felt my brother behind me. Caturix grabbed me by the arm, pulling me to a stop. A mix of anger and terror boiled behind his dark eyes. While the anger was something I was used to, the fear surprised me.

"I… I wanted to check Riv's saddle," I muttered.

"Boudica, you may be my sister, but if you speak a word of this to anyone, I'll…"

"You'll what?"

"You must swear your silence, Boudica. Do you understand me? You must swear it by the Great Mother and the Father God. You must swear it on our mother's spirit, on your love for Gaheris. You must swear it by the sun and moon that you tell no one what you have seen here."

Out of the corner of my eye, Kennocha appeared from the tack room, a confused and pained expression on her face. Her hands rested on her round belly.

I turned back to my brother. The dark look in Caturix's eyes reminded me of an animal caught in a trap. More than anything, Caturix was afraid. "What would I say?" I asked. "You should know me well enough to know that I would support you in such a matter. If Kennocha is carrying your child, you should tell Father you cannot marry Melusine. We can go togeth—"

"No! You will say nothing," Caturix said, giving me a hard shake. "You will say nothing, Boudica."

"Get your hands off me," I hissed, pulling my arm back. "Or by the Dark Lady, I'll get them off for you."

"Caturix," Kennocha called gently.

Caturix let me go. The fury in his eyes faded, replaced only by fear. "Boudica," he whispered, shaken. "You cannot tell anyone. You must not. You cannot say anything to anyone."

Confused and furious, I glared at my brother then turned and stormed away. My heart thundering in my chest, I walked until I found myself at the great oak at the center of Oak Throne. I sat down upon the roots protruding there. Pulling my legs toward my chest, I set my head on my knees.

What was happening? Why would Caturix ever think I would begrudge him his love? Especially a woman who was carrying his child. I didn't know Kennocha well, but I knew her reputation. She was well-liked throughout Oak Throne. Many had mourned with her when her husband had died. And she was a hard worker, known for her skill with goats. More than once, I had stopped to play with the baby goats at her home. If Caturix truly loved her, why hadn't he told Aesunos he had a lover and a child on the way? No wonder Caturix cared nothing for his upcoming nuptials to Princess Melusine. No wonder he was jealous of Gaheris and me. Caturix was trapped. He was letting duty get in the way. He had a woman and would soon have a child! How could he just abandon Kennocha like this?

Dashing the hot tears of frustration from my cheeks, I rose and stomped back toward the stable. Flinging the door open, I found Caturix on the other side.

Kennocha was gone.

My brother was holding his face with his hand, his fingertips pressed against his forehead. He turned and looked at me. "Boudica... Why did you come here earlier? To spy on me? To learn my secret?"

Willing my heart to be calm and steady, I replied, "Riv is not ridden often. I came to check Brenna's saddle, as I already told you."

Caturix looked away.

"Caturix, you cannot marry the princess if your heart is already given to Kennocha. And a child... Brother."

His expression icy, Caturix met my gaze. "Do you think what I want matters? Do you think my feelings for Kennocha or our child matter? I have already told Father. He has no interest in my *bastards*, as he called my unborn child. I must marry Melusine or risk insulting the Coritani. As Father so eloquently said, the Northern Iceni will not lose an ally over my lusty leavings with a goatherd."

I gasped. "Caturix..."

"There is nothing to be done."

"But you must—"

"I must nothing. We are not free. None of us. You are smart, Sister. For all your wildness, you are the smartest of my siblings. You know that Father only agreed to Gaheris's proposal because he wants our line to rule in Frog's Hollow. We are all under our father's thumb. You just got lucky."

"But if you love Kennocha, you will never be able to give your heart to Melusine."

"Melusine," Caturix said, spitting the girl's name.

"You and I do not always see eye to eye, but you are my brother. More than anything, I wish for you to be happy."

"My happiness is nothing. Not even my child matters," he said, the pain in his voice evident. "I must wed Melusine. I must do what is best for the family. I have no choice in the matter."

"And Kennocha? Your child?"

"I will see they are cared for here in Oak Throne. Father has forbidden me from acknowledging the child. I am—"

"A coward," I retorted. "You are a coward. You must stand up for your child, for Kennocha."

Fury rolled across Caturix's face. "We are not all as lucky as you, Boudica. You will win your love because you placed your heart strategically. You are not burdened by the responsibility the rest of us bear. You have always done as you wanted. With Gaheris, you were fortunate. Otherwise, you, too, would know what it means to do what is best for the throne—no matter the cost to yourself. It is a burden you will never have to face. You can live as selfishly as you wish. But it is not so for the rest of us. No more of this. You will say nothing more about it, Boudica. I will have your word. By the Dark Lady, you will swear to me that you will tell no one what you have learned here."

"But, Caturix…"

"Swear it, or I will stand in the way of everything you want. I will convince Father to marry you to someone else. I will twist him around my finger until he agrees with me. Now, swear you will be silent."

"How dare you threaten me?" I hissed at him. But then, I saw the terrified expression in Caturix's eyes. "Of course I swear it. But that isn't the point. Caturix…"

My brother stepped closer to me. "I will hold you to it, Boudica. I will hold you to your word. May Andraste punish you if you break your promise. May she take everything from you if you ever speak a word of what you have learned here. You have promised me your silence on this."

"I have," I said firmly. "But Brother"—I reached for his hand, which he reluctantly let me take—"do not condemn yourself to a life of unhappiness just to please our father. You will be king one day. You will be the master of your own fate. Don't do this."

"It is already done," Caturix said.

"And what of Princess Melusine? Is this lie fair to her?"

Caturix frowned. "It doesn't matter. She will get what she wants."

"A husband who is false to her, who cannot possibly return her affections? It's not too late."

Caturix pulled his hand back. "It *is* too late. We ride tomorrow. My fate is already tied to that girl."

"Whom you will never love."

Caturix stiffened. "We will not discuss this again." Caturix turned from me and made his way out of the stable.

"Caturix…"

Without another word, he departed.

I swallowed hard then shook my head. In one moment, so much of my brother's anger and resentment had been explained.

You gods, be gentle. Love is a rock on which we will beat ourselves to death.

To my great surprise, a soft, feminine voice answered in reply. *"Some loves are meant to burn."*

CHAPTER 11

Later that night, I made my way back to the roundhouse, going directly to my chamber. Brenna was already asleep. I changed into my bedclothes then slipped into bed. My head ached. Caturix's anger and fear had startled me but also evoked my pity. My heart ached for my brother. He was leaving behind a woman he loved. He would not even be here when his first child was born. As much as I pitied Caturix, I also felt angry at my father. How could Aesunos have done this? But Caturix was not wrong. Unlike my siblings, the gods had given me what I wanted. Caturix's life had been hard and was about to get more complicated. I sighed heavily then fingered the little frog amulet on my chest. Two emotions competed in my heart: deep sadness for my brother and great joy for myself. Feeling at a loss for how to process them both at once, I closed my eyes and went to sleep.

THE FOLLOWING MORNING, RIONA WOKE BRENNA AND ME, AND we dressed for riding. Brenna fidgeted nervously as she waited for me to get ready.

"It will be all right," I told her. "We'll be there by nightfall."

"It's just so terribly far. And… well, Father has had reports of bandits attacking small parties on the road."

"Luckily, we are no small party. Don't worry."

"Boudica is right," Riona said with a nod. "But pray to the Mother and the Forest Lord if you are worried, sweet Brenna."

Brenna nodded but said nothing more.

Once we were ready, Brenna and I made our way outside. We arrived in the center square to find two ox carts full of stones, two wagons brimming with supplies, and a party of at least three dozen riders preparing to depart. The sun had not yet risen. I watched as my father mounted. He tried to hide the fact that doing so made his leg hurt. Two years earlier, a strange lump appeared on Father's leg. It had grown larger over the years, and despite Belenus's treatments, more painful. While Belenus had implored him to go to Mona to the druids to remove the growth, Father would not listen. It was easier for him to pretend there was nothing wrong.

After seeing Brenna mounted, I went to Druda and tightened my saddle.

Ula appeared by my side. "Into the mist, you go."

"Sure you don't want to come with us?"

Ula laughed then looked at our group. "Like a faerie troupe. Who knows, you may wander into the fog and not come back out. Has been known to happen. The thin places… You walk in one day, walk out a hundred years later."

"Well, if that happens, know that I'll miss you."

Ula laughed, then slipped a satchel threaded on a piece of leather around my neck.

"What's this?" I asked, moving to open it.

Ula slapped my hand. "Stupid girl. It's a talisman. Wear that, and it'll keep the eyes of the greenwood off you."

"I'm starting to think you might actually care about me," I said, then moved to pull her into a hug.

"Get off. Get off," she told me, pushing me away. "Care about you? Bah. I only let you come around to keep myself in favor with the king. Now, be off with you."

"Of course," I said with a knowing grin. "Be well, Ula. May the Great Mother keep you."

"And you," she said curtly, then stalked back toward her cottage.

I fingered the talisman. I was glad Ula *didn't* care enough about me to bring the amulet.

At the front of the party, Varris, one of Father's warriors, sounded a horn, calling for us to move out.

I reined my horse in beside Brenna's.

"What's that?" she asked, pointing to the satchel hanging from my neck.

"Ula brought it."

"Where is she?" Brenna asked, looking toward the crowd that had gathered to say goodbye.

I chuckled. "Gone already."

Brenna smiled softly. "I spend too much time in the round-house. Everyone from Oak Throne to Frog's Hollow knows you."

"That's because I am too wild, remember? Don't worry. When you are queen one day, everyone will come to your hall to meet you."

"Queen? Queen of what?"

"I don't know, but I'm sure you'll be the queen of somewhere."

Brenna laughed.

"Unless, of course, you run off and join the bards like you should."

"A wish that cannot be fulfilled," Brenna answered lightly, but I heard the hint of sadness in her voice.

Father glanced behind him, making sure everyone was accounted for, then he and Belenus rode out at the front of our party. Caturix rode the line, making his way to the rear of our group.

Brenna waved to him.

He gave my sister a soft smile but didn't look my way.

At the back of the line, I spotted Bran and his warriors riding with the ox carts.

As we rode from Oak Throne, the people of the fort came to wave goodbye. In the marketplace, the children waited.

"Boudica! Boudica," they shouted.

I waved to them.

"Boudica," Eiwyn called excitedly to me. "Boudica! Will you bring us something from Stonea?"

"How about some mist? I'll trap it in a jar."

Eiwyn laughed, and a chorus of "no" came from the children who were now running alongside me.

"You don't want the mist?"

"No!"

"Very well. How about a great loon?"

"No!"

"Cattails?"

"We have that aplenty here," Phelan told me.

"All right. Then it will be a surprise."

"Don't forget," Eiwyn called.

I laughed. "How can I forget? Jars of mist for you all."

"No!" they all cried, but this time, they were laughing.

I gave them one last wave, then turned and faced the road.

As we neared the gate, I spotted Kennocha in the crowd. The woman met my gaze. Her eyes were red and puffy from crying. I gave her a soft smile and inclined my head to her. My heart broke at her pitiful condition.

Kennocha returned the gesture then looked away, her eyes searching for Caturix.

"What's wrong?" Brenna asked, studying me. "Did you see something?"

"No. Nothing."

"You're lying."

"I'm going to miss Ula, that's all."

At that, Brenna laughed lightly. "Fine, don't tell me. And despite your lie, you *will* miss Ula," she said, and then Brenna and I rode through the gate and into the pre-dawn morning.

THE RIDE FROM OAK THRONE TO STONEA TOOK MOST OF THE DAY. We rode across the flat green lands of the Northern Iceni. It was nearly midday when the ground began to slope toward the marshy fens.

A horn sounded at the front of the group, calling for us to break to rest the horses.

"There," I told Brenna, pointing to a clutch of trees with shade.

I clicked to Druda, and my sister and I made our way toward the shady spot. I slipped from my saddle and went to Brenna's side to help her down.

She dismounted with a wince.

"Why not ride in the wagon with Riona," I told her. "I can lead Riv."

Brenna shook her head. "If Father and Belenus can ride, so can I. We are Epona's people. I won't shame Father by being too delicate for the saddle."

I nodded, admiring my sister's spirit, but knowing that the stubborn blood that ran in my father's veins also ran through my sister's—and mine, when I was not too proud to see it.

Walking gingerly, my sister stretched then removed a packet of food from her saddlebags.

"I'll take the horses for water," I told her, grabbing Druda's and Riv's reins.

I led the horses to the nearby stream. Riv waded halfway into the water before he stopped to drink. Druda, always ready to drink half the creek by himself, stayed at the water's edge.

Leaving them, I went to the side of the small stream and stretched. Some of the younger boys came with buckets to get water for the oxen. Bran and his warriors came with their own horses and Father's and Belenus's. I went to join them. Bran and Cai, one of my brother's closest friends, were laughing about some joke Cai had made. Out of all of Bran's friends, black-haired, blue-eyed Cai was the easiest to look at. While my heart and soul belong to Gaheris, my eye didn't miss Cai's charms.

"Boudica," Bran said. "All well?"

I nodded. "Just tired of riding."

"You?" Cai asked. "You ride all day long."

"She has you deceived," Bran said. "Boudica only rides to Frog's Hollow then spends the day avoiding Oak Throne."

Cai grinned. "I see. I haven't had the chance to congratulate you, Boudica. I heard the news. Gaheris is very lucky," he said, giving me a brief, flirty look.

I guess I was not the only one who saw something pleasing to the eye.

"Now, Father will be after me," Bran said with a nervous laugh. "We need to find Brenna a king…"

Cai chuckled. "I'm always jealous of the four of you until I hear you talk like this. I could marry the tapster's daughter, and no one would care."

"Except the tapster," I replied with a wink.

Cai chuckled.

Downstream, I heard a familiar whinny. I turned to find Druda looking at me.

"Can you believe him? He's done. Now, he's hurrying me up," I said.

Bran laughed. "That horse is almost as willful as you. It's a wonder the two of you get along."

I scrunched up my face, giving Bran a look—and making Cai laugh—then turned and headed back. I collected Druda's reins then whistled to Riv. "Come on, Riv. I'm not wading in there after you."

My sister's horse huffed at me, then after a few moments, waded back out of the water.

Leading both horses, I rejoined the others. As I made my way, Father signaled to his man, who sounded the horn once more.

"No time to rest. The future of the tribe waits for no man, woman, or horse," I told the horses.

Druda huffed.

"Exactly."

Brenna joined me, patting Riv on the neck. "Ready, my friend?" she asked the horse.

I held Riv's reins while my sister mounted. Epona's people or not, Brenna would be sore tomorrow.

Once the party was reassembled, we headed out. As we rode into the marshy fens, the ground around us grew soft. Mindful to stick to the road, we made our way. The summer sun soon became occluded by the mist. The air cooled. Before long, the fog grew thick around us.

"Now I know why you offered the children jars of fog," Brenna said with a laugh.

We rode throughout the day, passing over several wooden bridges as the land around us became increasingly wet. Stonea, it seemed, was more island than a stronghold. As the sun set, the mist turned shades of gold, pink, and eventually faded into deep purple. Waterbirds called, their long, sorrowful notes sounding across the misty marsh. Despite the fact it was the height of summer, it felt cold. Frogs croaked in alarm as we passed, splashing back into the water for cover. Turtles ducked their heads under the surface of the pools of inky liquid. There was a dense, earthy smell in the air. It was not the loamy scent of the forest but the rich smell of mud and water. I was glad Father and the others knew their way. It seemed that any step in the wrong direction would lead us to be sucked into the muck. Tall cattails, waving grass, and islands of sod dotted the landscape that faded into darkness and mist.

As night fell, however, I began to hear sounds in the distance: the ringing of hammers, the sound of voices, and barking dogs.

Soon, a horn sounded from somewhere ahead.

Like fairy globes, blobs of golden light appeared on the horizon.

Our party sounded a horn in reply.

Like a ghost coming out of the fog, Stonea Fort soon

appeared. Tall walls rose out of the misty fens. The torches illuminated the watchtowers.

"Open the gate. It's the king!" a voice called, echoing through the misty darkness.

We rode toward the shadowy fort in the mist. As we approached, I could make out the stone walls surrounding the fort. Otherwise, the entire fort was surrounded by water. In a way, it truly was an island. We made our way into the massive fortress. I was surprised to discover that it was at least twice the size of Oak Throne. Sitting up on a hill at the center of the fort was another circular and walled embankment. I could just make out the silhouette of the chieftain's roundhouse at the center.

"Look," Brenna said, gesturing to the roundhouse. "The chieftain's house has its own fortifications. There is a whole village here behind the walls."

"Like a walled island," I agreed.

We made our way down the road that led to the chieftain's holding. As we went, villagers came out to greet us.

"King Aesunos, greetings! Welcome, King. Welcome to Stonea."

At the rear of the group, they called to Caturix.

Riding on, I spotted some shadowy figures in the distance. The strange stillness of the people standing in the darkness made my skin rise in gooseflesh. But the more I looked, the more I realized it was not people at all, but a small ring of stones. The moonlight slanted strangely upon them, casting an odd blue haze, making the stones shimmer.

Movement amongst the stones caught my attention.

There *had* been someone there. A figure appeared for just a moment then disappeared once more.

We rode up an earthen embankment, passing through an

interior set of walls before reaching the chieftain's house. I spotted several small buildings, a fenced area for animals, and other sheds inside the walled fort. The party halted.

A fleet of servants appeared from within.

I dismounted, then held Riv so Brenna could do the same.

Leading the horses, Brenna and I joined Father and Belenus.

"Very good," Father had just finished saying, waving off a servant who ran back into the roundhouse. He turned to Brenna and me, scanning us over, then looked into the crowd of servants from Stonea. He waved to a young man. "You there. Come, take the horses for the princesses."

The boy hurried to us, extending his hand for the reins.

"This is Druda and Riv," I told the lad. "I'm Boudica."

"I'm Innis, Princess. My father and I see to the stables."

I smiled at him. "It is good to meet you. Don't let Druda sweet-talk you into giving him more than his share. He can be very prone to moods and will try to make you feel sorry for him."

At that, the boy grinned. "Yes, Princess," he said.

I handed the reins to him.

"Be good," I told Druda, then turned back to the others.

Father frowned at me. "You don't need to learn the name of every servant you meet, Boudica," he told me waspishly. Waving to Belenus, he turned and went inside—limping heavily.

I gave my sister a knowing looking.

We entered the roundhouse to find it still under repair. The flagstones that had come from Frog's Hollow still needed to be laid on the floor in the main chamber. The roof overhead, however, had fresh thatch. Places where the walls had been recently patched told of the former state of the place.

My perusal of the hall was interrupted by an incensed voice. "Just look at this disaster," an angry voice called from the back of the hall. "What a cursed, forsaken shithole."

I sighed heavily.

My uncle, Saenunos, appeared from the back. He had put weight on since I'd last seen him, his belly rounding at the front. He'd cut his white hair short at the shoulders, making it curl more than it had when it was long. He glared at the meeting room, a look of disgust on his face. "If the Coritani get here before you get this place finished, they will take their princess back with them. It still smells like pig shite in here. Have you been working on this place?" Uncle asked Father.

"I didn't ride all day just to listen to you bitch. The stones are here and the men to work them. It will be fit for the Coritani girl soon enough," Father replied sharply.

Uncle Saenunos's lips curled as he looked around. "What did you do with the housecarl? Took his head for this, I hope."

Father said nothing.

"Of course not," Saenunos replied sharply. "What say you, Belenus? Here is the ancient seat of Can. What do you make of it?"

"Not the shine it used to have," Belenus said lightly.

"Not the shine... That's an honest truth, druid. My people have me set up in the guest house. At least we could get that cleaned and refreshed in a day. The new housecarl you have here is as useful as a heap of dung. I paid the women in the village to clean it and get it ready. I don't know where you and your lot will sleep," Saenunos told Father, then turned his attention to Brenna and me, eyeing us up and down. "Good. Good. They are grown now, women's bodies on them both," he said, eyeing mine and Brenna's shapes with such intensity it made my skin crawl. "Let's find someone's bed to put them in by winter. By the gods,

Boudica, you're a wild beauty, just like that mother of yours. You must find a hard man to tame her, Brother," Uncle Saenunos told Father. "She will need that wildness beat out of her."

I opened my mouth to protest, but Brenna grabbed my arm and gave it a squeeze.

Ignoring his brother, Father turned and scanned the crowd. "Riona," he called to our maid, who had just come inside. From the look of her gait, the long wagon ride had left her feeling creaky. "There is a chamber for the girls to share tonight. Go see if it's ready."

"Check for fleas," Saenunos told Riona, who looked like she didn't know what to do.

After a moment, Riona said, "Yes, Your Highness," then lumbered away.

Father went and sat on one of the benches by the central fire. Smoke twisted toward an opening in the roof. With a wince, he eased his leg toward the flames.

"If you're so miserable, go back to Holk Fort," Father told Uncle.

"I was the one who made this deal for the Coritani girl. I will see it through."

Father glanced at Brenna and me. "Surely someone will bring us something to drink," he said, glancing around for a kitchen servant—there was none to be seen.

"It's good timing for us too, snatching up Melusine," Saenunos told Father. "Have you heard the news from Venta?"

"What news?" Father asked distractedly, flexing his foot.

"Esu, Prasutagus's wife, has died."

At that, Father paused. "Is that so?"

Saenunos nodded. "Now, we must see who our neighbor to the south chooses. We must be careful, Brother. We cannot let ancient Antedios and his ambitious son, Prasutagus, expand their hold, or they will roll over us and take all we have in no time. Mark my words, he will marry strategically this time. The brother kings Caratacus and Togodumnus have a sister. Is she of marrying age?"

"She is, but they say she is mad," Father replied.

Saenunos shrugged. "Her mind is nothing if her womb still works. Prasutagus will wed her. We must cut him off at the root, marry Brenna to one of those brothers, and make our own alliance with the Catuvellauni before Prasutagus does. Both kings are looking to wed. You must remind them that you have two daughters of marrying age."

Ignoring him, my father scanned the room. "By the gods," Father grumbled in frustration. "Is there no one here to bring the King of the Northern Iceni an ale?" he bellowed to the back of the house.

A moment later, Bran arrived. "This is cozy," he said, eyeing the space.

"Bran, go and see where the kitchen servants have gone," Father barked.

Bran, looking confused, disappeared to the back.

"Where is Caturix?" Saenunos asked sharply, looking toward the door.

Father didn't answer.

Saenunos gave Father an annoyed look, then made his way toward the door, stopping to eye over Brenna and me. "Yes," he said, mostly to himself. "You'll do just fine in the bed of a Catuvellauni king," he told Brenna, giving her backside a squeeze.

Brenna gasped.

"Saenunos," Father said warningly.

Uncle Saenunos chuckled. He let Brenna go then left the hall.

Brenna exhaled deeply.

"Ignore him," Father told Brenna and me. "Brenna, go find Balfor. Ask him to see a bed prepared for me."

Brenna nodded then left. As she went, I saw her dash away the tears on her cheeks.

"Saenunos needs to be reminded of what is and is not his," Belenus told Father, his voice firm.

Father nodded absently.

Belenus sighed, then rose. "If you will excuse me, My King, I will go and find the druid Einion."

Father waved for him to go, leaving Father and me alone.

We stayed in silence for a long moment, then I said, "You didn't tell Saenunos about Gaheris."

"I will hear no end of his complaining if I do. Say nothing to him. My brother and I do not see the future in the same light. Everything I do must be strategically done...as *I* see fit, not how he sees it. Have you heard the whispers, Boudica?"

I stilled a moment. My father never spoke to me about matters of state, but there was only one meaning to his words. "The Romans?"

Father nodded slowly. "There are rumors that they are gathering in Gaul. Why, we don't know. All decisions going forward must be carefully weighed. Saenuvax, my grandfather, pledged the Northern Iceni as client kings to the Romans. But we have never paid our tribute or sent slaves, as Rome demanded. Perhaps the Romans are only expanding in Gaul. Perhaps the rumors are nothing. But if not..."

"Father, what can I—"

"Here we are, Father," Bran said, appearing from the back with a very harried-looking woman carrying a tray. She set it on the bench beside Father, half-spilling the cups thereon. A wooden plate with bread, meat, and cheese sat on the tray.

"Why is there no dining table here?" Father asked the woman.

"It was cleared for the stones to be put in, Your Highness," the woman told him. "I apologize for not having things ready. Chieftain Saenunos dismissed all the kitchen workers. He had his own people cooking his food. The servants, the ones Prince Caturix hired, were all sent home. I brought this plate from my own house. We hadn't had our supper yet. It's not much, but there is ale here and—"

"Saenunos dismissed my staff?" Father asked angrily.

"Chieftain Saenunos sent us away, but we are ready to work, King Aesunos. We'd been preparing the kitchens before the chieftain arrived, as Prince Caturix asked. There are people in the village who want to come to the roundhouse and work, those whose families took care of Can in the old days. My grandmother was a cook in the kitchen and I –"

"By the old ones," Father said, then rose. "Saenunos!" he yelled, then left the roundhouse with a limp, leaving myself, Bran, and the woman behind.

I watched my father depart, then turned back to Bran, who crossed the room to lift a tankard and a piece of bread.

"Thank you…" I said leadingly, asking for the woman's name.

"Brigthwyna."

"Brigthwyna," I repeated, then picked up a slice of bread. "Nicely baked," I told her. "Our cook in Oak Throne always underbakes things. She likes it better that way, so we all need to suffer raw dough," I said, then popped a bite in my mouth.

"Is this what bread is supposed to taste like?" Bran asked me, his cheeks full, a befuddled grin on his face.

I returned the gesture. "I think so."

The harried woman's expression softened. "'Tis a good grain we have here. We fen folk know how to make the marshland work for us."

"Of that, I have no doubt," I said, then drank the ale. It was a tart brew, different than what I was used to, but not bad. I finished the tankard and set it back on the tray. "What are the conditions of the kitchen here?"

"Oh, well," the woman began, "it's old, Princess. We started the work, but when Chieftain Saenunos arrived, he sent us out of here, calling us a pack of rats."

"I am so sorry for the insult. The chieftain spoke out of turn. Tomorrow morning, you and your people should return. Please get the kitchen ready, and see to it my father has his breakfast. There are supplies on the wagons if you need them."

Bran nodded. "I can show you if you like. My men can unload the goods."

"I...well, yes. I would like that very much."

"If the chieftain's people try to send you away again, tell them to come and explain themselves to me," I said, a firm expression on my face.

"Oh. Very well," Brigthwyna said, looking relieved.

Bran grinned at the woman then grabbed another hunk of bread. "Come. Let's get the supplies unloaded," he said, motioning for Brigthwyna to follow him outside. "This bread is excellent. What else do you make, Brigthwyna?" he was asking her as they left the roundhouse, Brigthwyna smiling once more.

I scanned the hall. The ancient pillars, carved with images of waterbirds, turtles, frogs, and tall grasses, needed a polish. Once the floor was redone and the place cleaned, it would be a lovely hall. Long ago, my family had built this fort in the mist. Now, it would be Caturix's new home.

With a wife he did not love.

Far from the woman and unborn child he had left behind.

On the marsh beyond the walls, a bird called, its voice sounding like a wailing cry.

CHAPTER 12

The next several days passed in a blur. Brenna and Riona busied themselves with preparing the hall for Melusine—as best they could with Saenunos's, Father's, and Caturix's input. Saenunos and Father bickered constantly. Bran threw himself into working with the men setting down the flagstones and thereby steering clear of the conflict, which left me adrift to wander.

As the days passed, I discovered Stonea's mist had its own pattern, like a living thing. In the morning, a dense bank of fog would cover the ancient fort. As the sun rose, the whole place would glow with golden and pink light, the strange hue illuminating the fort. By midday, the fog would burn off under the summer sun and reveal the walls and green spaces. At Stonea's heart was the chieftain's ancient roundhouse, which sat on an elevated mound above the rest of the fort, the whole place walled from the village that surrounded it. The village itself was protected by another set of walls. Beyond those were the marshy fens.

One morning, as I stood on the rampart of the roundhouse watching the activity below, Belenus joined me.

"Boudica? What do you see?"

"Goats, fishermen, and reeds."

Belenus laughed lightly. "Come with me, child."

Descending the wall, I joined the druid. We made our way out of the chieftain's fortifications, following the path back into the village.

"I lived here for many years when I was a young man," Belenus told me. "It was my first role as adviser to a chieftain. I advised Can, your grandfather's brother. Stonea is a special place. Come," he told me, turning from the path.

It was then I realized where we were headed: to the standing stones.

Belenus and I walked toward a small circle of stones that sat between the village and the chieftain's roundhouse. There were nine stones in all. The monoliths were twice my size. Sunlight shimmered on them, making the flecks of granite and other minerals buried in the stones shine. My skin rose in gooseflesh.

Belenus turned, giving me an assessing glance. "Do you feel it?"

I nodded.

"The mists are thin places. The stone rings doubly so. Stonea sits on a cusp. And this place," he said, gesturing to the ring, "is a doorway. In the bright light of day, that door is only open a crack, but you must be cautious at night. No one in Stonea dares come close to the stones save the druid Einion, who serves here. But you, Boudica, ever curious"—he chuckled lightly—"must have caution. The stones are ancient. They were here first. Then the village. Then the chieftain's roundhouse. The Fens are a low, flat place, except the plain of stones, as Stonea was once called."

Following the druid, I came to the monoliths. I set my hand on the ancient stones, feeling their power reverberate under my touch. "A doorway…to where?"

Belenus smiled knowingly. "Where do you think?"

I studied every inch of the stones, then looked within the circle, spotting—not an altar or bonfire—but a pool of water. Around it sat a ring of rocks. "To the realm of the Seelie," I replied, referring to the faerie people.

Belenus nodded. "The ancient people of this land are never far from us. They watch the movements of man. And these days, I feel their presence most keenly. Like a swelling in the air. Something is coming. There are signs of it everywhere. In the songs of the birds, in the shape of the stars, in the whispers of the trees."

"What are they saying?"

"There is fire on the horizon. And in my visions, I see you at the heart of it all."

"Me?"

"Come," Belenus said, motioning for me to step into the stones.

I hesitated for a moment, then followed him within. Belenus went to the pool, kneeling down at the side of the well. He gestured for me to join him. I knelt beside him then gazed into the water. To my surprise, it had a bluish-green color and was so deep, I could not see the bottom.

"The water is so clear, so blue…"

"This is no ordinary place. This is the well of Uaine, a mortal woman who fell in love with a fey prince. She went with her prince to the Otherworld, but a jealous rival thrust her back to the mortal realm. Uaine was never able to cross the veil again. She wept for her love, her tears forming this well. The waters are healing. But more, visions can be had here if Uaine is inclined to show you."

"Why didn't Uaine's prince come for her? If she couldn't come back, why didn't he come to get her?"

Belenus smiled lightly. "Perhaps he could not."

"Or maybe he didn't love her as much as she loved him."

"The fey can be fickle…"

"And humans are not?"

Belenus chuckled. "You're right."

I gazed into the water. "If a person finds the one they truly love, they should hold onto them with every ounce of their spirit. They should hold them so tight, not even death can part them, reuniting them life after life."

"You speak of soul magic. The deep love that spans beyond lifetimes. Not all of us are so lucky to find that one, Boudica. And even if we do, it is not so easy to hold on."

I turned to Belenus. He stared into the water, but his mind was far away.

"Have you ever had such a love?" I asked. In truth, while Belenus had been in Oak Throne since long before I was born, I knew little about his life. I knew he was a druid. I knew he was trained on Mona. He served my father, offered wisdom and council during the holy days, and led us in prayers on our sabbats. But Belenus himself? I knew almost nothing of the man.

"Once…" he said, then smiled softly to himself. "But that love was like catching the mist itself. It was the kind of love that crept into your very bones but could not be captured." He cleared his throat, as if trying to dislodge his words.

"I'm sorry," I said, realizing I had touched on something painful.

Belenus shook his head. "No, child. That love brought me many good things… Now, let us see what Uaine has to show us. Brenna is gifted with her lyre. She would make a proper bard. But you, Boudica, let's see what the greenwood has to show you. Still yourself. Let your eyes grow sleepy but do not close them. Breathe slowly, deeply, and close out this world. See only the water. See…and see beyond."

I did as Belenus instructed, gazing into the blue-green pool. While I tried to quiet my mind, I felt myself bristling at the story of what had happened to Uaine. She had been left behind, to suffer in sorrow, while her love simply forgot her. What a cruel fate. That was not love. I could not imagine the pain I would suffer being separated from Gaheris, but I also knew that I would never leave him behind—nor he me.

Gazing into the water, I waited. But all I saw was the water itself and the reflection of the clouds drifting overhead.

Again and again, I tried. Belenus had never endeavored to teach me anything. I knew that if I failed now, he would not try again. But the more I concentrated, the louder my doubt grew.

After a long time, I sighed. "Nothing but the wind and the clouds," I told him.

Belenus nodded slowly. "Perhaps today is not the day. I thought maybe…" He shook his head, then reached into his cloak, pulling out a vial. Whispering under his breath, he dipped the vessel into the water, filling it, then corked it once more. "For your father," he told me, then moved to rise.

I rose to my feet then offered him my hand. The old druid leaned heavily on me. Despite his bulking robes, I realized he was frail under the drapes.

"I will take this to your father now. Since he will not go to

Mona to see to his leg, perhaps the gods will be kind enough to bring a remedy to him here."

"Thank you, Belenus, for trying to teach me. I'm sorry I...failed.

Belenus smiled, then set his hand on the back of my head, meeting my eyes. "Even if we fail, there is nobility in trying. Through the effort, much can be gained. Don't forget that. Sometimes trying is the reward itself."

I nodded but was not sure I agreed with the druid.

We walked together back to the main road. Belenus inclined his head to me, turning toward the roundhouse once more.

Feeling frustrated with myself, I turned instead toward the village. Trying to set aside my frustrations with myself, I made my way down the path toward the village in time to hear a horn sound at the gate.

From where I was standing on the road, I was able to see the gates to Stonea swing open. The blue-and-gold pennants of the Coritani fluttering in the air, a party made their way through the gates.

Princess Melusine had arrived.

CHAPTER 13

I hurried back to the roundhouse to find the others waiting. I briefly met Caturix's eye. In that momentary glance, I saw the flash of terror—or was it heartbreak—just below the surface of his flat exterior before he looked away. Frustration washed over me. I remembered what Father had said. In his own way, he was trying to keep us safe from an unknown future. But if so, why did I feel like such a pawn? Even now, Saenunos was making his plans for my sister, despite her inclination toward the bardic skills. Caturix's perfectly contrived marriage cemented our relationship with the Coritani. Bran would be next to wed. But what of his affection for Bec? Had it not been for Gaheris, what would have happened to me? Caturix had been angry at me, but he was right. I'd gotten lucky. At the same time, I wouldn't have lain down like a sacrifice as my brother had done. No one would force me to wed anyone I didn't want.

And if Uncle Saenunos ever grabbed Brenna like that again, he'd find himself short a hand.

I debated going to Caturix's side. I was the only one who

knew his pain. But for that very reason, it was better if I stayed away. I joined Brenna.

"I saw them coming up the road," I told her. "All blue and gold."

"Did you see her?" Bran asked me.

I shook my head.

Soon, the gates of the roundhouse opened, and the party appeared. Two standard-bearers rode at the front. Behind them came the man I presumed to be King Volisios. He had short, golden hair and wore a blue cloak. Riding at his side was a man in druid's robes, his long, black hair hanging from braids at his temples. Behind them came a tall, lithe girl with long, yellow hair, wearing a blue cloak. Two dozen warriors rode behind them.

The girl surveyed our party with her light-colored eyes, giving us all a smile. For a moment, her gaze lingered on Bran, who stood to one side of Father.

"King Volisios," Father called, stepping forward.

"Ah, King Aesunos," the king replied as he swung from his horse. He strode to meet Father, the pair bowing to one another. King Volisios then turned to Uncle. "Saenunos," he said, embracing my uncle. "It is good to see you again. As promised," he said, turning to extend his hand toward the girl I presumed to be Melusine.

The young woman dismounted her horse with the aid of a footman then came forward. She was as tall as her father and very lean, her bright yellow hair reminding me of sunflowers. She smiled generously at Father.

"Melusine, this is King Aesunos," King Volisios said. "Aesunos, this is my daughter, Princess Melusine."

"King Aesunos," Melusine said, curtseying deeply.

"Princess," Father replied.

Melusine turned her sunny gaze on Uncle Saenunos. "Chieftain Saenunos. It is good to see you again."

Uncle, beaming with self-satisfaction, nodded to her.

Melusine's gaze drifted to Bran. She smiled at him.

Not noticing, Father turned to Caturix. "My son, Prince Caturix."

Melusine paused as if confused for a moment, then turned to my eldest brother. "Prince," she said, reining in her surprise. She curtsied deeply.

Caturix inclined his head to her, but the expression on his face was striking. He looked as though his spirit had fled his body.

"What's wrong with Caturix?" Brenna whispered to me.

I shrugged. In spite of our harsh words, my heart went out to my brother.

"This is my other son, Bran, and my daughters, Brenna and Boudica," Father said, introducing us.

Melusine gave Caturix one last smile, then turned to us. "I am pleased to meet you all."

"Shall we go inside?" Father said, turning. "The midday sun is scorching."

"You must try the ale, Volisios," Uncle Saenunos told the king. "It is like no other. Made with fresh spring water from the fens. The waters here have healing properties. You will not be thirsty for a month," Uncle said, slapping King Volisios cheerfully on the back.

"We are lucky we found our way," King Volisios told our uncle. "The man you sent to guide us was a great help. Surely, we would have been lost without him. I was beginning to think you were sweeping my daughter off to the Otherworld."

At that, Father chuckled. "She will be well protected here."

"As I told her."

Uncle, Father, and the king all made their way inside. Belenus left us to meet with King Volisios's druid. Soon, the four of us were alone with Melusine.

"This morning, the mists wove around us like a cloak," Melusine said. "My father kept making jokes that he'd wed me to a fairy prince. I confess, after a time, I started to feel a bit superstitious. Then the mist cleared, and I saw the light beaming from the walls. It was like the good neighbors set the fort before us. Then, I was twice as superstitious," she said with a laugh.

"Were you scared?" Bran asked her, a teasing tone in his voice.

"Bran," Brenna chided him.

Melusine laughed lightly. "Not in the least. I was only curious about my fey prince," she said, then turned to Caturix. "And here you are, with your raven-dark hair, looking so unlike your siblings that I was confused. Are you sure you aren't of the Otherworld?"

Caturix forced a smile. "Quite the opposite. I'm too much of this world, at times."

Melusine laughed, then took Caturix's arm. "Then I will be glad to have a husband well-grounded."

Caturix stiffened but did not pull away.

Melusine sighed happily. "May the Great Mother be thanked; what a fine roundhouse. And the village...so many good people came to greet us. My father said you have just recently begun repairs on Stonea?" Melusine asked Caturix.

Caturix nodded. "The fort was once the seat of ancient Can, but no one from the royal family has lived here in years. The roundhouse was in disuse. We've refurbished it for...for our home."

"I can't wait to see it. You must show me everything," Melusine said excitedly.

Caturix inclined his head to her. "Very well. Shall we have a look around?"

"Oh, please!"

Caturix nodded then led her away.

"Should we go with them?" Bran asked.

"No," Brenna replied. "Let's let them have some time to acquaint themselves with one another."

"She's a beauty," Bran said.

"So she is," Brenna said. "A fact, I hope, that is not lost on Caturix."

Bran blew air through his lips. "Caturix can find a reason to be sour about anything. He probably thinks she smiles too much. Maybe she's too beautiful and friendly for him."

"He's trying," I said, causing both Bran and Brenna to look at me.

"Truly, the gods are at work if Boudica is defending Caturix," Bran said, giving me a questioning look.

I blew air through my lips. "It's just hot. Father's right. Let's go back inside."

Leaving Caturix and Melusine to walk the compound, Bran, Brenna, and I went inside. Since our arrival, the stones from Frog's Hollow had been laid on the main dining room floor. The servants had cleaned the roundhouse from top to bottom, cleaning the cobwebs and any remaining signs that the place had recently been used as a pig shed. The colorful drapes and other décor we'd brought from Oak Throne hung from the walls, giving the room a cheerier glow. A table and chairs and benches now adorned the central meeting hall. The place was ready enough. In time, Melusine and Caturix could make it a home.

If my brother was able.

When my father spotted us, he waved for us to be seated at the benches while he, Saenunos, and King Volisios settled in at the table.

Brigthwyna appeared, offering the three of us mugs of ale. I drank it greedily. Something told me it was going to be a long day.

"What news?" Saenunos asked.

"Things are calm amongst the Coritani. Our triumvirate works well for us. Dumnocoveros, Dumnovellaunus, and I are keeping the peace. But to the north," he said, then shook his head. "Young Queen Cartimandua of the Brigantes just took the head of a Parisii chieftain. Trouble is brewing there."

"As it is to our south," Uncle said. "Cunobelinus's boys, Caratacus and Togodumnus, are finishing the work their father started. First the Trinovantes, then the Atrebates."

"Is it true that Verica has crossed the channel to elicit the help of the Romans?" King Volisios asked.

Father nodded. "That is the rumor."

"The last thing we need is the eye of Rome upon us once more," King Volisios said. "We already have enough conflict between our people. Every tribe in the west is at war with someone. And I will not be beholden to the lies my grandfather told to fend off the Romans when they last crossed the channel."

Father nodded. "Nor will we."

"And now that Prasutagus's wife is dead," Saenunos said, "let us see what that self-important, ambitious boy does."

"Marry one of your girls to him," King Volisios told Father.

Brenna flicked her gaze to me.

Saenunos spat on the floor. "I would die before giving Prasutagus a reason to finally take over all the lands of the

Northern Iceni. No. If those two sons of Cunobelinus ever stop fighting, we will wed them there."

"Hmm," King Volisios mused. "I dare say, Caratacus and Togodumnus show themselves far more ambitious than Prasutagus."

"Arrogant shit, Prasutagus. *Learned man of the druids*," he said in a mocking tone. "I cannot stand his smugness. No," Saenunos said.

King Volisios laughed. "I guess it is a good thing you are not those girls' father," he told Saenunos, then turned to my father. "What say you, Aesunos?"

"If it is true the Romans are building ships in Gaul, then there is much to consider," Father replied.

My gaze turned to Bran and Brenna. Brenna's brow was creased with worry.

A moment later, Caturix and Melusine appeared. Melusine held onto Caturix's arm, smiling and laughing as she took in every detail of the roundhouse. For a moment, I worried her display of happiness was all show, but something within me told me it wasn't so. Her mere presence in the room managed to break the growing tension.

Bran rose. "Melusine," he said, joining them. "Look here. The beams are carved with images from the fens."

Melusine left Caturix and went to Bran. "Is that so? Let me see," she said, studying the carvings in the wood. "You're right. How lovely. And is it true there are standing stones here in the fort?" Melusine asked Bran.

Bran looked unsure. "I don't know."

Motioning for Brenna to join me, I rose. "There are," I answered Melusine. "Would you like to see them?"

Melusine nodded then turned to Caturix. "Shall we all go?"

"Go on, Daughter," King Volisios called to Melusine.

"Caturix will stay here. Come, son-in-law, we are talking about the future of this land. One day, when these old men die, you will be king. Come plot with us," King Volisios called to Caturix with a good-natured wave.

"I shall return shortly," Melusine told Caturix, who gave her a stiff smile.

Brenna glanced at Father, who gave her an approving nod, motioning for us to go on. The four of us made our way back outside.

"It's so good to be out of the saddle," Melusine said, reaching up for a stretch. "I was starting to think unmentionable parts of my body might stay numb forever."

At that, we all chuckled.

"That is a beautiful necklace you're wearing," Brenna told her.

On Melusine's neck was a lovely woven piece with strands of silver and gold spun together to form an endless knot. Amongst the loops hung brilliant, polished stones.

"Do you like it?" Melusine asked brightly.

Brenna nodded.

"I made it."

"You?" Brenna asked.

Melusine laughed. "I know, it's not a common trade for a woman, but ever since I was a girl, I made such things— first of straw, then cloth, then leather. Our druid told my father the gods gifted my hands, so he allowed me to study under our artisans, who taught me how to work gold and silver. I'm always looking for stones to add to my pieces."

"That is such a rare talent," Brenna said in awe, touching the piece. "You *are* truly gifted by the gods."

Melusine smiled at her. "Thank you."

We wound down the path I had taken with Belenus to the stones once more. We all fell to silence as we approached them.

"There is a pool at the center," I told the others. "It's made from the tears of Uaine," I said, then recited the tragic story Belenus had shared with me.

"So sad," Melusine said, setting her hand on one of these stones. "Look. There are carvings here," she said, tracing her finger down the side of the stone. "Ogham, I think. I don't know how to read it."

I joined her. "Here is Duir, the oak," I said, touching the symbol of the oak carved into the stone. "He is the Father. And Muin, the vine, for the Maiden."

"Did Belenus teach you that?" Bran asked, a hint of jealousy in his voice.

I laughed. "No. It was Ula."

Bran and Brenna both laughed.

"Who is Ula?" Melusine asked, confused.

"An old crone in Oak Throne," Bran replied with a chuckle.

"Crone? Don't let her hear you calling her that," I told Bran, then turned to Melusine. "She is the wisewoman of Oak Throne."

"I swear I saw mushrooms growing from her cloak one time," Bran told me with a wink, then turned back to Melusine. "Boudica cannot be bothered to stay inside and learn from our druid; she has to chase every wisewoman, vagabond, and oddity she can find—all the way from Oak Throne to Frog's Hollow," he told me with a knowing wink.

Melusine laughed lightly. "I sometimes wonder about all these odd characters we see around. Who is to say they are not some god or fey thing come to test us?"

"You see," I said, gesturing to Melusine.

Bran shook his head.

Melusine looked into the well. "Do you think it would be proper to leave a votive in honor of Uaine?"

"I think, given you will soon be the mistress of this place, that is an excellent idea," I replied.

Melusine knelt beside the well. She pulled off one of her rings, a pretty gold piece with a pearl at the center. She held the ring just before her lips, whispering softly, then dropped the ring into the water. When she was done, she smiled brightly up at us.

Bran gave her his hand, helping her rise.

"Such joy in my heart," Melusine said happily. "I have all of you as my family and your brother as my husband. And one day, children..." she said with a wide smile. "All I can see is happiness before me. May the Mother Goddess be thanked."

Brenna took Melusine's arm and gave it a gentle squeeze. "May it be so."

Despite Melusine's fondest wishes, a prick of dread tugged at my heart. I looked back at the water, the blue-green waves rippling from Melusine's offering. But when I did, an image formed on the surface. Melusine sat huddled by the standing stones, tears streaming down her cheeks, and all around her, fire.

CHAPTER 14

The night passed merrily, Brenna playing her lyre, King Volisios's druid, Gwri, a lithe man with short, black hair, joining her on the flute. The warriors from the Coritani joined those of the Northern Iceni in the meeting hall, everyone eating, drinking, and laughing as we feasted in celebration of the nuptials, which would take place the following day when the sun reached its highest point.

Melusine laughed loudly after Bran told her a joke, the princess racing to tell a joke of her own. She was such a bright, lively thing. If things had been different, Melusine would have been an excellent match for Bran. As it was, I saw a fast friendship forming between them.

Caturix, on the other hand, was sitting on one of the benches, drinking one of many goblets of wine that night.

Filling a mug, I went and sat beside my brother.

Soon, the dancing began. Melusine laughed as Bran swung her in a circle, the princess's golden hair glowing in the firelight.

As I watched the scene, my mind turned to Gaheris once

more. Soon, we would be wed. There would be much mirth at the wedding. Everyone would come to dance and drink; we would roast a boar. Riona could fashion me a dark purple gown with orange and yellow flowers on the hem, fitting for a harvest bride. Yet, even as I dreamed of my own wedding, the despair wafting from my brother evaporated my joy, making me feel guilty for even thinking it.

I took Caturix's hand, entwining my fingers in his.

I said nothing.

Nor did my brother speak.

We simply sat and looked on—at a future he did not want.

After a while, Caturix lifted my hand, kissing the back of it.

Surprised, I met his gaze.

Both despair and gratitude swam in his eyes. He let me go, then rose and left the hall.

I sat watching the scene, feeling the sweeping sense of guilt for my own happiness. Who was I to be so lucky, to win the love I wanted while my brother suffered so?

After declining several invitations to dance, I suddenly felt it would be better if I left the hall altogether.

I slipped out into the night. Once more, mist draped Stonea. I could just make out the lights in the watchtower in the village below. I debated taking a torch with me but decided to leave it behind. Without the light, I could go unseen.

I made my way to the wall surrounding the chieftain's house, climbing the stairs to the palisade. I could hear the people in the village below, their voices soft as they called to one another in the dark. I walked the length of the wall. Behind the roundhouse, the wall of the chieftain's palace stood very near the outer wall of Stonea. The embankment was steep on this side. Beyond the second wall enclosing the fort was the foggy swamps.

Deep within the fen, waterbirds called their sorrowful songs. It was too misty to make out anything other than silhouettes of waterlogged trees.

But then, I saw the dancing lights on the water. Blobs of blue and green light bounced over the marshy moors. They seemed to have a mind of their own, spinning, twirling around one another, and then disappearing once more. Fairy globes. I touched the talisman hanging from my neck. The good neighbors could be kind or malevolent. One never knew their true intentions. But here, where one wrong step could lead you to be sucked into the murky swamp, it didn't pay to draw their attention.

I made my way around the palisade to the spot on the wall where I could just make out the standing stones in the village below. In the darkness, the stones had a faint blue glow. And just like the first night, I thought I saw…

Someone *was* standing there.

A soft wind blew, making the dress of the woman standing within the stones billow, her long locks dancing in the air.

And then, I heard her sorrowful weeping.

Wrapping my hand around the talisman, I turned back toward the stairs, making my way to the roundhouse.

Carried on the night's breeze was the sound of Uaine's cries.

CHAPTER 15

The following day, everyone was aflutter. Riona woke us just after sunrise.

"By Andraste's toe, there is too much to be done today. Stonea doesn't have half the kitchen it needs to feed all these people. And everywhere you step, there is someone beside you. Not a space to sleep or even turn around. Up, girls. Up."

"What does Andraste's toe have anything to do with it?" I asked the maid as I rose groggily. Brenna and I had been housed in a room that's former use was questionable. Something told me that if we had arrived in Stonea a week earlier, we might have been sharing the small space with sacks of grain and mice. But the place had been cleared and cleaned, and a small bed had been made up for us.

"Never mind that. I need to go back and help in the kitchens. Can you believe that? Your father will want you both in the hall pouring ale and making nice with the king's people. Belenus and those other two druids have the village working to make everything look festive. It will be a rowdy night tonight."

Leaving dresses out for us, Riona disappeared.

"Come, let's get dressed, then find Melusine," Brenna said.

"And what about pouring ale?" I asked teasingly.

"I'm fairly sure the men can pour their own ale," Brenna replied tartly.

"Brenna," I said in mock surprise.

"Don't chide me, Boudica. I'd swear this bed was made of potatoes, and I spent half the night trying to pry your elbow from my side. What were you dreaming of anyway? You thrashed and whined no matter how I tried to calm you."

I paused, trying to recall the dream. Faint and scant images danced before my mind. I saw the sea and Gaheris, but nothing more. "I don't know."

I shook out my dress, and Brenna and I—the two of us banging into one another to the point it became comical—got dressed. Once we were finally ready, Brenna snatched up the parcel in which she'd stored the necklace we had purchased for Melusine and slipped it into her pocket.

"Seeing what she can make on her own, I hope it's good enough," Brenna told me.

"She doesn't strike me as the ungrateful type."

"No. You're right. It's just, in these situations, I wish we had Mother to guide us. Caturix… He looks so unhappy. He is always sullen, but there is something in his gaze. He doesn't want this. I don't know what to do."

I paused. "It is in Caturix's hand to speak up if something is bothering him."

"And what can he say? What can any of us say? Uncle Saenunos is so determined to ally us to the Catuvellauni. I'll probably find myself in one of those brothers' beds before the year is done," she said, a distressed waver in her voice.

"Being in a man's bed is not an altogether bad thing. Depending on the man, of course."

Brenna turned and looked at me. "Boudica!"

I shrugged. "Gaheris and I will be wed soon enough."

"And if Father changes his mind? There are two brothers amongst the Catuvellauni. If Saenunos keeps talking, he will convince Father to break his agreement with Rolan, and you will find yourself alongside me in a strange man's bed. It is one thing, I am sure, to be with a man you love, but a stranger…"

I stared at my sister. "Father won't change his mind. It would ruin his relationship with Rolan."

"Do you think he cares about that?"

"I *will* marry Gaheris."

Brenna's brow furrowed. I could see she wanted to say more, but she held her tongue.

Once we were ready, we made our way out of the room and into the bustle. Riona was right. There were people everywhere, but there was no sign of Melusine. Scanning the room, I spotted Caturix. I made my way to him.

"Brother, we were looking for Melusine."

Caturix shrugged. "I have not seen her this morning."

"She is not with her father," Brenna observed. "Let's go outside. Coming?" she asked, giving Caturix a questioning look.

Vacant-eyed, Caturix shrugged, then drank his wine. Was he drunk already? Or still?

Brenna frowned at him but said nothing more. She turned to leave.

Feeling torn for a moment, I turned to my brother. "Caturix…"

"Say nothing, Boudica. Go on," he said, gesturing for me to follow Brenna.

Unsure what to do, I shook my head then went after my sister.

When I finally stepped outside, I felt like I was able to breathe at last. People milled about the courtyard. Through the open gate, I spotted Melusine and Bran on the road leading into the village.

"There," I said, pointing. Brenna and I set off at a quick pace, rushing to catch up with the pair. "Bran!" I called.

Catching sight of us, Bran and Melusine stopped to wait.

Melusine greeted us with a smile. "Caturix is so busy, but Bran offered to show me the village. It was too dark when I arrived to see anything. I wanted to stretch my legs a bit before the druids whisk me away. It seemed like a good idea to see the place where I will live the rest of my life," she said with a laugh.

I grinned at her.

Brenna gave her a soft smile and said, "Of course," but the lines around the corners of her mouth told me she was annoyed—probably with Caturix, who appeared only to be busy getting drunk this morning.

We made our way into the village, many people stopping to greet us as we went. The place was far larger than Oak Throne. The little roundhouses were spread out farther with more pastures for livestock. Passing several farms, we made our way to the market that sat near the entrance to the fort. Several dozen small stalls sold a variety of goods. Blacksmiths stoked their fires, hammers rang out, and vendors called to one another. One woman was selling apples, but her child was peddling the more exciting commodity.

"Princesses," the little girl called, holding up a puppy. "We have a dozen puppies. Would you like to buy one?"

"Oh! Look at it! It's so little," Melusine said, reaching for the puppy. "Like a tiny bear."

"They are terriers, Princess," the girl's mother explained. "Good for hunting smaller creatures like badgers or mink. Here on the fens, it's the small ones we're more likely to find. Good hunting dogs, sir," she told Bran, who lifted another puppy from the basket.

I looked into the little basket. An army of brown-and-black creatures staring back up at me. The dogs were very unlike the great, wiry hounds found in the north. I lifted one of the pups. The wiggly little fellow licked my cheek then bit my fingers.

"He's the wildest one," the little girl told me. "He's torn holes in all my stockings trying to bite my toes."

"Are you so wild? The roughest of the batch? Good. I will have you for Gaheris," I said, turning to show the pup to the others. "This one will terrorize all of Frog's Hollow, won't you?" I asked, ruffling the puppy's ears as he tried to bite my hand.

Melusine gave the puppy she was holding back to the little girl then bent to pet the others. "Would Caturix like such a gift?" she asked us.

Bran nodded. "Yes. I think so. My brother likes to hunt when he is not too busy."

Melusine smiled at the woman. "Will you save a pair of boys for me? Bring them to the roundhouse once the wedding is done? I will give them to my husband as a gift," she said, handing the woman some coin.

"Of course, Princess," the woman said happily. "We are pleased to have you and Prince Caturix here."

"I'm delighted to be here. I don't know what to do first," Melusine told the woman with a laugh, making her smile.

"Bran," I said, motioning for him to pay the woman on my behalf.

Bran half-sighed, half-chuckled then pulled out his coin pouch and paid the woman for the puppy I'd chosen.

"And the apples," I added, gesturing for Bran to give the woman more money. "Riona said we are short in the kitchens."

"Then Father should—"

"Apples," I said, gesturing with my chin.

Bran sighed then handed over more of his coins.

"We'll see them up to the roundhouse," the woman reassured Bran.

"Do you want to say goodbye to your brothers and sisters?" I asked my puppy, leaning him down to see his littermates once more. The wild creature paid his siblings no attention. Instead, he tried to lick the inside of my nostril.

"By Cernunnos, Boudica. Did you have to pick *that* one?" Brenna asked with a laugh, giving the creature a pat.

"Of course. Gaheris would have me choose no other."

Melusine moved to stroke the puppy on his ear, but in return, he tried to chew her fingers. "If you don't mind me asking, who is Gaheris?"

"The pesky creature to whom I am betrothed," I said with a laugh. "He is a chieftain's son at a village near the Wash."

"You know him well?" Melusine asked.

I nodded. "Since we were children."

"Oh," she replied, and this time, I caught the telltale tone of sadness in her voice. Once more, I was reminded of my good fortune. Melusine and Caturix were complete strangers. "That's very nice."

"Look," Brenna said, leading Melusine away to look at some pretty embroidered fabric pieces.

Bran took the puppy from my hands. "Father will complain about you adding this puck to the rest of the chaos," he said, making faces at the puppy.

"You honestly think he will notice?" I asked, then shifted my glance to Melusine. "She's very nice, don't you think?"

Bran smiled at the princess, who was laughing with the vendor. "Caturix is very lucky, although he doesn't seem to know it. He grows darker with each passing day and has hardly spoken to her. He should be the one out here showing her their new home, not me."

I agreed with my brother but found myself tongue-tied.

Bran studied my expression. "What is it?"

"What? Nothing."

"You're lying, Boudica."

"Never," I said, then took the puppy back from my brother.

Bran frowned at me. "I know better, and stop trying to distract me."

"If there was anything I could tell you, I would."

Bran frowned harder.

"Lick him," I told the puppy, lifting him to Bran's cheek. "Lick away!"

The puppy happily complied.

Laughing, Bran moved away from my puppy torture. "All right, sister. All right. All right."

"Lick him more!" I said, chasing after Bran.

"Boudica! Enough," Bran said with a laugh.

Having silenced my brother's questioning, we rejoined Brenna and Melusine. The four of us made our way through the market, Melusine greeting each vendor as she went. After we had met almost everyone, we finally turned back to the roundhouse. When we arrived, the Coritani druid Gwri was waiting for us.

"Princess," he said, bowing to Melusine. "It's time for you to prepare."

Melusine nodded.

"Before you go, we have a gift for you," Brenna told Melusine. "A little piece of our home to welcome you to our family." She handed Melusine the parcel.

"For me?" Melusine opened the wrappings then gasped. The sunlight glinted on the gold of the amulet.

"The oak tree is the symbol of our family," Bran told her. "Of which you are part of now."

Her eyes wet with tears, Melusine smiled at us. "Thank you all so much."

Brenna embraced Melusine. "You are our sister now. Don't forget."

When Brenna let her go, the princess turned to the druid Gwri. Giving us one more grateful smile, she turned and departed with him.

"See, she liked it. I told you," I told Brenna.

Brenna nodded. "Yes. She seems very happy."

Bran frowned. "I only hope Caturix cares as much about her happiness as we do."

CHAPTER 16

Bran, Brenna, and I returned to the roundhouse. Soon, we started to prepare for the midday wedding. Riona hurried us to our small bedchamber to get ready for the wedding ceremony. I was ready to return to Oak Throne where I could wear breeches and a tunic every day and never let Riona and her comb catch me. It felt like it took forever before Riona was satisfied that Brenna and I were dressed and adorned in our best.

"Boudica," Riona exclaimed, trying to push the puppy away from the hem of my dress with her foot, "why did you bring this monster here? Your dress will be rags by the time he's done with it."

"Aw, Riona. Be nice. He's just spirited."

"I'll spirit him away if he snags my embroidery. Shoo, you."

Brenna lifted the puppy and set him on her bed. From her things, she pulled out a leather glove and gave it to the pup to chew. "Here you go, you little bear. Be settled with that," she told him.

At once, the puppy pounced on the glove.

Riona adjusted the pins on the shoulders of my light green grown then stepped back. "Good. Good. Best we can do, getting dressed in this closet," she said then frowned, lifting the string to the talisman Ula had given me. "What's this?"

"From Ula."

"No. No. That won't do. It looks affright with this regal gown. Take it off."

"But—"

"Just for the wedding, Boudica. Surely the Sidhe won't come to snatch you in broad daylight," Riona said, exasperated, then pulled off the talisman and set it aside.

Riona then turned to Brenna, who was adorned in a gold-colored gown. The maid adjusted the pin in my sister's hair, fidgeting with the fresh flowers she had woven therein, then nodded, satisfied.

"All right. Let's be off. We're probably late already."

"Well, if you didn't braid and curl every strand of—"

"Hush, you," Riona scolded me good-naturedly then led us from the bedchamber—such as it was—back to the main room. "Not you. You stay here," she told the puppy who watched us, glove in his mouth. Riona closed the door behind her.

In the main chamber, the others waited. Only Belenus and Caturix were missing.

Father looked us over then nodded affirmatively, pleased with what he saw. "Very well. Let's go," he said.

"What a beauty you turned out to be, Brenna," Uncle Saenunos said, stepping in beside my sister. When he reached out to grab her arse once more, I pretended to stumble, knocking my uncle away from her.

"Boudica," he said with a hiss. "For as much as you look

like your mother, you don't have an ounce of Damara's grace."
With a huff, Saenunos stamped ahead of us.

My sister gave me a grateful glance.

Bran and Father walked ahead of us together. My father
was walking with a heavy limp.

"Father, do you want your staff?" I asked, my voice low so
Saenunos would not hear.

"No. Say nothing more of it, Boudica."

I frowned. *Stubborn, prideful man.*

We made our way to the ring of stones. As we approached,
we found a huge crowd gathered as the people of Stonea
waited. Saenunos, remembering himself, paused to let Father
go before him. He fell in line behind the rest of us, grumbling
under his breath. Belenus, Einion—the druid of Stonea—and
Caturix waited at the stones.

My brother's face was completely blank. He showed
neither happiness nor despair. He showed nothing at all. For
the good of the family, the good of the tribe, he was here. What
he wanted mattered nothing at all.

A prick of guilt stung my heart. In his way, Caturix was a
far better person than me. I would not give up Gaheris for the
sun or the moon. Only the gods themselves could take me
from him. If Father had not consented, Gaheris and I would
have fled north to Lynet's people, disappearing into the mists
of the rocky western coast and the Isle of Skye. All of my
father's and uncle's plotting meant nothing to me. I'd give it
all up to live in a hovel and eat roots, as long as Gaheris was at
my side.

We joined Caturix, standing beside my brother.

Then, we waited for the bride.

As the sun neared its highpoint, we spotted movement
coming from the roundhouse as Melusine's party approached.

Walking before them came their druid, who carried a smoking brazier. Blue-tinted smoke billowed from the bowl, filling the air with a pungent smell. Just behind him were Melusine and her father. Melusine had a dazed look, her face decorated with woad drawn in lines and other designs. She had redressed in a light blue gown, her hair braided and adorned with flowers.

King Volisios led Melusine to my brother, setting her hands in his.

Melusine smiled at Caturix, who did his best to return the gesture, then the pair turned to face Belenus.

"Great Sun Lord Bel, sacred Mother Goddess, we come before you on this high holy day to combine our tribes—the Northern Iceni and the Coritani—through the marriage of Caturix and Melusine. I call the eyes of the gods upon us now. As the sun reaches its zenith, may Bel's blessings shine down upon us. May Anu's fertility rise up from the earth and bless the bride," Belenus said.

Einion, the druid of Stonea, came forward, an attendant with him. The druid held a sword flat before him. The attendant placed two lumps of earth on the blade.

"This is the earth of Stonea. As the Lord and Lady of this place, you are sworn to defend the ground you stand upon. You and it are one and the same. In your marriage to one another, you also wed the spirit of Stonea. As you become one body, you will also become one with the plain of stones." Einion lifted the blade and held it before Caturix.

My brother took the small lump of dirt into his mouth.

The druid moved before Melusine who did the same.

"In the eyes of the spirits of Stonea, by the spirits of earth, your marriage is blessed," the druid called.

Gwri, the Coritani's druid, came forward next. Carrying his smoking bowl—Ula certainly would have approved—he circled the pair. Holding the bowl in one hand, a feather in the other, he waved the smoke over Caturix and Melusine. "Melusine and Caturix, may your love be blessed by the loon, the osprey, the gull. By the spirits of the air, your marriage is blessed," Gwri called.

Einion came forward once more. "The waters of the Fens," he said, lifting a loving cup. "May this loving cup, filled with the water of the sacred well of Uaine, bring you fertility. Drink, and your marriage will be blessed," the druid called, handing the cup to the pair.

Melusine and Caturix held the cup together, each tipping it so the other could drink.

When they were done, Einion took the cup then stepped back so Belenus could come forward.

Facing the sun, Belenus reached toward the sky. "Great Bel," he called, his hands in a U-shape, seeming to cup the sun. "Give your fire to Melusine and Caturix. Let it bring light to their marriage. Let your fiery spirit warm Stonea, giving it new life."

As he called to Bel, I swooned. For a moment, I swore I saw fire all around me. I gasped then bumped against Brenna.

"Boudica," she whispered, grabbing me, her soft voice shaking the visions of fire away.

"Bel!" Belenus called loudly. "Lend me your fire. Let me place it in the hearts of Melusine and Caturix, with the promise that as husband and wife, they will use those flames and serve as mother and father of this sacred land and to their children."

Belenus lowered his hands. To my stunned surprise, he held a ball of fire.

There was a gasp from the crowd behind me.

"Caturix, as you are husband to Melusine, swear to be a father to Stonea," Belenus called.

"I swear," my brother called firmly.

A flame dancing in his palm, Belenus set his hand on Caturix's heart.

Beside me, Brenna gasped.

Belenus turned to Melusine.

To my great surprise, the princess did not look afraid.

"Melusine, as you are wife to Caturix, swear to be a mother to Stonea," Belenus called.

"I swear it."

I stared in awe as a ball of orange flame danced in Belenus's palm. Without hesitation, he placed his hand on Melusine's heart, the flame disappearing into her body.

Einion stepped forward with an embroidered sash in his hands.

Caturix and Melusine lifted their joined hands.

"Let your hands be fastened together. I shall bind you," Einion said, wrapping the sash around their hands, "in this life and in the next, man and wife. May the spirits of the north, south, east, and west see your bonds. By earth, air, fire, and water, may they last for eternity. Under the eyes of the gods, on this sacred plain of stones, you are now handfasted."

Belenus turned back to the assembly. "By the Mother and the Father, I declare Melusine and Caturix protectors of Stonea, and man and wife under the eyes of the gods. Blessed may they be."

"Blessed may they be!" we all called in reply.

Belenus signaled to the pair.

Caturix and Melusine stepped forward to share their first—brief—kiss as man and wife. When they pulled apart, they turned to us.

At that, the crowd cheered happily.

Joyous, musicians started playing. The sound of flutes, drums, pipes, and stringed instruments filled the air.

Some of the ladies from Stonea threw flower petals into the air. The gold, red, and yellow petals scattered in the wind, blowing all around us like embers, landing on our clothes and in our hair.

The image made me dizzy once more.

Brenna caught hold of me. "We must get you into the shade," she whispered. "You, who spend the whole day long on horseback under the sun, sun sick at a wedding," she added with a light laugh. "Really, Boudica."

Taking me by the arm, Brenna led me to a shady spot under a pair of oak trees nearby. I leaned against the trunk, trying to shake off the dizzy feeling.

"I'll get you some water," Brenna told me, leaving me on my own.

Overhead, the leaves fluttered in the gentle breeze.

From above, a soft, feminine voice called my name.

"Boudica...

"Boudica..."

I looked up into the canopy of green. The sunshine made the leaves glow brightly. There, amongst the branches, I saw a tiny face. And then another. And then another. The whole tree was filled with piskies, so small... the size of squirrels. Tiny women in green garbs and red caps, their eyes piercingly green, looked down at me. One of them giggled, then braced herself on the branch. Hoisting an acorn, she took aim and lobbed it at me, hitting me square between the eyes.

Then everything went black.

CHAPTER 17

The water lapped on the sand. Back and forth, the waves rolled on across the glimmering shore. Mussel shells, their iridescent interior reflecting the blue of the sky, washed ashore with the seafoam. My mind felt lulled by the gentle back and forth of the waves. The water rolled in and out, in and out. But then, I saw debris in the waves: fishing poles, buckets, nets.

And then, the shoreline began to wash scarlet.

"Boudica."

I stared in horror as the blood turned the seafoam pink.

"Boudica, wake up."

Wave after wave of scarlet-tinged water rolled across the shore. Dancing with the waves, I saw a hand, then an arm, then a body. The person's hand drifted lifelessly on the bloody water.

"Boudica!" someone called, shaking my shoulder hard.

I opened my eyes to find myself face to face with Bran.

For a long moment, my brother studied me, then grinned. "Not dead," he proclaimed.

"I..." I began, looking around to find Belenus, Brenna, Father, Uncle Saenunos—with a heavy scowl on his face— Caturix and Melusine staring down at me.

I was lying in the grass under the oak trees. Overhead, the limbs shifted in the breeze.

"Banshees be cursed. In the trees...the good neighbors," I whispered.

"Drink some water," Brenna said, helping me sit up. "Boudica! Your skin is cold as ice."

"Of all the theatrics," Saenunos snarled, then stomped away.

Bran handed me his water skin.

"Banshees be cursed," I whispered, realization washing over me. I must have fainted from the sun. I looked up at Caturix and Melusine. "I'm so sorry," I told them both.

"The sun," Belenus said generously. "Nothing more than too much heat. Drink, Boudica. It will ease you."

Father frowned at me, then turned and limped away.

I took a sip of the water. The sun was blazing down, but I was shivering, the memory of the scene on the beach chilling me to the bone.

Melusine knelt beside me. "Are you all right, Boudica? You gave us all a scare."

"Melusine, I'm so sorry. I don't know what happened. In the trees, I saw..." I said, looking up into the limbs of the tree once more. But there was nothing there. I turned to Caturix. "I am sorry, Brother."

Caturix nodded once. "As long as you are well."

"Rest, Boudica," Belenus told me. "Make sure she stays in the shade and drinks water. She will be fine in no time. Caturix, Melusine, please come along."

Melusine took my hand, worry marring her features.

"I'm all right. Really," I told her. "I grew dizzy under the sun. It's ridiculous. I'm so sorry to spoil your wedding day. Please, go on."

Melusine smiled gently at me, squeezing my hand, then she and Caturix left.

Bran plopped down beside me. "Belenus went to all that work to put on a show, making a fire in his hands, only to be upstaged by a fainting princess. Really, Boudica."

I chuckled lightly. "I don't know what happened. I saw...something."

Brenna joined us on the ground. "Drink," she told me, tapping the water skin once more. "Saw what?"

I sipped again then set the skin down. "In the trees, I saw... No. You will laugh."

"Of course we will. Tell us anyway," Bran said.

"The good neighbors," I said, referring to the piskies I had spotted in the limbs of the oak tree.

To my surprise, Bran and Brenna said nothing.

"And when I was unconscious, I had a dream of the sea... It's faded now, but I saw something terrible. It's left me with such a terrible sense of dread. I can't shake it," I said, then shuddered.

"Like the dream you had about me being trampled by wild horses right before I was thrown and broke my arm?" Bran asked.

"Or the time you dreamed of smoke and fire right before the marketplace caught ablaze?" Brenna added.

"I'd forgotten that one," Bran told my sister. "Or the dozen others," he added, giving me a knowing look.

"I... I don't know."

Bran, Brenna, and I looked out at the crowd now moving off toward the village where the wedding festivities would take place. I could smell the roasting meat on the wind and hear the music coming from the square.

"We must never forget who our mother was," Brenna said. "*What* she was. It is Bel's day. If the sun lord can grant ancient Belenus fire, there is no telling what else he may have to say and to whom."

"All these whispers of Romans," Bran said. "Do you think it was them you saw? Was it a warning?"

"I don't know what I saw."

"Here you go, Princess Brenna," a little voice called.

I turned to find the stable boy, Innis, holding my tiny puppy.

Brenna smiled at the boy, taking the pup from his hands. "Thank you, Innis."

"Best hurry," I said, gesturing to the crowd. "Don't let the other boys get to the wedding treats before you."

At that, the boy gave us a short bow then ran off in a sprint. The puppy perked up, debating whether or not to give chase.

"No, no," Brenna told him, then handed the pup to me. "I thought if we couldn't rouse you, this one might."

I gave the pup's ear a scratch. "I'm fine now. We should join the others."

"Rest a bit more," Brenna told me.

I stared down the road, trying to shake the feeling of foreboding that held me.

"Do you have a name for him yet?" Bran asked, taking the puppy off my hands, rubbing his belly as the wild thing tried to bite.

"I will let Gaheris name him," I said absently.

A soft breeze blew. Overhead, the branches swayed.

"*Boudica...*

"*Boudica...*"

I ignored the soft voice calling to me and the laughter like a tinkling bell that went along with it. On Midsummer, it didn't do anyone any good to pay attention to the good neighbors. With a sigh, I took the puppy from Bran once more, then rose, ignoring the dizziness that wracked me as I stood.

"Come on, wild one. Let's get away from this piskie-infested tree and go find something sweet to eat," I told the puppy.

"Are you sure, Boudica?" Brenna asked.

I eyed the limbs of the tree above me, seeing movement. "Yes. Very," I replied, and with that, the three of us made our way to rejoin the wedding party.

CHAPTER 18

After several tankards of ale and a mug of wine, whatever had come over me passed. Soon, I fell into the celebration with the others. Everyone, from the village of Stonea to Melusine's people to our own group from Oak Throne, took part in the revels. Caturix was never without a mug or goblet in his hand, and by dusk, he was smiling widely and trying not to stumble as he stepped. His mood lightened, and for the first time, I saw him genuinely smile at Melusine.

Perhaps they would find their way after all.

My curiosity piqued, however, I found Belenus in the crowd. The druid was clapping as a group danced in the central square. With the bonfire lit and music playing, it was a merry event.

"Boudica," Belenus said when he saw me approach. "How are you feeling?"

"Fine now."

"Then why aren't you dancing?" he asked with a laugh.

"I will," I told him, "but I wanted to ask you something."

"What is it?"

"How did you do it?"

"Do what, my child?"

"The fire."

Belenus's expression suddenly turned serious. "That was not me but Bel himself."

"Did you ever do such magic before? I have not seen you perform the like."

Belenus paused, looking toward the bonfire. "A druid of my rank can perform many feats with practice and patience. I have been fortunate enough to have Bel's blessings in this life, but the skill does not always come to me as it once did."

"Do all druids learn such magic?"

Belenus smiled lightly. "We all have special gifts. And they are not all the same. Where some of us learned to bend the elements, others have *different* abilities."

"Such as?"

Belenus leaned forward and lifted his bushy, white eyebrows. "Some druids can shift form."

I stared at him. "Truly?"

He nodded. "That was how the druids terrorized Caesar when he tried to land upon these shores. The druids met Caesar on the white cliffs. They called upon the gods and drove Caesar into a remote cove where Llyr smashed the emperor's ships like toys. What soldiers did find their way to shore were tracked by owls and ravens and attacked by wolves. The druids spied on his movements, unseen from the trees, and reported on Caesar's doings to the chieftains. Each time Caesar reached into the land of the Britons, the gods struck back."

"And now? Do you believe the whispers from Gaul?"

Belenus tilted his head from side to side. "Since Caesar, the

Romans tried to invade once more. That time, the druids cursed the mind of Caligula. The great emperor ordered his men to collect seashells then marched his men home, most of whom returned to Rome half-mad from fear. They called us cursed people, our land one of stones and shadows. No, Boudica. I have no fear of Romans. I am more afraid of Caratacus's and Togodumnus's ambitions."

"Stones and shadows," I said. "I like that. As for the brothers, what do you fear those ambitions to be?"

"To make themselves High Kings of all of the Britons."

"Father will never allow it. Nor will ancient King Antedios and Prince Prasutagus."

"Ask the Verica of the Atrebates what he thinks of the Catuvellauni brothers' ambitions. Or Aedd Mawr, former king of the Trinovantes, who lost his crown to the ambitions of those boys' father."

The crowd behind us cheered, and I looked to find Father and Brenna dancing.

"Then it is good Father has allied us with the Coritani," I said.

Belenus nodded. "To be a good ruler often means putting aside the self—emotion, personal ambition, even love—to do what is best for the tribe. Even when those choices do not come easily."

I turned, raising an eyebrow at Belenus.

The druid gave me a careful look then shifted his gaze to Caturix.

Of course, he knew.

"But Bel works in mysterious ways, Boudica. Never forget. If his fires can melt stones, so too can they change a human heart," Belenus added.

"I hope you're right," I said, my gaze going to where Melusine and Caturix sat together.

To my surprise, my brother lifted Melusine's hand, giving it a kiss.

The music shifted once more, and everyone joined hands to dance around the fire.

I smiled at the old druid. "Will you dance with me, Belenus?"

"I am not as spry as I once was, but I think I can manage this reel," he said, taking my hand.

Together, we joined the others. Everyone was laughing and dancing—save Saenunos and King Volisios, who were huddled together in the shadows, whispering over their mugs of ale. The dancers formed two rings of people. The inner ring danced clockwise. The outer ring counterclockwise. Laughing, Belenus and I joined them. But the effect of the two rings moving in different directions was dizzying.

Across the fire from me, Brenna and Bran were laughing as they danced alongside Father. Caturix and Melusine joined in the fun, the princess's golden hair reflecting the firelight like polished bronze. The flutes, fiddles, and pipes bathed the misty moors around Stonea with song. But the strange sensation of our dancing circles spiraling around us made my head feel woozy. Images flashed before my eyes.

Clashing swords.

Screams.

Fire.

I was about to step from the circle when Brenna called out. "Father!"

The musicians paused.

Everyone stopped dancing.

Across from me, I saw my father bent on one knee.

"Father," I called, rushing to him, Belenus coming along behind me.

When I got to him, I found my father wincing but waving everyone off. "It's nothing. It's nothing," he said. "Get me up, Bran."

My brother helped lift him. When he did, I saw my father's pant leg was wet with blood.

"Belenus, look," I told the druid.

"Your Highness," Belenus said, his voice grave. "Your leg."

Father nodded. He already knew. "It's nothing. Please, carry on," he told the others. Waving to the musicians, he called, "Play on. Play on."

After a moment's hesitation, they started to play again.

"Get me to the hall," Father told Bran.

Not waiting for an invitation, I went to my father's other side and took his arm, helping him from the ground.

Father had gone absolutely pale.

A moment later, Melusine and Caturix appeared.

"King Aesunos, are you all right?" Melusine asked.

"Just my leg…ailment of an old man. Do not let it ruin your wedding night, Princess."

"Father," Caturix said, looking for direction.

"Enjoy the revels, Caturix. Keep them going. I'm fine."

In other words, distract everyone and minimalize the problem.

Caturix nodded to Father then turned back to the crowd. "All is well. Drink and dance, my friends," Caturix called, his voice slurring.

"All right, let's go," Bran said.

Taking my father's weight on me, we made our way back to the roundhouse.

I looked over my shoulder at the crowd. King Volisios had

gone off to talk to his own men, but Uncle Saenunos watched our retreat. His eyes glimmered in the firelight, a slight smile on his lips. His expression reminded me of a hungry wolf. If something happened to Father, Saenunos would become king of the Northern Iceni.

The smirk on his face told me what I already knew. Brother or not, he could hardly wait.

CHAPTER 19

B ack in the roundhouse, we took Father to his chamber, where we laid him down. Belenus rolled up the leg of his pants to reveal that the lump in his leg had burst. Blood and foul-smelling ooze poured down Father's leg.

Brenna gasped then took hold of my arm. Her face went pale.

"Get my case from my chamber," Belenus told Bran.

Bran disappeared at once.

"Brenna, hot water and clean cloths from the kitchen," he told my sister.

"Of course." Brenna left the room.

"Boudica, Einion and Gwri have gone into the fens. Go to Einion's house. It is the small cottage to the west of the standing stones. You will mark it by the well in the front. Find goldenseal, lightning mushrooms, and root of Taranus amongst his supplies. You know the herbs? Ula has shown you."

"Yes, but won't Einion—"

"We must have them now. Your father's life will depend upon it."

Not waiting another moment, I rushed from the round-house. Working my way through the darkness, I went to the home of the druid. The mist had settled in on the village once more. In the distance, I heard the music and sounds of laughter. Caturix had done what was needed—pretended nothing was wrong. The wedding party carried on, undisturbed by my father's grave condition. Eyeing the stones carefully, I passed them by then made my way to the cottage.

I knocked on the door of the round mud and wattle home. "Einion?" I called. "It is Boudica. Belenus has sent me." I waited a moment, but there was no answer.

I pushed open the door. The place was dimly lit by a dying center fire. The smell of herbs was pungent, assailing my nose the moment I entered. The druid had a long table on which he had bunches of herbs drying. Other herbs and roots hung from the beams of his little house. I jumped sideways when a shadow in the corner moved, revealing a cat. I must have woken the creature when I entered. The black cat, its eyes glimmering gold in the firelight, greeted me with a meow.

"Yes, I know. I am intruding. But I need herbs and roots, and the druid is off on his own business. I'm very sorry. Now, let me see," I said, then began fingering through the bunches lying about.

I found the root of Taranus first. Snatching a basket, I tucked it inside. Amongst the bottles on the wall, I also found the mushrooms Belenus had asked for. The cat jumped up on the table, watching me as I worked. Drying on the table, I spotted a bundle of goldenseal. Collecting what was needed, I turned to go when I saw some masterwort sitting out to dry. Remembering Ula's words, I took it as well.

I went to the door, the cat trotting alongside me.

Bending down, I scratched the friendly cat on the head. "Tell your master I mean no harm. I swear it by the Mother and Father. You have been a very good watchman."

The cat answered me with a meow then sat, watching as I exited the little house but not seeking to follow.

I closed the door behind me then I hurried back toward the chieftain's house.

When I passed the circle stones, I saw a figure standing there.

"Where are you off to in such a hurry, Princess?" a masculine voice called to me.

"My father is ill," I replied, cursing myself at once for answering a stranger in the circle stones.

"I know," the man replied. His voice was deep, but when he spoke, the sound like a ringing bell irritated my ears, the noise just on the fringe of my awareness. "I have something that will cure him. If you come with me, I can show you," he said, holding out his hand.

"I am no fool and have no time for your games," I said, reaching for the amulet Ula had given me, but it was gone. Riona had taken it off before the wedding.

"Hedgewitch magic," the man said. "But the talisman isn't there, is it?" While I could not see the stranger's smile, I could feel it. "Are you sure you don't want to join me, Princess?"

"No," I replied angrily then hurried on my way.

"Perhaps a drink, then? A dance?" he called with a light laugh.

I did not reply. Fey things. The high holy days always had fey things wandering in lonely places. Why they always seemed so interested in me, I didn't know. Today had been a strange day of omens.

I rushed back into the house, hurrying to my father's chamber once more.

Belenus had cleaned the wound and was holding a cloth to it, trying to stop the flow of blood. Brenna sat at Father's bedside, holding his hand. He was pale and sweating.

"Here," I said, setting the basket beside Belenus. "I found everything. And I brought masterwort as well."

"Very good. Very good. Set on a pot of water and start a draft of the root, mushroom, and masterwort together. Watch the proportions."

Understanding his meaning, I placed all the roots into a pot, added water, then combined two mushrooms and the flowers and leaves of the masterwort.

Belenus glanced into my pot, nodded affirmatively, then went back to work. He removed the bloody rags then began cleaning the wound with a tincture that smelled of lemon balm and mint. Still, the wound wept. Dipping into his things once more, Belenus removed an indigo-colored clay jar. Opening it, he revealed a salve. I caught the faint scent of mistletoe. My father winced as Belenus applied a pungent balm to the wound. I glanced quickly at the lump. The skin looked grey and unhealthy.

"Should it not be removed?" I asked Belenus.

The druid met my gaze, giving me a telling glance. It *should* be removed, but Father wouldn't let him.

"I will try to shrink it from the outside," Belenus told me—and my father. "Your Highness, if the mistletoe salve and the draught Boudica is preparing do not work, you will have no choice."

"You will not cut into my leg," Father said, a defiant tone in his voice. "It will heal soon enough. I just over-exerted myself."

Belenus frowned. "Or it will spread and kill you."

"Father," Brenna said, aghast.

My father did not reply.

With his free hand, Belenus pulled a small vial from his case and handed it to me. "Three seeds. Only three."

I lifted the vial and looked within. I recognized the herb. Ula often used it when she was seeking visions. "Gallowgrass?"

Belenus nodded.

I did as he told me, stirring the concoction gently.

Father groaned.

A short time later, the herbs had come to a boil. While I knew the drink would be more potent with some steeping, I measured out the first cup.

"Move the pot aside to simmer," Belenus told me, then took the cup from my hands. "Here now, Your Highness. Drink. This will help heal you from within."

Brenna and Bran helped Father up, and Belenus set the cup to his lips. When he was done drinking, Father nodded then laid down once more.

"Bran," Father said, "go back to the revels. Stay close to Saenunos. Let him see your eyes are upon him. Mark whomever he speaks with. Go now."

A dark shadow crossed Bran's face. "Yes, Father." He rose and left.

"You must rest now, Aesunos," Belenus told Father. "Caturix has everything well in hand. You must not think of it now. Brenna, your father will need his rest."

Brenna nodded. "I will go check on Melusine."

"Good," Father said lightly. "Yes. That's well done, Brenna. Go on."

Brenna kissed Father on the forehead, then rose to go. "Boudica?"

"I will need Boudica here," Belenus said.

My sister nodded then left.

"Boudica," Belenus said. "I will bind the wound now. Fetch me those clean linens," he said, pointing.

I handed Belenus a bundle then waited at his side, watching as the druid bound Father's leg. Blue, spidery veins twisted like ivy from the wound. Father's eyelids drooped.

"Another of the draught," Belenus said, handing me Father's empty cup.

I stirred the liquid then poured another portion into Father's cup. I then went to Father's side, helping him sit once more. I held his hand gently as he drank.

"When did Belenus teach you such herbcraft?" Father asked between sips.

"Not I," Belenus said with a chuckle. "Ula."

Father laughed lightly, then winced. "That old crone? At least you learned something from always following that old woman's shadow."

"Ula is as wise as any druid," Belenus said. "But Boudica also has natural inclinations."

"Yes," Father said drowsily. "She does. You're so much like your mother, Boudica. So much like Damara. Now, you want to marry the chieftain's son and take up the same role as Ula, the wisewoman of Frog's Hollow," he said with a chuckle.

The brew was working on him, the gallowgrass making him feel light and sleepy. And, apparently, loosening his tongue.

"Every village needs someone who can brew a tincture to rid you of a headache. Let's just hope I don't become as cantankerous as Ula. Now, drink," I said, helping him finish off the last of the drink.

"Saenunos wants you wed to King Caratacus," Father said drowsily. "He paid a visit to the Catuvellauni, my brother did, without telling me. They spoke of wedding you to Caratacus and Brenna to Togodumnus."

"Father."

"I told him no, Boudica," Father whispered drowsily. "I told him no. Boudica… If something ever happens to me, the family will need your stubborn willfulness. You will need to be strong. Bran and Brenna do not have it in them. Caturix goes along too easily with what others want. Be immovable. And watch your uncle…" And with that, Father closed his eyes and slept.

Stunned, I turned to Belenus.

"May the gods watch over us all," Belenus said. "And keep us from such a dark day."

CHAPTER 20

I t was late in the night when I finally left Father and Belenus sleeping in Father's chamber. I went outside to get some fresh air, only to find the wedding celebrations over. The music from the village was done, the central bonfire burnt down to mere embers. Only the guards milled about. Pressing my hands into my lower back, I gazed up at the sky to find the moon had a red tinge. The image so surprised me that I gasped.

"News is coming," a voice said.

I turned to find Einion, the druid of Stonea, approaching me.

"Ill omen," I replied.

He nodded. "I have just returned to learn that the king has taken ill."

"He's sleeping now, Belenus along with him. I must beg your forgiveness. Belenus sent me to your house to fetch some herbs. I let myself inside. I'm sorry."

Einion nodded, his eyes on the moon. "Think nothing of it,

Princess. Let me go check on the king," he said, then turned to go.

"Oh. And don't worry. I didn't let your cat out."

Einion paused. "My cat?"

I tipped my head then nodded. "Friendly little creature. The black cat with golden eyes."

Einion held my gaze. "I have no cat, Princess." The man frowned. "The gods are awake and moving. There are signs everywhere… Now, blood on the moon," he said, then went inside.

I inhaled slowly, then exhaled deeply. I would be glad to be done with this place and back home—and moreover, off to Frog's Hollow. I was sick of people and whispers and worries. I wanted the wind, and the sea, and the forest, and Gaheris's sweet kisses.

I sighed.

No more. I would find my bed and let what was left of this day pass.

Turning, I made my way back into the roundhouse to the small room I shared with my sister. When I entered, I found my little puppy sleeping in a basket beside the bed. He looked up, gave me a half bark, then fell over asleep once more.

I slid into bed beside Brenna.

"How is Father?" she asked tiredly.

"Sleeping."

Brenna wrapped her arm around me, pulling me close. "Where did you learn all those herbs, Boudica? From Dôn?"

"From Ula."

Brenna laughed. "Of course," she said with a heavy sigh then fell back to sleep.

Rest did not come easily for me. I lay awake, tossing and turning until I couldn't stand my own restlessness. As much as

I wanted to put everything behind me, I could not. From the vision of the ocean to the piskies to the strange man in the stones to Caturix's wedding to Father's leg and his words, it was just too much. I rose once more, slipping down the narrow hall back to the main chamber where—to my surprise—I found Bran awake. He was sitting at the table, staring into the fire.

I sat down across from him.

Wordlessly, he poured me a goblet of wine.

"What's wrong?" I asked him.

"Saenunos... Boudica, I think he is making plans for you and Brenna and not ones to which Father will agree. He was speaking to King Volisios."

"About Caratacus and Togodumnus?"

Bran looked surprised. "You know?"

"Father told me. He said he would not agree."

Bran frowned, then leaned toward me. "It's more than that. He wants the Northern Iceni and the Coritani to align with those brothers."

"Why? For what reason?"

Bran looked around him. "To take possession of the Greater Iceni lands."

"Father would never agree. Ancient Antedios has always been our ally. The Northern and Great Iceni have never been at odds."

"Saenunos wants to attack when old Antedios dies, taking the lands before Prasutagus gets the crown."

"What did Volisios say?"

"He laughed and reminded Saenunos that he is not king. Saenunos's ambitions are stunning. He even suggested I wed Imogen of the Catuvellauni."

"They say that poor girl is mad."

Bran nodded.

"I..." I began, but I was unsure what to say. "I am no druid, but there are dark signs everywhere. The druid Einion agrees. I have seen strange things, and the moon is soaked in blood tonight. You must tell Father what you have heard."

"When he is well enough," Bran said, then frowned. "He is so stubborn. That leg of his..."

"Perhaps this event will convince him."

"Boudica, you saw the wound. If he dies, we are all at Uncle's mercy."

I stared into my goblet. Dark thoughts spun through my mind. Caturix would make a good king, even if Father doubted him. But if our father died, it would not be Caturix who would rule, it would be Saenunos. Caturix would not take the crown until our uncle was dead. "No, we are not."

Bran gave me a questioning look.

"By Andraste, we are not," I repeated. "Saenunos is not our father. We are not beholden to him. Our loyalty is to the Northern Iceni. We must do what is best for the people. No matter what it takes. No matter what must be done."

Bran stared at me then nodded slowly. "No matter what must be done," he repeated.

I sighed heavily then polished off my wine. "I was already too anxious to sleep. Now, I am doubly so."

"Why do you think I am here? This bottle used to be full," Bran said, lifting an empty vessel of wine.

I chuckled, then clinked my glass against his.

Bran huffed a soft laugh.

"What is it?"

He shook his head. "Out of all of us, I never expected war-mongering from you."

"Did you not see how I beat Gaheris until he promised to

love me forever?"

Bran laughed. "That's different."

I paused. "Is it? I love the people of the Northern Iceni. Each of them. By name. I will keep them safe from machinations of men like Saenunos."

"May Andraste hold you to that promise," Bran said, lifting his cup.

"That is a burden I gladly accept. And one you should too."

"May the gods use me as they see fit."

"Be careful what you wish for," I said, then rose. "Get some rest, Bran. You'll need it if you want to keep up with all of Saenunos's plotting. Good night."

"Good night."

With a sigh, I headed back to my chamber. This time when I laid down, however, I drifted off into a dark, dreamless sleep.

CHAPTER 21

It was nearly midday when I woke again. Brenna was gone, as was the little puppy. I rose, redressed, then made my way to the central meeting hall, finding the place empty. Snatching a freshly made bannock and a mug of ale, I went outside. There, I found Brenna and Melusine tossing a ball for the puppy, the two of them laughing at the creature's antics. Lingering at the door, I finished my bread and ale then turned around.

I went back inside to Father's chamber. There was a candle illuminating the dark room. Father slept, his skin pale, his forehead wet with sweat. From the pot of herbs boiling over the fire to the scent of lemon balm in the air, I could tell Belenus had recently been there, but the druid was gone.

I wet a piece of clean linen with water then gently mopped Father's face. As I did so, I studied his features. There was little of me there. Only Caturix had Father's dark features.

Father's eyes flickered open for a moment.

"Damara," he whispered.

I swallowed hard, then said, "No, Father. It's Boudica," but he had already gone back to sleep.

I set the cloth aside then lifted the blanket to inspect Father's wound. Red blood marred the linens, but the angry veins and swelling had receded somewhat. I lowered the blanket then rose to go, turning to find Belenus there.

"Boudica," he said, his gaze shifting to Father. "He is better this morning. When he wakes, Einion, Gwri, and I will try to convince him to remove the growth. He cannot deny the risk any longer."

"With Saenunos and King Volisios here, there is no way he will comply. His pride will not allow it."

Belenus frowned. He knew I was right.

"Do *you* need anything?" I asked Belenus.

The druid shook his head. "You have been a great help already. I must say, you've learned much from Ula."

I chuckled. "Only to spite her."

"Then she found the perfect way to teach her pupil," he told me with a wink.

I set my hand on the old druid's shoulder then went back outside. This time, the puppy spotted me and made his way to join me. I picked him up, giving the curly-haired monster a scratch. "What have you been doing, you little bear?"

"He's been keeping us amused this morning," Melusine said, joining us, a smile on her face. She turned and looked toward the gate of the chieftain's compound where King Volisios and the other men from the Coritani were preparing the horses. "My father is preparing to go."

"So soon?"

Melusine nodded. "He says things are too unsettled these days to be gone for long. He has one eye on the Brigantes to the north and another on the Catuvellauni to the south."

"The Brigantes... Are they not ruled by a queen?" Brenna asked.

Melusine nodded. "Cartimandua has taken her mother's throne. She is no older than the three of us, but they say she is shrewd beyond measure. No one is quite sure what to make of her yet. Although, she has already engaged the Parisii in a skirmish. Thus..." Melusine said, gesturing to her father once more.

"It would be better for you and Caturix if we all go," Brenna said. "But with Father's condition..."

"How is your father this morning?" Melusine asked.

"Sleeping," I replied, "but the wound looks a bit better."

Melusine smiled gently. "I am glad to hear it. Has he had the ailment long—" she was asking when a horn at the lower gate interrupted her. The long, low sound echoed across the fens.

Caturix, who had been with King Volisios, stepped from the crowd and looked toward the village.

The horn sounded once more.

"That doesn't sound good," Bran said, appearing from behind us.

"Where have you been?" I asked.

With a frown, Bran gestured over his shoulder toward our uncle who passed us by, making his way toward the gate. We followed along behind him.

A sense of dread washed over me. Something was wrong. I could feel it. My heart began thumping in my chest, my hands sweating. Suddenly, I felt ill.

"Boudica?" Brenna said, taking my arm. "I swear, you are not yourself these days. What's wrong?"

"I don't know. I..." I began but said nothing more when

Balfor, Oak Throne's housecarl, rode into the chieftain's compound, a small party behind him.

Quickly dismounting, Balfor went to Caturix. The pair shared a brief word then promptly headed our way.

Caturix met my gaze. The look on his face sent a shiver down my spine.

I froze.

"Boudica?" Brenna whispered. She looked from Caturix to me then turned back to Bran. "Go tell Belenus that Father needs to be woken," she told my brother. "There is news."

Bran rushed back into the roundhouse.

"Who is that man?" Melusine asked.

"Our housecarl from Oak Throne," Brenna replied.

Caturix and Balfor met up with us, Saenunos along with them.

"When?" Saenunos demanded.

"Yesterday. We've been riding through the night."

"Caturix, what is it?" Brenna asked. "Is Oak Throne—"

"Oak Throne is well," Caturix said, then turned to me. "Boudica, come inside."

"Caturix," I whispered.

Belenus met us at the door. "Come," he said, waving for Balfor to follow him.

We all went to Father's chamber. He was sitting upright in his bed but still looked ashen and sweaty.

"My King," Balfor said, kneeling beside Father's bed.

"What has happened?" Father asked stiffly.

"There was an attack," Balfor said, his gaze shifting to me for a brief moment, "on the sea camp of the men of Frog's Hollow."

I felt my knees go weak. Brenna held on to my arm.

Father motioned for Balfor to continue.

"A rider came from Frog's Hollow. No one knows what happened. A group from their party was delivering the first barrels of fish back at the village when the attack occurred. By the time they returned, the attackers were gone, and the men of Frog's Hollow were left for dead on the beach."

I covered my mouth with my hand.

"Survivors?" my father asked.

"None."

Not waiting another moment, I turned and left the chamber, rushing to my room to gather my things.

"Boudica," Father called, but I didn't wait for him. Through the open door, I could hear Father's voice. "Bran, get your men. Saddle up at once and go with Boudica. Otherwise, she'll ride herself to death. Go with her. Find out what happened."

"No survivors?" Saenunos asked. "No one saw anything?"

"No one knows, Chieftain. Whoever did this overwhelmed the party, murdering them all."

"Bah," Saenunos said in frustration. "Our enemies grow bold. We must find whoever did this and punish them, Aesunos. Perhaps I should go—"

"No. Bran and Boudica will go," Father said sternly.

Slinging my bag over my back, I hurried back down the hallway.

"Boudica," my father called from within his chamber.

I paused. I could not think, nor feel, nor speak. I needed to ride. Now. I went to the doorway of Father's chamber.

"Bran will ride with you. Wait for him," he told me sternly.

"Father, I—"

"You will wait for Bran," Father said then turned to Balfor. "Any news of the family of Rolan? Of his son, Gaheris?"

"The rider from Frog's Hollow said Rolan is dead," Balfor

told Father, then turned to me. "I do not know the fate of Gaheris, Boudica. I'm sorry."

I willed myself not to cry.

"I will go to the kitchens and see rations are readied at once," Melusine said, swiftly departing.

Brenna held me by both arms. "The news will be the same whether you ride Druda out from under you or not."

"If he is hurt…" I whispered, my voice barely above a whisper.

Balfor said there were no survivors. Gaheris was not hurt. He was either alive or in the Otherworld, one or the other.

Brenna nodded. "I will pray to the gods. Be safe, my sister. Be safe." She kissed me on my forehead.

"Go to the stables and have the horses readied. I will get my men," Bran told me.

I nodded.

"Should I go, Father?" Caturix asked.

"No. Your life is here now. By Great Cernunnos, this leg. Boudica, keep your wits about you, and do what must be done. I entrust this task to you. We will come behind you as soon as we can."

"Yes, Father," I said, then turned and hurried outside.

Gaheris.

Gaheris.

Swift Epona, get me to my love.

CHAPTER 22

Along with Balfor and Bran's men, we set off within the hour. For days, I had felt something coming. Was this it? Was this the reason?

Druda, seeming to sense my nervousness, kept his pace quick and steady. It was nearly noon when we stopped at the stream, watering the horses and giving them a brief rest.

I sat down at the side of the stream, wetting my hands. Shifting my mountain of red hair, I wet my neck. The summer sun was scorching. Most of the horses waded into the stream to cool themselves. Splashing water onto my face, I tried to quell the nervousness of my heart, but there was no relenting.

Clasping the frog amulet hanging on my neck, I closed my eyes.

Gaheris.

I'm coming.

I gazed into the water. The crystal-clear waves trickled over the stones, reflecting the green of the canopy overhead. My eyes grew heavy. The birds chirping overhead seemed to call to me, calling my name in every warble.

"Bou-di-ca...Bou-di-ca...Bou-di-ca... They are coming.

My head grew dizzy. An eagle cried, and before me, a vision formed. I saw bonfires. People were laughing and dancing. A man appeared from the crowd wearing a mask made of green leaves and antlers. He was a hulking creature with tattoos on his chest and long, red hair.

"Bou-di-ca...Bou-di-ca...All of nature sings to the queen of oak. We call you. Defend us. Protect us... Bou-di-ca... Bou-di-ca..."

"Boudica."

I blinked hard.

"Boudica? We are ready to ride now," Bran told me, setting his hand on my shoulder.

I looked up at my brother. "Bran?"

His brow scrunched up. "Come on. We can make Frog's Hollow by nightfall if we bypass Oak Throne. There is no sense in going there."

I nodded.

Turning, I went to collect Druda, mounting once more.

Bran reined his horse in beside me, and soon, we rode off.

Each beat of Druda's hooves echoed the thundering of my heart.

Gaheris...

Gaheris...

Gaheris...

<hr />

THE MOON WAS HIGH IN THE SKY WHEN WE FINALLY APPROACHED the village of Frog's Hollow. I was surprised to see the place alight with torches.

But then, I understood why.

In the distance, I heard the sound of feminine voices lifted up in song.

The priestesses had come from the Grove of Andraste...to perform the rites for the dead.

As we approached, a horn sounded. Men guarding the entrance to the small village stepped forward.

"Halt! Who approaches?" a man called from the shadows.

I moved Druda ahead. "It's Boudica. I am with my brother, Bran, and the men of Oak Throne. We've ridden from Stonea."

In the shadows of their torchlight, I saw a young man run back into the village. The guard stepped forward, revealing Kentigern, one of Gaheris's friends.

"Boudica," he said, a pained expression on his face.

I dismounted Druda.

No sooner had I come forward, I found Bran at my side.

"Dôn and the priestesses are here. I've sent a boy to get Lynet," Kentigern told Bran and me.

"To get Lynet," I repeated. Not Gaheris. "Gaheris..." I began, but the question stuck in my mouth. A strange sensation, like someone had wrapped their hand around my throat, washed over me. I felt like I might throw up.

A moment later, in the shadow of the firelight, I saw Lynet making her way toward me. Her hair was wild, her eyes were red with dark circles underneath.

"Boudica," she whispered, meeting my gaze. She stepped toward me, her hands shaking as she reached for my face. "Boudica..." she said again, her voice cracking.

I backed up, not wanting her to get close. I bumped into Druda, who snorted at me but didn't move.

My gaze went to the village. In the distance, on the rise where the great oak sat, torchlight burned. I spotted the figure of Dôn.

"Boudica," Lynet said gently.

I shook my head quickly. "Don't speak," I told her. "Don't speak."

"Boudica," Bran whispered.

Nodding to me, Lynet took my hand. Her touch was as cold as ice. Feeling like I was floating, I followed the woman who would be my mother-in-law back into the village. We wound down the narrow paths, across the little wooden bridges, past the water wheel, and toward the rise.

They had gathered on the very spot where Gaheris had promised to build our home.

I looked behind me, finding Bran and the others following.

My brother met my gaze, a pained expression on his face.

As long as no one spoke, I would be all right. As long as no one told me anything, it would be okay.

But it was not all right.

Nothing was all right.

Rather than the home Gaheris had promised to build for me, the people of Frog's Hollow had constructed a burial mound made of stone and earth beside the great oak tree. It was as big as any roundhouse.

This house was not a new family with a brood of children.

This house was for the dead.

The priestesses of the Grove of Andraste stood before the entrance to the mound.

I caught Bec's gaze. She gave me a sorrowful expression full of empathy.

But as long as she did not speak...

Lynet lead me to Dôn.

"Boudica," Dôn said, inclining her head to me. "The moon is high. We must seal the mound now, but there is just enough time. Come," she said, reaching for my hand.

Lynet let me go.

Speechless, I followed Dôn.

The priestess bent low to enter the mound. I followed along behind her. Within, the place was illuminated with braziers that burned heady herbs. The scents of sage, mint, and lavender nearly choked me, but under them, I smelled death.

I suppressed a gasp as I looked around the room. Two dozen men lay with their grave goods about them. Dressed in their finest, they were strewn with flowers, their swords, axes, or spears on their chests. At the center of the room was Rolan, dressed in the same fine robes he'd worn the day he had asked Father for my hand.

And beside him…

"No…" I whispered, backing toward the exit.

Dôn held my hand firmly, not letting me go. "He has left this life, Boudica. But this is not the only life we live. You will see him again. The soul is bound to those we truly love. Life after life, we meet one another. Sometimes for a short while, sometimes for a lifetime. If you loved him truly, you will see him again. Do not shrink from death. It is only a passage. But you must bid him goodbye for this lifetime. Go to him. Promise to meet him in the next life. Show him your strength. Do not let him be afraid for you, now that he is gone," she said firmly, then let my hand go.

Moving slowly, I made my way to Gaheris.

Grief washed over me as I passed the men of Frog's Hollow. I knew them all, every name, so many who had been friends of Gaheris. Conal's wife had just had a baby. And Doran had three children of his own, his daughter just a few years younger than me. The bodies had been cleaned and dressed, but I still saw signs of their wounds. They had died fighting.

When I finally reached Gaheris, I knelt on the ground beside him. His mother had dressed him finely in his dark green cloak, pinned at the shoulder. His hair was brushed out long. There was discoloration under his eye and on his cheek where he had taken a blow to the face. His hands lay on his chest, clutching his sword.

"Oh, my love," I whispered. "My love," I said, and then the tears began to fall. Unable to stop them, I set my head on Gaheris's chest and wept. I could not control myself. The dream we had fashioned together was gone. Our home. Our life. Our children. They would never be. Everything we had planned. Everything we had hoped for. It was all gone.

"Who did this?" I whispered, turning to Dôn.

"No one lived to tell."

"No one?"

"Well," Dôn said, then paused. "That is not correct. There was one survivor."

"Who?"

"A boy, but the child does not speak."

"Tristan? Tristan saw who did this?"

Dôn nodded then gestured across the room. There, I saw the bodies of Tristan's father and brother. "The boy hid during the attack. He did not see much, and what he saw, he cannot say."

I turned back, touching Gaheris's cheek. "Oh, my love," I whispered. "I had a puppy for you," I said, then wept. I shook my head. "I'll meet you in the next life. I promise you. We'll have our animals and our children. We'll ride and hunt. You'll have your birds, and I'll have my horses. We will be happy. I swear, I will find you in the next life. I promise you."

Shaking my head, I dashed my tears from my cheeks.

"Come now, Boudica. We must seal the tomb before the

moon reaches its highest point. They will go to the Otherworld where they will drink and feast until it is time for them to return to this world again."

"I…" Pausing a moment, I pulled my knife from my belt. Moving carefully, I cut a lock of Gaheris's hair, slipping it into my pocket, then rose. "I love you," I whispered to him, then turned and rejoined Dôn.

The priestess turned to go, but I paused before the exit, looking back at the sorry sight.

"Boudica?" Dôn called.

"May Andraste hear my words. I will avenge Gaheris and all these good men. Even if it takes me until my dying breath, I will learn who killed these men, and I will make them pay."

"So you have sworn. So it will be done. May Andraste give you strength. You will need it."

CHAPTER 23

Feeling numb, I joined Lynet's side as Dôn, Bec, and the other priestesses performed the final rites, sending our dead on to the Otherworld. Lynet wept silently. She had lost her whole family. As I had lost my future with her son, so had she lost all those she loved.

When the rite was finally done, Lynet stepped forward.

"Please, everyone, join me at my home. We will eat and drink, honoring the dead."

Many in the crowd wept as we made our way back to the chieftain's house. A fire burned in the central bonfire. The whole of the village was illuminated with torchlight. Lynet and the other women worked setting food on tables outside so we could eat under the starlight. No doubt, many had fasted the whole day in honor of the dead.

Wordlessly, Bran came to me, wrapping his arms around me.

I tried to stay strong but wept on his shoulder.

It could not be.

How could this have happened?

"We will discover who is responsible," Bran whispered in my ear.

I nodded.

"Let's stay here tonight and ride to the camp in the morning. Perhaps there will be some sign," Bran suggested.

Wiping the tears from my cheeks, I nodded then pulled back.

Leaving Bran and the rest of the crowd, I slipped into Lynet's house and went to the small, draped alcove where Gaheris slept. The little raven hopped around the small cage, chirping when he saw me.

"Morfran," I said, greeting him. "Has anyone remembered you?" I asked, looking for the bird's food.

Of course, Gaheris had it sitting in a jar nearby.

I scooped some of the food from the jar, putting it into the palm of my hand. I reached into the cage. "Poor little creature," I whispered, my voice catching.

Once the bird had fed, I slipped my hand out of the cage then sat on Gaheris's bed. Gaheris's scent, a sweet mix of lavender and cedar, permeated the room. Lying down on his pallet, I grabbed a handful of his linens and pressed them to my nose.

"How will I go on without you?" I whispered. Weeping hard, I lay in Gaheris's bed, my mind reeling.

I must have fallen into an exhausted sleep, because I felt Lynet's presence when she covered me sometime later.

"Lynet?" I asked softly. "Should I—" I began, trying to sit up.

"Sleep, Boudica. You are the only family I have left. Let me look after you, sweet girl," she said, tucking the blanket around me.

I closed my eyes, wrapped in Gaheris's scent, then drifted off to dreams once more.

MY DREAMS WERE FITFUL THAT NIGHT. I WOKE WITH THE lingering memories of a nightmare. In my dreams, I'd been with two young women, both of whom looked terrified. I tried to help them, but no matter what I did, I couldn't move. I couldn't get to them. The fear in the girls' eyes broke my heart, even as I was in crippling pain. I howled because of it. And then, there was fire. Everything burned.

Exhaling deeply, trying to shake off the dream, I sat up.

It was quiet in the village.

All I heard was the croaking of frogs.

Wrapping myself in a blanket, I stepped back into the center of the roundhouse where Bran and his men lay sleeping on the floor. The drape covering Lynet's small alcove where she and Rolan shared a bed was closed. My heart feeling heavy, I went outside. The central bonfire had burned down to a low flame. Grabbing a couple of logs, I set them on the fire then sat on the bench before the flames.

It was not yet dawn.

Mist rose off the pond and river, drenching much of the village in fog.

I didn't know if Dôn and the other priestesses had gone back to the grove or if they were still in the village.

I stared into the flames.

I felt hollow. My whole future had been snatched away from under me. And worse, Gaheris's murderer was gone. No one knew what had happened.

No one except...

I rose, planning to go to Tristan's home, only to find the boy standing beside me.

"Tristan," I said, taken by surprise.

The boy met and held my gaze. Tears welled in his eyes. Sitting once more, I pulled the little boy onto my lap and held him close to me.

The gods only knew where the child had spent the night. From the scent of fern and earth on his clothes and the dampness of his hair, something told me he had been outside the whole night long. I took his hands between mine, rubbing them to warm them. I pressed my cheek against his head. I would speak to Lynet when she woke. What would be done with the boy?

Pulling Tristan closer, I wrapped Gaheris's blanket around us both.

"Did you sleep outside all night?" I asked.

After a long moment, he nodded.

I could chide the child, warn him not to sleep in unsafe places where the greenwood might snatch him, but what was the use? The world had already taken everything from him.

I whispered, "I feel like the whole world just stopped. Do you feel like that too?"

After a moment, he nodded.

I kissed him on the back of the head, then rubbed his hands again. They were warming up, finally. The pair of us sat there for a long time. Soon, deep ruby and pink colors trimmed the skyline as the sun began to rise.

I sighed.

Tristan rose. Taking my hand, he motioned for me to come with him. He went to the far side of the fire where the ashes were spread on the ground. He motioned for me to kneel beside him, then he picked up a small twig.

"You want to tell me something?" I asked.

He nodded.

"Show me something?"

He nodded again then pointed to the ash. In the ash, he began to draw. I didn't understand at first, but then I realized he was drawing waves.

"The beach?"

He nodded.

"You want to tell me what happened?"

Again, he nodded.

"Did you see the men who killed Gaheris and your family?"

Once more, he nodded.

"Did they come by boat or by horse?"

Tristan turned back to the ash. He drew a boat, then another, and then another.

"So many boats?" I asked.

Tristan nodded.

"Did you see their banners? Their colors? Who were they?"

Tristan frowned.

"I'm sorry. One question. Did they have banners?"

He tilted his head from side to side, as if unsure or the answer was not easy.

"How about a symbol? Did their people have a symbol that might signify who they were? At Oak Throne, we have our tree. Here in Frog's Hollow, your banners have a frog. The Greater Iceni have a horse. Did you see any kind of symbol on their shields or on their banners?"

He nodded. Wiping the drawings of the boats away, he began to draw once more. I watched as the figure in the ash transformed into a bird.

"A bird?"

Tristan nodded.

"Do you know what kind? A raven? A hawk?"

Tristan shrugged.

I looked back at the image of the bird. Its wings were spread wide, its head turned to the side.

Tristan tapped my shoulder. He then pointed to his mouth.

"Are you hungry?"

He shook his head then pointed to the bird once more. Then, he stuck out his tongue and made a movement, like he was sawing his tongue off. He closed his mouth and covered his lips.

Considering for a long moment, I asked, "They were silent when they came?"

He nodded.

"When did they come? Night or day?"

He drew a crescent in the ash.

They had come by night—in silence—and butchered the camp.

"How many?" I asked. "If this is all the men of Frog's Hollow," I said, setting a pebble before us, "how many were they?"

Tristan set three pebbles before my single stone.

I nodded then sat back. "Do you remember anything else?"

The child wore a frustrated look on his face. There was more he knew but didn't know how to express it.

Wrapping my arms around his waist, I pulled him toward me. "It's all right. You've done well. It's a start."

I stared at the image of the bird drawn in the ash. "Whoever they are, they will pay for what they have done. I will tear that bird from the sky and bathe it in fire."

CHAPTER 24

Sometime after sunrise, Lynet and the others woke, and the people of the village started about their work. Their expressions were grave. The whole village was in mourning. The women set out bowls and platters of food on the table for anyone who wanted to come. As it turned out, Dôn and the others had departed for the grove the night before.

"Let's help Lynet," I said, taking Tristan's hand.

Wordlessly, the little boy and I assisted the women setting out the food. When we were done, I sat Tristan down at the end of the table and filled a plate and cup for him. I kissed him on the forehead. "Eat," I told him. "Even if you don't feel like it."

He nodded, then pointed to me, then to his mouth, then to me once more.

"I will eat too. Soon. I promise," I replied.

He gave me a soft smile then nodded.

"He's always taken to you," Lynet said, joining me.

"He's a good boy. He told me what he saw. They came by

boat in the night, silent, in a large force, and killed our people."

"Tristan told you that…how?" Lynet asked.

"He drew it. And more, they had the emblem of a bird on their banners."

"Brigantes?" Lynet asked. "Their symbol is the raven."

I nodded. "I wondered that as well."

Lynet's brow flexed. "Farther north, in the Caledonian Confederacy, there is a tribe whose symbol is a crow. They are warlike people who live on the coastline, the Votadini—the crow people. This is just the kind of thing they would do."

"Your ancestors are from the north," I said. "Gaheris told me."

Lynet nodded. "Yes. But from the western coast, on the Isle of Skye. Boudica…" Lynet began then paused. "Do you know the dagger Gaheris wore?"

"Yes."

"Is there any chance he gave it to you?"

"His dagger was not with him?"

Lynet shook her head. "I had hoped maybe he'd given it to you, all things considered. It's a very special blade."

"He told me the story, about how the blade is passed to the daughters in a family, coming from Scáthach herself."

Lynet stared off into the horizon. "Then, you do not have it."

"No. I'm sorry. I know the blade, but he didn't give it to me."

"I have lost my ancestor's dagger, along with everything else I love," she said, tears welling in her eyes.

My heart ached. I wrapped my arms around her and pulled her close. She would have been my mother-in-law. In the future that would not come, I would have worked beside her every day, laughing and joking, teasing Rolan and Gaheris. We would have made food together, and she would have been there for the birth of my children—her grandchildren. And one day, my daughters would have wielded her ancestor's dagger. Now…

"Ah, Boudica," she said, pulling back. She kissed me on the cheek then turned, joining the other women who were pouring drinks for those who had come to eat—mothers, sisters, wives, and other children who had lost their parents.

Soon, Bran and his men joined us.

I took a seat beside Tristan, who set a round of bread on my plate then jabbed me in the ribs, pointing for me to eat. I took a bite, but only to please him.

"When we are done here, I will have the men saddle up," Bran told me.

I nodded then turned to Tristan. "We will go to the camp to see if there are any signs of who did this. It would be helpful if you came, but you don't have to."

After a moment, the boy nodded.

"I'll ride out as well," Lynet told us. "And these men will join us," she said, gesturing to some of the others who'd come. "Not only have these strangers taken our people from us, but we depend on the harvest of pilchards to survive the winter. We must see what we can salvage."

"We'll help," Bran told her.

Lynet nodded. "Thank you, Prince Bran."

It was good to see Lynet taking charge. I had worried what would happen to the people of Frog's Hollow now that Rolan was gone, but the answer was obvious. Lynet was just as capable as her husband. Father would let the people of Frog's Hollow choose their new chieftain. He was good in that way.

Saenunos would have sent one of his trusted dogs here to rule over these people.

After the others finished their meal, we made ready to go. Aside from the bites I had eaten mainly to please Tristan, I could not bring myself to eat otherwise. My stomach ached. I went to the stables and saddled Druda, feeling sorry to see Mountain looking forlorn in the corral as he looked on with anticipation for Gaheris.

Steeling my heart against the emotions that wanted to spill out, I led Druda to the center of the village, joining the others. Tristan joined me.

I waved to Bran. "Let me get on, then help him up?" I asked, motioning to Tristan.

"Boudica," Bran said carefully. "We may not find anything."

"I know," I replied. "In the least, we will help with the pilchards."

Bran nodded but said nothing more.

I slipped onto Druda then Bran helped Tristan mount in front of me.

Lynet appeared, a sword and bow on her back. She checked on the others then went to the front of the party. "Let's ride out," she called, then we rode from Frog's Hollow, taking the path to the sea.

"Hold on to his mane," I told Tristan. "And don't be scared. He's steady of foot," I said, then clicked to Druda. We had just neared the exit of the hollow when Mountain whinnied loudly, confused to see Druda off on an adventure without him.

And this time, I could not stop the flow of tears.

CHAPTER 25

A heaviness sat on my heart when I finally caught the light scents of sand and sea on the breeze. So much of mine and Gaheris's dreaming had been done beside the waves of the Wash. Now, the gods had taken those dreams with them on the tide.

Images flashed through my mind, memories of the visions I had seen.

The blood in the water.

The debris in the surf.

The hand on the water.

I had seen Gaheris die but had not known nor understood.

Great Mother, Forest Lord, why would you show me such things if I could not prevent them?

We kept to the forest trail for another two hours, riding adjacent to the surf, when Lynet finally led us across the dunes onto the beach. There, I spotted the little shanties of the fishing camp. Each year, the people of Frog's Hollow had come to harvest the pilchards, an annual reaping that ensured their very lives over the dark winter. Now, this place marked death.

Tristan leaned back against me.

"You're safe," I told him. "I promise you. Lynet will see to the pilchards, and we will leave."

We rode to the camp, finding it in disarray. Lynet dismounted, tying up her horse, then directed the men of Frog's Hollow to get to work. Nets lay strewn on the beach. Barrels and buckets were overturned. A haul of pilchards lay dead and dried up on the beach. The place was a mess. Righting the boats and other equipment and using the nets and tools they had brought with them, the remaining men of Frog's Hollow quickly got to work, heading back out to sea. From the number of birds hovering over the waves, the pilchards were still there—for now.

Bran rejoined me, helping Tristan down. "What can I do?" he asked.

"Ask some men to help with the fishing. And send two parties to ride the coast in both directions, see if there is any sign." The Wash touched Northern Iceni shores on the southeast of the inlet. The other side of the Wash to the north was ruled by King Dumnovellaunus, one of the triumvirate kings of the Coritani, along with Melusine's father, King Volisios. "When we return to Oak Throne, we must send word to King Dumnovellaunus, see if there have been any attacks on the other side of the Wash. Perhaps we should send a rider to King Antedios and Prince Prasutagus as well, see if there have been other incidents on the Iceni coastline."

Bran nodded. "Whatever you think is best. Father will be in no condition to ride from Stonea anytime soon."

"We will handle it ourselves."

"All right. I'll get my men ready and lead one of the parties," Bran said, then hurried off.

I looked down at Tristan. "Come. Let's walk together," I

said, taking his hand. We walked toward the surf. The dark blue waters were calm today, the waves lapping gently onto the shore. Down shore, the people of Frog's Hollow called to one another, identifying schools of fish as they began their work bringing in the harvest. I knelt down, meeting the boy's blue eyes. "Can you help me? Answer some questions about what happened?"

Tristan nodded.

"Which direction did they come from? North? East?"

Tristan paused, then shook his head.

"Was the camp awake or asleep when they came?"

Tristan closed his eyes.

"Your father, brother, Gaheris, and the others fought them?"

Tristan nodded, then pointed back to the camp.

"Over there?"

He nodded again.

"Why didn't they see you?"

Tristan took my hand then led me away from the water to a spot where the dunes met the forest. There, he led me to an old stump which was hollowed in the middle. Tristan crawled inside.

"You hid."

Tristan crawled out once more. When he looked at me, the expression on his face told the story—he was not sure if he had done the right thing or not.

"You did well," I told him. "You did very well. Your father would be very proud of your smart thinking."

He smiled lightly, then pointed to the stump, showing me a crack in the wood where he must have been able to see out.

"Ah. I see. Very good. This is a sad question, and I'm sorry to ask it, but did they…did they loot the bodies? Take our people's gold or weapons?"

Tristan paused, then nodded. He motioned to his neck and wrists.

They had taken the torcs and ringlets.

Tristan frowned, trying to think of how to express himself. He pointed to me then set his hand on my heart, repeating the gesture repeatedly.

"My…my heart," I said, then paused. "Gaheris?"

Tristan nodded.

A sick feeling rocked my stomach. "Go on."

He set his hand on the sword on my side. He then pointed to me and my heart once more.

"They took Gaheris's weapon?"

Tristan nodded.

I felt like my heart would break. I had held onto hope that we would find the dagger in the sand, that somehow, I would be able to recover it for Lynet.

My gaze shifted toward her. In the water to her waist, she worked casting a net. Her son and husband had died here, but she still worked to make sure her people were cared for.

I set my hand on Tristan's head. "Thank you. Thank you for telling me. Now, will you help me with something else?"

He nodded.

"We need to search the place where the battle happened. We need to see if we can find any sign of the attackers. Anything they may have dropped or left behind. Can you help with that?"

Tristan nodded, and together, we went back to the camp. I walked along the sand. The wind and waves had already disrupted any footprints or anything else that could be tracked. Still, there had to be something. Tristan gestured around, showing me where to look, and the two of us got to work. One of the older men from Frog's Hollow, Oran, returning from dropping a load of fish into a barrel, joined me.

"Princess," Oran said, his gaze shifting from Tristan to me. "I'm afraid the wind will have blown away any tracks. It's all just sand now."

I nodded. "I know. I just hoped to find some sign. Anything."

Oran nodded slowly. "The boy see anything?"

"He saw everything, but he cannot give the details. Whoever they were, they came by sea, attacked the camp, then left. And they had a bird as their emblem."

The old man's gaze shifted across the water. "Brigantes or Votadini, maybe…"

I set my hand on my hips and followed his gaze. "But why would they start a war with the Northern Iceni?"

"They wouldn't, which is why they silenced everyone who saw them. Whatever they were doing, they wanted to be secret about it."

I stared out at the water. "Maybe."

"I am sorry for you, Princess. We heard the news in the village. We were all happy for you and Gaheris."

"Thank you, Oran."

He nodded then went back, rejoining the others.

With a sigh, I rejoined Tristan, searching once more. My back and neck sweating, I combed the beach, looking for any sign. Aside from recovering some tackle, a pair of gloves, a pipe, and a bridle, there was no sign of anything—just the scattered belongings of men whose lives had ended prematurely.

I sat down on a bucket to drink some water.

Being in the place where Gaheris had died filled me with so much despair, I could hardly stand it. The earth itself seemed to mourn. There was a massive hollow pit inside of me. I felt like someone had dug my heart from my chest with their bare hands. My spirit ached. I closed my eyes. On the edge of my senses, I felt the visions that wanted to press themselves upon me. I saw blood in the water. And then an arm and hand, drifting back and forth on the waves.

"No," I whispered. "Show me who killed them. If you must show me something, show me that. If you cannot show me that, show me nothing at all."

The visions faded, and there was only darkness.

A moment later, I heard the sound of someone rushing toward me.

I opened my eyes to find Tristan coming my way.

I rose. "What is it?"

Tristan opened his hand to reveal a coin in his palm.

I lifted the piece. It was not Iceni—Northern nor Greater—in fact, I didn't recognize the markings at all. On the coin was a face, an image of a man with a beard. On the other side of the coin was a chariot.

"Where did you find it?"

Tristan pointed back to the beach.

"Well done. I don't know this coin," I said, then scanned the beach. Lynet was on the shore. "Let's ask Lynet."

Taking Tristan's hand, we joined Lynet.

"Boudica," Lynet said with a tired sigh, pushing back a stray lock of her hair that had blown loose. "It's going well here. We should be done by dusk."

I eyed over the nets. "The haul looks good."

Following my gaze, Lynet nodded. "It will have to do," she said with a sad smile. "The pilchards will all be back out to sea by tomorrow. How about you? Anything?" Lynet asked me, gesturing back to the camp.

"Tristan discovered a coin. Maybe something they dropped. I don't know the coin, nor do I recognize the name or face hereon," I said, holding the coin out to her.

Wiping off her wet, grimy hands, Lynet took the coin. She studied it for a moment, then shook her head. "I don't know it. Let's ask the others."

Lynet, Tristan, and I joined the group from Frog's Hollow.

"Boudica and Tristan found a coin. I don't know it. Do any of you?" Lynet asked, handing it to Turi, one of the older men in the group.

The man turned the coin over and over again then frowned. "I don't know, Princess."

The villagers passed the coin around.

No one recognized it.

"I can say one thing," Lynet said. "I have seen the coins of every tribe in the west and many in the north. I don't know this coin."

"Coins travel," Turi said. "It could have been in the pocket of one of our own men."

"Or buried in the sand for a generation," Oran added.

Sadly, they were not wrong.

"Yes. You're right. It was a good find anyway," I told Tristan. "We discovered a few other things: gloves, some tackle, and a pipe."

Lynet smiled sadly. "Guennola was asking after her husband's pipe. I'm glad to hear you've recovered it. Was there…there was nothing else?"

I guessed what she was asking. Lynet had harbored hope about her dagger.

"No," I said sadly.

She nodded. "Very well. Look, your brother and his party are coming back now," she said, pointing up the beach.

"Thank you all," I told the villagers. Setting my hand on Lynet's arm, giving her a gentle squeeze, I left her to meet Bran.

"Here," I told Tristan, slipping one of my own coins from my pocket and handing it to him. "We need to make it a fair trade. My coin for yours."

The boy smiled at me, taking my Iceni coin and putting it into his pocket.

We reached Bran as he dismounted.

"Anything?" I asked.

Bran shook his head. "We found an old couple who live in a fishing shack. They neither heard nor saw anything. Is Cai's party back yet?"

"No."

"Did you find anything here?"

I handed my brother the coin.

He turned it over and over in his hand. "I don't recognize it."

"Nor do any of them."

Bran frowned then handed the coin back to me. "Ah, there is Cai," he said, pointing down the beach. "Come on."

When we met the other party, the same news greeted us. No sign of anything. No news. Frowning, I looked back out at the sea. Whatever the waves knew, their secret was silent within them.

It was late afternoon when the people of Frog's Hollow finished their work. Two wagons were loaded. The villagers collected the other goods then prepared to leave.

I was just about to ride out when a sharp sound called above me.

I looked up to find Mavis, Gaheris's hawk, there.

Mavis circled above the camp then flew off toward the forest, calling one last time.

A silent tear rolled down my cheek.

In the very least, she was free.

When I looked back, Lynet met my gaze. She shook her head then dashed her tears from her cheeks.

Holding on to Tristan, I clicked to Druda then headed into the forest once more.

When we returned to Frog's Hollow, we discovered that the women had prepared a meal. It was set out at the table in the square. It was dark by the time anyone sat down to eat. I left Tristan with a big plate of food then joined Lynet.

"Won't you eat something? You were under the heat all day," she told me.

"I'm not hungry. Lynet, about Tristan…"

"I will move him into the roundhouse with me," she said. "He has no one now. His mother was my friend—though she has been gone for many years. I brought him into this world. I'll take care of him now. It is the least I can do in his family's honor."

"If Tristan—or you—need anything, you will not hesitate to ask us."

Lynet nodded. "Of course. Why don't you and your brother—and his men—stay the night. Ride home in the morning. I don't want you in the forest at night. My home is yours —just as much now as it would have been in the future. Never forget that."

I nodded.

"Good. Now, sit down and eat something. Gaheris would not forgive me if I let you go all day without a bite of food in your mouth."

"Lynet, I cannot. I…"

"You will try, Boudica. We both will."

Not arguing further, I sat down beside Tristan and let Lynet put a plate before me—just as I had done with the boy. When she was done, she sat across from me. She met and held my gaze, then gestured with her eyes for me to eat.

Though my stomach ached, rocked uncomfortable with misery, I stuck a bite of food in my mouth. And then another. And then another. My heart and mind felt numb.

I ate because Gaheris would have wanted it.

Because I would not offend the woman who should have been my mother-in-law.

Because I wanted to be a good role model for Tristan.

But for no other reason.

My eyes drifted across the village, resting on the mound where my love was buried. Not far from the burial mound was the ancient oak I had whimsically envisioned sitting in the center of my future home—a home where I would have raised my children and lived all my life, Gaheris's queen of oak.

Now the oak crowned my love's burial mound.

And my future had grown dark and uncertain.

I SPENT THE NIGHT HALF-AWAKE, HALF-ASLEEP SITTING ON Gaheris's bed and staring at the wall. The little raven, who had begun to lose his fluff and was a genuinely ugly-looking hodgepodge of feather and fluff, had roosted in my lap. I stared at the collection of things Gaheris had on his trunk: a seashell I had given to him, a wooden donkey his father had carved him when he was a boy, a stone he'd found that looked like a little man, a piece of amber—just the small treasures of life. Tears rolled down my cheeks, but I didn't stop them.

I had lost everything.

The grief was too much to bear.

Sometime the next morning, I heard Bran's voice in the roundhouse. I put the raven back in his cage, then remade Gaheris's bed. Afterward, I joined the others.

"I'll ready the horses for Oak Throne," Bran told me.

I nodded to him, then went outside to find Lynet. She was clearing away the bowls from the morning meal.

"You're not too late," she told me with a soft smile. "Just porridge. I can get you some."

I shook my head. "Lynet…can I ask a favor?"

She set down her plates. "Ask."

"The little raven…Morfran. Can I take him with me?"

She smiled at me then set her hand on my cheek. She nodded. "And anything else you want, Boudica. I will…I will give the room to Tristan. So, if there is anything else you want, take it."

I nodded.

"And come and see me. Often. All right?"

Again, I nodded.

"Good," she said, then let me go.

I went back inside. I placed the jar of bird food into my satchel then made sure the latch on the cage was secure. I looked around the room. What could I take? What would be enough to soothe the deep emptiness inside me? There was nothing. I opened Gaheris's trunk. Immediately, I was overcome by his scent. I gently touched his clothes. Closing my eyes, I remembered the feel of his body, warmed by the sun, on mine. The taste of his kisses. The feel of his flesh.

My heart aching, I lifted a simple tunic from the chest. I inhaled deeply of the fabric, then put the shirt into my bag. I rose and went outside. There, I found Tristan sitting on the bench. I went to him.

"Did Lynet tell you that you will stay with her now?"

Tristan nodded.

"She is a good mother. She cared very well for Gaheris. And she will be chieftain now. You will be safe with her, but if you ever need me, you can find me in Oak Throne."

Tristan smiled at me, a sad, broken smile.

I pulled him close and kissed him on the top of his head. "I love Lynet like my own mother. It's going to be all right."

Tristan hugged me tighter.

"Ready," Bran said, joining me.

"Here," I told Bran, handing him the birdcage. "Hand it up to me once I'm mounted?"

He nodded.

I slipped onto my saddle then reached for the little raven who squawked in complaint at being jostled about. Once I had myself—and the bird—steady, I reigned in beside Bran, and we rode to the front of our party.

Lynet joined us.

"Our father will be back from Stonea soon. Don't hesitate to send a rider to Oak Throne if you need anything," Bran told her.

"Thank you, Bran," Lynet said, then turned to me. "Don't forget what I told you."

I nodded.

She smiled from me to the bird. "Squawking thing. He's noisy, Boudica," she said, then chuckled softly.

I smiled at her.

Bran met my gaze.

I nodded to him.

"I'll see you both soon," I told Lynet and Tristan.

Tristan waved to me.

I returned the gesture. Then, we turned and made our way from Frog's Hollow. As I rode past the stone effigies at the village entrance, the depth of my loss sank in deeply.

I was leaving a future that would never be.

CHAPTER 26

The ride back to Oak Throne felt longer than it ever had before. We returned to greetings from the people of our fort, but I could see from their expressions they knew where we'd been. They knew what happened at Frog's Hollow. I did my best to greet the children with a smile and wave, but I could rouse myself for little more. I felt twice as sorry when I realized I hadn't brought them anything, as I had promised. After passing off Druda to one of the stableboys, I went into the roundhouse and promptly dropped onto my bed where I wept until I had no more tears in me, falling into a deep sleep.

I woke sometime in the afternoon the next day to the sound of the little raven complaining. I fed the small creature then laid down once more.

The following days passed in much the same way.

Cidna appeared with a plate of food, setting it beside me. "You must eat, Boudica. You have hardly taken a bite in days."

I stared at the plate of food but could not rouse myself.

Bran, too, tried to stir me. "You have to get up. Bathe. Eat. Gaheris wouldn't want to see you like this."

"Stop. Just stop," I told my brother.

"Druda nickers every time he sees me. He's looking for you. And this ugly bird of yours needs exercise."

I rolled over, not facing my brother.

Bran sighed heavily. "I've sent messengers to King Antedios and Prince Prasutagus in Venta and to King Dumnovellaunus, as you suggested. We should hear from them soon."

I didn't reply.

Bran sat with me in silence for a long time before he rose and left.

It was sometime late in the night, a few days later, when I heard movement in my bedchamber. I opened my eyes a crack when I heard someone muttering in annoyance. I found Ula there.

She must have felt me looking at her because she turned to me. "Your brother said you are wrung out. Expected as much after that business with the men at Frog's Hollow. Sit up," she told me.

I thought about arguing with her but relented.

She shoved a mug at me. "Drink this."

"What is it?"

"Stupid girl, don't ask questions. Just do as you're told."

Part of me wanted to argue with her, but I didn't have the will for it. Instead, I simply drank. The herbs were pungent, the bitter taste making me wince.

Ula studied me closely. "Not a complaint out of you."

I stared into the cup.

Ula harrumphed then took the cup from me. She then turned and started packing up her things once more.

After a few moments, my head started to feel fuzzy, and the room began to spin. "What was in that?"

"It'll shake you loose," Ula said. "Help you find your way out."

"I don't want to find my way out."

"Then that boy loses twice, first his own life and then yours —assuming he loved you enough to care about it."

"He did."

Ula nodded, then rose. "You will come to my house in the morning," she told me then left.

I lay back down.

Soon, it felt like my bed was spinning. I slipped off into a strange, half-awake and half-asleep state. I was struck with the peculiar sensation of falling. Holding on to my bed for dear life, I felt like my bed was spinning faster and faster.

Then, it threw me off.

I landed with a thump.

I lay on the ground with my eyes closed. I smelled the scent of loamy earth, ferns, and the faint, fragrant scent of flowers. Somewhere in the distance, I heard the croaking of frogs.

Opening my eyes a crack, I found myself in the depths of a forest I didn't recognize. The trees were enormous. It would take five men, hand in hand, to meet their circumference. The groggy feeling that held me had passed. In fact, my mind felt sharp, clear.

The night air was cool. Overhead, the leaves rustled, then an owl hooted. I looked up to see two yellow saucers staring down at me.

When the creature sounded again, its call sounded as if it were speaking my name.

"*Bou-dica, Bou-dica, Bou-dica.*"

The bird flew to another tree then turned his head all the way around, looking back at me.

"Bou-dica, Bou-dica, Bou-dica."

I rose. Dusting off my clothes and hands, I followed the owl.

The owl swept from tree to tree, leading me deeper into the glade. At first, I thought that maybe I was somewhere near the Grove of Andraste, but I soon realized this was no ordinary forest. Everything had a strange, silver sheen. Fairy globes danced under the moonlight, bobbing close to me, spinning around my body. At the heart of the orbs of light, I saw flickers like flames, but they moved too quickly for me to see them clearly.

"Bou-dica, Bou-dica, Bou-dica."

Following the owl, I made my way through the deep fern beds and under the canopy of trees until I saw the light on the horizon. There, in the middle of this great forest, sat a small stone cottage. The door to the building was open. The orange light within framed the open edifice. The building was covered in ivy and moss.

"Bou-dica, Bou-dica, Bou-dica."

The owl landed on the roof of the cottage.

A strange feeling of anticipation washed over me. Ula had sent my spirit into this strange in-between place. Was there danger here? I didn't put it past Ula to endanger me for my own good. And here, on the fringes of the Otherworld, peril lurked everywhere.

Moving carefully, I approached the door. Inside, I heard a woman humming. I recognized the melody. It was the same song Damara used to sing to me.

"Mother," I whispered, then entered the room.

The moment I did, I stopped cold. My skin rose in goose-flesh as I took in the sight.

It was the home from my dreams—my house in Frog's Hollow, the oak tree at the center, just as I had imagined it. Before the fire slept the little dog I had purchased for Gaheris in Stonea. On a perch over a chair, the raven sat resting. Beside the fire, however, was the most stunning image. A woman—no, not a woman, myself—sat holding a baby. My mountain of curly red hair trailed down my back. I held the bundle, singing sweetly.

But if I was here, so was…

"Gaheris? Gaheris!"

The singing stopped.

The woman—I—rose and turned toward me.

But it was not me.

And it was not my mother.

A creature with shimmering spring-green eyes looked back at me. While we had the same hair, she wore a different face. The stranger had blue-and-white markings painted on her skin. When I tried to look closely at them, my eyes grew blurry.

"Boudica," she said softly, her light voice ringing like a bell.

"I'm dreaming. Ula…"

"Ula serves me well," the woman said. Turning, she set down the tiny bundle into a cradle beside the chair. It was then that I noticed her stomach was round with pregnancy.

"Who are you?" I whispered.

"You don't know me?" she asked, then laughed lightly, "Yet you call for me. I am known by many names: Danu, Anu, Epona, Rhiannon, the Great Lady, Lady of the Forest, the Mother—"

I gasped then dropped to one knee. "Great Mother."

"Rise, Boudica," she said, extending her hand to me. "You are my champion. I will not have you on your knees."

"Your champion?"

She laughed lightly.

Taking her hand, which was surprisingly warm to the touch, I rose.

She gestured to the room around us. "It was a pretty picture. I am sorry that it ended before it could become a reality. But you already know that this is not your only life. You will see him again."

"It does not make the pain any less."

"No," she said, then set her hand on the tree. "But there is more that must be done. If this dream had come to life, how many others would have died?" She turned to me. "They are coming, Boudica. They will tear down my stones. They will chop down my trees. They will defile my waters. Their foreign gods will pollute my cities. You must rise from the green. You must strengthen your body and make ready to fight. You must teach others how to stand. It will cost you. But you must be ready."

"Who is coming?"

"Will you stand for me?"

"Against who? Who is coming?"

"Boudica," she whispered, then stood close to me, her lips pressed against my ear. "Will you stand for me?"

"Of course. But... Who is coming?"

She then let out a sound so sharp, so piercing, my hands flung up to cover my ears.

Gasping, I opened my eyes.

I was in my bedchamber once more.

My ears rang from the pain—from the searing cry of an eagle.

CHAPTER 27

T he next morning, I rose and flagged down one of the servants, asking for some hot water for a bath.

"Do you want me to get one of the ladies to attend you?" the young man who had fetched the hot water from the kitchen asked. "Cidna said she'd come with her potato brush, if you wanted."

I smiled lightly. "No. I can see to the water—and everything else—myself. My thanks to Cidna for her generous offer, though."

He chuckled softly, bowed to me, then left the steaming buckets at my door.

Pouring the hot water into the washing basin, I slipped into the tub and let the water wash away the sweat and despair that clung to me. The dream had rattled me. That was no ordinary nightmare. Ula had sent me into the Otherworld, and the message there had been a stark one.

Shadows clouded the horizon. Something terrible was coming. In the wake of Gaheris's death, it was not hard to imagine. The tribes were always on the brink of war. What if we discovered the Brigantes or Votadini were behind the attack of the camp? Would the Catuvellauni turn on the Iceni as they had done to the Atrebates and the Trinovantes? Would Saenunos's deepest fear that Prasutagus would finally seek to become ruler of all the Iceni come true?

And then, there were the rumors from Gaul…

But that could not be.

It was too unthinkable.

Not Rome.

Not again.

I slipped under the water, letting the warm liquid embrace me.

The Great Mother told me she needed me. Me. She needed a champion. While I did not understand her warning, I understood her request. With Gaheris gone, there was nothing left for me anyway. I would never be a mother. I would never marry. I would never love again.

I would give myself to the gods and let them use me as they saw fit.

When my father returned, I would ask him to send me to the Grove of Andraste or Mona. I would serve the gods. It was the Great Mother herself who asked it.

Who could argue with that?

AFTER I WASHED AND REDRESSED, I TOOK THE LITTLE RAVEN outside with me, setting the creature on my shoulder. The village was moving along in a quiet hum. It was clear that Father was gone. From the looks of the horse stall, Bran had already ridden out. Spotting me, Druda came to the fence and whinnied.

"I hear you," I called to him. I found him with his head hanging over the fence, waiting for me. I set my hand on his nose, stroking his face. On my shoulder, the little bird moved nervously from side to side. "Look," I told Druda, stepping back so he could see the little raven. "You see?"

Ignoring the bird, Druda snorted and then swung his head toward me once more, hunting for another pat.

I chuckled lightly. "I'm sorry, old friend. I know you've been kept inside. I'll get you out tomorrow. I promise," I told him, then patted him once more. "But for now, I have someone I need to see," I said, planting a kiss on his nose, then made my way toward Ula's house.

Druda, apparently satisfied his complaints had been heard, meandered off to join the other horses. I made my way down the village streets to Ula's tiny house, ducking as I entered.

The house was dark and quiet.

"Ula?" I called.

The fire had burned down in the brazier. While she had her usual herbs, mushrooms, and roots set out on her table, she wasn't home.

Frowning, I came back outside to find the usual pack of children rushing by. Seeing me, they stopped and gathered around me, hugging my waist.

"They said you were inside crying all these days," Eiwyn told me. "Oh, Boudica. I heard my da' talking about what happened in Frog's Hollow. Is it true that Gaheris died?"

I swallowed hard. "It is."

"We're sorry, Boudica," Phelan said.

The rest of the children chimed with their own condolences, all of them speaking at once.

"Death is a part of life," I said, forcing myself not to let my sadness show. "A hard part, but a part nonetheless."

"You will find a new husband," little Birgit said. She was just a small girl, no more than six years of age, with a mop of golden curls. "I saw it in my dreams. He will be very tall and have red hair, just like you."

"Boudica doesn't want a new husband," Eiwyn told her waspishly.

I smiled gently at Birgit. "That's very kind of you to have such nice dreams for me. Now, does anyone know where Ula has gone?"

"I saw her with her basket headed toward the mossy forest," Phelan said, pointing to the west.

"What is that bird, Boudica?" Eiwyn asked me.

"He is a raven," I said. "His name is Morfran. Here," I said, gently handing him to her. "Do you want to take him for a bit, see he gets a little exercise?"

"Of course," Eiwyn answered excitedly.

"He needs to flutter from person to person. Form a ring and see if you can get him to exercise his wings. I need to find Ula, but I'll be back."

"I've got him," Eiwyn said excitedly. "Let's go," she called to the others, and they ran to a grassy spot not far from Ula's cottage.

I made my way out of the fort, crossing the earthen bridge, and into the forest to the west. Upriver, a path led to the edge of a sacred forest. It was a special but feared place where moss covered the forest floor and boulders littered the woods. Legend said the good neighbors had enchanted the place to hide their faerie houses. From brownies to piskies, all manner of little people were thought to live in the glade. I remembered my mother telling Brenna and me a story of how the moss hid the entrance to the land of the hollow hills where the most ancient—and dangerous—of the good neighbors resided. All of us had been warned never to enter the mossy forest. In fact, no one hunted there for fear of striking down a shapeshifted creature of the greenwood. No one ever went there—except Ula—and me, dogging her shadow.

The moment I stepped from the sunny meadow into the trees, a wash of cool air came over me. I knew it was just the shade, but the experience was startling. I could feel I had moved into a thin place. The mossy forest was a borderland between our world and the Otherworld.

Making my way into the woods, I looked for signs of Ula's passing. If I knew her well, she would be deep in the forest where some fallen and rotting trees sprouted the best growths of mushrooms.

I paused, leaning against the timber of a wide oak, and pulled off my boots. Leaving them beside the tree, I pressed my toes into the green moss, feeling the sensation between my toes. Sunlight drifted into the thick green in slim shafts that broke through the canopy overhead.

I turned and made my way after Ula.

Songbirds called, and in the distance, I heard branches snap as animals darted off.

I looked up in time to spy the tawny coat of a deer as the animal trotted away.

A small stream that led to the river blocked my path, but a fallen log made a natural bridge. Like everything else, it was covered in moss.

Holding out my arms, I balanced as I made my way across. Soon, I moved toward the glen where I knew I would find Ula. As expected, she was there, basket in hand, plucking red-capped mushrooms from a log.

"You make so much noise in the woods, you sounded like a herd of horses approaching."

"Liar," I told her, pointing my bare foot in her direction.

"Then how did I know you were coming?"

"The good neighbors told you."

Ula harrumphed at me then kept looking over the mushrooms, selecting the best ones.

I joined her, looking into her basket. "Agaric?"

Ula nodded. "So, finally got out of bed, did you?"

"Obviously. Although, you drugged me into doing it."

At that, Ula chuckled. After tossing a couple more mushrooms in her basket, she turned and looked at me. "What did you see?"

"See?"

"Stupid girl. In your dreams. What did you see?"

"I…" I said, then paused. Somewhere deep in the forest, an owl called.

Ula and I both turned toward the sound.

Ula looked back at me, a questioning expression in her gaze.

"The Mother," I said. "She gave me warnings."

"Of what?"

"She wasn't clear. Of war, I think."

"The good neighbors are pulling back," Ula said, looking around the forest. "Something is coming. Shadows of danger everywhere."

"I was thinking of asking my father to send me to Mona."

Ula laughed out loud. "You have no patience for that. Your sister is the one who should go to Mona."

"Then what should I do with myself? With Gaheris gone, my whole future has unraveled. I must find a path, or I will go mad pining over what is lost."

"What did the Mother say?"

I furrowed my brow, trying to remember.

Ula slapped me on the side of the head. "What did the Mother say? Remember, you stupid girl. I didn't spend a week making that brew to send you to the other side for nothing."

I frowned at Ula. "That I would be her champion. I don't know what that means."

Ula nodded affirmatively. "Yes. Of course. The gods will show you. Even now, they whisper."

"Ula, what should I do?"

"What the Mother asked."

"Well, and no offense to the Great Lady, but she was less than specific. She told me to be ready, to strengthen my body, and to be ready because *they* are coming."

At that, Ula nodded knowingly. "Then do as she says."

"That's all well and good, but with Gaheris dead, my father and my uncle will maneuver me just as they did Caturix."

"Saenunos," Ula said then spat. "You should poison him."

"Ula."

Ula shrugged. "I'm not wrong. And you will be sorry for not agreeing." She reached into her pocket and pulled out a shiny blue stone she set on the log. "For the mushrooms," she called into the greenwood, then motioned for us to go.

We were silent as we made our way back through the forest. When we reached the fallen log over the stream, I took Ula's basket then offered her my hand.

"I can walk by myself," she said cantankerously.

I said nothing more but noted how slowly and carefully she came along behind me. When we reached the other side, Ula motioned for me to follow her. Rather than making our way back to the field, we moved toward a shadowy ravine. Moving carefully, we walked toward an outcropping of rocks. As we drew closer, I saw that hidden by the moss, ivy, and lichen, there was a small entrance to a cave. We approached the entrance, Ula pausing to push aside a web of ivy that hid a face carved into the stone at the cave entrance.

"What is this place?" I whispered.

"An entrance to the hollow hills."

I stared at the dark crevice, no more than waist-high, that disappeared into the hillside.

"Dark creatures," Ula said. "They despise mankind, but sometimes, they will whisper to you, tell you things, especially at dusk and dawn. They'll sneak up on you like robbers and speak terrible truths."

I looked from the cave to Ula, who was staring at the face in the stone.

"What do they say?"

"The stones will fall. The trees will bleed. But the false gods will burn. All will come to pass through her, with hair like fire."

I looked at the stone face. "Me?"

"The Mother has plans for you, Boudica. Do not be ruled by your father or your family. Stand strong in the face of that force. The Mother will move you. Rely upon her."

I looked back toward the cave.

"Now, come on." Motioning for me to follow her, she entered the cave.

"Ula!"

"Come on!"

When we entered, Ula paused to take a torch from the wall. Striking the tinder, she lit the torch then stepped forward, gesturing for me to follow her.

"Where are we going?" I whispered. "This isn't safe."

"I'll show you. Follow close behind me. Stay left. At every turn, stay left," she said then we entered the cave.

The light behind me faded. Moving carefully over the rocks

—and cursing myself for leaving my boots behind—I followed her. The place smelled of minerals and mud. In the flickering light of the torch, I saw flecks of granite and crystals in the cave walls. Small tunnels disappeared off the main path. I bent to look down the offshoots. They wound deep into the earth. I could almost feel eyes on me, Ula and I kept left. We had walked a good distance when I saw light at the end of the tunnel and smelled fresh air. Soon, we came to an opening in the cave. I looked up.

"Where are we?" I asked.

"Climb up and see," Ula told me, pointing to the rocky wall.

I tied her basket to the back of my belt then reached for a handful of rock and began the climb.

"Ula? Can you—"

"I'll take care of myself. Go on, now."

I frowned then kept climbing. Soon, I saw a bucket and a roof overhead. When I reached the top, I realized where I was. Pulling myself up, I swung my legs over the ledge to find myself standing in the garden behind Ula's house. The cave exited from her dry well.

A moment later, Ula appeared at the top of the well. I turned and offered her my hand, helping her out.

"A secret entrance into the fort," I said, looking all around.

"An entrance now. Once, there was water…long ago," Ula said, brushing off her robes.

I unhooked the basket and handed it to her. "Why did you show me?"

Ula shrugged. "Because they told me to."

"They?"

She gestured to the well.

"Why?" I asked.

"You know as much as I do. Now, get to work. The Mother didn't deliver her message for nothing. I have my own things to attend to," she said then turned and went back to her house.

I looked back at the well. What the greenwood wanted from me, I didn't know. But I knew one thing for sure, given the good neighbors' prankster ways; there was almost no chance I would ever see my boots again.

CHAPTER 28

I returned to the roundhouse, slipping on another pair of boots, then headed back outside in time to see Bran leading his horse toward the stables.

"Boudica," my brother called happily. "Are you... How are you?"

"As well as can be expected."

He nodded thoughtfully. "We went hunting. I just left a doe with Cidna. Where have you been?"

"With Ula."

Bran nodded. My normally loquacious brother paused then seemed unsure what to say.

"What are you doing now?" I asked.

He pointed to Cai and the others who were lingering outside the stables. "We were going to do some sparring."

"I'll join you."

"You?"

"Yes, me. Gaheris was training me to work with a spear. You can pick up where he left off."

Bran looked puzzled, then a sad expression crossed his

face. "Of course, little sister," he said, putting his arm around my shoulder. "Gaheris was always good with a spear. I once saw Gaheris throw his spear through the crook of a tree to get a hare. No one could make a shot like that except Gaheris."

Smiling sadly, and willing the river of emotions with me to stay locked behind their dam, I nodded.

Bran kissed me on the side of the head then led me to join the others.

To my surprise, none of Bran's warriors said anything as Bran and I began our training. Perhaps it was out of respect for my grief or maybe an understanding of my fury over the manner of Gaheris's death, but either way, no one teased me. Instead, they offered tips as we worked. First with spears, per my request, and then with sword and shield.

"Watch your stance," Bran told me, positioning me. "You're a good rider, and you have good aim with the spear, but with the sword, you lack strength."

I frowned at my brother.

He chuckled. "Running through the forest like a nymph doesn't make you strong, but it does make you fast," Bran said, then continued his instructions.

Bran and I worked back and forth, practicing shield and sword.

Balfor appeared a moment later. "Bran," he called. "A messenger for you."

"I'll be back," Bran told me. "Practice on the straw dummy."

I turned, making my way across the yard to the practice dummy, but was waylaid by Cai.

"I was watching you fight," Cai told me. "Bran is right. You are fast. This," he said, reaching out for my shield, "is getting in your way."

"What do you mean?"

Cai set the shield aside and put a dagger in my hand instead.

He moved in front of me, a shield in his hand. "Use your speed to your advantage," he said. "Attack with the sword."

I attempted a thrust, which Cai deflected with his shield. "Now, what are you doing with your left hand?" he asked.

"I… Nothing, I guess."

"Exactly." Cai looked down at his side, where his shield was no longer covering him. "You see here? This is your real target. Come at me—slowly—with that dagger."

I nodded, then did as he instructed.

"Good, Boudica. Well done. Use your speed to your advantage. Keep yourself agile. That's how you can win."

I smiled at Cai. "Thank you."

He inclined his head to me.

Bran rejoined us, eyeing the dagger in my hand. "You're deadlier than you were when I left you."

I smiled lightly at him.

"You'll want to come," Bran told me, gesturing behind him toward the roundhouse. "There is a rider from the Coritani. We'll meet with him together."

I nodded, then turned back to Cai, returning his dagger to him. "Thank you."

Cai took the blade, inclining this head to me. "Any time. Feel free to ask."

Bran and I returned and headed back to the roundhouse. When we arrived, we made our way to Father's meeting chamber. There, a well-dressed man waited for us. He was a slim, dark-haired man with a long nose. He rose when we entered, bowing politely.

"Welcome," Bran told him. "I am Prince Bran, and this is my sister, Princess Boudica."

"I am Varden, messenger for King Dumnovellaunus."

"You are welcome here in Oak Throne," I told him.

"Thank you," he replied genteelly.

Bran motioned for the man to sit, then gestured to one of the servants to pour us all an ale.

"King Dumnovellaunus was disturbed to hear of the attack on your people," Varden said carefully. "And he sends his regrets for the loss."

"Thank you," I replied. "The incident was most unexpected."

"King Dumnovellaunus took the liberty of speaking to Chieftain Fimbul, whose people live on the northern shore of the Wash, on your behalf. We have had no instances of raids this season."

"What of warbands? Any incursions into your lands?" Bran asked.

"The Parisii... The Votadini..." I added.

"May I ask, where is King Aesunos? I am sure the king would be interested in what King Dumnovellaunus has to share."

"Surely you are aware our brother has wed Princess Melusine, daughter of King Volisios," I replied. "Our father is in Stonea for the wedding."

There was no way one of the three kings of the Coritani would not know Caturix and Melusine were wed at Midsummer, but this man was fishing. Why did even our allies feel like enemies?

"Naturally, King Dumnovellaunus offers his felicitations," he said. "You asked of the Parisii and the Votadini. Both are currently at war with our northern neighbors, the Brigantes. I suspect they are likely distracted by that issue. That said, in seasons past, some sects of the Votadini have raided our coastal villages. Although, we have not had such problems this season."

"Which sects from the Votadini were responsible for such raids?" I asked.

The messenger considered me for a long moment then said, "The crow people who live along the coast, Princess."

I nodded. "We thank King Dumnovellaunus for this news."

The man inclined his head to me. "What little of it there is, Princess. We are sorry we cannot be of more help. Perhaps if you have any other information to share about the attack? Any witness? Survivors?"

"Sadly, there was none. We don't know anything about the culprits," I said.

The man nodded slowly. "Alas, all the more reason to grieve."

I gave him a tight smile. While the man's words were all pleasantries, my skin crawled in his presence. Nonetheless, hospitality dictated that I offered, "Please, will you take your rest here tonight? We can have our servants see to your lodgings."

"No. But I thank you for your gracious offer."

"Will you at least let me see you fed before you return?" I asked.

The man smiled. "I would be obliged."

"I'll speak to Cidna," I told Bran, then left the meeting room. Behind me, Bran shifted the conversation from political tensions to the sorrel horse the messenger had ridden in on.

I made my way to the kitchens where I found Cidna salting the deer Bran had struck down on his hunt.

"Cidna, there is a messenger from the Coritani. Can you fix him something to eat before he rides back out?"

"I've had my hands in this carcass for the last hour. My fingers are burning from all the salt. Good reason to stop. I'll see to it, Boudica."

It didn't escape my notice that she hadn't complained or fussed at me.

Nini rose from her bed in the corner long enough to lick my hand, then went to lie down once more.

I made my way out the back, pausing at the animal pens to scratch the pigs' ears. But mostly, I was trying to control the swell of emotions inside me. My eyes drifted across the compound to the palisades where the guards patrolled back and forth. The messenger's news brought me no solace. Gaheris was dead, and no one knew how or why. Everything felt so...unfinished. One day, I would learn what had befallen my love. One day, someone would pay.

CHAPTER 29

I spent the next several days hiding from my feelings by jabbing and whacking straw dummies, imagining that each was the mysterious assailant who had taken Gaheris from me. With each strike, I buried the pain of not knowing what had befallen. If I thought about it too much, it was going to kill me. Bran and Cai both took the time to train me. It was not uncommon for women from the tribes to fight alongside the men, and all the Iceni women had a fierce streak. Even Brenna carried a dagger in her boot.

But now… Now, something was awake inside of me. Half the time, I didn't know whether I wanted to run deep into the woods, never to be seen again, escape to the Grove of Andraste, or simply learn how to murder every bastard I ever met.

Instead of choosing, I walked a little of each path.

After spending the morning with Cai, working with my spear, I mounted a very put-out Druda and headed into the forest.

"Stop acting cranky," I told him. "You're going for a ride

now. Pouting won't help that," I told the horse. But still, a prick of guilt stung my heart. Before, I'd ridden almost every day, even if I wasn't going to visit Gaheris. Many times, I would ride to the sea for a swim then come back. No wonder Druda was upset with me.

It was not a far ride to the Grove of Andraste. I turned down the woodland path toward the grove, which was hidden deep in the forest. As I passed a fern-filled glen, a hare poked its head above the leaves. Its ears twitching, it watched me as I passed.

My skin rose in gooseflesh.

"Fey things," I whispered to Druda.

The horse snorted. Leaving the fern glen, I rode through a hawthorn stand, then on to the little village. When I reached the stones that stood sentinel on either side of the path leading into the village, I dismounted then led Druda inside.

The usual pack of barking hounds greeted me, alerting the others to my presence. The massive, shaggy beasts' heads were as tall as my waist. I gave each a scratch. "Such fierce protectors. Licking and wiggling all around. A fearsome lot you are."

The priestesses worked at a bench in front of Dôn's house. They waved to me. Bec left them, joining me.

"Boudica," Bec called as she crossed the green. "I'm glad you've come. I thought we might see you sooner."

"I've been...adrift."

Bec nodded sadly. "It was a terrible loss. We all liked Gaheris. How are you?"

I shrugged. "As expected."

Bec set her hand on my arm. "I am sorry, my friend. It is no consolation to say that it is fate, or that the gods have plans, or even that you will see him again. All I can say is, I'm sorry."

I nodded, choking back my emotions, then looked over her shoulder. "What are you working on?"

"Bundling and prepping herbs. Tedious work removing the flowers and stems."

"Dôn?"

Bec gestured to the hilltop nearby upon which sat a circle of oaks.

I followed her gaze. "I was hoping I…"

Bec nodded. "Come on," she said, and we set off for the forest shrine.

We made our way up the path that wound around the hilltop to its crown where the oak trees grew in a circle. We both paused at the entrance. There stood two tall menhirs. The ancient stones were covered with green moss and silver lichen. But on the stones, I spotted the carvings of the ancient people. Images of the Forest Lord, seated with a cauldron in his lap, were carved into one stone, along with other swirling designs. On the other stone was an image of the Great Mother. Above her was a carving of a spiral. I reached out and set the tip of my finger on one of the stones, tracing the spiral pattern there. Under my touch, the stone felt gritty. My finger worked its way from the outer loop inward. As I traced, I began to feel dizzy.

"All life spirals in endless loops. Our spirits are like the circles hidden within the oaks. Each new life, a new circle," Bec whispered as she watched me. "One life after the next, we spin and spin. We live, die, and are born again. Over and over."

"Together? Born again together?"

Bec nodded. "Like trees in the same forest. Forever."

"Until we come to the center," I said, my finger reaching the end of the trail. I turned to Bec. "And then what?"

Bec grinned at me, then gave me a wink. She would not say. Instead, she motioned for me to follow her into the stones.

I set my hand on the image of the Mother Goddess for just one moment, remembering the vision Ula had evoked, then followed Bec.

The moment I passed through the trees, the skin on my arms rose to gooseflesh. My heartbeat quickened. This place, much like the mossy forest near Oak Throne, was ancient. Knowing. Here, I felt the eyes of greenwood on me.

Dôn sat on a stump near the center of the ring of trees. Her long, white hair was neatly braided. It trailed down her back. She sat looking into the fire that burned at the center of the grove. She wore a faded bluish-purple gown, the same as Bec's and the others. But the discoloration of the dye spoke to how long she had been at the grove. The long walking staff she used leaned against her shoulder.

"The fire started crackling as soon as you entered the circle," Dôn called.

"Ancient Dôn," I said, joining her. I knelt on the ground beside her.

"Arise, Boudica. Arise," she said, waving her hand at me. She turned to Bec. "I hate it when they call me ancient," she told Bec.

"I think they mean it as a matter of respect," Bec replied.

"I'm sure they do, but it just makes me feel old. I am not old yet."

I smiled lightly. "I am sorry, wise one."

"Wise one," she mimicked behind me. "That's better."

"Dôn, I..." I began, but I didn't know what to say. Why had I come?

"You don't know why you are here," Dôn said, then smiled. "You are half unmoored from yourself. Gaheris was the anchor keeping you in this world—in the best of ways. But that is a dangerous way to live. The greenwood has coveted you since you were born. You must come back to yourself, Boudica. There are too many shadows moving these days. I have seen them here," she said, pointing to the fire.

"The men of Frog's Hollow... Who did it? Have you seen any sign?" I asked.

Dôn shook her head. "The gods will not show me. No matter how many times I ask. And that is telling enough. After all these years, I know Andraste well. When she hides the truth in darkness, it is a deadly and dangerous thing."

I turned and looked toward the flames. "I have seen things as well. Omens. Warnings. None of it makes sense to me."

"You are Damara's daughter. It is no wonder. She once told me she'd had visions of you, Boudica. She saw great things for you."

The notion that my mother had spoken to Dôn about me surprised me. Father spoke so little of Mother, I often forgot that other people knew her well. But that was, in part, why I had come.

"Dôn, with Gaheris gone..." I said, then sighed heavily, the weight of the truth hanging on me like it weighed a million pounds. "Already, I can feel Saenunos's plotting. I cannot bear the idea of being forced to wed someone else. If you would have me, I would take my mother's place here."

Bec looked from Dôn to me and back again.

"Ula always tells me—"

Dôn chuckled. "Ula tells you exactly what you need to hear when you need to hear it. Vexing woman. There is more power in one of her fingers than in half the druids on Mona."

"Is that so?" Bec asked in surprise.

"Do not be so startled by the idea, Bec. That suggests arrogance."

"You're right," Bec replied, a hint of embarrassment in her voice.

Dôn nodded to herself, as if agreeing with her thoughts. She motioned for us to be silent then stared into the fire. Her eyelids grew heavy, her gaze glossy. After the longest time, she said, "Tell your father he will let you grieve until Beltane. That is the word of the gods," she said, gesturing to the fire. "By next Beltane, your path will become clear again. The king must honor the Dark Lady's wishes. As for Saenunos, he can tempt the will of the gods all he wishes. Their eyes are already upon him."

"Is there a possibility I can come to the grove?" I asked.

Dôn smiled lightly. "There is a chance of anything, Boudica."

"Thank you, Dôn."

She nodded then gestured with her hand that we should depart.

Bec and I both turned, making our way from the shrine, but before I got to the exit, Dôn called to me.

"Boudica, tell Ula we don't have enough scarlet elf cup. When she is next this way, ask her to bring some."

"I'll tell her," I reassured the high priestess, imagining Ula's waspish reply to such a request.

Smiling to herself, Dôn simply nodded.

At that, Bec and I went back downhill once more.

"Dôn is a master at indirect answers," Bec said.

I chuckled. "Is it Dôn or the Great Lady Andraste?"

Bec laughed lightly. "Or both."

"Both."

When we reached the bottom of the hill, Bec took my hand. "How are you? Truly?"

I shook my head. There were no words to describe how I was.

Bec smiled sympathetically at me. "Come as often as you like. You are always welcome here."

"Thank you. Right now, I feel like I have no place. I don't belong anywhere."

"You're unmoored, as Dôn said."

I nodded.

"She is right to caution you. Be careful, Boudica. Fey things always want to use someone like you. Be on your guard."

"All right," I said, but even I felt the hollowness of my words.

We walked back to Druda, whose ears pricked when he saw me once more. He knickered lightly.

"All he likes to do is go, go, go," I said, smiling at the horse.

Bec set her hand on Druda's nose. "Then you fit one another very well. Boudica, how is Bran? I have not seen him in some days."

I slipped onto Druda. "He's well. Managing Oak Throne was more work than he imagined, I think. I'll tell him you asked."

Bec smiled but didn't protest. "We'll see you soon. Lughnasadh, if not before."

Lughnasadh, when Gaheris and I would have wed. "If not before. Be well, Priestess."

"And you, Princess."

Turning in my saddle, I waved to the other priestesses who still stood working at the bench then left the grove.

The Dark Lady Andraste had bought me nearly a year of peace. A year to mourn. For that, I would be forever grateful.

Andraste.

Shadowy one.

You have my eternal gratitude.

While there was no reply, in the depths of my mind, I swore I heard a woman snickering.

CHAPTER 30

Druda and I took the long way back to Oak Throne, following the river. I lengthened the ride as much as I could, giving myself time to reflect on Dôn's words. Stumbling across some blackberry bushes, I paused to pick a sack full as I thought it all over. Dôn's words brought me comfort, but it was a small light in the darkness. It was late in the afternoon when the fort finally came into sight. Our warriors and others were milling about everywhere. I was surprised to see so much activity. Had Father returned?

I clicked to Druda, quickening his pace.

Only when I got within eyesight of the bridge did I catch sight of a black-and silver-banner, the image of a running horse thereon. Oak Throne had a visitor from the Greater Iceni.

"Banshees be cursed," I whispered, then spurred Druda forward, trotting across the bridge and into the fort. In the distance, I spotted Bran talking with someone from the Greater Iceni's party. Bran was laughing and joking with a tall man who had hair as red as my own. Judging from the heavy, sparkling torc on his neck, I guessed him to be Prince Prasutagus.

Reining in Druda, I joined them.

Bran smiled when he saw me.

"Ah, Prince Prasutagus, here is my sister, Boudica," Bran said, gesturing to me.

Prasutagus turned, his gaze meeting mine.

In that single moment, I was struck by such a sense of familiarity, it startled me. Had I met the prince before? Perhaps I was remembering him from when I was a child.

Prasutagus paused, a surprised expression on his face, but he quickly dismissed it. He bowed to me.

I eyed the prince over. He was taller than Bran and more broadly built. His red hair, though the same shade as my own, was wavy rather than curled. He was richly dressed, his cape pinned at the shoulder with a fine, gold pin in the shape of a running horse—as on his banners—the symbol of the Greater Iceni. He had a light smattering of freckles across his cheeks. His chestnut-brown eyes sparkled. I was surprised to see the markings of a druid on his brow. A stag's head with a wide set of horns covered his entire brow. Tattooed in a line from his lower lip to the bottom of his chin were the phases of the moon.

I slipped off Druda.

"Prince Prasutagus," I said, bowing deeply.

"Princess," Prasutagus replied politely.

"You are welcome in Oak Throne," I said.

"Thank you. I received a messenger about the incident at your village. We, too, have had some signs of raids on the coast. I thought it best to speak in person. King Aesunos…" he said, looking back toward the roundhouse.

"Our brother, Caturix, is recently wed," I replied. "The king and the others are still in Stonea. I'm afraid you've ridden this far for nothing. It's only Bran and me. All the same, won't you come inside?" I asked politely. "It is a hot day, and it was a long ride from Venta. In the very least, let me fill you and your men up on Northern Iceni ale as a reward," I said with a smile.

Prince Prasutagus chuckled lightly. "That is an offer I cannot refuse. I see I am not the only one riding today," he said, his eyes drifting to Druda. "I've always liked a dapple grey," he said, coming closer to Druda. He lifted his hand, moving to touch Druda's nose, then paused. "May I?"

I nodded.

Prasutagus set his hand on Druda's nose, giving him a soft pat, then stroked his neck. "I had a horse that looked much like him when I was a boy. His name was Garwin. He was a spirited creature. What about you, friend? Are you full of spirit too?"

"Moody as the weather. This is Druda," I told the prince.

Prasutagus nodded. "Druda."

Druda snorted at him.

Prasutagus chuckled. "I see. He's a very fine horse, Princess."

"You hear that, Druda? The prince thinks you are very fine. Good thing he doesn't know you as well as I do."

Druda nosed my chin as if trying to silence me, making Prasutagus and me laugh.

A moment later, Tadhg, the stableboy, appeared. "Shall I take Druda along with the others, Princess?" he asked, gesturing to the prince's men's horses.

"Yes. Thank you, Tadhg," I replied.

"Shall we?" Bran said, gesturing to the roundhouse.

We turned, heading inside, but I only got a few steps before I remembered the parcel I had stashed in my saddlebag.

"I'm sorry. One moment," I told Prince Prasutagus, then hurried back to Druda, retrieving the bag full of blackberries.

I waved to the children who had gathered nearby to watch the excitement.

They rushed to join me.

"Boudica," Birgit said, wide-eyed, "who is that?"

"Prince Prasutagus of the Greater Iceni."

"He's so tall," Eiwyn agreed.

"Yes. Now, here. These are for you," I said, opening the bag to reveal my winnings.

"Boudica! Thank you, Boudica! Oh, thank you, Boudica!" they yelled in tandem.

"Who among you can count?"

"Me! Me!" Phelan shouted.

I handed the bag to him. "Measure them between you all fairly."

"I will, Princess."

Nodding, I ruffled his hair, then hurried across the square to rejoin the others.

Smiling, Prasutagus gave me a quizzical look.

"Blackberries," I said, holding out my hands to reveal the stains thereon. "I picked them for the children. They like me to bring them back surprises." I laughed, then wiped my hands on the hem of my tunic only to realize a moment later how completely ill-mannered I must have looked in front of the prince. Brenna would have been horrified.

Prasutagus merely chuckled lightly.

As we made our way to the roundhouse, I spotted Ula sitting on a woodpile nearby. She was studying the prince's party, looking at them through something pressed against her eye. After a moment, I realized it was a hagstone.

I gave her a scolding look.

At that, Ula laughed.

Prasutagus looked her way, eyeing Ula with curiosity.

Still chuckling to herself, Ula rose and returned to the village, muttering to herself as she went.

I didn't say anything. Someone like Ula was well below the interests of Prince Prasutagus, but then he said, "Your wisewoman was watching me through a hagstone."

Bran gave me a worried glance.

"That's Ula. She's a very learned healer but also a bit of an eccentric."

Prasutagus smiled softly. "It's the eccentric who often prove the most interesting."

I cocked an eyebrow at him. "In that, we are in agreement."

The prince inclined his head to me.

We made our way into the roundhouse. Cidna had everyone working quickly to set our food, ale, and wine for the unexpected royal visit. She was huffing with the exertion. Nini pranced around the room worriedly, as if wondering what all the fuss was about.

"Pssh," Cidna hissed at Nini. "Don't get underfoot. Back to the kitchen."

But Nini rarely listened. Instead, she came to greet the prince herself.

"Nini," Cidna called weakly, trying to stop the wiry hound, but to no avail.

Prasutagus bent to give Nini a scratch on the ears. "So, you are the protector of the kitchens? I could have guessed by that round belly of yours."

"Your Highness," Cidna said, stepping forward in stunned embarrassment. She shifted her glance to me, her eyes begging for me to help.

"This is Nini," I told the prince. "Professional scraps eater and greeter of princes."

Prasutagus laughed. "Fine dog. I have many myself. My wife—" he began, then paused. After a moment, he said, "My late wife, Esu, used to complain there was no room on the bed for her because of the dogs. It's good to meet you, Nini," he said, patting her once more, then rose.

"She's no hunting beast, that is certain," Bran told Prasutagus, gesturing for the prince to join us at the table. "But she never misses a dropped morsel."

"She hunts in her own way," Prasutagus said with a light chuckle then took a seat.

Lifting a pitcher of ale, I poured cups for Prasutagus, Bran, and myself before sitting once more. At the other end of the table, Cidna saw to Prasutagus's men.

"How is your father, King Antedios?" I asked the prince.

Prasutagus sighed heavily. I could hear the weight of his answer in his breath. "Aging, I'm afraid. Some days, he is very sharp and attends to tribal matters. The next day, he calls for my mother, who has been dead for twenty years. The shadow of the crone is upon him."

"I am sorry to hear it."

"It is sad to see someone you love in such a state," Prasutagus said, then drank heavily.

Bran, sensing the prince's sorrow, sought to change the subject. "And Venta? My men tell me the city is bigger every time they visit."

Prasutagus nodded. "We are growing. I have much to be grateful for, even amongst the difficulties of this year. In fact, I have been speaking with the druids. Next Beltane, we will hold a great festival at Arminghall. The druids of Mona will come. It shall be a meeting of the tribes like we have not seen in many years. Together, we shall honor Bel with a great ceremony."

"Let's hope there is anything left of the Atrebates and Trinovantes to join us—soon, they will all be Catuvellauni," Bran said carefully.

"And the Iceni pinched in our little corner," Prasutagus replied. "I had hoped to speak on that matter, amongst other things, with your father."

Bran shifted his gaze to me.

I eyed the prince. My head told me to be silent, but Prasutagus had a trustworthiness to him that loosened my tongue. Despite Saenunos's ramblings that Prasutagus would sooner cut our throats than make peace, there was nothing about this man that suggested my uncle's paranoid worries were to be heeded.

"Our father took ill in Stonea," I said. "Nothing life-threatening, but he can't ride at this time. Bran and I came to see to the matter at Frog's Hollow."

Prasutagus stroked his chin thoughtfully. "I am sorry to hear such news. I hope he recovers soon."

"Thank you."

When Prasutagus lifted his cup to drink, I met Bran's gaze. His expression told me that he, like me, could feel the ice on which the pair of us were now dancing. We had to be careful what we said. Bran and I—a second son and a second daughter—would never be rulers. But we could sink our family by talking too much. Yet, I had not been wrong to be honest with Prasutagus. My heart assured me of that.

"I was greatly disturbed to learn of the attack on your people," Prasutagus said. "Two weeks ago, at the mouth of the River Yare, a small band of fishermen were similarly killed."

Bran and I exchanged a surprised glance.

I turned back to Prasutagus. "Any sign of the culprits?"

Prasutagus shook his head. "None. And no survivors. Much of the trade in Venta comes via the Yare. I thought it a simple matter of robbery—the entrance to the Yare is a ripe spot for such problems—until I received your message. And your people? Were there any survivors? Any sign?"

"One survivor," I said. "A mute child who can tell us little, only that the raiders came by night. And we found this," I said, handing Prasutagus the coin.

The prince studied the coin. "I don't know this currency."

"Nor does anyone else we've spoken to," Bran said.

After studying the coin closely, Prasutagus handed it back to me. "I'm sorry, Princess. I don't know. Was there nothing else?"

"No. Nothing. They killed the men, and they looted the… they looted the…" I said, the words sticking in my throat as my mind bubbled up with images of Gaheris lying dead amongst the waves, his blood coloring the wash, his hand drifting on the water.

Prasutagus studied me closely, his eyes searching my face.

I looked away from him, tears welling in my eyes.

"The bodies," Bran finished for me. "They took their coins, torcs, weapons, and any other valuable goods. There was no sign of who did it, but the child was able to tell us that the culprits had a bird on their banners."

"A bird?"

Bran nodded. "We had a messenger from King Dumnovellaunus a few days ago. They've had no attacks like what we have seen. But in the past, the crow people of the Votadini have raided their shores."

"A bird…" Prasutagus mused.

"Perhaps some rogue faction of the Brigantes," Bran suggested.

Prasutagus turned his gaze from Bran to the candle burning at the center of the table. His eyes lingered for a time on the flames. After a long pause, he said, "Or the Romans."

It felt like a chill had wafted through the room.

"The Romans," Bran repeated. "Those are just rumors," he said dismissively. "Ever since I was a boy, people have been worrying that the Romans would return and force us all to make good on the oaths our ancestors made."

Prasutagus blinked hard, then shook his head. "The Yare... the Wash... These are places to penetrate our lands, to get deeper inland. The Romans are building up their forces in Gaul. Every day, more men arrive at their camps. And they are building. Lighthouses. Boats."

"Rumors," Bran said.

I studied Prasutagus's face. His gaze revealed his certainty. "Not rumors," I told my brother, looking from the prince to Bran and back again. "The prince is certain."

Prasutagus nodded to me. "I have been in Gaul. I heard the rumors, so I went to see for myself. I traveled with some merchants, hid my identity. What they are saying is true. The Romans *are* building their forces in Gaul. Their camps stir like a hive of bees," he said, then paused. I could see he was considering his next words. Finally, he said, "My father had word from King Verica. He has asked for our support in reclaiming his throne from Caratacus and Togodumnus."

Bran looked from Prasutagus to me. What the prince was sharing with us went far beyond anything Bran and I had ever been privy to, and the implications of Prasutagus's words were unthinkable. Verica, the deposed king of the Atrebates, had run to Rome for help. If he was making plans to take back his throne, had he convinced the Romans to send some men to help him?

"You must speak to our father," Bran said in all seriousness.

I nodded in agreement to Bran, then turned to Prasutagus. "Did you see Verica in Gaul?"

Prasutagus shook his head. "No. As much as I dislike the sons of Cunobelinus, I detest Verica more."

"Yet, if Verica is on the move and the Romans have offered him help…"

Prasutagus nodded. "You understand the problem correctly, Princess. Perhaps there is nothing to it, merely Verica looking for allies, but there is also the possibility that Rome might lend him some troops. In that case, we must all be wary. It is time to keep our friends close. We are all the Iceni. The Northern and Greater Iceni have always been allied. In the days to come, may we remain that way."

"May we remain that way," I said, echoing the prince. "And may the gods be with us," I added, lifting my cup.

"May the gods be with us," Bran and Prasutagus replied, the three of us clicking our mugs together.

It was late when we finished our meal. My heart was heavy with the thought that not only were the Northern Iceni threatened by the moves the Catuvellauni brothers, but also by the news that Verica was planning a bid to retake his lands. If he did, he would drag all of us into war. And then, there were the Romans. Were they simply establishing themselves in Gaul, or did they have their sights set across the channel once more?

"You are welcome to stay with us tonight," Bran told Prasutagus. "We would not have you ride back to Venta in the dark."

"I would be grateful," Prasutagus said. "And, if I might impose on your hospitality, I would appreciate it if you could provide a guide to take me to the Grove of Andraste tomorrow. I would give my prayers to the Dark Lady. If that is appropriate."

Bran turned to me.

The Grove of Andraste was the holy place of the Northern Iceni and not one usually visited by outsiders. But Prasutagus was druid-taught. Much to Saenunos's annoyance, Prasutagus had been trained on Mona. Of course he would have an interest in holy things.

I smiled lightly. "If Andraste summons you, I am happy to take you there."

"Thank you, Princess," Prasutagus said, inclining is head to me. His eyes lingered on mine. And once again, I felt that same sense of familiarity.

"Let me speak to Balfor. I'll see to you and your men's accommodations," Bran told Prasutagus, then rose and left the room.

I refilled the prince's cup. "I was sorry to hear of the passing of your wife."

Prasutagus nodded. "Thank you. It has been a difficult year," he said, then met my gaze. "You lost someone close to you in this attack on your people, I think."

Surprised by his observation, I nodded. I willed myself not to, but I could not hide the play of emotions on my face. "I did," I said, my voice catching.

Prasutagus, in a gesture of empathy, moved to take my hand but held back. When he did so, I noticed his fingers were tattooed with Ogham, the secret tree language. "As I remind myself, a person lives many lives, and those we love the most always return to us—one way or another."

"I... Thank you. I wish the same for you," I said, lightly touching his fingers.

"Prince Prasutagus, your lodgings are already ready," Bran said. "Apparently, our housecarl is more astute than I am," he added with a good-natured laugh.

"Very well. Thank you," Prasutagus said, rising. He turned to me. "Good night, Princess."

"Good night."

With that, Prince Prasutagus followed Bran from the dining hall toward the guest chambers. Balfor motioned for the prince's men to follow him to the guest house just outside.

I sat frozen.

The moment our hands connected, a vision had danced through my mind. I saw Prasutagus and myself standing on the shore of an icy river. Prasutagus held my waist, his arm around me protectively. Yet, we looked different—different eyes, different hair, different everything. But inside of us, we were the same people.

And what I felt for him...

The ramifications of such a vision shook me to my very core.

CHAPTER 31

Before Bran could return, I left the center hall and went to my chamber. There, Morfran waited for me. The raven squawked at me when I entered. I removed him from his cage and set him on Brenna's bed where he hopped back and forth, practicing his wings.

I dipped into the chest at the foot of my bed, pulling out a bag. I removed Gaheris's shirt.

Clutching it, I breathed in deeply, inhaling his scent.

Hot tears welled in my eyes.

Why had the gods taken Gaheris from me? And why would they show me such visions? Ula was right. There were shadows everywhere. I was sick of seeing things that made no sense to me. Who was Prince Prasutagus to me? No one. My father's ally. Nothing more. Why in the gods' name would *that* man appear in a vision?

"Gaheris," I whispered.

But once more, Prince Prasutagus's eyes came to mind— and this time, not the visage of the man from my vision, but the chestnut-colored eyes of the prince sleeping down the hall from me.

"No," I whispered.

Feeling miserable, confused, and just exhausted by all of it, I laid down, squeezed my eyes shut, and wept.

⁂

I WOKE EARLY THE NEXT MORNING. I ROSE QUIETLY AND DRESSED for riding. The raven was perched on the end of Brenna's bed. I returned him to his cage then made my way outside. A mist had settled on the fort, but the sun was about to rise. The morning light would soon clear the fog away.

Making my way across the compound, I climbed the steps of the rampart and watched as the mist rose off the river.

My heart felt heavy. The strange vision that had flashed before my eyes left me with a crippling sense of guilt. I had no interest in the prince. I had no interest in anyone. Anything. My heart was wed to Gaheris, and it would remain that way until I found him in the next life.

The sky turned shades of pale pink and yellow. I heard voices at the stables as the workers saddled the horses in preparation for our ride to the grove. I made my way back down the steps and toward the roundhouse. I needed to make sure Bran was awake and the prince and his people fed.

While the mist had burned off the river, it was still rising from the fort. I walked through the fog, nearing the great oak. When I did so, I saw a figure standing in the mist, looking up into the tree branches. I slowed my steps and set my hand on my sword. As I neared, however, I realized it was Prasutagus standing there.

"Prince Prasutagus," I said, approaching. "I'm sorry I was not within to greet you."

He gave me a soft smile then turned back to the tree. "I am early to rise when I sleep in a new place. They say this oak comes from Mona."

I nodded. "That's the story I always heard."

"Have you been there?"

"No."

Prasutagus studied my face a moment then turned back to the tree. "I was on Mona for five years. If I weren't an only child, I would have stayed. While I am far from Mona, sometimes the gods still whisper to me. I hear their voices in the winds and the trees."

"Is our oak speaking to you, Prince Prasutagus?"

"Oak Throne has many voices. But I think you know what I mean?"

Had he, like me, have a vision?

"I…" I began, unsure what to say. Thankfully, Bran arrived in time to save me.

"Ah, here you are," Bran called, jogging over to join us. "A bite to eat before riding?"

Prasutagus inclined his head to Bran, and we made our way back inside. After a quick morning meal, the prince, two of his men, Bran, myself, and a small party from Oak Throne made our way out of the fort and set off for the Grove of Andraste.

Bran and Prince Prasutagus rode ahead of me. Bran leading the conversation, he spoke to the prince about hunting.

Saenunos had painted Prasutagus as a pompous, arrogant, would-be killer. Nothing could have been further from the truth. Prasutagus struck me as an earnest and thoughtful man. He carried the same air about him as the druids. Saenunos had cursed Prasutagus's *learned* ways, but what was wrong with being close to the gods? What fault was there in a man who knew things about the world? Was Saenunos intimidated by Prasutagus's contemplative manner? Was he envious of the prince's education? Did he take Prasutagus's reflective nature as conspiring? Saenunos saw conspiracy everywhere, even from his own brother. In the end, perhaps Saenunos simply felt small in the presence of all great men—such as my father and the prince—and it was a feeling he would not tolerate. It was easier to hate.

We arrived at the grove by mid-morning. I could smell the wood smoke coming from the central bonfire as we approached. In the trees overhead, a raven cawed then flew toward the sacred oak circle on the hill knoll.

Prasutagus watched the bird, then lifted his hands to his forehead in a gesture of respect I had seen Belenus make before. I narrowed my gaze, looking for the raven, but it had disappeared into the green canopy overhead.

When we arrived, Bec approached us, wiping her hands on her apron as she went. She smiled at Bran then she looked over the rest of the party, her eyes settling in on Prasutagus.

When she saw him, she stopped. Waving to one of the children nearby, she whispered in the child's ear, then the little girl set off in a flat run toward Dôn's small home.

I dismounted, finding myself surrounded by the pack of hounds once more. "Pack of traitors. Can't you even be bothered to bark at strangers?" I told them, giving them all a pat.

"Prince Prasutagus," Bec said, bowing to him. "Welcome to the Grove of Andraste."

"Thank you, Priestess. I am truly honored to be here."

From her roundhouse across the square, Dôn appeared. She took the measure of our group and then approached, her walking staff in front of her. Her long, white hair was unbound and she was dressed in her dark robes. She looked the very image of a servant of the gods.

When she joined us, Prasutagus bowed deeply to her then greeted her in a language I did not understand.

Dôn returned the gesture, uttering the exact phrase to him. Dôn eyed the prince carefully. "You are far from Mona, but the glow of the green still surrounds you, Prince Prasutagus."

"I carry it in my heart," he told her, making Dôn smile.

"Come," she told him. "We shall speak before Andraste's great fire."

Prasutagus inclined his head to her. "Thank you, Mother."

Dôn turned to Bec. "See to the prince's men and our friends from Oak Throne. Welcome, Prince Bran," she said, nodding to my brother.

"Good morning, ancient Dôn."

Dôn huffed in bemusement, then smiled at him, shaking her head.

"If you please," Bec said, motioning for the rest of us to join her. "The children will see to the horses."

I moved to follow Bec and the others, when Dôn called to me. "Boudica?"

I turned toward her.

"Come," she said, then she and Prasutagus began their slow walk up the path leading to the shrine.

Confused, I turned and looked at Bec, who motioned for me to go on.

Who was I to question Dôn?

I made my way behind the pair. Dôn and Prasutagus spoke in low tones as they walked ahead of me. I could only make out snippets of their conversation, which mainly revolved around Prasutagus's ancient father, Antedios. I also heard Dôn mention Esu, Prasutagus's late wife.

When we reached the entrance to the grove, Prasutagus paused before the menhirs. His hand drifted from the image of the Great Lady to that of the Forest Lord, his gaze lingering long on the image of Cernunnos.

A small voice, ringing like a bell, whispered from the trees around me.

"Druid king. He is a druid king.

"A child of the forest.

"Another champion of the greenwood."

I turned to find its source but saw only flashes of light zipping through the trees.

Dôn motioned for Prasutagus to follow her into the ring of trees.

I watched the lights as they darted between the leaves. Fairies?

"The Stag King.

"The lord of Bel's fires."

Then, I felt something close to my ear. There was a soft hum, like the sound of a bee, then a ringing voice whispered. *"A king needs a queen."*

"Boudica," Dôn called. "Come, child. Help *ancient* Dôn."

I turned my gaze from the canopy above and back to Prasutagus and Dôn. Dôn was settling in on her stump before the fire, but Prasutagus was watching me, a strange expression on his face. When I met his gaze, he looked away.

I joined the pair.

"Add two logs to the fire, Boudica," Dôn told me. "Let Andraste have a little more flame."

I did as she asked. As I set the second log on fire, a spiral of embers drifted upward. I watched the flames dance toward the green overhead.

A raven called.

I spotted the bird sitting amongst the limbs.

"I hear you," Dôn said with a laugh. "I hear you, Dark Lady," she said, then turned to Prasutagus. "Come, Prasutagus of the Greater Iceni. Come and see what the Dark Lady has to show you," Dôn said, motioning for him to stand before the fire.

He stood there for a long time, his eyes on the flames. I watched as his lids grew heavy.

Then, my gaze drifted from the prince to the fire.

When I looked within the burning inferno, I saw a building on fire. I saw people running. I saw warriors fighting. I saw a strange statue of a smooth, painted god I didn't recognize being toppled by woad-painted warriors. I saw a young woman with raven-black hair fighting with shield and sword against armor-clad warriors. Along with the girl, I saw another woman with pale blonde hair, a foxtail clipped to her long locks, howling in rage then battling with two swords like a wild thing.

I meant to move away.

I knew I should move away.

Whatever it was Andraste wanted to say to Prasutagus, surely, I was getting in the way.

But I could not take my eyes from the scene of destruction that unfolded.

The fire popped, sending embers upward once more.

The image shifted.

I heard lively music and saw women dancing. Their hair unbound, rings of flowers on their heads, they hopped on their bare feet around a bonfire. The music chimed happily, and the girls spun faster around the flames. Beyond them, in the shadows, stood a tall man with the horns of a stag, his face made of green leaves.

I gasped, pulling myself from the vision.

Blinking hard to push the image away, I looked to Prasutagus, who was still lost to the flames. I turned from him to Dôn, who met my gaze.

She inclined her head to me then looked back to the fire once more.

When I looked back, I found Prasutagus's gaze on mine.

"The fire is speaking with many tongues today. The Dark Lady speaks of shadows creeping across the land and of the champions who will protect our world," Dôn said.

"What does it mean?" Prasutagus asked her.

"It means you should be ready, Prince Prasutagus. Ready for the dark times ahead. You must keep our allies close, and do what you can to secure the future of all of the Iceni. Even if the price you must pay is in blood."

THE THREE OF US RETURNED TO THE VILLAGE, MY MIND STILL spinning with the images Andraste had shown me. I had seen battle. And more. I had seen the Horned King. What great Cernunnos wanted with me, I had no idea. But to see the god alongside Bel's fires...it was a potent symbol of life. Yet all around me was death.

Well, perhaps not everywhere. When we reached the little village once more, I spotted Bran and Bec talking. They stood close to one another, Bran holding Bec's hand, making the priestess laugh.

My eyes flicked to Dôn, who said nothing, merely smiled to herself.

Prasutagus had been stone silent on the way back from the shrine. Whatever Andraste had shown him, married with Dôn's words, had given the prince much to consider.

But what had he seen?

Admittedly, I was curious.

Prasutagus was nothing like what I expected.

Truth be told, I liked him.

I had not expected that.

Prasutagus turned to Dôn. "I am honored to speak with you today. Thank you for your time."

"It is the gods to be thanked. I am only their mouthpiece."

Prasutagus smiled gently at her. "We will all gather at Arminghall this Beltane. I've had word from the druids of Mona that they will attend. We shall have a great meeting of our people. I would be glad to see the priestesses of the Grove of Andraste there."

"It shall be as the gods will," Dôn replied with a nod.

Prasutagus motioned to his men to make ready to leave.

Bec and Bran joined us.

"It is always good to see you, young prince of Oak Throne," Dôn told Bran. "Remember that you are always welcome here," she said, then flicked a glance at Bec, whose cheeks reddened.

"Thank you, ancient one," Bran replied.

At that, Dôn chuckled, then turned and made her way back to her cottage.

Bran and Bec began saying their goodbyes as the others readied the horses to leave.

After a moment's hesitation, I followed Dôn.

"Dôn," I called lightly.

She stopped, turning to me.

I cast a glance over my shoulder. "Dôn, I know I should not have looked. The vision was intended for Prasutagus, but—"

"But the Dark Lady spoke to you as well."

I nodded.

Dôn chuckled. "Two souls. One fire. It is no surprise to me, Boudica."

"What do you mean?"

"Nothing, my dear," she said, then patted my cheek playfully. "Nothing at all. Now, go on."

"But the visions. I saw—"

"Precisely what the Dark Lady wanted you to see. Do not question the gods, Boudica. We are all servants of their will," she said, then set off on her way once more.

I turned back to rejoin the others. When I did so, I noticed Prasutagus watching me.

When he saw me look his way, he turned away.

Was it really wise not to question the gods? What if their will did not match our own? What if their nudges were contrary to our own hearts and minds?

My gaze went to Prasutagus once more.

And what if they weren't?

CHAPTER 32

We followed the river on the way back to the grove. Bran fell into conversation with Prasutagus's men. Prasutagus slowed his black charger to ride beside Druda and me.

"And what is this fine beast named?" I asked, motioning to the horse.

Prasutagus smiled then patted the animal on his neck. "He is my Raven."

"That's a good name for him. Under the sun, his coat shimmers blue."

"Even purple, in the right light."

"Raven," I called to him.

The horse turned his ear toward me.

Druda puffed with frustration, making both Prasutagus and me chuckle.

"Jealous," I chided Druda.

"Funny creatures. On Mona, some worked with animals, learned to speak their language."

"I'm not sure I'd want to hear everything Druda has to say.

My mother was born on Mona. She lived there in her youth before coming to the Grove of Andraste."

"Your mother was a priestess?"

I nodded.

Prasutagus paused. "I remember your mother. Just a little. I was maybe fifteen or so when your family came to Venta."

"So I'm told, but I was too small to remember."

Prasutagus nodded. "She was like us," he said, gesturing toward my hair and then his own. "Marked by Bel's fires."

"That is one of my clearest memories, of her hair."

"Esu used to say that Bel marked people likely to be stubborn at birth." He chuckled lightly, but there was sadness just below his words.

Trying to distract him from his pain, I asked, "*Are* you stubborn, Prince Prasutagus?" I cocked an eyebrow at him.

At that, he laughed. "The fiercest mule cowers in comparison. Though I confess, there is nothing my father can't ask of me."

"Then you are a dutiful son."

"I try," Prasutagus said then sighed heavily. "His days are short, so I do my best to please him. If he lives until the winter solstice, I will be grateful."

"May the gods watch over him."

"Thank you, Princess."

When we arrived at the bridge leading into Oak Throne, Prasutagus signaled to his men to hold.

"We will ride back to Venta from here," he told me.

"Are you certain? I'd be happy to see you and your men fed before you go."

Prasutagus smiled lightly. "I must admit, I am still full from the morning meal. Your cook does nothing by halves."

"I'll be sure to pass on the compliment."

Prasutagus smiled lightly. It was a soft expression rather than a wide, loud grin. It suited the prince's quiet nature.

Bran joined us. "Can my men ride along with you to the border? I would feel better to see you safely into your own lands once more."

"As you wish."

Bran turned to me. "I'll go as well."

"Of course you will."

Bran winked at me.

"I hope we will see you in Venta in the spring," Prasutagus told me.

"I hope to come," I replied with a grin, evoking that smile from Prasutagus once more.

"Please send word if there is any news of the bandits. I will do the same. I am disturbed by these events. I'll try to learn if anyone knows anything."

"Thank you," I told him.

Prasutagus held my gaze. "It was a pleasure to meet you, Princess." The look in his eye puzzled me. I felt like the prince was looking both at me and beyond me. What was he trying to see?

"And you, Prince Prasutagus. May the Great Mother and Forest Lord watch over you."

He smiled at me. "And you."

At that, Prasutagus turned his horse and rejoined his men.

Druda snorted unhappily as he watched Bran and the others ride out.

"No, we don't need to ride to the border of the Greater Iceni lands," I told Druda, but the horse pawed the ground regardless. "Grumpy creature."

I watched as the band headed off. Bran turned in his saddle to wave once more before disappearing from sight.

To my surprise, Prasutagus also turned back.

I smiled at him, giving him a light wave. He returned the gesture by bowing in his seat to me, then he rode off.

Frustrated, Druda pawed the ground once more then breathed heavily.

"Making sure I know you're aggravated, eh? Message received. Come on," I said, turning him back toward the fort. "I've had enough adventuring today—and that's saying something for me. I promise to find you some apples to repay you for the great disservice I've done to you," I said as we crossed the earthen bridge back into the fort.

For the first time in a long time, I realized I was smiling. Truly smiling.

But the sudden realization—and the why—plucked the strings of guilt and misery on my heart.

Prasutagus was intriguing. What of it? I was allowed to think so. Noting that a man you expected to be boorish and cruel was actually earnest and easy to talk to—and not hard to look at—did not make me disloyal to Gaheris.

Annoyed with myself, I shoved the thoughts away and went to the stables. There was work to be done, royal visits or no.

And I had no business thinking of Prasutagus anyway.

CHAPTER 33

A month later, I was in the square near the sacred tree, working with Morfran, when a horn sounded at the gate. The weeks had passed slowly. I attended to small matters in the running of the fort while Bran spent his days off doing as he pleased—as I once did. Now, that time was done. From the sound of the horn, it could only be one person. Father had returned. The raven, who I had thought was likely to fly off at the first chance he got, proved to be clingier than any dog I'd ever owned. When he saw me step away from the tree for a better look, he flew to me at once, landing on my shoulder.

The young bird's fuzz was gone. Now, he had his midnight-dark feathers, which reflected blue and purple in the morning light—much like the coat of Prasutagus's horse.

For a brief moment, the memory of the prince and his soft smile wafted through my mind.

I frowned, shaking the memory away, then made my way toward the gate.

Soon, I saw the standard-bearers pass through. And behind them, I spotted the chariot that carried my father. Brenna rode on her own horse, Belenus alongside her. The rest of the party followed behind them.

I hurried to meet them.

The people of Oak Throne poured out of their houses, all of them cheering and calling. Father gave them a stilted wave, but Brenna smiled at everyone, waving and calling to many people.

"Father," I called, waving to him.

My father gave me a wave in greeting—slightly warmer than he gave the rest of the villagers, but not much—then carried on.

I hurried to Brenna.

"You have a growth," Brenna told me, eyeing my shoulder with a laugh.

"This is Morfran," I replied, gently patting the bird. I reached for Brenna's hand. "I'm glad to see you back."

My sister took my hand, giving it a squeeze.

"Welcome returns, Belenus," I called to the druid.

"Ah, Boudica. It is good to be home."

I looked up at my sister. "How is Father?" I asked her in a low voice.

"In mood or body?"

"Both... Either?"

Brenna shook her head. "The answer is the same either way. Not well. But how are you, my sister?"

The look of empathy in Brenna's gaze struck me hard. These past weeks, I had been struggling with the implications of my new reality. Gaheris was gone. Not only had I lost the person closest to me, and with him, my plans for the future, but now, things would be uncertain. Only Dôn's words would protect me until Beltane. And then, if the gods did not intervene on my behalf, my father would find someone else's bed to stick me in.

The thought made me feel ill.

For a time, I hoped I was carrying Gaheris's child, but it was not to be. My courses had come again. And with them, all hope that some piece of the life I'd dreamed of with Gaheris was truly gone.

I turned, scanning the party.

"Saenunos has not come," I said.

Brenna leaned toward me. "He and father had a terrible argument. Saenunos left in a fit of fury."

"Why?"

Brenna shook her head. "I don't know, but they argued shortly after Father had a messenger from King Antedios. Is it true that Prince Prasutagus came here?"

I nodded. "He came expecting to speak to Father."

Brenna nodded. "How was he?"

I shrugged. "Not what Saenunos painted him to be. He asked us to take him to the Grove. He was well-received by Dôn."

Brenna's brow flexed, her expression showing the same confusion I felt.

We rode to the square just outside the roundhouse. I helped Brenna dismount then went to Belenus.

"You are like the Morrigu with that raven on your shoulder," Belenus told me with a laugh, taking my hand as he slowly swung his leg over the side of the saddle. I offered him my other hand then braced myself as the old druid slid from his saddle.

"He's a smart creature. He likes to make a game of fetch. Just like a dog."

"Speaking of," Brenna said with a smile, then motioned for me to come with her.

We went to the wagon where the servants had ridden along with the supplies.

I found Riona there.

"Ah, Boudica. It's good to see your face and to be home."

"Welcome returns, Riona."

"Here you are, Brenna. He slept the afternoon in my lap," Riona said, lifting a tired puppy off her lap.

I swallowed the hard lump that had risen to my throat. I'd forgotten about the little dog I'd bought for Gaheris. And now, here he was, his intended owner lying dead in the mound.

Brenna took the puppy from Riona. The little creature greeted my sister by licking her cheek and chin, making Brenna laugh.

"Thank you, Riona," she said, then turned back to me. She had a worried look on her face. "I wasn't sure if I should bring him or not. I'm sorry if I should have left him. It's just... He's just the sweetest thing. Melusine and I had such fun with him. Even Caturix liked the puppies Melusine got for him. I swear, it was the only time I ever saw him smile. When it came time to leave, I couldn't leave this little one behind. But I know you had intended to give him to..." Brenna said, her words falling short as she hesitated.

"Gaheris."

Brenna nodded.

I set my hand on the pup's head. He really was a sweet little thing. Wild as ever, he gave me a bite for my trouble.

"Still a little monster," I said.

"Melusine and I were calling him Bear."

"Bear, eh?" I asked, patting him again. "Keep him, Brenna."

"Oh, no. Maybe Lynet or—"

"No. He has taken to you and you to him. It's good to see my sister guarded by a bear, little and furry as this one may be."

"Boudica, are you sure?"

I nodded.

"So, you will stay with me, little bear. I suppose I will need to train you properly now."

I patted the puppy once more, causing Morfran to squawk in protest.

Bear perked up, looking at the bird.

"Don't even think about it," I told the pup, shaking a finger at him. I turned to Brenna. "Come, let's get you inside. Surely, you're parched."

"Where is Bran?" Brenna asked, looked around the compound.

"He set off this morning."

"Hunting?" Brenna asked.

"Perhaps."

My vagaries did not slip past my sister. "Perhaps?"

"In the direction of the grove."

"Ah," my sister said. "You hear that, Bear? Very curious," Brenna said, giving the puppy a scratch on his tummy, then turned to me. "I've not spoken more than a dozen words to Bec, but you know her well. How is she?"

"She and Bran would make one another happy. And right now, I'm sure Dôn is enjoying the opportunity to use Bran's muscles to get work done at the grove."

Brenna laughed. "May the sisters entwine their fates to a happy end."

"So mote it be."

BRENNA AND I MADE OUR WAY INTO THE ROUNDHOUSE. WITHIN, I heard Belenus and father talking. My father had a tone in his voice that told me he was in a foul mood.

"We should redress the wound," Belenus was telling him.

"I will sit for a while and eat something first. My leg will not fall off all at once."

Turning, I gave Brenna a worried look.

"Belenus does not like the way the wound has been weeping. It's not healing as it should, and Father refuses to have the lump removed. Father's health was not good in Stonea. He slept most days after you left. Maybe now that he's home and away from Saenunos…"

I nodded.

Putting on the best smile I could muster, I joined my father in the hall. "Welcome home, Father."

Father nodded to me. "Thank you, my daughter. All seems well here. Has there been any news?"

"Nothing of importance since Prince Prasutagus left," I said. As soon as the prince departed, I sent a rider to Stonea with a message for my father, relaying the details of his visit. Neither Bran nor I heard anything of the matter after that. No doubt, my father had taken the issues into his own hands. "There were some small issues regarding crop rotations, storing grains, and the like, which I settled. A family came to see us over a squabble over bride-price. I ensured that the matter was resolved to everyone's satisfaction."

Father nodded slowly. "Where is Bran?"

"Hunting."

"Always hunting. At least one of you managed to stay put

long enough to see the fort is still standing," Father said waspishly.

"How is your leg, Father?" I asked.

"Healing," he said stiffly, stretching his leg out with a wince.

Belenus, seeming to note my father's lack of empathy, stepped toward me and took my hand. "We were all very sorry to hear the news from Frog's Hollow. Gaheris was an honorable young man. I am sorry he is gone."

I swallowed hard. "Thank you."

"The rites were held..." he asked leadingly.

I nodded. "Dôn came from the grove, and she and the priestesses saw to it. They built a mound in Frog's Hollow."

Belenus nodded.

"What of the pilchards? Did they get the crop in? Otherwise, we'll be dealing with hungry mouths in Frog's Hollow all winter," Father remarked.

Brenna uttered a soft gasp of protest but bit back her words.

"Yes," I said stiffly.

Father nodded.

Belenus met my gaze. "I am sorry for your loss, Boudica."

I nodded, willing myself not to cry. Despite my best intentions, tears welled up.

"Cidna!" Father bellowed. "Your king is parched! Where is that woman? I hope Prince Prasutagus was not left waiting like this."

"No, Father."

"Cidna!"

"Your Highness," Cidna called, appearing from the back. She was sweating and puffing hard. She carried a tray laden with food and drink. "My apologies, King Aesunos," she said, a worried expression on her features. "I was in the smoke-house laying out the meats. I didn't even hear the horn."

Father huffed at her. "We need to get someone younger in the kitchen. You are moving too slowly these days," he said gruffly.

Cidna said nothing, simply set out her food and returned to the kitchen.

The puppy, smelling the meat, struggled to get down.

Brenna set the pup on the floor. At once, he bounded toward the table.

"Nuisance, this one. You should have left him in Stonea," Father said, glaring at the dog as he turned to eat.

Brenna took Belenus's arm, and they both went to the table. Neither my sister nor the druid replied to my father.

"You're right, Father," I said, unable to keep the edge from my voice. "Cidna has cared for this entire household on her own with far too little help for too long," I added, feeling the dam around my frustrations with my father shaking loose. "It was always too much of a burden to place on one woman and a handful of helpers anyway. Alone, with all her aides in Stonea, she saw Prasutagus royally fed. Many women in the village would be happy to assist Cidna in the kitchens. Tomorrow, I will employ two women to come help," I told him, my voice hard.

My father, his eyes on his plate, did not reply.

Agitated, I left the hall and went to the kitchen. There, I found Cidna patting her eyes with the corner of her apron.

"Cidna…"

She waved her hand at me. "No. He's right. I should have been at the ready."

"You are human. And you are one person. I will see you get more help. But no one will replace you. Ever."

Cidna merely nodded then dabbed her eyes once more.

"What can I do to help?"

Cidna waved at me dismissively. "We'll attend to it. Albie, get that bread out," she told one of the kitchen boys who rushed back to the hall with two baskets full of bread.

"Are you sure?"

Cidna nodded then turned to the cutting board, chopping carrots with vigor.

Snatching up Cidna's ale tankard, I hurried to the back and filled her mug. When I returned, I set the ale on the corner of her workbench then paused to kiss her on the cheek.

"Boudica," she said appreciatively, patting my arm.

Leaving her, I made my way out the back door. Lifting Morfran off my shoulder, I sent the bird flying. Working my way across the yard, I climbed the stairs of the wall and looked out over the field. It was late summer now. Goldenrods and purple asters dotted the fields, the first summer flowers fading. Lughnasadh was next week.

I would have been a bride.

I would have woven purple and gold flowers in my hair, danced, drank wine, and wed the man I loved.

Now, he lay rotting in his tomb.

After Lughnasadh, winter would come once more. And with it, darkness.

My eyes drifted toward the woods and the path to Frog's Hollow.

I hadn't been there for weeks now. I could not get myself to go. Gaheris's absence was so palpable, I couldn't bring myself to face it. Turning, I looked off toward the south. Summer was fading, and soon, Samhain would be here and the long nights after that. All would be darkness. There was little to pin your hopes to... except when spring came once more, we would all go to Venta to meet with Prasutagus and the druids for Beltane.

At least, there was that.

Once more, the prince's soft smile came to my mind.

At least, there was that.

CHAPTER 34

The silence that fell over our house after my father's return was practically deafening. The only sound that punctuated the darkness was Brenna's lyre. The trip to Stonea had awakened something inside my sister. She had always been a gifted musician before, but now, there was a special kind of magic to her music.

We were sitting under the oak in the waning days of autumn, the children listening as Brenna played. When she was done, my eyes were wet with unshed tears. Several of the children around me quickly dashed hot tears from their cheeks.

"That was so beautiful, Princess. Where did you learn that song?" Eiwyn asked.

Brenna smiled. "One day, in Stonea, I went up on the walls and played. From deep in the mist, a voice sang back to me. I played its song. Over and over, we played this game, the voice and I."

"Whose voice was it?" Birgit asked.

"I don't know. Who do you think?" Brenna asked with a grin.

"The goddess of the marshes," Eiwyn said matter-of-factly. "She gave you her magic."

"Yes. That's it. That's what happened," Phelan agreed.

All the others nodded.

"Perhaps," Brenna mused.

"You should go to Mona," Eiwyn told her. "Let the bards teach you. Did you know that is how they moved the standing stones into rings? They used song magic."

"How do you know that?" I asked her with a grin.

"Ula showed me."

"Showed you?"

Eiwyn nodded. "One day, she lifted a rock from her hand by singing to it. Ask her, Boudica. She will show you."

"Or she will lie and say she can't do it," I said with a grin.

At that, all the children laughed.

A cool breeze blew across the yard.

Brenna rose. "It will be cold tonight, children. You should get home now."

"Thank you, Princess," Eiwyn said, the other children echoing their thanks before they set off back toward their homes.

Bear, thinking a game was afoot, sprinted after Eiwyn, who took off in a run, making the little dog rush after her even faster.

From his perch overhead, Morfran squawked at the dog in irritation. The bird and the dog had developed a fierce rivalry, Morfran seeming irritated with everything Bear did.

Brenna chuckled. "Bear is a spirited thing. You picked the best pup of the litter, Boudica."

I nodded. Gaheris would have loved him.

Lughnasadh had passed. With Father feeling ill, no revels were held that day. Belenus performed a simple ceremony, but our usual fall festival never manifested. For once, I was happy about my father's indifference. On the holy day, I'd ridden to the seashore and spent the day staring out at the same waves on which strangers had come, taking my love from me.

Now, I was in the abyss beyond that marker in time. After Lughnasadh, everything was a confused darkness.

"What I told the children was true," Brenna said, interrupting my thoughts.

I turned to her.

"There *was* a voice in the mist. It did sing to me. Ever since" —she looked down at her lyre—"my music has been different. I dream of songs. I hear music in the wind, in the forest. I try to play what I hear."

"What did Belenus say?"

"He would agree with Eiwyn. I... Boudica, I asked Belenus to petition Father once more to send me to Mona. If the spirits of the land themselves call, perhaps Father can be convinced."

"Father seems to be in no mood for anything."

Since his return from Stonea, Father had grown increasingly foul-tempered. He spent most of his time huddled away in his meeting chambers, sending messengers all over our land. But he shared nothing with us. Every scrap of news we got came from the merchants or the people in the village. Still, Caratacus and Togodumnus warred with the Atrebates. More than that, I didn't know. How long would it be before the brother kings turned their attention to the Iceni?

"You're right about that," Brenna agreed.

The wind blew across the square once more, carrying with it the chill of the winter to come. Brenna pulled her cloak tighter around herself.

"Come on. Let's go back. Your bear will find you once he's given up the chase," I said.

Brenna nodded, and we turned back toward the roundhouse. "Do you think Ula really lifted a stone with her voice?"

"Of course she did."

"Do you think she would show me?"

I smirked. "I have no idea, but we can ask."

I whistled to Morfran, who flew down, landing on my arm, then bounced up to my shoulder.

Brenna chuckled.

We had almost reached the roundhouse when Bear appeared once more.

"Chased them all home, did you? Like a little herding dog. Well done," Brenna told him, giving him a pat.

But before we could go within, a horn sounded at the gate. A messenger had come.

Balfor appeared at the door.

Curious, Brenna and I waited.

Soon, a rider with the standard of King Antedios of the Greater Iceni appeared. The messenger spoke a few words to Balfor then the housecarl led him inside.

"What's all that about, I wonder?" I asked.

Brenna shook her head. "Father exchanged messengers with the king several times in Stonea. I don't know what the issue was, but something about Antedios caused the rift between Father and Uncle."

I frowned. "The prince said he did not expect his father to live long. Do you think…"

Brenna shrugged.

Inside, the messenger had already disappeared into the meeting room with Father and Belenus.

Eating an apple and looking far too nonchalant, Bran appeared. "What's all that about then?"

Brenna shook her head. "I don't know. A messenger from King Antedios."

I sighed. "I'm in no mood for intrigue," I told my siblings. "Let me go see what the eccentrics are busy with today."

"Ask her if she will show me," Brenna said.

I nodded.

"Ask who what?" Bran asked.

Brenna chuckled. "Never mind. You missed everything already. Where were you all day anyway?"

"I...um...hunting."

"Hunting. Why is it you never return with anything? You must be a terrible hunter," Brenna teased.

"Oh, don't worry. At this rate, we're very likely to see the results of all his *hunting* by spring," I said, giving Bran a knowing look.

"Boudica," he chided me.

I winked at him, then went outside.

Behind me, I heard Brenna tell Bran, "She's wicked, but she's not wrong. Will you ask Father's permission to marry Bec?"

"I need to ask Dôn first. I'm still working up the nerve," he replied with a laugh.

I smiled lightly. Something told me my brother would have little difficulty convincing the high priestess. It was Father he needed to concern himself with.

I pulled my cloak tight around me and made my way to Ula's cottage. Ducking under her talismans, I knocked on the door.

"Be quick about it. Don't let the cold air in."

I chuckled lightly then entered. Ula was seated at her small, rickety table, scratching with a quill on a piece of birch bark.

"What are you doing?" I asked.

"Talking to the gods."

"And what are you talking about today?"

"The House of Aesunos."

"Nosey of you."

Ula laughed then continued her writing. I went and stood over her shoulder. She was noting down some words in Ogham.

"When Prince Prasutagus came, I noticed he had the tree language marked on his fingers."

"Druid born, that one. He should serve the gods, not be king."

"He's not king; he's a prince."

"He will be king by spring."

I paused for a moment, letting her words sink in. King Antedios would soon be dead. "Wouldn't you say that to serve the people is to serve the gods? In a way, a king is an intermediary between the gods and the common folk."

"You riddle like Belenus today," she said, then rose, taking her strip of birch with her.

The birch bark in her hands, she pressed it close to her lips, whispered something, then threw it into the fire.

Rather than watching the birch burn, I watched Ula. Her eyes grew drowsy as she watched the flames. She stood still for a very long time, nodded, then turned to me. When she met my gaze, she had an odd expression on her face. It was a look of sympathy. Out of all the things she could have said or done, for some reason, that felt like the worst. Not wanting to know why, not wanting her to say anything, I went and sat down at the table. I shifted Ula's small pot of ink toward me. I lifted a piece of birch and set it in front of me. "This winter, you will teach me all the Ogham letters and what they mean," I said, drawing the marks of Ogham I knew.

"Is that so?"

"Yes."

"You want to know what they mean?"

I nodded.

Ula took the quill from my hand. Taking another strip of bark, she drew a symbol thereon and slid it back to me. "Duir. Oak," she said. "A simpleton can learn this."

"But there is more, isn't there? Duir is the Father. He is Cernunnos. The great oak. The father of druids and the druid himself. That is the meaning. Am I right?"

Ula laughed. "Maybe you're not so stupid after all." She lifted the piece of bark and handed it to me. "Listen. If you want to truly learn, listen…"

"Listen?"

Ula nodded.

I lifted the bark toward my ear.

Ula slapped the side of my head. "A head full of dung. Not with your ears, you stupid girl. If all you do is listen with your ears, you will learn nothing of this world. Take it and go. Come back tomorrow and let me know what you've heard."

"Ula…"

"Go on."

Slipping the bark into my pocket, I went to the door, pausing just a moment before I left. "Eiwyn told us that you lifted a stone with the sound of your voice."

"That girl. She is full of lies and—"

"Brenna will come back with me tomorrow. You will teach her." I sucked in my lips, trying not to laugh. I had never told Ula to do anything. I could barely stand waiting for her reply.

Ula sighed heavily then began shifting pots on her table, muttering as she went. "A druid in the house, but still they come to me—cursed with them—a grove full of priestesses— the gods dump Damara's girls on me…"

Chuckling, I opened the door. "Right. See you tomorrow, then."

"You're letting the cold air in," Ula yelled at me.

Slipping back outside, I laughed lightly, then returned to the roundhouse to share the good news with my sister that she, too, could have an abusive tutor.

CHAPTER 35

Before heading back to the roundhouse, I went to the stables to check on Druda and to practice with my spear. Setting my cloak on the side of Druda's stall, I pulled one of the practice spears from the rack and began practicing the moves Gaheris had shown me and Cai had helped me refine. The grain barrel that was my opponent was soon taking a beating.

As I worked, my mind went to Gaheris. Soon, it would start to snow, and we would all be trapped in the house. There would be no winter hunts with Gaheris, no snuggling close together beside a campfire to share warmed wine, no more anything. Now, it was just me and whatever fate the gods decreed for me. Rather than spending my time in Frog's Hollow, I would be here in Oak Throne, waiting...

It was going to be a long winter.

But for Prince Prasutagus, it would be worse. His father would die. Knowing it was coming would not ease the ache. From what I could see, he loved his father. I still mourned a mother I barely remembered. With his wife gone, the prince

277

would be alone in his grief. Surely, he had people around him to ease his pain. His druids. His warriors. The thought of him on his own in his sadness evoked a sense of deep pity.

I paused.

I was sweating hard, my heart beating fast. I had been practicing my jabs as my mind wandered.

But why had it wandered *there*?

I turned to Druda. "What do you think? Am I getting any better?"

The horse, who had been drowsing, huffed at me, then closed his eyes once more.

I nodded, then lifted my spear once more.

Prasutagus would soon be alone, just like me. While I had my siblings around me, they did not understand my grief. Perhaps, in that, I felt sympatico with the prince.

Shaking myself from thoughts of Prasutagus, I lifted my spear once more, spinning it between my fingers. I remembered how Gaheris twirled his spear around himself to impress me—which it did.

Remembering the move, I gave it a try.

The spear bounced from my hand and across the floor a moment later, clattering against the stall doors.

This time, several of the horses expressed their annoyance with whinnies and exasperated huffs. One of them even kicked the stable door.

"Sorry," I said, then picked up the spear once more, beginning my practice again. I planted my feet firmly, balancing myself, then began to thrust and jab. I moved back and forth, working hard and trying hard not to think about Prince Prasutagus anymore.

It was well after sundown when I finally left the stable. When I stepped outside, the cold wind startled me. I was drenched in sweat. The sharp wind chilled me. Hurrying, I made my way back to the roundhouse. When I entered, I could feel a pall hanging over the place. Something was not right.

I was on my way to the dining hall when Bran appeared in the hallway, gesturing for me to follow him.

I joined my brother.

"What's happened? Is there bad news from King Antedios?"

"There was news, that is certain," Bran said, leading me to my chamber. He scrunched up his nose at me. "Ach, Boudica. You smell of sweat and horses. Where have you been?"

"Practicing with my spear in the stables."

"Figures."

When we reached the door to my chamber, I could hear Brenna weeping on the other side. Alarmed, I opened the door in a hurry to find my sister sitting on her bed, her eyes red and puffy. Morfran squawked when I entered.

"Brenna?" I said, rushing to her. "What's happened? Are you hurt?"

"No. I'm all right," she said, patting my hand. Brenna looked up at Bran then nodded to him.

"There was an argument," Bran explained to me. "Belenus asked Father to send Brenna to Mona in the spring so she may train with the bards for a year. Father—"

"Said no, of course," I finished for him.

"It's worse. A marriage contract is already settled for me," Brenna said in a despairing moan.

"To whom?"

"To Prince Prasutagus," Brenna said sadly, then sniffed once more.

I felt like a chill wafted through the room. I froze, and my words evaporated. I stared at Morfran.

"Apparently, King Antedios asked for Brenna after Prasutagus's visit here. That must be why Father and Saenunos quarreled. Uncle would never want to see the Iceni unite," Bran said.

"Oh! You're right. That must have been the cause," Brenna told him.

"Father would hear nothing from Belenus. He even shouted at the druid," Bran told me.

"I will never go to Mona," Brenna said sadly.

"I don't know what King Antedios said that convinced Father, but he sent the messenger back tonight with his word that he would bring Brenna to meet the prince at Beltane."

Both Bran and Brenna turned and looked at me.

"Boudica?" Brenna asked.

"I..." I began, but found myself at a loss for words. I felt like someone had reached into my stomach and grabbed my insides, squeezing hard.

"It is a shock," Brenna agreed.

"I tried to tell Brenna that she shouldn't be afraid. I liked Prasutagus. He's a quiet sort, honorable. He reminded me of the druids," Bran said.

"He studied on Mona," I said quietly.

"Yes," Bran replied. "That makes sense. You spoke to him at length, Boudica. How did he seem to you?"

How did he seem to me? The answer my heart whispered to that question terrified me. Pulling myself together, I said, "He's amiable. Given he is druid-taught, I'm sure he will let you study music with a bard."

Brenna sniffed. "That gives me reassurance," she said, taking my hand. "I'm glad you liked him. As far as partners go, there was no one better than Gaheris. I trust my sister to know a good man when she sees one."

"He spoke honorably of his late wife," Bran told her.

Brenna nodded then dabbed her eyes. "At least I will have the winter to prepare myself."

I rose and went to Morfran, stroking the bird's soft feathers.

"Boudica," Bran said carefully, "after the talk of Brenna, Father and Belenus spoke of you as well. Belenus told him that Dôn has dictated that you be left on your own until Beltane."

"Belenus said that? He knew?" I asked.

"Belenus has been to the grove since our return," Bran replied.

"What did Father say?"

"He was furious," Brenna replied.

"Why?"

"Because Father has had word from King Caratacus. He asked to make you his bride."

CHAPTER 36

Bran and Brenna began to discuss what Brenna remembered of the conversation between Aesunos and Saenunos that had caused the rift in Stonea, both of them theorizing about the matter.

Struck by the news, I stammered, "Why... Why don't I get us some...some wine," then backed out of the room.

But instead of going to the kitchens, I rushed back outside.

Leaving the roundhouse, I raced to the wall. My breath came quick as panic gripped me. My hand shook. My heart pounded in my chest. I ran up the steps to the palisade then looked out on the landscape. The moon shimmered down on the fields around the fort. Under the moonlight, the waves of the Stiffkey looked black with silver swirls on the surface. The whole world had taken on a dark blue and silver sheen. The goldenrods and asters, which had been so colorful in the sunshine, had lost their luster. Now, they were only shades of grey.

As I stared out at the countryside, a terrible sense of anguish washed over me. I felt like I could barely breathe.

Setting my shaky hand on my chest, I tried to slow down my short breaths. I felt confused and miserable and angry all at once. When I questioned myself as to why, the answer horrified me.

It was not the news about Caratacus that had me so upset.

No. It wasn't that.

Prasutagus had asked for Brenna.

Not me.

He had asked for Brenna.

I loved Gaheris, but the fact that he was gone was not lost on me. I knew my father well. It was only a matter of time before he would find a place for me. Dôn had bought me time to grieve, time to find my footing once more. At the end of it, I hoped to be strong enough to find a new path forward. But Caratacus?

And if I was honest with myself, truly honest, there had been something about Prasutagus that had intrigued me. He was so familiar. I had felt an ease around him I hadn't known since...

I heard a rustling overhead, and a moment later—much to my surprise—an owl landed on the rail of the rampart not far from me. It turned its great, moon-round eyes toward me.

My body shuddered. "Owl mother," I said with a miserable sob, feeling hot tears trickle down my cheeks. I should be happy for Brenna, but...

With a sigh, I looked out at the field.

I was selfish. I should want my sister to be wed to a good man. And that was what Prasutagus was, a good man. It was just, while I had not let the thought break the surface, Prasutagus was...

The owl ruffled its feathers more.

This time when I turned, I found a woman standing there.

She had large, golden eyes and long snow-white hair. She was dressed in a white gown trimmed with feathers.

I stilled.

The land had many voices. The gods. The goddesses. But the greenwood and all its fey inhabitants were never far from me. What this creature was, I didn't know. But everything in me told me to be wary.

"Why do you weep, firebrand?" she asked in a soft, silver voice.

"Everything seems so dark," I said in a broken voice.

She laughed lightly. "Dark? To you? You, who are nothing but flames?"

I shook my head, not understanding.

"Have faith in the gods, queen hereafter. Have faith in the wyrd sisters. But most of all, have faith in the greenwood. We will have our champion."

"Boudica?" a voice called.

I turned to find Ula there.

Beside me, I heard a rustle once more. I turned just in time to see the owl lift off from the wall and fly toward the field, the moon shimmering silver on her wings until she flew out of sight, into the forest once more.

Turning, I made my way back down the steps, joining Ula in the courtyard.

Ula was staring at the spot on the wall where the woman had appeared, chewing the inside of her cheek as she considered.

"Who was that?" I asked.

"Oak, broom, and meadowsweet—flower face."

I scowled, not understanding.

"Blodeuwedd, the cursed flower maiden. A creature of the greenwood," Ula explained. "Dangerous creatures are stirring. We are too close to Samhain for you to wander about at night. The worlds are growing thin, Boudica. Beware."

"Then what are you doing wandering around at night?"

Ula laughed. "What would they want with an old crone like me?" she said, then wandered away, leaving me in the darkness.

I turned back toward the wall.

Have faith in the greenwood. I would try. But, at the moment, everything felt like darkness.

WEEKS PASSED. AND WITH THEM, I FOUND MYSELF FEELING DULL and lifeless. I took Brenna to see Ula. Even though Ula complained endlessly about it, she endeavored, all the same, to teach my sister what she knew about song magic, while nagging me to listen to the Ogham.

I tried but heard nothing.

Whatever I was supposed to hear was not speaking to me.

Instead, my worried heart faced the south.

Caratacus.

Would my father really wed me off to that ambitious king? I had never seen the man. I knew little of him. What I did know was that he was a fighter. He and his brother were dominating their way south. What would I do with a ruthless creature like that?

The thought filled me with despair.

Soon, Samhain approached. A week before the festival, Lynet arrived at Oak Throne. I was busy sparring with Bran and the others when she joined us.

Leaving my spear aside, I went to her.

"Lynet," I called. "And Mountain," I added, pausing to give Gaheris's horse a pat. "Well met. Both of you."

Mountain nosed my chin and gave my hair a whiff in greeting.

"I missed you too, old friend," I said, stroking his nose.

"Well met, Boudica," Lynet said. She slipped off the horse then embraced me. "It is good to see you."

"Is everything all right?"

Lynet nodded. "I just need to talk over some issues of the winter stores with your father. And I wanted to ask you to come to Frog's Hollow for the Samhain rites. Dôn and the priestesses will join us. We thought, given what we have all lost this year, it would also be good for you to come."

I nodded, feeling a lump rise in my throat. "I'll be there."

"Good. You can stay with me."

"Thank you. How is Tristan? The other children?"

"He's very well. They all are. But they miss you. We all do."

"I'm sorry. I wanted to come, I just…"

I didn't know what else to say. The truth was, the idea of going to Frog's Hollow had been too painful. There was nowhere in that place that didn't remind me of what I had lost.

Lynet lifted the frog pendant on my chest. She studied it, a sad smile on her features. "I understand, but it's still your place. Remember that."

I nodded.

"Lynet, he is ready for you," Balfor called.

Lynet winked at me before following Balfor inside.

A few moments later, Brenna appeared, her lyre case in her hands.

"I saw Lynet," she told me brightly.

I nodded.

"I'm going to see Ula now. Want to come?"

I shook my head. "Maybe later."

Brenna laughed. "All right. She's easier on me when you're there to mistreat instead. Oh well," she said, then headed off.

I took Mountain's reins. "Come on, old friend. Let me find you something to eat. Druda will be glad to see you," I told him, then led the horse across the square to the corral, tying him near the water trough. I whistled for Druda, who appeared a moment later. When he spotted Mountain, he ran across the green to meet him.

The pair exchanged whinnies, then nosed and nipped playfully at one another. I went to get Mountain some grain. When I returned, I fed the horse then leaned against him. The scent of the animal was so familiar it sent a twinge of pain through me.

"Ah, my old friend, are you missing him too?" I asked Mountain.

I stayed with the horse until Lynet appeared once more.

"All right, big guy," I said, untying his reins. "Time to say goodbye."

As I led Mountain to Lynet, Druda whinnied in protest, Mountain returning the gesture.

Lynet was chuckling when I joined her.

"Whining like playmates sent home for supper," she said.

"So true. He's fed and watered. All go well?" I asked, looking back toward the roundhouse.

Lynet nodded. "Yes. Your father looks very thin," she said, passing a concerned look over her shoulder.

"The leg wound has not healed properly, and he will not listen to Belenus's advice."

Lynet tilted her head to the side then nodded. "Men like to hide their ailments. Rolan was the same. Every time he pulled something, he'd walk around limping for a week but claim everything was *fine*. All fine," she said, smiling lightly before her memory was clouded by heartache. She shook her head, patted my arm, then remounted Mountain.

I handed her the reins.

"I will see you soon," Lynet told me.

"Yes. I'll be there."

"Good," she said, then patted Mountain. "Come on, old boy. Hopefully, Boudica didn't spoil you so much you're slow going home."

I laughed.

Lynet gave me a wave then rode off once more.

I sighed heavily as I watched her go, reminded again and again of the life that had passed me by.

When I turned to go back to my training, however, I saw someone passing down the lane—another whose life had slipped away from them.

Her stomach protruding heavily, Kennocha clicked at a pair of goats as she struggled with two very-full baskets as she made her way back into the village. I frowned when I saw her, a swell of pity washing up in me. I chided myself for not visiting her sooner. Lost to my own grief, I had kept putting it off. But the truth of the matter was that she was carrying my niece or nephew, even if Caturix could not claim his child. Surely we owed her more than any of us were giving her—particularly my brother.

I hurried to catch up with her.

"Kennocha," I called.

The woman stopped, looking around in confusion to determine who had called her name.

When she saw me coming her way, she looked confused. "Boudica," she said, then tried to curtsey.

"No. Don't," I said, gesturing for her to stop. "From the looks of you, you may drop your burden from the effort."

She smiled weakly. "I confess, I expect this one any time now," she said, glancing down at her stomach. There was such sadness in her eyes. Kennocha's family was all dead. Now with Caturix in Stonea, she was truly on her own.

"Here, let me," I said, taking the baskets from her hands. They were full of jars and baked goods. I recognized the items from our own stores.

"I traded with Cidna," Kennocha explained quickly. "I gave her two goats. Unfortunately, she didn't need these two fellows."

"I..." I began, feeling sorry to think the woman thought she had to explain herself. "Yes, Cidna is too particular. These gents look frisky and fine," I said, smiling at the goats. "You always have the best goats in Oak Throne."

Kennocha gave me a grateful smile, but it was punctuated by a wince.

"Are you all right?"

"The labor pains have been coming off and on for a few days now. Much worse today. I wanted to get my trading done before this little one got here."

"Have you seen Ula?"

She shook her head. "Not until it's time, otherwise she'll chide me for being overly excited."

I chuckled. That sounded like Ula. "Either way, let's get you home. You should not be out and about carrying such heavy things so close to your time."

With that, we made our way back into the village. Kennocha walked slowly, her hands pressed against her back. When we finally got to her little house, she clicked to her goats, sending them back into the pen then turned to take the baskets from me.

"I'll set them down for you," I said, eyeing her door. Truth be told, I wanted the widow to invite me inside. For Caturix's sake, I needed to make sure she was all right.

Kennocha nodded then went to her door. "Please," she said, opening the latch. "Come in."

The little house was sparse but clean and cozy. A fire burned in the central firepit. Over it sat a pot of porridge. The widow's cot had been neatly made. Warm blankets and skins covered the bed. Not far from it was a small cradle. I set the baskets on her table then went to the cradle. It was a beautiful, carved piece. On the headboard had been carved the oak tree symbol of my family.

"It's beautiful," I said.

"A gift from the child's father."

I looked back at her.

Kennocha met and held my gaze.

"I am sorry about how things unfolded," I said, struggling to find the right words. "Caturix does not love easily. To have been with you, made this child... He must love you very much. Like all of us, he is tied first to his duty to the family," I said, but immediately regretted my words. Caturix should have fought for this woman. As much as I liked Melusine, Kennocha's sorry state broke my heart. "Not that I agree with that or my brother's choices. He should be here with you. And I am sorry that he didn't fight for you."

She swallowed hard then nodded. She wiped a tear from her cheek. "The fact that you think so is more comfort than you can ever imagine, Boudica."

Frowning, I looked around the room. "Do you need anything? Do you want for anything?"

She gave me a broken smile. "Aside from your brother? No. Caturix left me with money, and there is a trader who travels between here and Stonea who always brings me a small bit of silver and a word or two from Caturix. What more can a woman like me ask for?"

Fury swelled up in me. "You are carrying Caturix's child. I think you have the right to ask for quite a lot."

"If only things were that easy, Boudica. But you have known your own hardships. These many months I wanted to tell you my sorrow on hearing what happened to Chieftain Rolan's son, but I didn't know how you might receive me."

It was my turn to swallow my feelings. "I... thank you, Kennocha. But you need not have hesitated. If you ever need anything, you may ask me. I have sworn to my brother to keep your relationship private, but that doesn't mean we can't be friends."

She set her slim hands on her lips. "Thank you," she whispered then winced again.

I frowned. "Are you sure I can't fetch—"

"Ahh," Kennocha said, setting her hands on her lower back.

"I'm going to take that as a yes. I'll be back soon," I told her then rushed to the door.

"Boudica," Kennocha whispered, fear on her face.

"Rest. I'll be back with Ula in a moment," I said then raced toward Ula's cottage.

Dodging down the narrow village streets, I made my way to Ula's small roundhouse. From within, I heard the sound of Brenna's lyre music and my sister's voice. Something about it seemed different. It made the hair on my head feel like it was standing on edge. I flung open the door to find Brenna sitting on the floor, her lyre in her hands. And all around her, feathers floated in the air.

The moment she saw me, the music stopped. "Boudica," she said.

The feathers fluttered gently toward the ground.

"Banshees be cursed," I whispered, watching them in awe.

"Nosey girl, what are you about?" Ula asked waspishly.

"I… The widow Kennocha's child is coming. She needs you."

"The *widow* Kennocha," Ula said then chuckled to herself. "Very well. Brenna, clean up this mess and come back tomorrow. Boudica, fetch a basket and help me."

"Me?"

"Yes, you. The *widow* Kennocha," Ula muttered to herself as she began collecting her things.

Brenna began collecting the feathers and putting them away. "I don't know this woman, Kennocha. If she is a widow, who is her child's father?"

I looked away from my sister, not wanting her to see my face.

"Puck, Seelie, or Selkie, it makes no difference," Ula grumbled.

I handed Ula the basket.

When Ula met my gaze, I saw the look therein. She knew very well who the child's father was. Ula slipped her supplies in the basket then nodded to me.

"Let's go," she said, then the two of us set off.

We worked our way through the village back to Kennocha's house. As we drew close, I heard her call out in pain.

Without knocking, Ula entered. The widow was sitting at

the side of her cot. Her face was wet with tears, the skirt of her dress wet.

"You waited too long," Ula scolded her then set down her basket on Kennocha's small table. The jars inside rattled. Ula pulled out an apron and tied it on. "Boudica, boil some water then wash your hands well. Lie back, Kennocha, or you'll be birthing the new prince or princess of Oak Throne on the floor." Ula pulled a bottle from her basket and cleaned her hands with a sharp astringent that smelled of lemon and alcohol.

"You... you know?" Kennocha asked, looking from Ula to me.

"Boudica didn't tell me anything," Ula scolded her waspishly. "I have eyes of my own. Now, lie down."

Kennocha did as Ula instructed.

Ula got to work examining the woman while I banked up the fire then set on some water to boil. I then went to Ula's basket and set out the jars of salves and ointments she had there.

"You're coming to it already. Why did you wait so long?" Ula asked Kennocha. "Boudica, brew a draft of raspberry leaf for afterward. It will help with the bleeding."

I did as she asked, working quickly as the woman's cries started coming more frequently.

"Oh, Caturix," Kennocha moaned softly.

"No good calling for him now. He's busy in another woman's bed. At least his sister is here to see you through. Thank the gods for that. Hold her hand, Boudica. The hard part is coming soon."

I went to Kennocha and sat beside her, mopping her forehead with a damp rag.

"When I tell you to push, do as I say," Ula told her.

Kennocha nodded. "Yes."

And then the difficult part began. Ula guiding her, Kennocha began her laboring. The sight of it was horrifying and wonderous all at once. Kennocha grunted and strained as she labored for what felt like hours.

Finally, with one last cry, the child was delivered.

"There we are. There we are. Bring my basket, Boudica. And the linens," Ula called.

"The child?" Kennocha asked weakly.

"A girl," Ula said. "You have a daughter." Taking a knife from her basket, Ula cut the umbilical cord then wrapped the baby in the linens, handing it to me. The child cried heartily.

Dipping a piece of cloth in warm water, I wiped the child's face clean. My niece. She had a full head of black hair, just like her father.

I went to Kennocha, handing her the baby. "Your daughter," I whispered, setting the baby in her mother's arms.

"Oh, sweet one," Kennocha said, stroking the baby's cheek with her finger.

"Do you have a name for her?" I asked.

"Mara."

"Mara," I whispered, stroking the baby's soft hair.

I sat with Kennocha as Ula worked. After a time, Ula declared the work done then began packing up her things and washing her hands.

"You will need to rest now. There was tearing," Ula told Kennocha. "I will leave a salve for you. Put it on three times a day. I will spend the night here, and in the morning, see that one of the girls from the village helps you."

"Thank you, Ula," Kennocha whispered tiredly.

Ula merely harrumphed then went to Kennocha's stores and poured herself a mug of ale.

"Can I do anything?" I asked them both.

"Make sure her father knows he has a daughter," Ula said, a sour tone in her voice.

I nodded. "I will. And I'll come again to check on you both."

"Thank you, Boudica," Kennocha told me.

I smiled gently at the woman then set a kiss on the baby's forehead. "Sweet Mara," I said then rose to go.

"Do you need anything?" I asked Ula.

She shook her head. "A rest. Be off with you now. Your blood has given me enough trouble for one day."

I nodded then turned and left the cottage. When I stepped outside, it was night once more. The air was cool. Not expecting to be out so late, I'd left my cloak behind. I returned to the roundhouse and made my way to my father's meeting room. The king had already gone to bed. There, I found a slip of paper and a quill. I was suddenly glad Belenus had taught the four of us what Latin he knew. I composed a short note to Caturix then sealed it with wax. I went outside in search of Cai, finding him at the stables.

"Boudica," he said, looking confused. "What is it?"

"I need someone I trust to make a trip to Stonea. I have a message for Caturix. It's urgent, but I don't want to ask my father's men. Will you make the trip?"

Cai paused. "I... of course. But I will take Dougal with me. He knows the path to the fort very well. I don't want to get lost in the mist. Is that all right?"

I nodded. "But say nothing, not even to Dougal, about who sent you. You must promise me."

Cai nodded.

I handed the note to him.

"Is everything all right?" Cai asked, looked me over carefully. "Are *you* all right?"

I couldn't miss the caring expression in Cai's gaze. More than once during our spear training, I had seen him looking at me with admiration. While he was handsome and sweet, my heart was already a mess. Gaheris was gone. Prasutagus was—no, just no. I needed no further complications in my life.

"I'm fine. Thank you for your concern. I just need to get this to my brother."

"We'll go at first light," he said with a nod. "But this is no excuse for you to be lax on your spear practice while I'm gone, you know."

I gave him the best smile I could muster. "I wouldn't dream of it," I told him. "Thank you, Cai. You have always been a good friend. I appreciate your help."

He smiled at me. "Whatever you need, Boudica."

Not wanting to prolong a conversation which was taking a rapid turn into a place I didn't want to go, I nodded to him then turned and went back to the roundhouse.

I had a niece.

My brother's first child had been born.

But he was gone, married off at my uncle's maneuvering.

Just like I would be if the gods did not intervene.

Andraste.

Dark goddess.

Watch over me.

CHAPTER 37

Over the next week, I paid several visits to Kennocha and Mara. The tiny baby was doing well, and the mother was recovering. Ula had ensured a young girl from the village came to help Kennocha, and I arranged in secret for her payment. On top of that, I worked with Ula to make sure the widow's stores were fully stocked and that she wanted for nothing. The fact that I was attending to such matters, not my brother, not my family, annoyed me beyond reason.

It was late one evening after the others had gone to bed that I found myself alone in the dining hall with my father.

He rose to leave when I said, "There is a new child in the village."

My father grunted, bobbing his head in acknowledgment, but asked nothing.

"The widow Kennocha has had a baby girl. She named the child Mara."

My father paused. "What of it?"

"What of it?" I repeated sarcastically, as if the answer was obvious.

Aesunos turned and looked at me. When he met my gaze, he could see that I knew. "That child is nothing to this house. Nothing. To none of us, including you. Do you understand me?"

"No, Father. I don't understand you at all."

He huffed at me, flinging his arm in annoyance, then walked away.

His callousness chilled me to the bone. But what more could I do? The child would never be acknowledged. The best I could do for her was see that she was well-fed and cared for. One day, my brother would be king. Perhaps then things would be different. Yet, now there was Melusine to think of, and no one would want to hurt her. I was glad my brother's troubles were not my own. I had my own heartaches to nurse, as I was about to be reminded.

A week later, Bran and I rode to Frog's Hollow. It was near midday on Samhain eve when we arrived. Father had begrudgingly let us go, but only because Belenus had intervened, suggesting to Father that our presence there would serve as a reminder of his leadership.

We would be emissaries of Oak Throne.

He could not argue with that.

Before we left, Father managed to get in one last barb. "That boy is gone, Boudica. Say goodbye to him tonight. I will not argue with Dôn, but when Beltane comes once more, you will do your duty to your family—as I see fit."

"Don't we all," I replied waspishly then left without waiting for his reply.

With each passing day, my father's mood grew darker. In whatever game he was playing to ensure his own power, we, his children, had become pawns, not people. Not even an infant girl, named after our mother, could touch his heart.

That was why, when I saw Bran's face light up when he spotted Bec at Frog's Hollow, I was struck with sadness.

There was no way Father would allow Bran to marry a priestess.

He had wed Caturix to Melusine. While Melusine was beautiful, kind, and charming, my brother had to give up the one he loved—mother and child—to do as Aesunos saw fit.

Aesunos had only agreed to wed me to Gaheris because the marriage had been strategic.

And he'd promised Brenna to a man she'd never met.

And every time I thought of it, pain pricked at my heart. Prasutagus hadn't struck me as the kind of man who would just marry a woman for her title and power. The fact that he'd agreed to marry my sister without meeting her...perhaps I had misjudged him.

But below the surface of my questions lay deeper feelings of jealousy I didn't understand. If Prasutagus wanted to marry someone from my family, why hadn't he asked for my hand? Perhaps in my grief, I had fooled myself. I thought I'd felt a kinship between the prince and me. Maybe in my mourning for Gaheris, I'd been confused. Or perhaps it had all been in my mind.

Either way, Prasutagus would marry Brenna.

And I would be carted off to wed some Catuvellauni cutthroat.

But tonight was not about the future. It was about the past.

"Boudica! Boudica! Boudica!" a chorus of voices called as I entered the village.

I smiled when I saw the children rushing toward me. Everything had been so dark and miserable when I had last been in Frog's Hollow. I was glad to see their smiles returned.

"Ah, here is my fairy troupe," I said, bending down and holding out my arms, hugging all of them at once.

"Look," Henna said. "We've made masks for mumming so the fey will not take us tonight," she said, proudly displaying a mask made to look like a hare.

"Oh, well done," I told her. "Surely the Unseelie will never recognize you. Now, let me see all the others."

In turn, the children showed me the masks they had made of bark, clay, leather, feathers, and paints.

"Mine is an owl," Kendrick told me, trying on his mask.

"Let me hear your hoot," I said.

He hooted loudly, making the others laugh.

"Well done. I was visited by flower face some weeks ago. Do you know her legend?"

"Blodeuwedd? The flower maiden?" Aife asked, her eyes wide.

I nodded. "Blodeuwedd was created from flowers, made as a gift to the god Llew, who was cursed. It was said that Llew could never love a mortal woman. So Gwideon, the son of Cerridwen, made Blodeuwedd for Llew. She was the most beautiful maiden in the world. Llew loved her at once, but he loved her too fiercely—jealously, protectively. He smothered that delicate flower with his love—and when he was unhappy with her, with his rage. Weeping, Blodeuwedd wandered the forests. One day, she came upon Gronw, a hunter, with whom she fell in love at once. The pair promised to run away together. But when Llew learned of this, he turned Blodeuwedd into an owl, parting her from her lover. As an owl, she is deprived of the sunlight all flowers need to thrive. He cursed her to a life of misery."

"What a bad, jealous man," Henna said.

I nodded in agreement with her.

"Did you really see her?" Glyn asked, suspicion in his voice.

I nodded. "A snow-white owl visited me. And come to think of it, she did smell of flowers."

"What did she say?" Henna asked.

I grinned, then hooted, making the children laugh.

Turning from Henna, I smiled at Tristan. Taking his hand, I pulled the boy closer to me. I pointed to him and to the masks. He handed the mask in his hand to me.

I studied it closely. It was well covered in black feathers.

"A bird?"

He nodded.

"A raven?"

He pointed at me.

"My raven?"

He nodded.

I tousled the boy's hair. "Well done. The Unseelie will never know you are not Morfran and will leave you alone tonight." I turned back to the others. "Let me go and greet the priestess and Lynet. Have you gathered gifts for your dead?"

"We were working on that when you arrived," Henna told me.

"Very well. Carry on, then," I said, rising.

Before he sprinted away, I pulled Tristan toward me and kissed him on the head.

"Missed you," I told him.

He paused to kiss me on the cheek. He then tapped his chest twice and pointed at me—he missed me too—before sprinting behind the others.

I made my way to Lynet, Bec, and Bran.

"Boudica," Lynet said happily, embracing me. "I'm so glad to see you."

"And you."

I turned to Bec. "Priestess," I said, giving her a short bow.

"Princess," she replied with a smirk.

"Dôn isn't here?" I asked.

Bec shook her head. "She said she had things to attend to, so she sent Grainne and me."

"What can I help with?" Bran asked Lynet.

"The men are building up the bonfire and drinking ale—mostly drinking ale—if you'd like to join them," Lynet said, motioning in the direction of the center square.

Bran nodded to her then turned to go, his gaze lingering on Bec's for a long moment before he left us.

"Come," Lynet told us.

Bec and I followed her to the long table before the chieftain's house. It had been set for supper and beautifully adorned. The table had been covered in green moss and flowers. Candles bathed the table in golden light. Small trinkets like shells and beads glimmered in the firelight. At each of the place settings, cloaks had been laid on the backs of chairs. Plates and cups sat ready, as did jugs of wine. Amongst the goods, I also spotted a familiar pipe—the one I had recovered from the beach. Other personal items were laid before each seat.

The table was set for the dead.

Lynet went to the seat at the end of the table, touching the fabric of a cloak hung here. "Rolan's winter cloak," she said, her eyes on the material. She stayed in one place for a long time before setting her hand on the back of the chair beside Rolan's. "For Gaheris," she told me.

I nodded, feeling my stomach knot with the same ache I had been nursing for months.

Lynet smiled lightly. "We're cooking inside," she told me, gesturing to her house. "You are welcome to join us."

"If you don't mind, I will borrow Boudica for a time," Bec told Lynet.

"Of course, Priestess," Lynet said, inclining her head to her.

With that, Lynet turned and went back inside.

Bec looked down at the table. "Already, I can feel the spirits drawing close. In the face of such tragedy, it is to be expected." She set her hand on my shoulder. "He will be eager to see you tonight."

I swallowed hard. "And what will he find?"

Already, even in noticing Prasutagus, I had been disloyal to Gaheris's memory. I chided myself once more. It was good the prince was going to marry my sister. I had no business being married to anyone but Gaheris. And if I could not be with him, it was better to serve the gods. I needed to convince Dôn to bring me to the grove come Beltane.

"The woman he loves," Bec said simply.

I looked at her.

Bec smiled softly at me. "Time passes. You cannot grieve forever. Gaheris would not want it. No matter what fate has in store for you, Boudica, it is not in your hand. Gaheris will understand that."

"I don't like it when you read my mind."

Bec laughed. "Only the expression on your face. Your mind is quite the mystery to me."

I chuckled lightly.

"Come," Bec said, gesturing for me to follow her.

Bec led me away from the heart of Frog's Hollow and down a

narrow path that led, not to the mound where Gaheris was buried, but to an older shrine beyond the village. A trail led away from the village, beyond the pond, and deep into the woods. I had seen the cave-like shrine before but had never been inside. Gaheris said it was ancient, enduring there beyond anyone's memories. If the legends were to be believed, Frog's Hollow existed long before Oak Throne. And the shrine, or so Gaheris said, had once belonged to the ancient people of our land. We made our way down the path along a hillside until we reached the entrance. The skulls of Frog's Hollow's earliest members guarded the gateway. The skulls lined the arched gateway from the ground up, the eyeless bones staring out at any who would enter.

Bec set her entwined fingers on her forehead, motioning for me to do the same.

"Ancestors, I approach in the name of the Dark Lady, Andraste. With great reverence, Princess Boudica and I will pass into your sacred resting place. We offer you our love and respect in these thin hours before Samhain."

My hands were pressed against my forehead, but my eyes were fixed on the skulls. I waited.

Bec lowered her hands then motioned for me to follow behind her.

I paused. "Are you sure?" I whispered. Thin places. Ula had taught me all about the thin places. On Samhain, the veil between our world and that of the Otherworld grew thin. We had no business in a cave.

"Andraste will guide us," Bec said. Ducking, she went inside.

I hesitated a few moments, then followed her within.

Bec lit a small brazier, carrying it before her. Once we made our way through the entrance, the passage widened. Bodies lay on shelves cut into the walls. Between the ledges were skulls. They looked out at us, their black eyes wide. The air inside the cave was cool and damp. The sunlight faded behind us. Soon, only Bec's orange flame lit the way. We made our way deep into the earth. Soon, we approached another doorway. Ducking low, Bec entered.

I followed her to find myself standing in a domed room. The cave widened here. While I expected the space to be filled with bodies, instead, I found a cauldron hanging over a cold fire. Turning, I looked around the room. The walls had been painted. Amongst the images there, I spotted Cernunnos seated with his cauldron on his lap, his horns extending into the sky, a crescent moon painted between his antlers. Images of animals—deer, hare, birds, frogs, horses, and a great serpent that was so large, its tail encompassed the entire room—decorated the walls around the horned god. On the other side on the ceiling was an image of the Great Mother in her celestial form, with stars in her hair.

Bec went to the cauldron and knelt.

She began whispering in a low voice, calling upon Andraste.

A chill washed over me, my skin prickling to goosebumps.

"What is this place?" I whispered.

"It is the oldest shrine to the gods in your lands, Princess," Bec told me. "Older than the trees in the grove. Older than your oak around which the fort was built. Older than your menhir deep in the forest. Older than the seahenge. Older than them all. And closest to the Otherworld," Bec replied, then set the fire under the cauldron to light.

"This is a shrine to the dark ladies," Bec said, standing back.

As the flame flickered to life, I saw an image of three

women carved into the wall. Wearing long robes, they stood around a cauldron.

"The cauldron goddess," I said. "Cerridwen?"

Bec nodded. "And Andraste and the Morrigu, the dark triad."

I scanned around the room. Two doors led from the chamber, deeper into the cave.

From one of the doorways, a soft voice called to me, giggling as it whispered my name, the sound like a ringing bell.

"Boudica…

"Boudica…"

"Do you hear that?" I asked.

Bec's eyes shifted toward the doorway. "Yes. The greenwood watches you wherever you go, Boudica."

"Why?"

Bec cocked an eyebrow then turned to the cauldron. "Let's ask and see."

"Maybe…maybe not tonight," I said, hesitating.

Bec reached for me. "But that's why we've come. That's why Dôn asked me to bring you here. She wanted to see what the gods had to say to you, what path they wish for you."

"Dôn said that?"

Bec nodded.

"Does this mean she will consider letting me join you?"

"I don't know. I hope so. Ula says you have the sight, but your skills are like that of a wild horse, bucking and running heedlessly," she said, then pulled a vial from her pocket. She handed it to me. "Now, we shall see."

I looked at the vial. "Ula told you that?"

Bec grinned, then shook her head. "Ula told Dôn. I just happened to be there. Now, drink."

"What is this? And when did Ula come to the grove?"

Bec chuckled. "She blusters our way, clicking her tongue at us and telling us what we're doing wrong quite frequently. Drink."

Uncorking the vial, I did as she instructed, the bitter taste of the brew making me cough. I handed the empty vial back to Bec. She slipped it into her pocket, then drank one herself. We stood there for a long time.

My head began to feel heavy, and the images on the walls blurred.

The fire under the cauldron crackled. When I looked at it, I found the flames burned purple.

"When did... Why is the fire purple?" I whispered to Bec.

Bec gave me a knowing look.

They weren't really flames as we knew them. It was faerie fire, a false fire made of magic rather than elemental flame.

"Still yourself. Let your eyes grow heavy, and look into the cauldron. The veil is thinning. The draft will help us navigate the thin spaces, allow us to hear better. If they will, the goddesses will speak."

I did as Bec instructed, staring into the cauldron. What I found there, however, was not liquid but swirling smoke.

"Dark Lady Andraste, on this Samhain eve, we call you to this sacred, holy space. Cerridwen, goddess of the cauldron, and the Morrigu, lady of battles, speak to us. Show us visions of what will be. Guide me, a priestess of Andraste's sacred grove. Guide Boudica, daughter of Oak Throne, on her path. This has been a year of darkness and loss. Show us what light still exists. Show us what will come," Bec called.

My eyes on the swirling smoke, I opened myself to any message.

But there was nothing.

We stood there for the longest time.

Still nothing.

I cast a quick glance at Bec. Her eyes were steady on the cauldron, her lids heavy. She watched something. I could just see the light reflected in her eyes. But when I looked, there was only darkness.

I tried once more, letting my mind open to the gods.

Still, no visions appeared.

"Boudica…

"Boudica…"

Turning, I noted the images on the ceiling. They had started moving. The great serpent slowly began to twist around the room. Figures on the walls danced and moved. Cernunnos ran, a spear in his hand, chasing a boar. The Great Mother danced, stars spiraling around her. The sisters of the cauldron stomped in a circle around their fire. The moon, sun, and stars on the walls drifted across the ceiling.

From the door where I'd heard voices came the sound of crashing waves and the scent of the sea.

"Boudica?" a voice called.

The sound was so distant, so far away…

But I would know his voice anywhere.

"Boudica?"

"Gaheris," I whispered.

"Did you hear him?" I asked, turning to Bec. But to my surprise, she was gone. "Bec?"

My voice echoed through the chamber.

On the ceiling overhead, an owl floated toward the door through which I still heard the sound of waves. The bird settled on a rock above the entrance then moved its wing, gesturing for me to go on.

"Boudica?" Gaheris called once more.

"Gaheris," I whispered, then turned and rushed through the door.

Everything was black for a slim moment, then I burst forward into the blinding sunlight. The rays of the sun were so intense, I winced, barely able to open my eyes. When I finally was able to open them a crack, I saw the tossing blue waves. The sun shimmered so brightly on them, it made everything around me fuzzy. I couldn't see. Half my vision was blurred by the bright sunlight.

I looked down to find myself standing on the seashore.

I was in the same camp spot where Gaheris and I often met in secret.

"Boudica," Gaheris called gently.

I turned to see him walking toward me.

He looked every bit the same as he had the last time I saw him. He was nicely dressed in his best clothes. His hair was neatly pulled back from the temples with braids.

"Gaheris," I whispered, feeling tears well in my eyes.

He stepped toward me, setting his hand on my cheek.

"Don't cry."

"How can I not cry?"

He stroked his thumb across my cheek. "No. You must be happy. You must live. That is what you must do."

"Without you?"

"Without me. At least, for this life."

"What happened to you? You must tell me. You must speak. You must tell me who did this to you."

Gaheris smiled softly. "Don't speak of that now."

"I must. I have to know."

"One day you will learn. And when you do, you must be as strong as I know you are. But don't chase that. Be happy. Live. I want you to follow your heart. Do you understand me? Do not think of me. Follow your heart."

"What are you talking about?"

"Promise me."

"Promise you?"

He laughed. "Are you a magpie? Yes, promise me you will listen to your heart. We will be together again. Do not doubt. But in this life, you must live passionately, wildly, for both of us."

A bubble of laughter escaped me, and a tear streamed down my cheek. "There were never any bounds to your wildness."

"Nor yours," Gaheris told me. "I love you, Boudica," he whispered, leaning toward me. "From this life to the next," he said, then leaned in and kissed me.

The sound of the waves crashing around me startled me, jolting me away from the kiss.

I opened my eyes to find myself standing in the shrine beside the cauldron once more. Alone. A small, orange fire burned under the vessel.

"Gaheris?" I called, my voice echoing through the near darkness. "Gaheris?"

Tears rolled down my cheeks.

"Oh, my love," I whispered.

My heart felt both heavy and light from seeing him. I missed him more than words could say, but he had also set me free to live without the burden of his death weighing upon me.

I exhaled a deep, shuddering breath, then looked around the room. "Bec?" I called, but she was nowhere to be seen. My eyes drifted up to the walls where the painted figures sat motionless once more.

Bec had left me alone in the tomb.

Scanning around the room, I saw a torch on the wall.

Snatching it, I lit the end from the fire under the cauldron then turned to leave.

"*Boudica…*

"*Boudica…*"

My eyes drifted to the gateway leading into the darkness. From within, I caught the scent of flowers and saw a shimmer of green light.

"*Boudica…*"

"No. That's enough," I said. I would not be tricked into any more unexpected journeys into the Otherworld.

Taking my torch, I went outside. I wasn't surprised to find it was dark. The tonic Bec had given me had loosened me from my spirit, allowing me to walk between the worlds. Time moved differently in the Otherworld. Who knew how long I was gone?

I made my way down the narrow path back toward the village. I didn't like that Lynet had been left on her own tonight. Certainly, the others would be there for her, but I should have been too. It was only fitting.

As I neared the pond, I felt a chill in the air. My skin rose in gooseflesh. The wind shifted, and with it, I heard silvery bells once more.

Out of the corner of my eye, I saw movement.

I paused.

There was someone in the shadows.

"Hello?" I called.

There was no reply.

In the darkness, I saw movement once more. Stepping off my path, edging a little closer to the pond, I finally spotted the culprit: a stag.

The deer picked his way slowly along the grass surrounding the water, weaving in and out of the trees.

Against my better judgment, I moved closer, trying to get a better look at him.

The King Stag in the wood.

The Forest Lord.

Would he speak to me?

Slipping behind an oak, I slowly looked around, but did not spot him.

The wind rolled through the valley, causing the water on the surface of the pond to stir. I shifted my gaze to the water. The silvery moon overhead was reflected on the waves. And there, on the water's surface, I saw the silhouette of a man standing at the edge of the pond.

I looked up to find Prasutagus standing across from me.

"Boudica," he said, as if he, too, were surprised.

"Prasutagus?"

"I…" he began, then paused. "I'm not surprised to find you here…"

I stared at him. "Who's to say where we are?"

Prasutagus smiled softly, that same gentle smile I had appreciated in person. "You are right. Boudica, I—"

"We shall see you in the spring, Prince Prasutagus," I replied stiffly.

He inclined his head to me. "Yes. I am looking forward to it."

Not knowing what else to say and feeling a flurry of strange emotions cropping up in me, I turned to go, climbing the slope to the trail once more. When I reached the top, I looked back.

The prince—and the stag—were gone.

CHAPTER 38

When I finally returned to the village, I discovered the rites had already been concluded. The feast for the dead had already been laid out. Grainne was playing a game with the children in the center square. She was sitting at the center of a circle. The children, all decked out in their masks, danced around her. Many had already returned to their homes. Lynet and the other women who had lost their husbands were gathered around the bonfire. Bec and Bran were nowhere to be seen.

Working my way across the square, I took a spot on the bench beside Lynet.

"I am sorry I missed—"

Lynet raised a hand to stop me, a gentle smile on her face. "The priestess told us you would not return for some time. There is nothing more to be said."

"I..." I began but stopped. Already, this night was painful for Lynet. Nothing I could tell her would ease that.

"Boudica, you did not get a chance to meet her earlier, but this is my sister, Cien." She gestured across the fire to a woman

I had not noticed before. She was dark-haired, like Lynet, but wore kohl around her eyes. Her neck and arms were heavily tattooed.

I inclined my head to her. "I am very pleased to meet you."

"And you, Princess. I have heard much about you," Cien told me. "I understand you intended to become a part of my family."

I swallowed hard then nodded.

Cien looked toward the fire. "The spirits are awake. It is my nephew, not my sister, who speaks of you. The love of his life…" she said, then smiled softly.

I did not know what to say, but I could sense the Otherworld about this woman. I had no doubt that she was able to feel and see Gaheris.

"My sister is a priestess of our tribe in my homeland on Skye," Lynet told me.

"You've come from Skye?"

Cien inclined her head to me. "I sensed my sister's need."

The sisters exchanged a loving glance.

"That is a long journey," I said.

Cien shrugged. "Not as the raven flies."

Lynet chuckled.

"You are welcome in the land of the Northern Iceni," I told the woman.

"Thank you, Princess."

"Come, let's sing," Lynet said with a broken smile. "Our loved ones would not have us sit and weep in sorrow. Let them dine. And we shall sing to them." At that, Lynet broke out into a sweet song about lovers in May.

The other women gathered there chimed in, their words painting a pretty picture of a maiden and her love meeting on

Beltane and the promises made between them to never be apart once more. Despite my desire to please Lynet, my thoughts drifted to the seashore where my love had told me goodbye.

And then to the pond.

Why in the name of all the gods would Prasutagus find his way to me?

The women passed around a bottle of wine.

Not missing a note, Lynet poured me a goblet then passed the vessel on.

I sat, sipping the heady brew as my eyes rested on the fire. Soon, my head felt dizzy. Perhaps it was Bec's tonic or the combination of it and the wine, but the world around me started to spin. Time seemed to speed and slow in bursts. Each time I looked up, more women had gone. The children and Grainne disappeared from the central square. The candles on the feasting table grew low. When I looked again, only Lynet and Cien remained with me at the fire.

I heard a loud bubble of laughter.

When I followed the sound, looking toward the table once more, I saw the men sitting there, laughing, drinking, and enjoying the food that had been set out for them.

Catching my eye, Gaheris smiled at me. He lifted his goblet, toasting me, then gave me a playful wink.

The logs in the bonfire shifted, capturing my attention. Embers floated from the fire into the air. As I watched them, I heard screaming and the sound of battle. Shaking my head, I turned back to the table, but it was empty once more.

Lynet was gone.

Only Cien remained.

"The shadows of the future gather around you like moths to a flame. No wonder my nephew loved you. Do not forget

Skye when the time comes. Through the fire in your blood, we will all be avenged."

"How..."

Cien opened her mouth once more to speak, but only a loud caw came from her lips—the shrill cry of a raven. And then, she shifted form into the bird itself and flew off into the night's sky, leaving me alone beside the Samhain fire.

⁂

I woke the next morning when a soft hand gently shook my shoulder. I looked up to find Lynet there.

A breeze blew through the valley, making the chimes hanging outside Lynet's house nearby tinkle. I looked around, finding the square deserted. The bonfire had burned down to red and white coals.

"The fire has grown cold," Lynet said. "Come inside and warm yourself."

I nodded then followed her. When I entered the house, I was surprised to find it empty. "Where is your sister?" I asked.

Lynet smiled knowingly. "Gone. She has returned home."

"But it's such a far journ—"

Lynet gave me a knowing look. It was then I remembered what I had seen. The woman had shifted form into a raven. "I dreamed..."

"It was no dream. There is great magic on Skye." Lynet sighed. "I had many visions of you, Boudica. I saw a young girl beside you, a child with raven-black hair like my sister. I saw this girl on Skye with my people. I thought that girl was my granddaughter. But now, I don't know what I saw."

"A memory, perhaps, of another life?"

"Perhaps." Lynet set her hand on my cheek. "You have the

316

old magic in you. Something deep within. I see it every time I look into your eyes." She shook her head. "I mourn the future denied to us both."

"As do I."

"Sit. There is honey mead warming by the fire. Pour yourself some. I will make you something to eat."

"My brother…" I said, looking around.

"I'm sure they will be back soon," Lynet said. While her back was toward me, I didn't miss the smile in her voice.

It was as I suspected. Bran and Bec had disappeared together into the night.

Lynet returned with a plate. The pair of us sat side by side, finishing our breakfast, then went back outside to clear the banquet for the dead. The spirit of the food had been consumed by the lost. What remained was just the empty shell. We cleaned the food, goblets, and platters. I was busy washing the plates when Bran and Bec appeared hand in hand. I flicked my gaze in their direction but said nothing.

I was happy for my brother. I only hoped that my father found it in his heart to give Bran what he wanted. Caturix had been too afraid to ask, I had been denied by the gods, and Brenna—well, Brenna did not wish to marry Prasutagus. I understood her reasons. She had dreamed of a life on Mona amongst the bards. If Prasutagus had asked for me…

I stopped cold.

If he had asked for me…then what?

Gaheris was not six months dead. I had no business entertaining thoughts like that. And all the same, Prasutagus had *not* asked for my hand. Clearly, I had meant nothing to him. Turning my attention back to the plates, I scrubbed harder.

Behind me, Bran and Lynet spoke, Bec disappearing to fetch Grainne. Bran joined me.

"What did that platter ever do to you?" he asked, watching me.

"Nothing. Just helping Lynet."

Bran looked over the remaining work, then rolled up his sleeves and started washing goblets.

For once, my brother was quiet. He simply did the work. He was on the last dish when he asked, "What do you think Father will say?"

I paused. "With Caturix wed and Brenna promised, your chances are better."

Bran began washing once more. "Brenna doesn't wish to wed Prasutagus. Belenus should have intervened."

I said nothing, merely scrubbed harder.

"I will ask Father's permission to marry Bec."

"Speak to Belenus first. He knows what plans Father has already made without your permission. If there are none, maybe he will say yes."

"And if there are?"

I raised an eyebrow at my brother.

Bran cursed under his breath then began washing the bowls, scrubbing with a vigor equal to my own.

Trapped.

We were all trapped under my father's thumb.

Great Mother. Forest Lord. Help us find a way to escape.

But I already knew better. There was no way any of us could escape our fates.

For good or ill.

CHAPTER 39

After wishing farewell to Lynet, Tristan, and the other children, Bran and I made ready to ride back to Oak Throne. Bran and Bec made a short visit to the pond to talk in private while I made the climb to the mound. With a handful of wildflowers and herbs tied with a leather strap, I went to the entrance.

"In the next life, my love. Until then, don't wander far. Something tells me I'll need your strength in the days to come."

I kissed the bundle of flowers, leaving them behind, then returned to the village and mounted Druda.

Bran and Bec joined me, Bran mounting Foster.

"I wish you well, Priestess. Hopefully, sister hereafter, if the gods are kind."

Bec's cheeks flushed pink. "Thank you, Princess. Hopefully, sister hereafter."

"You realize, of course, that if you marry Bran, that will make you a princess too."

At that, Bec laughed. "I hadn't thought of it."

"I'll call upon you soon," Bran told Bec.

She nodded to him.

I turned and looked back toward the village, giving Lynet one last wave, then Bran and I rode off toward Oak Throne.

The dark months were now upon us. And while Bran was full of hope, I felt the last rays of sun on my back as I rode from Frog's Hollow.

Ahead of me was only night.

IN THE DAYS FOLLOWING OUR RETURN FROM FROG'S HOLLOW, I spent most of my time training with my spear, fussing over baby Mara, or dogging Ula to the point of annoyance. I returned one day from the stables to hear the sound of Bran's and Aesunos's raised voices coming from Father's conference chamber.

"What's happening?" I asked Brenna, who sat plucking the strings on her lyre, her attention fixed on a feather lying before her.

"I'm trying to ignore them. Watch," she said, then strummed again and again. And then, she hummed a very low note then plucked a string hard. The two sounds merged, making my ears ring. And for a brief moment, the feather lifted off the table.

Bear, who had been sleeping nearby, lifted his head then barked at the feather, breaking Brenna's concentration.

The feather fluttered down once more.

"Bear," Brenna complained at the dog, then exhaled heavily. She turned to me. "Did you see?"

I nodded. "For a moment, it was alight. That's amazing."

Brenna smiled but then a sad expression crossed her face.

"Belenus said very few bards on Mona can do this, that it is a rare talent."

I said nothing. I was not indifferent to my sister's plight. Still, every time I remembered that Prasutagus had asked for my sister's hand—having never met her—I felt angry. And jealous. And mad at myself for feeling both.

A door slammed.

I rose in time to see Bran turn the corner in the hallway and head out the front door.

"What's happening?" Brenna asked.

"Bran..." I began, guessing the matter very easily. I was about to say more when my father appeared.

Grumbling to himself, limping as he walked with his staff, he made his way into the dining room.

"Father," Brenna said, rising.

"Willful lot. Both you and your brother," Father said, turning his anger on me. "First, that village boy. Now you want to go to the grove. You and Bran would ruin the Northern Iceni. Only Caturix and Brenna have the sense to listen. That boy will do as he is told and you... Dôn's word or no, come Beltane, you will wed Caratacus of the Catuvellauni."

"Only if the gods agree," I shot back.

"What did you say, girl?"

"I said, 'only if the gods agree,'" I retorted, raising my voice. "If Dôn calls me to the grove to serve like my mother, there is nothing more you can say on the matter. And if you want a marriage to the Catuvellauni, you can wed them yourself."

Turning, my father struck me across the cheek. "Off whoring yourself with that chieftain's son, and now this? You will learn obedience."

"We are not game pieces for you to move as you wish," I shouted at him.

Father moved to strike me again, but this time I grabbed his arm. His staff shifting, he nearly fell, his weight falling toward me. Had I not been holding on to him, he would have landed on the floor.

His face close to mine, I met his gaze and held it. "We are our mother's children as much as we are yours. Remember that," I said, then shoved him off of me.

Father caught himself with his staff then pulled himself to his full height. "I will not lose everything my father built—not to Saenunos or anyone else—because of my willful children and their whims of love!"

"Was not Caturix born of a whim of love?" Belenus asked from the doorway. "You forget yourself, Aesunos."

"Nor will I be lectured by old men," Father said, then turned and left the hall, returning to his chambers.

For a moment, the three of us were still, then Brenna said, "His leg…"

I glared at my sister. "Stop making excuses for him. Bran is not Caturix. He will not set Bec aside because Father wants him to. Bran will leave, and we will lose our brother," I said, then turned and went after Bran.

When I emerged in the square, I discovered I was too late. I spotted Bran on his horse riding from Oak Throne.

He would be back.

But I was right. Bran had the same wild streak I did. He loved Bec, and he would have his way—even if that meant setting the family aside for her.

I felt someone draw close behind me. I turned to find Belenus there.

"Brenna is not wrong about your father's leg, but it is worse than she fears," he told me.

"What do you mean?"

"Boudica… Your father is dying."

"What?"

"The growth on his leg has poisoned the blood. That is why his mood has soured so. I don't know how long he will live, but his days are short. That is why he endeavors to place you all securely before his time is done."

"He knows? He knows he is dying?"

"He can sense it, but he has never spoken the words."

"Well, he can stop worrying about Bran and me. We don't need his help. Nor do we want it."

"Be careful with your anger, Boudica. It is easy to regret words and deeds spoken in fury," Belenus said, then turned and went back inside.

Leaving the roundhouse, I went to the wall, where I stood, watching the waves on the river.

My father was dying.

Sorrow whispered in my heart, but I also felt confused. We would all be out from under his thumb if he passed. But if my father did die, a worse fate awaited us. Saenunos would become king of the Northern Iceni. I understood Father's plan better now. He was trying to secure our futures.

My father was dying.

In his effort to look after us, he would burn all our hopes to the ground. How quickly good intentions turned into sorrow.

CHAPTER 40

In the following weeks, a storm blew in, covering our land with snow. Life in the village ground to a stop as people worked to stay warm. Winter had truly come, and with it, the shadow of the hard times ahead. Father kept to his meeting room. When he did appear, he looked thinner and grew more irritable with each passing day.

"I don't know if he will even make it to spring," Brenna whispered to Bran and me one evening as we sat beside the fire in the hall.

"Good," Bran retorted waspishly.

"Bran!" Brenna protested.

"What can you say against me? Father has shamed me."

As it turned out, Father had already been plotting on Bran's behalf. He had offered an alliance to the young queen of the Brigantes, Cartimandua. Apparently, the queen had no interest in the second son of the Northern Iceni.

"Now that Cartimandua has rejected me, Father has threatened to wed me to Imogen of the Catuvellauni, poor mad girl. He will hear nothing of my feelings for Bec."

"That is no reason to wish death upon him," Brenna retorted sharply.

"Don't you realize what could happen if he does die? You could go to Mona. The wedding to Prasutagus could be called off. Honestly, I was surprised by the whole thing anyway. I thought Prasutagus had taken a liking to Boudica."

I kept my gaze low, not wanting Bran to read my expression. I simply shook my head. But his words gave me some comfort. Maybe it hadn't been all in my head.

"Does Caturix know about Father's health?" Brenna asked.

"I don't think so," Bran replied.

"We should send word when the weather clears. In the meantime, we should pray to the gods that he recovers. Whatever our disagreements, he is still our father."

"You sound like Caturix," Bran told Brenna.

"Well, then Caturix is right."

"Caturix is *always* right," Bran grumbled. "Except in his treatment of his wife. He hardly noticed Melusine. I wonder how that poor girl survived the winter alongside him."

"At least she had the dogs," I commented.

Bran laughed.

"Boudica," Brenna scolded me.

I shrugged. The tense situation with my father had me feeling on edge. While my logic kept telling me that he was working to secure our future and that of the Northern Iceni, his callous attitude was more than I could stand.

But there was worse than my father.

"In the end, if Father dies, we still will not be free. You are forgetting one very dire thing," I said.

"And that is?" Bran asked.

"Saenunos will become king of the Northern Iceni. And then, may the gods protect us."

And with that, we all fell silent.

Later that night, after Brenna and I had gone to bed, I lay awake staring at the ceiling as I listened to the wind howl outside. The winter winds were fierce. Snow piled up outside. Yesterday morning, Cidna and I had barely been able to push open the door to the kitchen. Poor Druda was stuck in the stables, and we were trapped in the house. Part of me couldn't wait for spring once more.

Apparently, I wasn't the only one who couldn't sleep.

Brenna sighed heavily, then asked, "What did Bran mean about Prince Prasutagus taking a liking to you?"

I felt like someone had closed a hand around my heart. "I don't know."

"Did he... Did he strike you as the flirtatious type?"

"No."

"Was he forward with you?"

"No, Brenna. He just made conversation with me, that's all. Bran spoke out of turn. There was nothing."

"What did you talk about?"

"Family. Horses. Just...nothing, really."

For a long time, Brenna was silent.

I rolled over, my back to her. I prayed to all the gods that Brenna would just fall asleep, but after a time, Brenna asked, "Did you like him?"

"Well enough."

"I mean, I know your heart is heavy for Gaheris, but was there any spark betw—"

"No, Brenna. Good night."

We lay there in the darkness for a long time. The wind outside the roundhouse howled. Even with our brazier burning, it felt cold. I thought Brenna had fallen asleep, but eventually, she whispered, "I know when you're lying."

I stared at the wall. "He's handsome, Brenna. And earnest. And easy to talk to. All women want a man like that. I'm glad you will marry him. You will be happy."

"Oh," Brenna said lightly.

I squeezed my eyes shut once more.

May the gods forgive me for lying to her.

CHAPTER 41

Yule came once more, and with it, merriment in Oak Throne. The villagers decorated the square with garlands of greens and red winter berries. A center bonfire was readied. Father had shown nothing but disinterest in the festivities, but given the holiday was Brenna's favorite, she took over the duties usually performed—or at least organized—by the king.

I found Brenna in the kitchens the day before Yule looking over all the goods Cidna—and her two new helpers, Ystradwel and Arddun, a mother and daughter pair—had been baking. The whole house smelled of roasted nuts, baked sweets, and meat. It was all Bran could do to stay out of the kitchen. More than once, I'd heard Cidna shouting at him.

"What else do you need, Cidna? Shall I see about more anise spice?"

"I'm well supplied, Brenna. Just need to finish baking the last of the sweets today."

"Eiwyn and her little pack will honor you as a goddess

when they see all of this," I told Cidna, picking up a small, spiced cake and taking a bite.

"Boudica," Cidna scolded me lightly. "Those are for tomorrow. You're as bad as Bran."

"Come now. That's unfair. No one can reach Bran's level. He was in here this morning stealing sweets when you were in the supply cupboard."

Cidna threw down the dough she'd been working. "He was not."

I giggled. "He was. You see. You are lighter on that platter," I said, pointing behind her.

When Cidna turned to look, I grabbed two more of the cakes and stuck them in my coat pocket, making Ystradwel and Arddun laugh. Brenna rolled her eyes at me.

"I'll tan that boy's hide when I see him next."

I nodded. "As he deserves. Anyway, I know when I am underfoot. I'll see you later," I said, waving, then turned to make my way out of the back of the roundhouse.

While the walkways from the kitchen to the sheds behind the roundhouse were cleared, the snow reached my knees. It was a crisp, cold morning. The sunlight shimmered on the pristine blanket that had fallen the night before. I made my way into the village. As I went, I saw many of the villagers adorning their doors. Others worked in the square. They waved to me as I passed.

I wound my way to Ula's little cottage at the edge of the village.

I knocked on the door then waited. "Ula. I love your Yule decorations," I called.

A moment later, the door flung open. "What decorations?" she asked cantankerously.

"Precisely my point," I said, gesturing to the door. "Not a sprig of holly to be seen."

Ula shook her head then gestured for me to come inside. "Come on. I'm almost ready."

I entered the small cottage, heading to the fire where I rubbed my hands together, trying to get warm. I then dipped into my pocket and pulled out the sweet breads, setting them on a plate on Ula's table.

"Compliments of Cidna," I said.

I expected Ula to complain or have some grumpy retort. Instead, she took one of the breads and sat down by the fire.

"Take the other one," she told me.

I did as she said, then sat down across from her.

Ula grabbed a flagon of wine and uncorked it, pouring a cup for each of us. Then, she sat still, looking into the fire as she ate. "My mother made hers just like this. Underdone and too heavy on the anise."

"I'll be sure to tell Cidna."

Ula chuckled.

"Your mother…"

"Wylla. She was a healer, like me."

"And your father?"

Ula huffed a laugh. "I'm a child of a greenwood marriage."

I nodded. Like my own mother, Ula had been conceived by the Beltane fires.

"Perhaps you are the child of some god," I said with a grin.

Ula laughed. "What splendid comforts my father has afforded for me," she said, gesturing around the room.

I shook my head.

"Have you heard Duir yet?" Ula asked.

I frowned. Ever since Ula had given the Ogham symbol to me with an edict to listen, I had failed to understand her meaning. I knew nothing more than I had the day I'd asked her to teach me.

"No."

Ula smirked. "Perhaps he will speak today," she said then polished off the rest of her wine. "Let's go." She rose and grabbed her cloak.

I quickly drank what was left of my wine and popped the last bite of cake in my mouth. Ula's wine, made from a mix of fermented fruits and roots, was stronger than the wine we had in the roundhouse. When I rose, I felt dizzy. I swayed a little.

"Better keep your footing about you today, Damara's daughter. You'll need it," Ula said with a laugh.

I followed Ula out as we made our way out of the fort. As we passed the center square, I saw the men had gathered around Cole, one of the woodcutters, who was carving the Yule log. A pile of wood chippings at his feet, the man had carved the face of a woman from the log.

"It's beautiful, Cole," I called to him. "Even better than last year."

"The lady of winter, Princess."

"May she warm us in her fires."

"Indeed," he replied.

Ula had carried on without me. With a sigh, I turned and hurried after her. Once we exited the fort, we turned off the path and into the deep snow, making our way to the mossy forest. The trek was difficult. While Ula didn't complain, her pace had slowed. In the least, the fresh snow was powdery. Finally, we entered the forest. The trees were bare. The moss was hidden under the snow. But today, what we were after was in the limbs of the trees.

"Where do we look?" I asked.

"I know the place," Ula replied, motioning for me to follow.

Ula and I went deep into the forest, getting some relief from the snow as we passed through a thick glade of tall evergreens. The sharp scent of the evergreens filled the air. Ducking low under the branches, we finally made our way to the other side of the forest where we came upon a stand of oak. The wide trees rivaled the width and height of those at the grove. As we approached, I stopped.

Ula paused and looked back at me.

I studied the oaks. They grew in a strange, concentric ring.

"Ula..."

"They are in a spiral. We must walk the path. Follow," she told me, then we entered the forest.

Ula was right. The trees grew in such a way that they spiraled inward. Ula and I followed the path until, at last, we reached a massive old oak at the center of the spiral. The old tree grew in such a manner that it almost appeared to have a face on its trunk.

"There," Ula said, pointing upward.

I followed her gesture, spotting many bunches of mistletoe growing in the branches.

I sighed heavily. "I should have brought Bran."

"You are just as spry. Go on," she said then handed an empty satchel to me. "And you will need this," she added, handing me a small, golden sickle.

"Ula," I said. "This is a druid's knife."

"So it is. Unless you want to offend the gods, you will use it."

"Won't it offend the gods that I'm not a druid?"

"You don't know what you are. Princess. Priestess. Chieftain's wife. Queen. Warrior. Who knows what you are,

Boudica? Today, you are a druid. Besides, I don't see Belenus climbing this tree, do you?"

I chuckled then slid the knife into my belt. I removed my cloak and pulled off my gloves. I had climbed a thousand trees a thousand times each as a girl. This one was no different. Besides, the old oak had wider limbs. Quickly scanning for a path, I jumped up to the lowest limb, maneuvered my arm around it, then swung until I pulled up the rest of my body. Balancing myself, I stood on the branch, holding onto a branch above me.

I glanced down at Ula who was grinning at me.

"Bran always says I'm a dryad. Maybe he was right."

Ula chuckled.

Working carefully, mindful of the patches of ice and snow on the limbs, I pulled and swung my way up to the first bundle of mistletoe.

"Be sure to thank Duir," Ula called.

"Thank Duir. Sure. And don't fall to my death," I said, setting aside a branch. I slipped the golden sickle from my belt. "Father oak. King of the forest. I thank you for your sacred mistletoe. It will bring healing and good fortune to the people of the Northern Iceni. With great reverence, I thank you," I said then cut the bundle of mistletoe, sticking it into my satchel.

When I was done, I climbed up once more. Setting my foot on a branch, I gasped when I slipped on a slick of ice I hadn't noticed. I clung to the branch for safety. Once I stopped quaking, I firmed my footing and tried again, lifting myself even higher to the next branch. Working myself into a crook in the tree, I took out the knife and said my thanks once more, this time adding, "Duir, Ula has been chiding me all winter because I don't understand your symbol. While I'm here hanging from your branches like an acorn, please feel free to enlighten me." And with that, I cut the next bunch of mistletoe. And then the next. And then the next. Soon, I realized I was so high in the tree that I could see over all of the other trees in the forest.

I rested a moment, staring out at the snowy landscape.

The wind was sharp here, but clean and fresh. In the distance, I spotted the fort and the roundhouse. I watched as the River Stiffkey trailed off. In the far distance, I spotted the tall oaks that crowned the Grove of Andraste. And farther on, I saw other tall stands of trees.

"The king tree," I said, looking across the land. "You are the king tree. The master of our land. The Father. The Stag King. But more...the voice of the land itself. Like a wise druid, you speak through the ages as you stand sentinel—our lives passing as you live on for hundreds of years, until your progeny grows to replace you. I think I understand."

"Come down, girl. It will snow soon," Ula called from below.

I shifted my gaze to the west. Ula was right. Snow was coming. I could smell it in the air.

Working carefully, I began making my way back down. When I got halfway and had a clear view of Ula, I shifted my very full satchel of mistletoe. "Let me drop it to you," I called to her.

"No," Ula called back in a hurry. "It cannot touch the ground."

Sighing heavily, I shifted the bundle once more as I swung my legs over another limb, wiggling my feet as I searched for the branch below. Step by step, I made my way back toward the ground. I was more than halfway down when the sack of mistletoe got caught on an errant branch. I gave the bag a tug, but when I did, I changed my footing. To my horror, my left foot landed on a patch of ice.

For a split second, I gasped, realizing my mistake.

I reached out for a nearby branch, only to be surprised by what I saw sitting thereon.

A tiny group of men and women dressed in red caps and green cloaks watched me. One of the little women with long, silver hair pinned up in buns met my gaze. I caught the branch on which they sat with two fingers. Grinning, the little woman hopped over to me.

She met my eye, gave me a wicked grin, then stomped on my fingers as she waved goodbye.

My weak hold faltered.

My foot slid.

And a moment later, I was tumbling down.

And then, everything went dark.

CHAPTER 42

I opened my eyes to find myself standing before a bonfire. Beside me, a woman I didn't know was nattering on about the gods only knew what. I studied her face, realizing I had seen her in a vision before. The fox tail clipped to her pale blonde hair gave her away. She was laughing and gesturing wildly at the fire, the bottle of wine in her hands sloshing onto us and the ground before us.

I glanced across the fire to find a man staring at me—well, something like a man.

He wore a mask made of leaves and the horns of a stag.

"I am the land itself.

"I am the unending flow of magic below your feet.

"I am the pulse of life.

"I am the King Stag searching for my queen."

The man, and the ground below me, both seemed to speak.

The oak.

The Forest Lord.

The land.

It was all the same.

Powerful but incomplete. With the May Queen, the magic became whole. One.

The man standing across the fire reached his hand out. "Boudica, come to me…"

<hr/>

MY EYES FLICKED OPEN.

Overhead, I saw a bank of stars, the moon silhouetted by the bare limbs of the oak tree. And then I heard an angry caw. From the branches overhead, Morfran looked down at me. He cawed at me then made a series of clicks and whistles he often sounded after I fed him…his happy chirps.

"Enough, you noisy thing. I see," Ula groused at him.

I was lying in the snow, but wrapped in my cloak once more. Ula had made a small campfire. The flames popped, embers twisting upward toward the bare limbs of the great oak…from which I had plummeted.

"Seems I'm still alive," I said, sitting up slowly, rubbing my shoulder which protested at the effort.

"Popped out," she told me, pointing to my shoulder. "I got it back in while you were out. It will be sore for a couple of days."

"Glad I was unconscious for that," I said, wincing as I worked my shoulder. "Remind me to send Bran next year. Or maybe Phelan. He's spry." I gestured to Morfran. "When did he show up?"

"A bit ago. Probably wondering where his dinner was."

I chuckled. "No doubt, you're right."

I scanned around me, spotting the satchel of mistletoe hanging from a branch nearby.

"Oh no. Ula, did I drop it? Did it touch the ground?"

Ula laughed. "No. You landed on your back, holding it up so it wouldn't touch. That's what did your shoulder in."

"Well, I dedicate myself to my tasks."

She blew air through her lips then shook her head.

"I do," I protested. "I understand Duir now, I think," I told her. "The Ogham symbol is easily understood as a letter. And it is a quick reference to the druids and Cernunnos. But there is more. Duir is not just part of the land. Duir is the masculine spirit of the land and the voice of the past and the future. Duir manifests the sacred energy of the land."

"Duir's roots run deep," Ula said. "The oak remembers old things. Those who follow Duir are the keepers of our world. Witnesses and guardians. Protectors of the greenwood. Oak is the king, the Father. Yet there must be balance to make things whole. A king is nothing without his queen."

The same sentiment the man in my vision had shared. "What does that mean?"

"The months behind you have been hard. What lies before you will be harder, Boudica. You must call upon the strength of the greenwood and stand for what is right."

"You couldn't have just told me that? Did you really need to make the piskies push me out of a tree for that lesson?"

"What piskies?"

"What piskies," I repeated, as if she didn't know. But then Ula gave me a confused look. Hadn't she seen them? I sighed. Queen. "My father will make me queen of the Catuvellauni."

"Will he?" Ula asked then huffed a laugh.

I looked up at her. "Won't he?"

Ula smirked. "It is the gods who make or unmake you. Do not forget that. And do not forget Duir's message."

"And the piskies?" I asked with a laugh.

Ula rose then kicked some snow on the fire, extinguishing

its flames. "Irksome creatures. Let's go before one of the good neighbors calls the mists and traps us here forever."

"What, you don't want to be stuck with me for all eternity?" I asked with a wince as I tried to roll my shoulder.

At that, Ula laughed.

With my good arm, I grabbed the bag of mistletoe and slung it over my back. I turned to Morfran. "Fly back now. Tell Brenna I'm fine," I said, giving the bird a sprig of the plant. "For Brenna. Bren-na."

The raven cawed in return, a two-syllable sound that was vaguely reminiscent of my sister's name, then flew off.

With that, Ula and I turned and headed back toward the village.

As I walked away from the tree, I looked back, up into the limbs of the oak. There, silhouetted by the moonlight, I saw little figures sitting on a branch, their legs dangling. And on the wind, I heard the soft sound of laughter.

By the time I got back to the roundhouse, it was late. I'd stopped by Ula's house where she'd prepared a sling for me. Leaving her, the knife, and the mistletoe behind, I went home.

I found the others, including Father, in the dining hall.

"Boudica," Brenna said, rising when I entered.

Morfran squawked loudly, Bear following my sister to see what all the fuss was about.

"What happened?" Brenna asked.

I flicked my gaze to Father who was watching me carefully.

"I fell on the ice. My shoulder just needs a rest for a day. I'll be fine."

"Where were you?" Father asked.

I moved to shrug then winced. "Looking for holly."

"It is winter, and it is very late. Brenna was worried to death," Father said sharply.

"I sent Morfran," Brenna said.

"Sorry to worry you," I told my sister. "The ice was hidden under the snow. A stupid mistake."

"You should stay in the fort," Father said waspishly. "Wandering around like a village girl at all hours…"

I met Brenna's gaze.

My sister sighed. "Does it hurt?"

"A little."

"Let me get you some wine. Cidna had some spiced wine warming," Brenna said then hurried toward the back.

"That girl has everyone upside down," Father said, tossing a bone onto his plate. "The whole fort is turning themselves inside out to appease Brenna's whims."

"It's Yule, Father. We always celebrate," I said.

Father blew air through his lips.

I frowned at him. "It would be wise for you to make an offering to the gods."

"And why is that?"

"First, because you are king. And second, because you are not well."

"What do you know of it?"

"What my eyes see. And they see that your health is failing you."

"You sound like Belenus."

"May the gods forbid a king listen to his druid."

Father pounded his fist on the table, but said nothing more.

The smile on Brenna's face faded as she entered the room. "Here you are," she said, handing me a goblet. "Can I… Can I bring you some mulled wine, Father?"

"You can quit spending all my wealth and eating up my stores on foolishness," Father shouted at her then rose. Leaning against his staff, he hobbled out of the room.

I took the cup from Brenna's hand. "Guess it's a good thing I didn't tell him how I actually fell about twenty feet from a tree Ula made me climb."

"Boudica!"

I laughed, took a drink, then handed the goblet back to my sister who drank as well.

"Happy Yule, sister," I told Brenna with a wink.

CHAPTER 43

I woke the following day to the sound of Brenna singing lightly. I woke up, feeling drowsy after partaking in far too much spiced wine the night before. My shoulder still ached. I rotated it slowly. It was better than it had been the day before, but still sore. My sister was sitting on her bed, her lyre in her lap. Her fingers were going through the motions of playing, but not plucking the strings.

"Ah, you're awake. Finally. Watch this," she said, then sang a soft melody, her fingers moving quickly across the strings.

In my sleepy state, I swore I saw a shimmer of color like a rainbow. It rippled from the strings as heat waves from the ground on a hot day. "Did I just see…"

"You did. Isn't it beautiful?"

"That's not possible."

Brenna laughed. "The world is full of things that are not possible. But all the same. That said, Ula told me she has only seen someone manage it once before."

"You should go to Mona."

Brenna set down her lyre. "There is no hope of that. I can

only hope Prasutagus will be kind enough to let me continue my studies."

"He will. No doubt, he will bring a bard to teach you. He won't ignore such talent."

"You speak so well of him."

I shrugged. "It was an honor he earned, not one I bestow upon him. He's a good man," I said, trying to keep the pinch of pain out of my voice.

Brenna, mistaking the source of my pain, set her lyre down and came to sit on my bed. "Surely, this match with King Caratacus will come to nothing. Dôn may intervene yet—or the gods themselves."

I nodded. "You're right."

Brenna kissed me on the side of my head. "Let's forget these men for the day. It is Yule! Let's celebrate."

Brenna and I redressed and joined Bran and Belenus in the dining hall. There, a hearty breakfast was set out for the family and the servants—as was customary. Brenna had spent the entire day before working with the staff to decorate the hall in evergreen, holly, pinecones, and other trimmings. The smell was heavenly. The stacks of food Cidna had been making heaped the tables. After the morning meal, we would take the baskets full of baked goods to the square where the Yule log would be lit at midday and would burn for the next twelve days.

"Happy solstice," Brenna said, greeting everyone.

Everyone called their cheer in reply.

"The king sends his apologies and asks us to partake in the morning meal without him," Belenus said. "Now that Boudica and Brenna have joined us, let's join together and thank the gods for the return of the sun."

We joined in a circle around the central hearth, all of us

holding hands.

"Bel, sun lord, the long nights of winter will soon be behind us. Day by day, your rays will warm our land. Under the blanket of snow, the Great Mother sleeps. The land slumbers, making ready to awake once more. In spring, she will shed off her wintery coat. We celebrate this day, honoring Bel's slow return and the Mother who nurtures this land during the darkness to prepare it for the light. May all those in this house be blessed by Bel, and may all the gods be honored. Blessed may we be."

"Blessed may we be," we all called in reply.

At that, Brenna cheered. "Please, everyone. Take your fill," she said, gesturing to the tables.

"Where is Father?" I asked Belenus.

He motioned for me to step aside with him. "Abed. He has a fever. Ula was here this morning before the house woke—I'm surprised you didn't hear her complaining—we have given him herbs, and Ula treated his leg. Damned, stubborn man."

I frowned. "The people will wonder where he is," I was saying when Bran joined us, both of his hands loaded with sweets.

"Yes," Belenus agreed, "but it cannot be helped."

"Father?" Bran asked.

"Ill with fever," I told him.

Bran frowned.

"Ula had fresh mistletoe...retrieved from a special tree in the forest. We are hopeful it will bring your father back to health."

"Ahh," I said with a nod.

"Doesn't mistletoe grow high up in a tree?" Bran asked.

"So it does. And it's quite a climb to retrieve it," Belenus said with a knowing look. "How is your shoulder this morning, Boudica?"

I grinned. "Much better, thank you very much. Now, I have some tasks to attend to. I'll find you all later."

Belenus and Bran laughed.

"Be careful, Boudica. Ula may get you killed yet," Bran called.

Ignoring him, I took one of the small baskets of baked sweets and went back to my chamber. First, I set packages on Brenna's and Bran's beds—just small trinkets I had purchased as gifts for them. There were maple sweets for Bran and an embroidered coin pouch for Brenna. Then, I grabbed two other parcels and the basket and went outside.

The morning air was crisp and cold. The powdery snow sparkled. In the village, many people had trimmed their homes with evergreen boughs and winter berries. Smoke trailed out in curling fingers from the fireplaces of the little homes. It was quiet in the village, everyone cozy inside with their families.

Finally, I reached Kennocha's small roundhouse. Her goats welcomed me with bleats when I knocked on the door.

When she opened the door, I found Kennocha red-eyed and puffy-cheeked.

"Kennocha? What's wrong?"

"Boudica... I... It's nothing. Please, come inside."

I entered the small roundhouse, setting the basket and parcels on the table, then went to the crib. Inside, little Mara lay sleeping. Her dark hair curled around her ears, her lips were poked out in a pout.

"She looks so beautiful," I whispered.

Kennocha gave me a pained smile.

"What is it?" I asked.

"It's nothing... I'm just being foolish," she said, then sighed. "I miss him," she said, then shook her head, dashing tears from her cheeks. "I should have known it would not go as I dreamed. The thought that he is with another breaks my heart, but knowing he is not with her"—she gestured to her daughter—"not this solstice. Not on any birthday. Not ever. He is not here and will never be... It's almost too much to bear."

I pulled the woman into an embrace. How thin she was. The winter had been hard on her. "I am sorry. I am so sorry," I said, then turned toward the table. "Please, won't you sit down? I have a small gift for Mara. And look, I have brought you the best of Cidna's cakes. You need to eat something." I led her to the table and pushed the basket of baked goods toward her, uncovering it to reveal a bounty of cakes, biscuits, loaves of bread, and other sweets, including pots of honey and jams.

"You are too kind to think of me, Boudica. And a gift for Mara? It's too much."

I shook my head. "No. It is still not enough." I gazed back at the cradle where Mara lay sleeping. "I know what it means to lose someone you love," I said. "There is nothing harder in this world. Even though Caturix is not with you, at least you still have a piece of him... you have someone who can remind you each day of the love you once shared. It is so much better than the yawning void that could be there," I said, my voice trembling.

"Boudica," Kennocha said gently, setting her hand on my arm. "I'm sorry. I should not have complained. At least your brother is still with us. Gaheris..."

I nodded.

Gaheris was gone.

And next year, at this time, my sister would be in Prasutagus's bed. And me... Well, the gods only knew what would happen to me.

I huffed a light laugh. "We're both wrong to lament. It's solstice. The sun will return. How can we be sad?"

Kennocha laughed lightly, then pulled two sweet biscuits from the basket, handing one to me. "Instead, let's cheer Bel," she said.

I clicked my biscuit against hers in toast and turned to drown my sorrows in delicious concoctions of honey, anise, and cinnamon.

I LEFT KENNOCHA A FEW HOURS LATER AND JOINED THE OTHERS IN the central square. Everyone had come to watch Belenus bless the Yule log and partake in wine and sweets. Bran and Brenna stood at the front with Belenus. I joined Ula at the back of the crowd.

"Happy Solstice," I told her, slipping a small packet into her pocket.

"What's that?" she asked.

"A gift."

"I don't need a gift."

"No, but you need new gloves. And you're welcome."

Ula laughed lightly, then took my hand and placed something therein. I opened it to find a hagstone strung on a leather strap.

"Next time, use this to see the piskies before you get into trouble."

Chuckling, I slipped it on. "I will. Thank you, Ula."

"Pssh," she said, waving her hand at me. "Your shoulder?"

"Sore, but better."

"Your father will be feeling better, in body at least, by tomorrow. The mistletoe will do its work."

"Belenus told me you'd come. Thank you."

"Woke me too damned early."

I chuckled.

Ula and I watched as Belenus called his prayers to Bel. When he was done, three strong men carried the carved Yule log, which honestly looked like a woman, to the bonfire. They banked the wood around her then set the whole thing aflame. Bel's fires would melt away the winter snows covering the Great Mother, and soon, the land would wake once more.

Once the ceremony was done and the fire was lit, the villagers came to collect kindling for their hearths. Others went to drink wine and eat with their friends. Bran and Brenna worked their way through the crowd, talking and laughing with the others.

I spotted Cai cradling a steaming goblet of spiced wine. He lifted it to me in a toast.

I inclined my head to him.

"Fine-looking boy," Ula said, her gaze on Cai.

I chuckled. "So he is."

"Bed him. It will ease your sorrows."

"I have no desire to bed anyone."

"No?" Ula asked, a knowing tone in her voice.

I frowned. "Stop spying on me in your weird mushroom smoke."

Ula laughed. "Come Beltane, you will change your mind. You'll see. Happy Yule, Boudica," she told me, then wandered off. I watched as Ula gingerly grabbed a half-burned stick of wood from the fire, then went back to her house.

Leaving the others behind, I crossed the courtyard and climbed the wall to the palisades. I stared out at the frosty landscape. My eyes turned south, my mind traveling all the way to Venta where Prasutagus would be without his wife this Yule, as I was without Gaheris. Did he feel the same ache I did? Did he feel deep loneliness and heartache?

Did he hope Brenna would fill that void?

I frowned.

I *should* hope that Brenna would ease his loneliness. I *should* wish that she would take away his pain. And I *shouldn't* be thinking of him in the first place. But I was. Cai *was* a fine-looking boy and a good friend, but I would never be with anyone who didn't move my heart, my spirit. After Gaheris, I never dreamed I'd care for anyone like that again. But most of all, I never expected that if I *did* feel like that for someone, that the man I cared for would ask to marry my sister.

CHAPTER 44

The weeks after the winter solstice celebration dragged on slowly. The long winter seemed like it would never end. I went outside one morning to check on Druda not long after Imbolc. Bran and Brenna had ridden to the grove to take some food supplies to the priestesses. I doubted Dôn actually needed them. Most likely, Bran had conjured up an excuse to go and made Brenna his culprit. While I was usually up for an adventure, I felt out of sorts today. For the last few weeks, a strange sense of sorrow had come over me. Hoping to shake the darkness, I left the roundhouse. The sun shimmered like gold on the icicles hanging from the eaves of the roundhouse. The ice dripped in the sunlight. Soon, the spring equinox would come. And with it, life would begin again.

Deciding the snow wasn't too deep, I saddled Druda and set out for a ride. The snow had turned from thick, white blankets to slushy and brown along the edges of the road where wet mud seeped through. Having no particular path in mind, Druda and I headed south. Perhaps, if the road was clear, we could send a messenger to Stonea. Little Mara was doing well. Did Caturix even care? And then, there was Father's health. My brother should know Aesunos was not well. Rather than showing any signs of healing, Father seemed to be holding on to life through sheer bitterness. An inner power fired him, carrying him forward. As spring approached, so too would come his meddling.

King Caratacus.

No.

Never.

I was about an hour south of Oak Throne when I spotted a rider galloping in my direction. I stopped, watching as he approached. He wore a black-and-gold cape in the colors of the Greater Iceni.

Pulling my spear, I turned Druda, blocking the man's path.

As he approached, he slowed his horse.

"Hold, rider. I am Boudica, daughter of King Aesunos," I called. "What is your business?"

"Princess," the man called, reining his horse to a trot. "I am Elidir, messenger coming from King Prasutagus with a message."

"*King* Prasutagus?"

"Great Antedios passed two weeks ago. I am carrying the news to King Aesunos."

"That is sad news. I'll ride with you," I said, then strapped my spear on my back once more.

"I almost thought my welcome in the lands of the Northern Iceni would be short-lived," the Elidir said, eyeing my spear. He chuckled lightly.

"You can never be too careful."

"No, Princess. You cannot," he said, tapping the sword on his belt.

We turned and rode back to the roundhouse. My heart ached for Prasutagus. The loss of his father, following the loss of his wife, would be hard for him.

As the thought occurred to me, my own relationship with my father came to mind once more. I loved my father. When I'd been a girl, I used to ride with him on the front of his saddle and follow around behind him, listening as he gave council. Even more than my brothers, I watched his every move—he was king, and I wanted to be like him. But now... the angry, inconsiderate man who limped around our roundhouse shouting orders and striking his children was not the man I remembered. This father was a stranger to me.

When we arrived at the roundhouse, I met Balfor at the door. "A messenger from Prasutagus," I told the housecarl.

He nodded then motioned for the man to follow him inside. When we got to the door of my father's meeting room, Balfor motioned for the messenger to wait. He disappeared within, returning a few moments later.

"The king will see you now," Balfor told Elidir, opening the door for him.

Curiosity getting the better of me, I followed him inside.

Within, Father and Belenus sat at the table, a map spread before them. I was able to catch just a glimpse of it before Belenus rolled it up. From what I could see, it was a map of the Catuvellauni tribal lands.

Father's eyes flicked toward me for a moment, then turned toward the messenger. "Well, what is your message?"

"Great King Aesunos," the man said, bowing to Father. "I am sorry to share the news that ancient King Antedios has died. Prince Prasutagus was crowned king on Imbolc."

"I see," Father said.

"So, it has come to pass at last," Belenus said sadly. "Would we all be so lucky to live to nearly a hundred years. We are sorry to hear the news. We shall hold a rite of remembrance in his honor, and in the honor of your new king."

"Thank you, Druid Belenus," the messenger replied, his gaze going to Father, who sat staring into the fire.

Belenus turned to me, giving me a coaxing look.

"Won't you take your rest, Elidir?" I asked the messenger, gesturing for him to follow me from the room. "Come, let me see that you have something to eat and drink."

"Please send King Prasutagus our condolences on the death of his father and our best wishes on his rule. I trust the king intends to hold the Beltane rites as planned?" Father asked.

"Yes, King Aesunos. King Prasutagus wanted me to reassure you that the gathering would still be held. He also wished me to relay that he has had confirmation from Kings Caratacus and Togodumnus that they, too, shall attend the rites, along with the druids from Mona. He looks forward to your talks about the future of all of the Iceni."

"We shall be there. Anything else?" Father asked.

"No, King Aesunos."

Father bobbed his head then waved for the messenger to go.

"This way, please," I said, motioning for Elidir to follow me.

I led the messenger back to the dining hall. There, I asked the servants to see he was given food and drink. I sat down with him while we waited.

"I hope the ride from Venta was not too difficult," I told Elidir.

"The streams are beginning to flood with all the melting

snow, but not too high to cross yet. The deer are busy. Even saw a bear."

"Spring."

"Spring," the man agreed, then paused. "Princess, is King Aesunos altogether well?"

I paused. Prasutagus was a friend and ally. What happened to the Northern Iceni affected our southern neighbor. Prasutagus had warned me that he feared his father would die. Did I owe him the same courtesy? Would it change his plans? I wasn't sure. In the end, I simply said, "It has been a long winter. But we will see King Prasutagus at the Beltane rites. Of that, Prasutagus can be assured."

"I understand your brother, Prince Caturix, is settled in Stonea."

I nodded. "Yes, wed to Melusine of the Coritani."

"I've never been to Stonea. They say you have to be part fey to find it."

I chuckled. "An excellent way to keep the fort safe."

The man laughed lightly.

Cidna brought food and drink, and Elidir and I spoke of idle things while he took his fill. When he was done, I walked Elidir outside once more.

"We look forward to seeing you in Venta come spring, Princess," Elidir said. "King Prasutagus spoke of it very often over the winter."

"We'll be happy to see him again. Our thoughts are with him during this difficult time."

"Thank you, Princess. I'm sure it will comfort the king to know your heart is with him," he said, then mounted.

"I… Safe travels, Elidir. Mind those streams."

Elidir inclined his head to me, clicked to his horse, then set off south once more.

Standing in the courtyard, I watched him go. Suddenly, I found Ula at my side.

"King Antedios is dead," I told her.

Ula nodded. "So the ravens told me."

"And Prasutagus is king…"

"Of course he is. Did you expect someone else to be king?"

"No."

"Now he just needs a queen," Ula said with a laugh, then wandered off, muttering to herself as she went.

A king needs a queen.

Brenna would make a beautiful queen.

My sister… Queen of the Greater Iceni.

Wife of Prasutagus.

Partner for his bed.

Mother of his children.

While I wanted to feel happy for Brenna, the thought was like dust in my mouth. I turned toward the stables—and my training spears. Something told me that stabbing straw dummies to death would be the only thing that would take the feeling away.

CHAPTER 45

It was evening when Brenna and Bran returned from the grove. While I had expected Bran to be cheerful, his mood was sullen. My brother disappeared back outside. Brenna joined me, warming herself by the central fire while I shared the news from Venta.

"It is a pity, but Antedios was very old, wasn't he?" Brenna asked.

I nodded. "Belenus said he was nearly one hundred."

"Such an ancient thing. Do you remember him at all?"

"No. I have little memory of our trip to Venta, just scant images. Do you recall him?"

"Me? I never went to Venta. I had a fever when all of you went when we were children. Don't you remember? Mother left me with Riona."

"I'd forgotten."

"We were so little. Perhaps Caturix remembers, but you and Bran were very young."

"Is everyone at the grove well?"

Brenna nodded as she rubbed her hands together. "Bran,

Bec, and Dôn disappeared together. I spoke with the priest-esses. Grainne is such a pleasant girl. She always has something funny to say. I don't go often enough. It was a sharp reminder of that. As it is, I'm glad I was able to leave the house. I'm sure the news from Venta didn't sit well with Father."

I shrugged. "Who can say? He barely reacted to the messenger and hasn't been out of his room all day."

"Dôn sent this for him," she said, pulling a jar from her bag. "A balm for his leg."

"Give it to Belenus."

Brenna nodded, her gaze cast in the direction of Father's meeting chamber. "*My* father would have been grateful for such a gift. That man in there…who knows how he will react?"

Bear, who had been keeping Nini company in the kitchens, came in barking excitedly having heard Brenna's voice.

"Oh, you wicked little creature. There you are. What have you been doing all day?" Brenna asked, scooping him up.

Bear, licking his lips, gave himself away.

"Eating," Brenna said with a chuckle.

"Let's only hope he was eating something Cidna gave him, not something he helped himself to," I replied.

Brenna looked worried. "You don't think…"

A moment later, we heard a clatter in the kitchen and the sound of Cidna cursing. "Bear!" Cidna yelled angrily.

I grinned at my sister then waved to her. "I'll see you later."

"Boudica," she said, looking worried.

I laughed. "Good luck."

"Figures she would leave us to our fate. Now, what have you done, naughty boy?"

Leaving my sister, I grabbed my cloak then went outside in

search of Bran. I found my brother practicing archery in the fading sunlight.

I went to the nearby cabinet and grabbed a bow and a quiver as well. Standing beside him, I took aim and shot, both of us emptying our quivers. When we went to retrieve the arrows, I paused to admire Bran's hits.

"Well done," I said, looking over the murdered strawman.

Bran nodded, looking to mine. "And you."

"King Antedios is dead. There was a messenger."

Bran paused, then turned and looked at me. "I feel like a storm is rolling toward me. I won't let it sweep me up. Dôn says to be patient... I won't marry anyone but Bec. Do you think Lynet would help me? Bec said she is willing to go away with me if Father refuses. Do you think Lynet would help me get to her people in Skye?"

"But if Dôn urges patience, then be patient."

"You put too much trust in Dôn."

"It is the gods I trust."

"Perhaps in them too."

I laughed. "If I cannot trust my father, the high priestess of Andraste, or even the gods, who can I trust?"

"Me. You can always trust me," Bran said with a laugh.

"Of that, there is no question," I replied with a chuckle, embracing my brother. "And you can always trust me. If Dôn is wrong, we will go to Lynet together. I will get you and Bec to Skye."

"May the gods hear your words, Sister."

CHAPTER 46

L ate one night in the weeks following, after I had sat far too long in the dining hall with a flagon of wine trying to forget everything—Gaheris, the sting of pain and jealousy I felt over Brenna's engagement, the idea that my father and uncle were already plotting a place for me in Caratacus's bed—I rose to go. My legs were wobbly, and my head spun. Intending to see if Ula was still awake, I turned to make my way toward the door when I found my father standing there.

"Boudica," he said stiffly. "Where are you going?"

I pointed behind him. My head twirling, and I knew well enough not to get into a conversation.

My father didn't move. "We will go to Venta soon," he said.

"I'm aware." Aware that my sister would soon be the one to wed King Prasutagus. Aware that Gaheris had rotted to bones by now. Aware that his murderer was still free to roam out there, their identity unknown. Aware that my father was planning to marry me to a cutthroat.

"I will meet with Caratacus and Togodumnus in Venta. I must do something to protect the Northern Iceni. I must protect Caturix's claim to the throne—assuming I can manage to outlive my brother. I must win the Catuvellauni's loyalty by any means necessary. No matter what Dôn has to say on the subject. Do you understand me?"

"Ah," I said lightly. "So, which brother did you decide I should bed on behalf of the tribe?"

My father's face hardened, but now my tongue was loose.

Before he could speak again, I added, "Are you certain you have thought this through? With me wed to one of these brothers, what's to stop them from riding to Oak Throne the moment you're dead? After all, they will be married to a princess of this house. How long before these brothers decide Saenunos and Caturix are inconvenient obstacles to what they could otherwise easily take? I thought you were smarter than that, Father."

"Saenunos has long been an ally to—"

"Every time my uncle looks at you, he has daggers in his eyes. This was his idea, right? That I marry Caratacus. Did you ever wonder why? Why did he propose this match? How does it benefit him? Why was he so opposed to Prasutagus, who is a noble man? You're blind. Your brother is trying to out-maneuver you. He is playing his own game. If you don't die fast enough to see Saenunos's plot the whole way through, he will have you murdered."

"He wouldn't."

I blew air through my lips. "Do you really think so well of him?" I was drunk. As much as my conscience fought to silence my tongue, I couldn't stop. "And just what did dear Uncle think of Brenna's match?"

"I only suggested the match. That was enough to start a war. The marriage was arranged between King Antedios and me."

"Between you and King Antedios? Not between you and Prasutagus?"

"The ancient king said his son spoke favorably of this house."

Of this house. Not of me. "If you didn't tell Saenunos, then you already know your brother is not to be trusted."

My father's eyes shifted to the space behind me. I could see he was reflecting on my words.

"You may think little of me or what I want, but mark my words, Father. Saenunos is dancing to his own tune. In his mind, he *will* be king. He doesn't love you. He doesn't care about you. He wants to be king. When he learns you have aligned us to the Greater Iceni, you had better watch your back. And if you marry Bran to that poor, mad girl and me to Caratacus, you'll be sticking your head—and ours—into a noose. Saenunos is too blinded by ambition to see the truth. Even if he does out-maneuver you, and he might unless you start paying attention, those brothers will have him murdered the second he is crowned king. Caturix too. You'll be gone, and I'll be left to push out babes to your murderer, and Bran will be wed to a mad woman. In the end, we will all be Catuvellauni. Brenna too, when they turn against Prasutagus. Now, if you will," I said, motioning for him to step aside.

Wordlessly, Father moved out of my way.

My head still spinning, anger making my hands shake, I made my way past him.

"You are a mirror of your mother," Father said, making me stop cold. "Especially when you are angry."

Fury gripping me, I turned toward my father. "Why did you marry her?"

He didn't answer me.

"Why did you marry my mother?" I demanded.

"I... I loved her."

"Then you are a hypocrite in the eyes of the gods."

"What do you mean?"

"You married for love but you deny the same to Bran. Don't make Bran suffer just to assuage your own fears. Let Bran marry Bec."

"Every choice I make is to protect all of you. How can you not see that?"

"Your choices are poor, Father. People fight for what they love, not what's been forced on them. You forced Caturix to wed Melusine, and you don't even care about the *real* consequences of that—the flesh and blood that suffers just outside your door because of what you dictated. You've forced Brenna into a match she doesn't want, depriving her of a future on Mona. Now, you would take Bran's future from him and try to force me into a Catuvellauni bed. But let me assure you, Father, I am made of iron. I will not bow down to your will or anyone else's. I know you want to protect the Northern Iceni. But hear this: despite all Saenunos's plotting and the Catuvellauni's ambitions, no one will touch the Northern Iceni while I still have breath in my body. Shackling me to a miserable life will not make my resolve any stronger. My tongue is sharp enough to make my own allies. And my spear arm is strong enough when words fail. I don't need what's between my legs to make alliances. You've already sacrificed two of your children on that altar. Leave Bran and me alone," I said, then turned and headed for the door.

Before I exited, I heard Father softly call out my name, but I didn't turn back.

Once, I had loved my father.

I knew he thought he was doing what was right.

But tonight, I didn't care. Gaheris was gone. Brenna would wed Prasutagus. And me...well, only the gods knew what would become of me.

***

DRUNK AND FULL OF SPITE, I MADE MY WAY TO THE RAMPARTS where I stood, watching fairy globes dance across the fields as the moon moved across the sky. Misery swept over me. I should have been pregnant with my first child by now. Gaheris and I, and our house full of animals, should have been blissfully happy. Instead, I would leave soon for Venta and the Beltane rites. I didn't want to go. I didn't want to be there when Brenna and Prasutagus made their plans for their future. The idea of watching that man share jokes and smiles with my sister made me feel sick.

Everything just felt wrong.

It was well after midnight, the dullness in my head from the wine finally starting to abate, when I turned to go back to the roundhouse. To my surprise, I found someone standing on the rampart, half-hidden in the shadows.

I pulled my sword. "Show yourself."

To my surprise, Prasutagus appeared. The moonlight showed through him, making him shimmer with blueish light.

"Prasutagus?" I whispered.

The king appeared confused. He looked from me out at the landscape.

"You are on the walls of Oak Throne," I told him.

Prasutagus turned back to me. "Boudica…" he said, then lifted something small, holding it up in the light of the moon.

Feeling wary, I stepped closer toward him to see he was holding a coin—the same coin Tristan had found.

"Is that…"

Prasutagus nodded. "I drew the coin's likeness when I returned from Oak Throne in the autumn. My most trusted merchants have watched for me, seeking the coin. I have an answer for you. The coin is from Gaul."

"Gaul?"

He nodded. "Yes. We should speak more of this, but the casting is taxing. I will see you soon in Venta. Let's talk then."

I stared at him. This man had crossed the barrier between the worlds to see *me*. And this was not the first time. Why? Confusion washed over me and then pain. I cared for Prasutagus. I had tried to deny it, but the moment I'd learned Brenna would wed him, misery and jealousy had taken over me. It felt like my last hope for happiness had been snuffed out. But I could not blame Prasutagus. Perhaps he was simply a good person. Maybe he connected well with everyone he met. He would make a good brother-in-law. The proof of it was before me. He'd only met me once, but still, he sought to help me find Gaheris's murderer. "Thank you, King Prasutagus."

Prasutagus's brow flexed as if he was confused. "Boudica…"

"We shall see you soon."

He nodded. "I… Yes. I will see you again very soon. I look forward to it. Beltane," he said with a soft smile, then faded.

I stared in his wake.

Why had he bothered to exert the effort to see me?

Dipping into my pocket, I pulled the coin Tristan had

found. It had come from Gaul. In the pocket of a trader? A raiding tribe?

Or worse?

There was so much worse.

In the pocket of a Roman.

CHAPTER 47

In the weeks that followed, the weather warmed significantly. Brenna's constant chatter about her nervousness at her upcoming nuptials was beginning to become maddening. I wanted my sister to be happy. I knew that Prasutagus would be a good husband. And try as I might to bury my jealousy, I could not shake it. Prasutagus was always—annoyingly—on the edge of my awareness. To escape them both, I resumed my daily rides to the beach.

It wasn't the same without Gaheris, but visiting the places we had haunted together brought a sense of familiarity—even if tinged with grief. I mourned the fact that I was there alone. At the same time, I was well aware that down the beach a day's ride, my love had lost his life. I didn't know what I would find on the shores of the Wash. Some sign. Some comfort. In my daydreams, I hoped to discover the raiders. Maybe, I just wanted an escape...some place to be close to Gaheris's memory.

A place that belonged to me.

Somewhere away from the reality that Brenna would soon wed Prasutagus.

I arrived early in the morning, swimming out to the shoals where Gaheris and I often found oysters. I collected oysters and fished—a more arduous task without Mavis's help—then made up a small fire to cook my meal. Then, I would practice with my spear, occasionally stopping to listen to the sound of waves, the wind blowing my red curls into a wild, tangled mess.

Day after day, I escaped Oak Throne to make my journey to the sea.

And every day, I saw nothing.

No one.

No sign.

Only my memories waited for me.

And despite my hopes, they did little to ease the ache in my heart.

In the days before we rode to Venta, I visited the beach once more, keeping to my same routine. But rather than returning directly to Oak Throne, I made a detour to the grove.

Druda's hooves pounded on the golden sand, the sea spray splashing up on my face as we sped down the beach. Druda loved to chase the shifting tides as much as I did, racing to splash through each wave before it receded once more. He and Mountain used to race. My hands, grimy with sand, held tightly to the reins. Tapping on my horse's sides with my heels, I coaxed more speed. Overhead, an eagle called. I watched as the bird hovered in the air, holding itself in place aloft as it surveyed the unsuspecting fish below. Then, it dove. A moment later, the great bird lifted off with its catch. The fish, suddenly snatched from its natural habitat, wriggled in the eagle's grasp. But it was no use. Even if it did escape, it would plummet to its death. Momentarily, I felt bad for the creature. The eagle changed its course toward the forest. And so did I.

"Come on," I told Druda. I turned the horse, leading him from the beach to the marshy wetland and the forest beyond.

As we worked our way carefully through the marsh, a blanket of mist began to envelop us. A rider unfamiliar with these lands would surely be lost. I wondered for a moment if that was by nature or by the design of the gods. In the distance, a marsh bird called. Frogs jumped into the still water as we passed by. Picking our way, Druda and I finally approached the line of trees at the forest's edge then followed the narrow path away from the marsh and into the forest. The mists receded as we passed the ancient oak, ash, and thorn trees, working our way into the heart of the woods. Soon, I could smell the scent of smoke in the air.

Druda sneezed.

"You smell it too? Even with all the mist and magic hiding this place, the smell of their bannocks cooking on the fire will give them away."

I eyed the horizon, making out the stand of oak on the knoll in the distance. The moment I saw them, an unexpected memory of my mother came to mind. Brenna and I had been lying in bed. My mother sat at the edge.

"But why don't they have walls at the grove? If someone tries to attack them, the priestesses will not be safe," I declared indignantly.

"They don't need a wall," Mother replied, spinning the leaf she held between her fingers. "If any enemy ever tries to attack the ancient grove, the trees rise from the ground," she said, twirling the leaf faster and faster. "Their roots like feet, their limbs like weapons, they will stand together like soldiers guarding the place."

"That's not true," Brenna said with a laugh.

Mother's hazel eyes grew wide. "Of course it is. How can you doubt such a thing? Swinging their branches, they will attack the enemy," she said, tossing the leaf into the air and tickling us both by surprise.

Brenna and I both laughed.

"I believe you," I told her.

Mother nodded. "It is always wise to believe the old tales, my Boudica. Those who believe will learn to hear the whispers of the greenwood."

"Even the Seelie? What about the little people?" I asked.

Mother nodded. "And more. There are so many more. A hundred different voices make up the greenwood. Now, good night, both of you." Kissing us both on the foreheads, she left us.

The memory faded. To my surprise, tears had welled in my eyes. I rarely remembered my mother. In these dark days, all manner of strange thoughts had gone twisting through my mind. None was more surprising than such a solid memory of Damara.

The gods were playing with me.

Each day we grew closer to Beltane, I felt their presence more and more.

Dôn had bought me time, but it would soon run out.

But not all was darkness. Something had shifted in my father after our terse discussion. In the very least, he did not speak of mad Princess Imogen to Bran again. Of course, he did not speak of wedding Bran to Bec either, but at least my brother would not be forced to wed a crazed woman—or to run away to escape that miserable fate. What he planned for me, however, I still had no idea.

Instead of Bran and Bec, maybe I should be the one to run

off to Skye...especially considering Brenna was marrying the only man I had cared for since Gaheris's death.

I slowed Druda to a stop.

For a moment, we stood motionless.

I felt stunned by the admission.

I did care for Prasutagus.

The fact made me angry with myself.

Clicking to the horse once more, I made my way into the grove.

Soon, Prasutagus and Brenna would be wed. I needed to let go. I would think on the king no more.

"Come on, Druda. Let's see if they have anything good to eat cooking on that fire."

CHAPTER 48

Druda and I were greeted by the hounds who wiggled around my legs with excited whines.

"All right, all right," I said, giving each one a pat. "I'm sorry. I don't have anything for you to eat."

"You assume they want something from you," Bec called.

I looked up to see Bec making her way toward me. Her own two hounds followed her, their tails wagging when they saw me. She had her long, brown hair pulled back from the temples with braids. Her gown was pinned at the shoulders, showing off her tanned and muscular arms, which spoke of hard work.

"Don't they?" I quipped back at her. "Could have fooled me."

"Just your attention," Bec said with a grin. "Aren't you supposed to be at home getting ready for the trip to Venta?"

"Why do you think I'm here? If you listen hard enough, you can hear Saenunos complaining from here," I said, referring to my uncle. Saenunos had arrived in Oak Throne two days earlier to ride with us south to Venta. Coincidentally, my trips to the beach had started earlier and lasted longer for the last two days. I swore if I heard King Caratacus's name one more time, I would ask Ula for a brew to make myself deaf.

"And what is your uncle complaining about today?"

"That he has to wait for the swelling in Father's leg to calm before they can ride south," I replied. While Father's health had stabilized a bit—coincidently, after he had received Dôn's healing balm—the warm weather had his leg swollen once more. Belenus warned Father that if he traveled too soon, before the druid could treat the leg, he'd repeat the disaster he'd experienced in Stonea. Father, begrudgingly, listened.

Saenunos was far less patient.

"How dare the king's health be such an inconvenience?" Bec said with a shake of the head. "So, you left Bran and Brenna to deal with him?"

A sting of guilt pricked my heart. "Bran escaped going hunting. Brenna… She's able to ignore his moods."

"Is she?" Bec, who had been playing with the dogs, looked up at me, raising an eyebrow.

A pang of guilt pricked at my heart. Bec was right to point out my error. I had left Brenna on her own to save my own sanity. But doing so, perhaps I had wronged my sister. "I hear you, Priestess."

"I'm glad, Princess. Be that as it may, I'm happy you're here anyway. Dôn told me to bring you when you arrived."

"She knew I was coming?"

Bec nodded. "She told me this morning."

My eyes flicked to Dôn's small roundhouse.

"She's not there," Bec said then sighed. "Come, let's hear what Dôn has to say."

Bec and I made our way up the hillside. The path between the village and the grove was well worn. A soft wind blew, causing the leaves to shift. In the trees overhead, a raven called to us as it hopped from limb to limb.

Bec gave the bird a quizzical look. "Andraste is watching."

I followed her gaze.

The bird ruffled its feathers and, with a caw, flew off.

The new green leaves shifted overhead. The sunshine made the loam of the earth effervesce, perfuming the air. Ferns unfurled their fingers, and purple violets dotted the forest floor. It was nearly Beltane. Soon, we would all travel south to Venta and the nearby shrine of Arminghall Henge for the rites of Bel. I could already feel the fire of spring in my blood. The world around me felt alive.

"Boudica...

"Boudica...

"*Play with us in the green...*"

I paused, looking around for the source of the voice.

Bec looked back, then stopped. "What is it?"

"Did you..." I said, then hesitated, looking deeper into the woods. A nearby hedge rustled, and a fawn shot off. The sunlight shining on its dappled coat, it disappeared into the forest.

Bec watched the animal retreat, then turned to me. "It's that red hair of yours... The greenwood's eyes are always on you."

"I'd prefer to be carried off by some Seelie prince than end up the wife of King Caratacus."

"You shouldn't jest about such things."

"I really *don't* want to be the wife of Caratacus."

"You know what I meant."

"Yes, Bec."

"I mean it."

"Yes, Bec."

"Boudica, are you listening to me?"

"*Yes*, Bec."

Bec smiled lightly, then shook her head. Turning, she made her way back up the slope. When we reached the entrance to the shrine, Bec raised her hands and called out her prayer. I copied the gesture then entered behind the priestess, passing the effigies that stood sentinel at the entrance to the shrine.

Dôn stood beside the fire, leaning against her tall staff. She looked up at us, giving me a smile. "Ah, Boudica. Welcome returns."

"Wise Dôn," I said, bowing to her—and remembering not to call her *ancient* this time.

Dôn smiled lightly then turned to me. "So, we shall travel south for the rites of Bel. Already, the sun lord is calling the spring maidens. Even I, *ancient* as I am, can feel his pull. If I was your age, I would strip naked under the moonlight and call on the horned lord to take me as a lover."

Grinning, Bec shook her head.

"Why not do it now?" I asked.

Dôn chuckled. "Perhaps I will, Boudica. Perhaps I will. We will ride from the grove in the morning. Tell your father we request an escort. We'll leave at sunrise."

"My father's leg has swollen again. Belenus will not let him travel yet, even though Saenunos is insisting."

"Bec will give you another jar of ointment to take to him," Dôn said, then turned to Bec. "You know the one?"

"I do."

Dôn nodded. "We women of the grove must be on time, even if our king is not."

"I'll be sure he sends someone," I reassured her. While I tried to hide the disappointment in my voice, I was well aware

I'd done a poor job. Was this why she wanted to see me? So I could relay a message to my father?

"Ah, Boudica," Dôn said. "I know your heart. I have no answers for you. The fires whisper, but they do not yet tell me what you want to know," she said, then motioned to Bec. "Throw on another log. Let us see if the Dark Lady will speak today. Come, Boudica," she said, motioning for me to join her.

I went to the priestess's side.

Bec added another piece of wood to the fire. After a few moments, the flames grew higher as the bark caught fire. Embers spiraled upward. I watched the fire burn, feeling its heat on my brow. My lower back began to sweat, and I felt overly warm.

Dôn raised her hands into the air, hoisting her staff with one hand. Her bracelets made of stones, bone, feathers, and shells clicked. "Great Andraste," Dôn called, her voice echoing through the grove. "Queen of battles. Lady of dark places. Weaver of fates. Kingmaker. We honor you. Ancient one, it is nearly Beltane once more, what would you have of the daughter of Aesunos and Damara?"

The fire crackled and sparkled. A log fell, causing cinders to drift upward.

Dôn watched the flames. I could see the orange glow of their light reflected in her eyes.

I cast my eyes toward the fire, searching for some answer.

Andraste... Great lady... My love is gone. My sister will wed the king who, if I am honest, moved my heart. My father wishes me to marry a man I do not want. What can I do? Can I join Dôn here at the grove? I would gladly serve you my whole life long. What do you want of me?

But no answers came.

Beside me, Dôn was silent for a long time. When she grabbed my arm, she startled me.

I turned to look at Dôn, but her face had contorted. She had fire in her eyes. I realized then it was not Dôn at all looking back at me—it was Andraste. "Fire," she croaked in a voice that was not hers. "Beware, Boudica. Eagles are flying. You will be the shield protecting the oaks. You will be the champion of the greenwood. What do I want from the daughter of Aesunos and Damara? Fire. I will have fire. Fire!" she called then laughed, loudly and hoarsely, in a voice that echoed across the forest.

CHAPTER 49

I stared at Dôn.

The fire in the center of the grove popped and snapped. The sound distracted Dôn who turned toward the flames. When she looked back, she was herself once more.

"Dôn," I whispered.

"I saw you before an army. So many people. So many…" she whispered, shaking her head. "Your hair was flames," she said, then shuddered. "You will be the defender of the people, Boudica."

"Against who? The Catuvellauni?"

"Eagles…" Dôn said quietly.

"The Romans," Bec said with a gasp.

Dôn shook her head. "I don't know. The vision wasn't clear. I will speak with Selwyn when we get to Arminghall Henge."

"Who is Selwyn?" I asked.

"The high priestess of Mona," Dôn replied.

I frowned then looked back toward the fire. "The Dark Lady did not truly answer. Will I come to the grove? Will I be forced to wed Caratacus? As much as I revere her, it was not an answer."

"Andraste riddles," Dôn said. "That is her way. I cannot ask your father to let you join us until Andraste directs it."

"In the vision," Bec began, "whose army did you see? The Northern Iceni? When?"

"Not just the Northern Iceni. All of us. It was all of us," Dôn said, then shuddered. "We must leave for Arminghall Henge at first light. You have a great fate before you, Boudica. Of that, there is no doubt."

"One of fire," Bec said warningly.

"Yes," Dôn replied thoughtfully, then added, "Do not give up hope, Boudica. Call upon Cernunnos, on Bel, on the May Queen. Ask them for help. They, too, listen. And on Beltane, they may be inclined to grant your wishes."

"Thank you, Dôn."

She inclined her head to me then turned to Bec. "Go on. Get the ointment for the king. I will sit a while longer," she told her, returning to her spot beside the fire. With a tired groan, she sat down on a stump. "Remember to tell your father, Boudica. An escort. By sunrise."

"I will see to it," I told her.

With that, she nodded to me.

Bec motioned for me to follow her, and the pair of us departed the shrine.

The sense of disappointment made my stomach ache.

Bec, sensing my distress, said, "Don't give up, Boudica. All things happen as they must. We all follow our fates. Andraste may still call you here. And the grove is only one place. There is still Mona."

"I have given up all hope of Mona."

"At the Beltane rites, there will be a group from the Isle of Glass," Bec said leadingly.

"The holy isle? Avallach?"

Bec nodded. "Andraste rules this place, but on Avallach... Pray to the Maiden. Dôn is right. On Beltane, she may listen."

"Either place takes me far away from here."

"It does. But it also takes you a good distance away from the bed of Caratacus," she said with a laugh which I joined.

We continued on our path to the village once more.

As I walked, I turned over Dôn's words. She had seen me —*me*—before a great army. How was such a thing even possible? But more importantly, why was such a thing necessary?

"Dôn's prophecy..." I said, unsure what else to say.

"It is a dark omen."

"Is she ever wrong?"

Bec bobbed her head from side to side. "It is not always easy to understand what we see. The gods do not always make things clear. Especially Andraste. After all, I don't expect your hair to really turn into flames unless the sun god has given you powers you never told me about."

I chuckled. "I don't imagine I'd be very effective as a warband leader if my hair burst on fire. 'You there, mind the chariots—never mind why my head is smoking!'"

Bec chuckled, but after a moment, she added, "But still... It is a warning, Boudica. And when Andraste shows her face, it must be taken seriously. Heed her words."

"Yes, Bec."

"Boudica."

"*Yes*, Bec."

When we finally returned to the village, we found Grainne and Tatha readying the wagons. Grainne paused her work to join us. "Boudica, are you ready to ride south? I've never attended the rites at the Arminghall nemeton before."

Bec motioned to me that she was going to get the ointment, leaving me with Grainne.

The girl, who was five years or so my junior, had come to the grove after a fever had wiped out her entire family. An orphan, she had been under the care of the priestesses. But unlike many other children in the same situation, the goddess had called Grainne to serve, so she had stayed when she came of age.

Grainne's bright blue eyes flashed with excitement.

"I went to Venta when I was a little girl, but I have almost no recollection of it now. And I was too young to attend the last gathering at the nemeton." That, and my mother had just died, but I did not say so.

"I've never been farther south than Oak Throne," Grainne said with a laugh.

"They're all giants south of here. Best be on your guard," I told her with a wink.

Grainne laughed.

Bec returned, a jar in her hand.

"I wish you both a safe trip south," I told the priestesses. "I'll see you there. Remember, giants," I told Grainne with a laugh, then joined Bec.

"Ride safe, Boudica," Grainne called in reply.

Bec and I went to Druda.

"For your father," she said, handing me the jar.

I slipped it into my satchel then mounted Druda.

Bec untied the horse then handed me the reins.

"There is sand caked on your legs," she told me.

"It was a good swim, though."

"Too soon for swimming. The waters must have been freezing."

"They were. But that was the only way to get what I was after."

"Do I dare ask?"

"You can. But that doesn't mean I'll answer."

Bec gave me a knowing look.

"Something for Melusine."

"Will she and Caturix come for the rites?"

I nodded.

"Bran..." she began, then paused. "It would be good if Bran rode with us tomorrow."

"I'll be sure to mention it to him. Bec..." I said gently.

"Say nothing, Boudica. I'll be glad to spend time with him, if I can. I must be content with that."

"You're forgetting something vital, Priestess."

"What is it, Princess?"

"No one is married on Beltane."

At that, Bec's cheeks redden. "As the gods will."

"Then may the gods will that you feel the same tug that even Dôn feels."

"Boudica," she replied with a laugh.

"For my brother's sake," I said with a chuckle.

"Watch yourself, or Cernunnos may move you next."

I laughed. "My heart is buried in Frog's Hollow. There is no one for me."

"That's exactly what someone says right before fate undermines all their plans."

"I'll keep that in mind," I said, then clicked to Druda. "See you soon, Priestess."

"And you, Princess. Blessed be."

"Blessed be."

CHAPTER 50

Druda and I followed the River Stiffkey back toward home. Druda was usually quick to go back, but today, his mood matched my own. He dragged his feet, meandering slowly. The last thing I wanted was to return to Oak Throne. My head ached at the thought of listening to my uncle and father bicker all night. Instead, I looked up at the trees, feeling the warmth of the early summer sun on my face.

I exhaled deeply, thinking of Dôn's words and the wretched sense of disappointment.

I felt like all the pieces of a future I didn't want were about to collide, smashing me in the middle. Once Brenna was wed, everyone would turn to me. And still, Andraste did not call me to the grove. Instead, she wove tales of armies and fire and war. What did any of that have to do with me?

Druda snorted then shook his head.

A moment later, I realized why.

There was a strange scent in the air, a heady smell of flowers unlike any I had ever smelled before. The perfume was so pungent. I looked around for the source only to realize we had ridden through a hedge of elder trees. The scent of the bright, white blossoms was lovely, but under it was a deeper, headier smell that reminded me of roses.

The hedge shifted.

Druda came to a stop. His nostrils flared as he breathed in heavily. His withers shivered.

"Easy," I whispered, patting his neck, then pulled the spear on my back. "Show yourself," I called commandingly.

There was no reply, but I saw movement in the brush. A moment later, a pure white stag stepped out of the green, stopping on the path in front of me.

"The King Stag," I whispered breathlessly.

Yet, as I looked at the beast before me, I did not get that same sense of Cernunnos I always felt whenever the Father God drew near.

This was something different.

Overhead, an owl called.

I looked up, surprised to hear such a creature at this time of day. The snowy owl lifted off the limb of a nearby rowan tree and disappeared on silent wings back into the forest.

When I turned back, I found a man standing in my path.

The stranger had long, raven-black hair and was impeccably dressed in a deep green silk tunic trimmed with gold and silver thread. His leather was finely crafted, beautiful designs pounded thereon. He wore a sword on his hip and a silver ringlet on his head.

"Hail, Boudica, princess of the Iceni," he called, his voice ringing like a bell through the forest.

Druda's withers shook once more, but he stood perfectly still.

"I am Boudica, princess of the *Northern* Iceni, not all the Iceni. And you are?"

"I stand corrected," he said, bowing genteelly to me.

"*And you are?*"

"Don't you know? You called me," he said with a smooth smile. His eyes flashed silver. He was, by far, the most handsome creature I had ever seen. Something deep within me was pulled toward him. I studied his chiseled features, a square jaw with high cheekbones. Overhead, the dying sun began to color the sky shades of rosy pink, fiery orange, and deep purple. The colors played on the man's dark hair.

Druda snorted then pawed the earth.

The man's gaze shifted to the horse.

The moment he broke eye contact, I felt like I could breathe again.

And then, I realized...

Seelie.

A faerie prince.

"It was only a jest," I said, my heart pounding in my chest.

Bec had been right. I had been a fool to tempt the Seelie this close to Beltane.

"Is that so?" he asked in a smooth voice. "I know your heart, princess of the *Northern* Iceni. You do not want the things of this world. The machinations of man. You want to swim naked in the icy waves of the Wash, to race your horse down the beach, to ride in the greenwood. You would find much pleasure in my court. Why don't you come with me for just a little while? We will eat and drink. I will have you home by dawn—if you still wish to go."

Never eat and drink with the fey.

Never accept faerie gifts.

And never tell them your full name.

Banshees be cursed!

I cleared my throat. "As tempting as the offer may be"—

and Andraste forgive me, it was very tempting—"I must be going."

He gave me that charming, sultry smile once more. "Are you certain?"

I met his gaze. "Give me your name, faerie."

At that, he grinned then shook his finger at me. "Clever princess. If you want to know, then come with me."

"I think we both know that is a horrible idea—for me."

He smirked. "Very well, Boudica, princess of the Northern Iceni. Then I wish you good cheer this Beltane tide."

I swallowed hard, but my mouth was dry. He knew my name. He knew my full name and title.

I inclined my head to him.

"If you ever change your mind, simply call," he said with a grin.

At that exact moment, the last rays of sunlight broke through the clouds and shone into my face, making me squint. I blocked the sun with my hand then looked back, but the stranger was gone—taking my name with him.

"Andraste," I whispered. "Protect me from the machinations of both fey and human kind," I said, then patted my nervous horse. "Come on, Druda. Let's get home before the piskies join in on the fun."

CHAPTER 51

It was dusk when Druda and I approached the gates of Oak Throne. As I made my way through the market-place, I was set upon by the usual horde of children.

"Boudica! Boudica, did you bring them?"

"Boudica, did you bring us some? Boudica!"

"Boudica, what did you find?"

Laughing, I dismounted Druda—who began his own slow walk back to the stables—then knelt to meet the children face to face. I sighed heavily, then shook my head. "Too many waves," I said sadly. "Not a single one today. I'm sorry."

"Oh," the children said, letting out a collective sigh of disappointment.

I grinned. "You are too easily fooled," I told them, then removed the pouch hanging from my belt and opened it. Within, glimmering in the light of the torches that illuminated the road, was the treasure they were so eager to win: shells.

"Yay!" they screamed happily, dancing and jumping around.

With a smile, I rose. "All right. Hold out your hands. Like

this," I said, modeling how they should form their hands into cups. Then, digging into the bag, I portioned out my finds. It had taken nearly an hour to collect the shells for the children, but I hadn't minded. They rarely got to go to the water. The shells were treasures that would stir their imaginations.

"Whoa, look at this one. So pink!" Birgit screamed in delight.

After I passed out all my shells, the children huddled around one another, examining their wins, a few of the shrewder children aiming to make trades.

"Thank you, Boudica," Eiwyn called.

"Thank you, Boudica!" the other children echoed, all of them pausing to give me a hug—all at once—before they went back to fawning over their wins.

"You're welcome," I said, stashing the sack. I jogged to catch up to Druda. "What? Tired after your long ride? Can't wait to get back to your stall?" I asked, walking alongside the horse.

He nosed my ear then continued on his path.

When we got to the stables, I found Moritasgus, the stable-master, waiting. "The king sent a boy to see if Druda was here."

"Hmm," I mused, handing Druda's reins to the man. "You suppose he was worried about the horse?'"

Moritasgus laughed. "I doubt that was the case, Princess."

I sighed. "I'm not even inside, and I'm tired of listening to Saenunos already."

"I'm sure the people of Holk Fort are delighted to see their chieftain away for a time."

"Moritasgus, what are you implying?" I asked with mock shock.

The man chuckled.

I patted Druda. "Let's see how it goes. Perhaps you'll find me sleeping in the stables tonight. Good night, Moritasgus. May Epona keep you."

"And you, Princess. Good luck.""Thank you. I may need it," I said with a laugh, then crossed the green.

Avoiding the main entrance, I slipped around the back of the hall and entered through the kitchens. The smell of baking bread and roasted meat filled the air. My stomach growled hungrily, reminding me that I hadn't eaten since morning. I tried to skulk quietly through, bypassing Cidna, whose back was turned to me, but Nini gave me a bark in welcome.

"Traitor," I told Nini, then gave the wiry-haired beast a pat.

"Your father was looking for you," Cidna warned.

"Really? I've been here all day."

Cidna gave me a knowing look. "Then why do you have sand on your cheek?"

I brushed my hand across my cheek, feeling the grime there. "Must have been the wind."

"The wind," Cidna said with a laugh.

I plucked a round of bread and slipped it into my pocket. "You're one to talk, Cidna. You have flour on your cheek," I told her.

"Of course I do! I've been in here cooking for the lot of you all since sun-up." The woman looked down. "On my face, my hands, arms, clothes, and even in my hair," she said with a laugh. "I'll be glad when you all ride to Venta. Now, be off with you. I won't get an earful accusing me of hiding you in the kitchens," she said, waving her fleshy arm.

Grinning, I slipped out of the kitchens and followed the hallway that led like a labyrinth through the circular roundhouse, finding my way to the bedchamber. Just before I entered, one of the serving boys from the hall spotted me.

We stared at one another a long moment before the boy grinned then ran off.

Caught.

With a sigh, I entered the chamber.

Brenna sat on her bed, shifting through her necklaces. She looked up when I entered. A tangle of emotions—worry being the foremost—warred on her features. Her brow was furrowed. "I don't know what to take with me."

I shrugged then sat down on the bed beside her. "Does it matter?" I asked, picking through the strings of amber and pearls.

"Of course it matters. I must make a good impression on King Prasutagus. Unlike you, I can't win him over with talk of horses and dogs."

I chuckled. "Even if you make a bad impression, he will still marry you."

"How do you know?"

"Because you are the *first* princess of the Northern Iceni," I said. While I was trying to jest, there was a waspish tone to my voice I hadn't intended.

Brenna, her mind distracted, misunderstood the tone. "You're right. It doesn't matter who I am. He is marrying me for my family."

I swallowed hard, feeling sorry for my words and the emotion behind them. Brenna didn't deserve it. If my sister knew I truly felt something for the king, she would have refused to marry him. I wasn't being fair. As it was, I needed to forget Prasutagus. Apparently, he'd already forgotten me. "I'm sure you will grow to love one another. After all, who could not love Brenna?"

She looked up at me, her eyes glossy with unshed tears. "It's just... I see how it is with Melusine and Caturix."

"It will not be the same with Prasutagus. He and Caturix are like night and day. You will like him, Sister. I promise."

Brenna sighed a deep, shuddering breath. "I won't be his first wife. If he loved her, how can I ever compare?"

"What is a memory compared to a warm, loving, and wonderful creature like you? Brenna, everywhere you go, people love you. And Prasutagus is a good and honorable man. Just talking to him makes a person feel calm and happy. He's eager to laugh and has a soft smile that makes all the hardness of his masculine face fade into sweetness, even with his druid tattoos on his face. You will see."

Brenna stared at me. "Boudica…"

Realizing I'd said too much, I lifted the string of multi-colored pearls. "This. With the green gown," I said.

From the hall, I could hear Saenunos screaming.

"Father told him about my betrothal. Saenunos is beside himself. He and Father have been warring the whole day long."

"And Bran?"

"He spent most of the day hiding, like you. But he got ensnared earlier when Father informed Saenunos he would not wed Bran to Imogen. It was a terrible scene and why I'm in here."

"I must face the tempest on Dôn's behalf. Want to come with me?"

Brenna began scooping up the jewelry then paused. "If I must. Boudica…"

I could feel her unasked question. It wrapped around my throat and threatened to choke me. "Coming?" I asked.

Brenna sighed, then nodded. She placed her jewels in a box, then followed along behind me.

I exhaled deeply, grateful to all the gods for letting me escape Brenna's question.

The two of us exited the bed chamber and returned to the main meeting space at the center of the roundhouse. We found Bran lingering at the door. Father and Saenunos were in a heated debate when we entered.

"Your reasons have no logic," Saenunos told Father darkly.

"Still going..." Brenna whispered under her breath.

"And your arguments are growing thin, Brother," Father told him. But I could see from the look on my father's face that the conflict was making him weary. What little strength he had regained, Saenunos was draining.

Saenunos's eyes shifted from Brenna to me. "Ah," he said with a sharp smirk. "Here they are. One will be the ruin of all of us, and the other behaves like a wild thing. You won't be so wild once Caratacus is done with you, girl," Saenunos told me.

I glared at him.

"Where have you been all day, Boudica?" Father asked waspishly.

"I went to fetch something for Melusine."

"Aesunos," my uncle told my father darkly. "You have let Boudica live too freely. You must convince Caratacus to agree to the alliance when we are in Venta. Wed Boudica to him at the festival."

"They are my children. I will wed them where I see fit," Father said, slamming his fists down on the table.

Frustrated, my uncle rose. "You will be the ruin of the Northern Iceni, Aesunos!" he shouted at Father, then stormed out of the house.

My father sat staring in the vacant distance before him.

"Father," I said carefully. "Dôn sent this for you. It is the same as before. It worked very well, if you remember," I said, setting the jar before him. "And she has a request. The priestesses will leave for Arminghall at sunrise. She asked for an escort."

"Did she?" Father asked absently. "She will not wait for her king?"

My gaze flicked from Bran to Brenna. I felt like I was walking on a thin sheet of ice. "I think our holy people have matters they must see to that are dictated by the schedule of the sun, moon, and stars, not kings."

Father huffed a laugh, then grabbed the jar and slipped it into his pocket.

"I'll ride with them," Bran offered. "I can take my men. Six of us should be enough to secure their passage."

"Of course you will," Father said. While his words were dripping in sarcasm, Bran brushed them off.

"Very well. I'll have my men ready to go at sunrise," Bran replied. "Perhaps Boudica can ride with us," Bran offered. "She's always anxious for a stretch. It would be good for the members of this house to be seen alongside the holy sisterhood of the Grove of Andraste."

Father turned to Brenna. "I suppose you want to ride too?"

"No, Father. I am content to wait for you. I am in no rush to get to Venta."

"Go ready your men, Bran. Brenna, please fetch Belenus."

"Thank you, Father," Bran said, then departed.

"Yes, Father," Brenna said, also leaving us.

Father turned to me. "What did you fetch for Melusine?"

"Hold out your hand."

With a half-smile, the first I had seen in days, he did as I asked.

Slipping a pouch from my pocket, I poured the contents into his hands: pearls.

Father started at them. "From the Wash?"

I nodded.

"How did you... Did you swim to get them?"

"Yes."

After a moment, Father laughed lightly, taking me by surprise. "Wasn't it cold?"

"I shivered to my core, but Gaheris once showed me a good spot to find the best pearls. It wasn't a far swim."

"Gaheris..." he said in a soft voice, nodding to himself. "You are good to think of Melusine. Make your preparations to ride with your brother."

"Thank you, Father."

"Boudica..."

"Yes?"

"We will meet with Caratacus in Venta. But that is all. You are right. Saenunos is an ambitious fool. But to keep the peace, we must at least speak to King Caratacus. I am mindful of Dôn's words. And I am sure King Caratacus will understand that even kings do not interfere in the will of the gods. Do we understand one another?"

"Yes, Father."

"Very well," he said, then motioned for me to go.

My heart feeling lighter than it had in months, I departed the hall. Perhaps my father would not wed me to Caratacus. Maybe, between Dôn and Andraste, I would be spared.

For now.

CHAPTER 52

I t was late in the evening when Bran and I finally returned to the roundhouse. From the hall, I heard the soft strumming of Brenna's lyre.

Bran and I entered to find what remained of the evening meal still sitting on the table. Brenna, Father, Saenunos, and Belenus were sitting on the benches surrounding the circular fire pit. The ancient druid sat staring into the fire as Father and Uncle bickered. Bear was circling the table, one eye on Brenna and one on the food.

"What is this I hear about you riding south *tomorrow*?" Saenunos demanded as soon as we entered.

"Dôn asked for an escort. I will ride with the ladies of the grove," Bran said.

"Not you, boy," he spat at Bran then turned to me. "You."

"I'm going with Bran. What about it?" I asked pointedly, sitting down at the table. Taking pity on Bear, I handed him a big hunk of meat. Like a guilty thing, he took it and ran.

"You're not riding with your father?" Saenunos asked.

"Correct. I am riding with my brother."

"Such a smart mouth on this one," Saenunos said.

Father, who looked pale, sighed heavily.

"As it is, Brother. You have given the throne to Prasutagus. When we are gone, it is Prasutagus and his progeny who will rule on. You curse your sons in this choice of marriage. There is a reason our father and grandfather never wed the Northern Iceni to the *Greater* Iceni."

"Neither Egan nor Saenuvax ever managed to produce any female offspring. That is why we were never married to the Greater Iceni," Aesunos replied tiredly.

"One must look beyond their own mortality," Belenus told Saenunos. "Prasutagus's heirs—and Brenna's—will have the blood of this house. This only strengthens the Northern Iceni. You lose nothing in this arrangement."

"And how many heirs are you planning, Sister? I need to know how many nieces and nephews I will have to battle to keep my lands," Bran asked Brenna with an impish grin.

Brenna shook her head, a light smile on her face, then kept strumming.

Saenunos frowned at Bran. "Joke now, boy. But when we are gone, it will be up to you and Caturix to hold the line in the face of Prasutagus's ambition."

"Is he so ambitious?" I asked. "He's not attacking us now. In fact, how many generations have the Northern and Greater Iceni tribes known peace? We must be one of the few tribes who've managed not to kill our neighbors."

"What do you know of it?" Saenunos snapped at me.

"Peace, Saenunos," Belenus said. "You cannot move what the gods have ordered. It is the will of the gods that Brenna is engaged to marry the Greater Iceni king. Ancient Antedios wished for this marriage as a final gesture of love for his son.

Soon, the blood of this house shall be in line to inherit their throne."

"All this talk of Prasutagus…" Bran said. "What we should be talking about is the Romans."

Brenna ceased playing.

It felt like a chill washed through the room.

"There is more gossip about Verica," Bran said. "I heard it in the market tonight. The Atrebates's ousted king has been seen in Gaul with the Romans by many people. And some of the Atrebates chieftains—those Caratacus and Togodumnus didn't kill—were also spotted in Gaul."

"We should have no fear of the Romans. The gods protected us from the eagle once," Belenus said. "They will do so again."

"May the gods forgive me for saying so, but I'd rather not leave it solely in their hands," Father told him. "In Venta, we will hear what news there is of Rome."

"May the Lord of the Forest and the Great Mother protect us," Belenus said. "There is plenty of infighting in our own lands to worry about. We must keep the faith in our gods," Belenus said.

"One thing is certain," Father said. "If the Romans come again, it won't matter who sits on the Iceni throne—Northern nor Greater. They will try to crush us all."

THE FOLLOWING MORNING, I WOKE TO BRAN SHAKING MY shoulder. "Boudica, get up. We must make ready. Dôn said sunrise. Would you be late?"

I opened my eyes a crack, spotting my brother's mop of

curly hair—which had, since last night, been neatly trimmed. "Did you cut your hair?"

"No."

"Yes, you did."

"No, I didn't. Brenna cut my hair."

Brenna chuckled. I rose to find my sister dressed and waiting.

"Why are you up?" I asked.

Brenna laughed. "Bran needed a haircut, and you didn't even pack a bag. What will you wear before King Prasutagus? The same clothes as yesterday, which smell like seaweed and sweat?"

Bran laughed.

"Go away," I told him.

My brother grinned at me. "I'll go see to the horses. Druda doesn't like it when we saddle him if you aren't around. He acts like he's worried someone else will try to ride him. Better hurry," he said then left.

On Brenna's bed, my sister had laid out my riding clothes. A bag sat at the foot of her bed. "Everything is here. Riona checked it. And I've already evoked Cidna's ire by having food prepared for you all. I'll go fetch it and meet you outside."

"Thank you, Brenna."

Brenna nodded then left me.

I rose to discover my sister had set out my teal-colored riding tunic, leather trousers, and a leather jerkin. But she'd also added a pretty silver pin with an oak tree thereon for my hair and earrings to match. Working quickly, I changed into my riding gear, even adding the adornments Brenna had selected, then grabbed the bag. I quickly belted my sword then snatched my spear from the corner. Once I was done, I left the roundhouse.

It was still dark outside. Bran's warriors and a saddled but irritated Druda were ready in the square before the round-house. Father waited alongside Bran and Brenna. Amongst Bran's men, I spotted Cai. I joined my family.

"It's not far, even in the dark," Bran was telling Father.

"Father," I said, inclining my head to him.

"Boudica. Ride safely, and mind yourself in Venta."

"Yes, Father," I told him, biting my tongue.

Brenna walked with me to the horses. "I gave the food to Cai, but here," she said, slipping me a round of still-warm bread.

I slid it into my pocket. "Thank you."

Brenna smiled, but the corners of her lips twitched nervously.

"Don't worry. Everything happens as the gods wish. Remember that," I told her.

Brenna nodded.

With that, I strapped my bag onto the back of my saddle then mounted Druda. He huffed at me, voicing his protest to the early wake-up. "Don't take your frustrations out on me. Blame Dôn."

Bran whistled to the others that it was time to go.

I squeezed Brenna's hand. "I'll see you in Venta."

She nodded. "In Venta."

With that, I turned Druda and followed the others, waving one last time to Father and Brenna as I departed.

The village was quiet. Not even the vendors in the market were awake yet. But under the moonlight, I spotted a familiar form standing at the end of one of the streets. I reined Druda toward her.

"Ula," I said, stopping beside the old woman.

She handed me a small pouch on a string. "Put that on."

"Protecting me from faeries again?" I asked, taking it from her hand.

Ula laughed but didn't answer—which was the worst answer she could have given.

I slipped it around my neck. "Want to come with me? You could ride behind me," I said, gesturing.

"Bah," Ula said. "What business do I have with druids and kings?" she said, then studied me closely. "Everything happens as the gods wish. Remember that," she told me, repeating the same words I had just spoken to Brenna.

I lifted an eyebrow at her.

The old woman smirked then turned to go.

"Ula," I called.

She paused a moment.

Dipping into my pocket, I pulled out the round of bread Brenna had given me then tossed it to her.

With a laugh, she caught it, then lifted it to her nose, taking a deep breath. "Smells good, but Cidna never grinds the flour fine enough."

"I'll be sure to tell her."

With that, Ula laughed then trudged off.

I fingered the pouch hanging from my neck for a moment, wondering what she'd put inside. If I opened it to look, I'd break the enchantment. I trusted Ula. For whatever reason, she wanted me to have the item. I slipped the talisman inside my shirt then clicked to Druda.

We rode off toward the grove.

It was just before sunup when we arrived. While the sky was grey, the first shafts of golden light trimmed the horizon.

Bec was busy in the village square organizing the others. As it turned out, only Bec, Grainne, Tatha, and Dôn were coming. Dôn and Grainne would ride in the wagon. Tatha and Bec had already saddled their horses.

When we rode into the square, Bec stopped her tasks long enough to cast a glance at Bran. She smiled at my brother, her serious demeanor cracking for a moment.

Bran returned the gesture, giving Bec a goofy grin.

Dôn crossed the square to greet us.

"Ancient Dôn," Bran called.

Dôn and I exchanged a glance, both of us suppressing a chuckle.

"We are pleased to accompany you on the voyage south," he added.

"Very well, Prince Bran," Dôn said with a smirk. "We are ready, are we not? Bec?"

"Yes, Mother. We are ready."

"Then let's be off," Dôn said.

Grainne helped Dôn climb into the wagon.

Bec and Tatha mounted their horses.

The other priestesses and the children gathered to wave farewell.

Bran directed the men, sending four of them to ride at the front, two in the back. Bec and Bran reined their horses toward one another, the pair taking a spot at the back of the group. I rode Druda alongside the wagon.

"Blessed morning to you, Dôn," I told her.

"Boudica," she said with a laugh. "Now, tell me, how did you manage to convince your father to let you come?"

"It was Bran's doing. Although, I think my father was trying to save me from Saenunos's plotting."

Dôn chuckled. "Let him plot all he wants. All things come to pass as the goddess wills."

"Let us hope that what the goddess wills is good for us," I said, giving Dôn a knowing look.

"How do we know what is good for us, Boudica? Sometimes the things we want so desperately are the things that end up hurting us the most. And, sometimes, the things we ignore are the things we need. We mortals are fools. When you reach my age, *ancient* as I am, you will see. Our vision is clearest when we look backward. How many things I wanted were repaid with sorrow?"

"Then I'll be sure to want nothing henceforth," I told her.

"If only it were that easy," Dôn said, then turned serious. "Want makes us hungry. Remember that. Patience. In all things, patience."

I gave her a smile. "Yes, *ancient one*."

Dôn laughed, then shook her head.

I cast a glance back at Bran and Bec. Bec reached out and touched my brother's newly trimmed curls.

Want.

Very soon, the question of what Bran and Bec wanted would have to be faced. I only hoped my brother could win Andraste's blessing. But as Dôn warned, we are all the victims of want.

CHAPTER 53

The ride south took most of the day. While my father, uncle, and sister would travel directly to Venta, the seat of King Prasutagus, Dôn wanted to go on to Arminghall Henge where the rites would be held. The nemeton was the holy site just outside the city of Venta. There, we would all gather—the chieftains and their families, the holy people, and the common people of both the Northern and Greater Iceni—to celebrate Beltane.

"My work is at the nemeton," Dôn had told Bran. "There is nothing in Venta that interests me."

It was nearly sundown when we arrived. The vast, grassy plains surrounding the nemeton were filled with people. Camps had been set up everywhere. Bonfires burned brightly. The sound of music filled the air. Drums, horns, and lutes sounded as people danced around the fires. I heard rowdy cheers, and everyone was drinking. On the banks of the River Tas, men—stripped down until they were practically nude— spun fire. Everyone's faces had been painted with blue woad or other chalk designs.

Now I knew what Dôn had meant about the pull of Beltane.

With each beat of the drum, I felt it myself. Yearning washed over me, and suddenly, I felt lonely for Gaheris. The gods were awake. The Horned Lord was calling. As my eyes danced over the fire-spinners, I felt the prick of that call most keenly. Sweat dampened my back. My eyes lingered for a long time on a young man dressed only in breeches, his dark hair pulled back from the temples. His body moved gracefully as he spun the fire around him, the trail of it leaving echoes in the darkness. He wove spirals and the never-ending pattern of the double-disc. I exhaled deeply, trying to blow out the feeling, then turned away, my eyes drifting to the shrine.

On the hill nearby, sitting at the crossroads between the Tas and Yare rivers, was the nemeton. Like our hillfort, deep ditches surrounded the shrine. In the center of the rise were tall timbers arranged in a crescent shape, high as five men, reaching into the sky. A fire burned at the center of the shrine.

"There," Dôn called, pointing for us to ride closer to the shrine.

We picked our way through the encampment. In one corner of the field, a group of men engaged in a game of javelin throwing. I watched as one man cast his spear so far downfield it was lost to sight. His comrades cheered loudly. We passed a row of women sitting with pots of woad painting symbols on revelers.

Riding beyond the camps, we passed through a busy marketplace. Vendors sold a dizzying array of wares. From skins to jewels to dogs to food to horses, everything a person could imagine was on sale. Beyond them, in a makeshift square, someone had erected a maypole. The tall shaft of wood reached into the night. A crown of flowers encircled the pinnacle of the pole. Bright-colored ribbons had been strung from the top. Already, maidens my own age were dancing barefooted around it.

"Look," Grainne said, pointing to the maypole. "What great fun!"

"The Father God's phallus, erect and alert, reaches toward the maid of the sky," Dôn said. "It is in Cernunnos's honor that they dance, coaxing out his fertility—whether they know that or not," she added with a laugh.

Grainne's wide eyes twinkled with excitement.

Turning my horse, I joined Bran and Bec.

"Well?" Bran asked, a smirk on his face.

"Well, what?"

Bran laughed, then gestured around us.

"The May rites Belenus leads at Oak Throne are rather tame by comparison," I said finally.

Bran chuckled. "That's an understatement. This is nothing. They've only started drinking. Soon, things will get…interesting. You must be wary, Sister. Some say you are very pretty…"

"*Some* say?" I asked indignantly.

Bran gave me a playful wink.

"Leave her be," Bec told Bran with a knowing grin. "None of us know what the gods have planned for us."

Bran raised an eyebrow at her. "Is that so, Priestess?"

"So it is, Prince."

At Dôn's instruction, we rode to a section of the encampments where other holy people had gathered.

"Dôn," a woman with black-and-silver hair called, moving to meet us. She wore a long, dark blue gown trimmed with silver embroidery. She had painted spirals and twirling triskelion shapes in woad on her forehead. "Fair greetings, sister."

"That is Dindraine," Bec whispered to me. "She is the high priestess of the Catuvellauni."

If the holy people of the Catuvellauni were here, did that mean their brother kings were already here too?

I frowned.

Dindraine went to the side of the wagon and helped Dôn down.

Bran motioned to us to dismount.

"Your people can place your tent here," Dindraine told Dôn, gesturing to an open space nearby. "We have saved you a place."

Dôn inclined her head to Dindraine then motioned to Bran and me.

"Sister," Dôn told Dindraine, "please meet Bran, second son of Aesunos. And this is Boudica, second daughter of the Northern Iceni."

"Well met," she said, inclining her head to us. She turned back to Dôn. "You keep good company."

Dôn passed her a knowing but mirthful look.

Dindraine raised and lowered her eyebrows in reply, then said, "King Caratacus and King Togodumnus are amongst this wild crowd somewhere. They left Princess Imogen in Verulam. For the best, no doubt."

I gave Bran a quick glance.

Dôn nodded. "I am getting too old to ride this far south. This will be my last Beltane at the nemeton. I'll surely be dead by the next one."

"Nonsense," Dindraine said. "Andraste will not let you die. But come, take your rest by the fires anyway. You and your priestesses—and the prince and princess, if they wish."

"Let us see to your tent," Bran told Dôn.

I nodded in agreement. "I'll help."

Dôn chuckled. "These two never just sit. It is against their natures," she said, then waved for us to go on.

"I should join Dôn," Bec whispered to Bran. "I'll find you later?"

Bran nodded to her then turned back to the wagon.

"Great Dindraine," I said, giving the priestess a bow. "I am glad to have met you."

The woman inclined her head to me. "And I, you, Princess."

I flicked my gaze to Dôn, who nodded to me. I left them, joining Bran, who had a worried expression on his face.

"What is it?"

"I can't shake this terrible feeling of dread in my stomach."

"That's just hunger," I said with a laugh. "Let's get the tent up so we can go eat."

Bran laughed. "Do you ever take anything seriously?"

"I take everything far too seriously. Right now, my own stomach is knotting because of *your* sense of dread. Maybe it's better if we ignore all inklings of trouble. I find that serves me better. I push them all down into a tiny invisible ball inside me so I can pretend they don't exist. Losing Gaheris? Pushed down. Forced to marry Caratacus? Pushed down. Father's illness? Pushed down. Prasutagus..." I began, then caught myself. "Anyway, I just keep pushing it down. It works better that way."

"You know what happens when you do that, right?" Bran asked.

I cocked an eyebrow at him.

"Eventually, it will all explode."

"Pressing that comment down with the rest."

"Boudica?" Bran asked.

"Hmm?" I replied, pulling a bundle off the wagon.

"What about Prasutagus are you pushing down?"

Caught. "Nothing."

"But you said—"

"Just Saenunos's war-mongering," I lied.

I turned to find Bran studying me closely. He sighed heavily and sadly.

"I knew it," he said, giving me a sorry look.

"Knew what? There is nothing to know."

"There was a kinship between you and Pras—"

"Say nothing. Nothing. It doesn't matter. He will wed Brenna. He *asked* for Brenna. It doesn't matter."

Bran frowned, then shook his head. "I don't understand it. I'm a man, Boudica. I can see when a man likes a woman, and Prasutagus very clearly liked *you*. It doesn't make any sense."

"Bran," I said, my voice sharp. "You will say nothing more about it. Do you understand me? Nothing. Right now, all that matters is that I find a way to avoid being forced to wed King Caratacus. That is the only thing that matters right now. Go ahead and feel dread about that! Now, let's get to work so we can go eat. Someone was roasting chickens on a spit. Let's get going. Cai?" I called to the warrior lingering nearby. "A hand?"

"Boudica," Bran said, his tone low.

"Not. Another. Word," I told him, then went to the campsite.

The days before me would not be easy. And now that Bran knew… It was easier to pretend I wasn't jealous when it was just me who knew. And Bran's words did nothing to assuage my mind. If anything, now I felt more confused. If Prasutagus had felt something for me as well, then why… No. Not. Another. Word.

Ah, Gaheris. Why did you leave me to all this mess?

CHAPTER 54

B ran and the other warriors busied themselves with setting up the tents. I took the horses to the river for water. I stood patting Druda's neck as I watched the raucous scene in the field. There was so much life. Music drifted across the field. People were singing, cheering, and talking. Everywhere I looked, people were rejoicing. The bonfires grew brighter, higher. The fire-spinners drew sacred shapes in the very air. The presence of the otherworld was so strong here. Everyone seemed to feel it.

But that was only to be expected.

The nemeton sat on the plain above the twin rivers—a crossroads of betwixt and between.

Both the nemeton and the holy day itself were thin places and times. No wonder I felt the pull of the gods.

"What do you think?" I asked Druda as he drank from the river. "Suppose I should go to the market, find that roasted chicken, and have a look around?"

The horse's ear twitched in my direction, his dark eyes picking up the glint of firelight.

"Good. We agree."

I stared at the water, seeing the reflection of the stars overhead and the fires from the spinners who stood upstream. They merged into a collage of color before me: the inky dark blue of the night's sky, the silver shimmer of the stars, the golden red of the fire.

I could just make out my reflection in the water, a dark silhouette framing my shape and my mountain of unruly red hair.

My gaze narrowed when I saw a figure appear behind me in my reflection.

A man.

With horns.

My heart beat quickly.

My spear in hand, I turned. But there was no one there.

I chided myself for somehow drawing the attention of the fey at a time when the veil between the worlds thinned out. I fingered the talisman Ula had given me. "Whatever this is, let it keep the eyes of the fey—especially the piskies—off of me," I said, briefly eyeing the limbs of the trees overhead. "All right, you lot," I said, taking the horses' leads. "That's enough for now. Surely Cai and the others packed some grain for you. Come on."

By the time I brought the horses back, Bran and the others had the tents erected. I tied up the horses then joined my brother.

"Done?" Bran asked.

I nodded.

"Let's go," Bran said. "I've been dreaming of roasted chicken since you mentioned it. And strawberry wine. And sweet bannocks."

"Bec?" I looked back toward the nemeton.

Bran frowned. "I suspect she will be busy for a time. If the gods are kind, I will find her later."

"Cai," Bran called to his friend. "I'll meet you at the ale tent."

Cai waved to Bran, Cai's gaze shifting to me for a brief moment, giving me a smile, then we set off.

Leaving the area where the holy people had gathered, we made our way into the market. As we passed, vendors shouted out to us, selling all manner of goods.

"A new saddle for you, sir?"

"Pretty lady, a bouquet of flowers?"

"A new rug for your home, miss?"

"Young lady. Young lady with the red hair…a jewel for you, my dear? A pin for your hair?" an old woman called to me.

Soon, Bran and I arrived at the tent where the vendor was selling jugs of wine.

"Here," Bran said, giving me a small money pouch. "This is for you."

"Are you giving me coins?" I asked in surprise, weighing the sack.

"Father is giving you coins. I am only the messenger."

"That's a surprise. Let me see the pouch he gave you."

"Why?"

I stuck out my hand, motioning with my fingers for him to hand it over.

With a laugh, Bran complied.

I weighed the two bags in my hand. "As I suspected," I said, giving him back the lighter bag which he'd given to me.

Bran laughed. "Not so quick," he said, switching the bags back. "I have the men to see to. But this is *only* for you. If anyone should be offended by Father's unfair generosity, it's me. Now, go on, my rich sister, and buy us some fresh bannocks," he said, gesturing to the vendor across the way.

With a roll of my eyes, I went on my way. The smell of sweet bread filled the air. The man had a large, flat iron sitting over a fire. He stood flipping the cakes.

"How many you want, Red?"

I chuckled. "A dozen. Sweet ones."

"Oh, pretty girl, everything about me is sweet."

"Would your wife agree?"

At that, he laughed. "Depends on the day...and her mood."

"And your mood has nothing to do with it?"

Chuckling, he wrapped up the cakes.

I handed the man a coin.

He looked it over, spotting my father's image engraved thereon, along with his name. "Northern Iceni?"

I nodded.

"I hear their princess is going to wed King Prasutagus."

"So I've heard," I said, trying but failing to keep the sharp tone out of my voice. "Thank you," I said, then with a wave, left the man.

"Enjoy them, Red."

I turned and rejoined Bran, who was holding three bottles of wine.

"Three bottles? Very nice."

Bran grinned. "I felt thirsty."

"Roasted chicken," I told him, my stomach growling in agreement.

Bran laughed, and we made our way down the thoroughfare once more.

"Give me one of those," I said, taking a jug and pulling out the cork. I took a swig. The taste of the sweet strawberries mixed with the sharpness of the fermentation burned my throat.

When we reached the vendor selling chickens, I bought two, one for each of us. Juggling my purchases, I rejoined Bran.

"Let's go sit," Bran said, directing us toward a bonfire not far from the ale tent.

Settling in on the grass, the bottles of wine and cakes between us, each of us with a whole roasted chicken for ourselves, we ate and watched as some musicians played. Three girls danced, their feet bare, around the fire. They carried long sticks with flowers and ribbons tied at the end, waving them as they danced. One of them paused to play with Bran's curls before pivoting off once more.

Bran stuffed the first bite—more like half of it than an actual bite—of the cakes into his cheek. "Ouch. They're hot," he told me in a muffled voice.

"What do you expect? They just came off the fire," I said, then tore into the chicken, well aware how horrified Brenna would be to find me and Bran sitting in the grass eating like two undignified gluttons. But when the taste of the delicious roasted bird hit my tongue, I couldn't care less what anyone thought.

Drinking wine and eating, Bran and I clapped and cheered for the musicians as they played reel after reel. I had nearly finished one of the bottles of wine—and all the chicken—when Bran's men finally found us.

"Come on, Boudica," Davin, a blond-haired warrior who was the same age as my brother, called, holding out his hand to me.

Rising, I took his hand.

"Your hands are slippery," he complained with a chuckle.

"Chicken," I replied, wiping my hands on my trousers, making everyone laugh.

Giggling, Davin and I joined the others, spinning around the fire. The rich strawberry wine had my head buzzing. Soon, the others in our band joined the merriment, twisting around the roaring fire, dancing to the sound of the drums, flutes, and strings.

We danced until the sweat made my tunic stick to my back. My hair broke free of its proper binds. I stuck the silver brooch into my vest so as not to lose it, then spun with the others, feeling the call of May. I raised my hands above my head and twisted and jumped, the heat from the bonfire reddening my cheeks. Around us, others clapped and cheered.

The fire crackled and popped, sending embers into the sky.

As I twirled, I saw that Bec had joined us. She and Bran were talking, passing a jug of wine between them.

Soon, I became breathless.

"I have to rest," I told Davin, giving him a wave.

The warrior returned the gesture then plucked another pretty maiden from the crowd.

I joined Bran and Bec. "How did you get away?" I asked the priestess.

"Dôn told me to come to join you," Bec said with a smile.

I nodded. That was a good sign.

"Come on," Bran told Bec, and the pair of them joined the other dancers.

Grabbing the last jug of strawberry wine, I left the others and made my way back into the market.

"Pretty girl! You, with hair as red as Bel's fires. Come, let me mark you for the gods," an old woman called to me.

She was sitting on a skin not far from a fire, a collection of pots before her.

I went to the woman, settling in on my knees before her. She was an ancient thing, her face deeply lined. She had long, silver hair. Even in the firelight, I could make out her twinkling blue eyes and the mischievous sparkle therein.

"You are Northern Iceni," she said as she began to stir the blue woad in one of her clay pots.

"How did you know?"

"The gods whisper to me," she said with a laugh.

"All of them or one in particular?"

She laughed. "I like your wit," she told me with a grin. "I shall mark you out so the Stag God finds you this night," she said, then began drawing on my forehead. "He will come to you in human form. His mortal flesh will be drawn to you. You will entrance him, and your flames will singe his heart so he loves no other."

Prankster. I grinned at her. "What am I supposed to do with such a man?"

"Oh," she said, then grinned. "What does any maiden do with the Forest Lord? Don't you know, Boudica of the Northern Iceni?"

At that, I raised an eyebrow at her—not at the suggestion of sex—but at the fact that she knew my name. "I *do* know. I had such a man once. I don't need another."

"Who says we are to have but one love in each life?" she asked as she marked my cheek.

"A real love, a true love…no one gets more than one of those."

"You mean the old magic. The love of lifetimes."

"Yes."

"Never doubt what the Forest Lord can bring you—especially on Beltane," she said, then lifted a small, round piece of polished metal for me to see myself. She had drawn the triskelion at the center of my brow. And beside it, I spotted Ogham staves along with other swirling designs. Below my eyes, on my cheeks, she had drawn other symbols.

I handed her back the looking piece then dipped into my pocket for a coin.

"No need, Princess," she said, stopping my hand. "But I'll take that," she told me, motioning to my wine jug. "I can't remember the last time I had a sip of wine."

"May I buy you a new one? I confess, my brother drank half of it already."

"No doubt he did. Let the prince enjoy the pleasures of life. This wine is enough payment for me."

I gave the jug to her. "Then I thank you, Mother. And I wish you a blessed Beltane."

"And you, Boudica."

I rose. Casting a glance back at the bonfire, I spotted Cai, Davin, and the others still dancing, but Bran and Bec were gone.

Pausing, I turned back to the old woman. "How did you know my na—" I began to ask, but the old woman—and her pots and the wine—were gone.

The hair on my arms rose, and a prickle ran down my spine. The gods were at work tonight. I only hoped they had my best intentions in mind.

CHAPTER 55

F iddle music filled the air along with the pounding of
drums. As I made my way down the festival rows, I
paused to watch the fire spinners. One man thrust a
flaming torch into his mouth only to pull it out still ignited.
Along with the rest of the crowd, I cheered. Others filled their
mouths with alcohol and blew flames like the great dragons of
lore.

I passed the javelin hurlers, then paused to watch some
chariot races. Each chariot had a two-man team. The teams
sprinted down a stretch of green. Around me, people wagered
on their favorite duos, cheering or moaning as the chariot they
were backing crossed the finish line.

I bought myself another jug of wine and paused to dance
along with some other women around a bonfire. This time, I
pulled off my boots to feel the earth below my feet. Dancing
and spinning, I felt the power of the night and let the fires
have their way with me.

A woman worked her way through the crowd, a basket in
her hands. Within, she had crowns of wildflowers and oak

leaves. The branches had been woven together, the new green leaves and colorful meadow flowers making a pretty adornment. I bent my head as she passed, letting her place a crown on my head, then went back to dancing once more.

The gods called me. Round and round I went, my hands in the air, dancing and laughing with the other women. We leaped and spun, the embers of the fire rising into the sky.

As I danced, I spotted a man standing on the other side of the fire. He was tall and firmly built—for a moment, I swore I saw a pair of antlers protruding from his head. But when I spun around that side of the fire once more, he was gone.

Giggling, I carried on with the merriment. We ladies twirled and danced, hopping in the air, whirling. The wine made my mind feel loose. The drumming, the fires, the spirit of the night, everything set my soul on fire.

When I spun again, I spotted the man standing in the shadows watching me, his arms crossed on his chest. Dancing, I made my way around the circle to him, then, on a reckless impulse, I stepped away from the others to see *who* was there.

I stumbled into the shadows only to be met with a familiar face.

"Prasutagus," I said with surprise.

The king lifted a finger to his lips.

I looked around me. No one seemed to notice him.

"How… But…" I said, gesturing around.

"Druid magic," he said with a soft laugh. "They will not know me from a beggar. You, however, saw right through the enchantment."

I smirked at him. "I saw the Horned Lord in the woods."

"No doubt you did," Prasutagus replied with a grin. He looked behind me. "Where is your family? I heard a rumor the Northern Iceni had come, but instead of having the pleasure of your company, I spent all day listening to Caratacus and Togo-dumnus bending the truth and plotting until I got a headache."

"Please, no offense intended. It's just Bran and me. My father and his party will be here soon. They will come directly to Venta. Bran and I rode as an escort with the holy women of the grove."

Prasutagus nodded slowly. "I see. I'm sorry you did not come anyway," he said, a strange, confused expression on his face. His eyes went to the shrine in the distance. "Have you been to the nemeton?"

I shook my head.

Prasutagus smiled lightly. "It is astounding. Magical. But I know of something even better. May I show you?"

"Show me what?"

"If I tell you, that will spoil the surprise," he said with a grin.

I paused a moment. Everything in me told me to go with him. In all this crowd, Prasutagus had found me. Of course I wanted to go with him. But still... he was meant to be my sister's husband. Perhaps I should not. Yet, what was the harm? If Prasutagus had really cast an enchantment on himself, no one would know it was him anyway. And truth be told, my curiosity was piqued.

"Boots," I said, pointing over my shoulder.

He nodded.

I snagged my boots, pulled them on, then rejoined the king. Prasutagus took my hand then led me through the crowd. In the shadows, I discovered Raven, the king's horse, waiting.

"Is the horse enchanted too? One can hardly miss this giant, handsome lad," I said, giving the horse a pat.

Prasutagus chuckled. "The magic extends as far as I wish it."

"Make me look like an ugly, old crone," I told him.

Prasutagus laughed. "Such a thing would be impossible. Beauty like yours would only break through. How else could I find such a firebrand in this crowd? Come on," he said, motioning for me to slip onto the horse.

I slid my foot into the stirrup but wobbled, reminding me that I'd drunk my weight in wine. My woozy head and lack of reason should have been proof enough that I was drunk, but it was my lack of surefootedness in the saddle that reminded me. What was I doing with Brenna's future husband?

Prasutagus held my waist, helping me up. The sensation of his hands on me felt like fire. Once more, I felt the pull Dôn spoke of and again questioned my reason. This could very soon prove to be a bad idea.

Prasutagus mounted behind me. Taking Raven's reins, he clicked to the horse, and we rode off. Prasutagus turned the horse toward the River Yare, and we rode along the bank, passing several camps as we went.

"I spent far more time in these rivers as a boy than my father would have liked. Even before I went to Mona, I discovered that there are many holy places across our land. Some are so old, they are nearly forgotten," he said, then turned the horse toward a stand of trees sitting on the top on the plain in the distance. The sounds of music and laughter grew softer but were still audible. I looked back, watching the fire-spinners. From such a great distance, the artistry of their work was even more evident. The flames lingered in the air, making symbols in the night's sky.

"Look," I told Prasutagus, gesturing. "The fires."

He pulled Raven to a stop then dismounted. Offering me

his hand, he helped me down. We stood side by side, watching the raucous scene below. "Bel is whispering to them, telling them what magic to create. The whole camp is steeped in magic. Even now, I can feel it. The deep tug of our land, our gods. Do you feel it, Boudica?"

"Yes," I whispered.

"The Lord and the Lady call, reminding us what it means to be full of life. To be alive. It was a long, dark winter. But spring has come again, and with it, new life."

I looked up at him. "I was so sorry to hear of your father's passing. Following the death of your wife, this has been a hard year for you."

Prasutagus looked out at the fires in the valley below. The glimmer of the flames made his eyes sparkle. "Yes," he said, then stood in silence for a long time. "But there have been moments of light in the darkness," he said, turning to me. "Such as meeting you."

I stared at him. The look in his eyes told me that Prasutagus felt for me every bit of what I felt for him. But if so, why was he going to marry Brenna?

I looked away. "I… What did you want to show me?"

"Ah. Yes. Come," he said, then we made our way toward the rise, Raven plodding along behind us. "When I was a boy, I found this place by following a hare. The druids later told me it is one of the oldest holy sites in all the land. You will see why."

As we approached the top of the rise, I spotted something in the tall grasses. As we went toward it, I realized it was a half-ring of standing stones. Many of the stones were broken, some missing. But a single stone stood at the very center. And on it had been carved ancient designs. Under the moonlight, I spotted the double-disc shape, a crescent moon, a serpent, and horses—the symbol of the Greater Iceni.

"This is the King Stone," Prasutagus explained, gesturing to the engraved stone. "It looks out over the valley, watching over the Greater Iceni," he said, then gently took hold of my waist, moving me so I could see the view.

The sensation of his touch sent a shiver through my body. From here, I realized, the stone was perfectly aligned to the intersection of the rivers, and beyond that, the nemeton. "It's all in alignment."

"Yes," Prasutagus said. "And two hours ride northwest, another ancient circle of stones. They all stand in a perfect line. There is a path of energy flowing under them all. Can you feel it?" he asked.

"I think so."

"Do this," he said, then moved his arms to his sides, his palms facing the ground. Again, I saw the shadow of horns about his head. A yearning within me contracted so hard, my stomach hurt.

"Prasutagus," I whispered.

"Try it," he told me.

I did as he suggested. After a long moment, I felt the energy he spoke of. A sensation, like the pulse of a beating heart, thumped from the ground. "I feel it," I whispered. Grinning, I looked at Prasutagus. "I *do* feel it. It pulses."

"The lifeblood of our land." Prasutagus held my gaze. He studied my face, then reached out and set his hand on my cheek. "I wondered why you did not come to me at Venta," he whispered, "but now I know. You are my May Queen. Naturally, you would be dancing by the fires amongst our people."

He stepped toward me, setting his hand on my hip, then pulled me close. When he leaned in to kiss me, my mind protested. I knew I shouldn't allow it. My loyalty to my sister demanded I step away. And my heart whispered, in the tiniest voice of protest, Gaheris's name, but I didn't step back. I couldn't. I felt the pull between Prasutagus and me. It was so powerful, I could not resist.

When he set his lips on mine, a thousand emotions flowed over me, but the deep sense of safety, home, and love were the strongest. I had not felt anything like it since Gaheris. But there was more. More. The sense that I belonged with Prasutagus was so deep, I fell into it like falling into the ocean.

His touch felt so right, so familiar. I fell into the kiss, feeling his touch. His mouth had the fruity tang of wine, and I caught the sweet scents of soap and sage on his clothes and body, mixed with the delightful, salty scent of his skin.

My head felt light.

When he pulled back, I swayed, spots of light swimming around my head.

"The gods are whispering," Prasutagus whispered. "I see your face before me in visions—you, but not you. Boudica…"

Involuntarily, I slid my hands down his back and under his tunic, feeling his flesh.

A soft moan escaped my lips.

"Boudica…" he whispered once more, placing kisses on my neck.

The scent of night-blooming jasmine perfumed the breeze. It was warm, and the moon was nearly full. Music drifted up to us from the valley below. The heavy beat of the drum made my body quiver—that and Prasutagus's touch.

I let myself be swept up in the moment. Soon, my hands were roving across his strong back, my tongue tasting his mouth, my body yearning. Amongst the wildflowers in the fields around us, other lovers called. I could just hear their soft moans. In the distance, the drums and flutes sounded out the song of Beltane. The whole world was alive. We were not Boudica and Prasutagus. We were the Forest Lord and the Maiden.

But still… Despite all my want, my love for my sister overshadowed the will of the gods.

I stepped back. "I cannot," I whispered, feeling like I had to break some invisible tie between us to wrench myself away. The gods knew I wanted Prasutagus more than I had desired anything this long, dark year. But I couldn't. It wasn't right.

"Did I… Did I do something wrong?" he asked, a pinch of pain on his face. He reached toward me, taking my hand. "Boudica, what did I do wrong?"

"It's just… I can't do this to Brenna," I said, then shook my head.

"Brenna?"

"Prasutagus, if you feel as I do, *why her*?" I asked, unable to hide the pain in my voice.

Prasutagus stared at me for a very long time, saying nothing.

"Will you not answer me? Why didn't you ask for *me*?" I said with far more passion than I had intended, the words coming out in a sorrowful moan, all of my pent-up despair finally breaking loose.

Prasutagus set his hand on my cheek and met my gaze. "You must explain to me. Who is Brenna?"

"Who is… Who is Brenna?"

He nodded.

I lifted my hand slowly, covering my mouth. Brenna had not been in Oak Throne when Prasutagus had come. Nor had she gone to Venta as a child. King Antedios was old, forgetful. Could it be…

"Brenna is my elder sister to whom your father and mine arranged your betrothal."

"You have... you have a... Brenna?"

"Yes! Your father arranged for you to wed my elder sister."

"No," Prasutagus said, then stepped back. "No. That's not right. I spoke to my father of the princess of the Iceni. I told my father about you, Boudica. I told him how, after many months of darkness, I felt a spark of life once more in your eyes. My father didn't tell me his plans. He made the arrangements with King Aesunos. Only once the matter was settled did he tell me he had made the arrangement. My father arranged the marriage as a last kindness to me. A chance for me to love again..."

"Your father agreed to wed you to my elder sister. My father comes with Brenna in a matter of days. Brenna is expecting to become your wife!"

"By the gods," Prasutagus whispered. "Boudica, I swear by the sun, moon, and stars, by all the gods, I believed I had asked for your hand. You, whose face I know across a hundred lifetimes," he said in a broken voice, reaching out to touch my cheek once more. "You, who my heart knows already."

"You are betrothed to my sister," I said in a soft moan.

"No. It cannot be. I will fix this."

"How? How, without offending my father? Without making him and you look like fools? How, without dishonoring our people and your father's words? How can you fix this? How can this be undone?"

"I..." Prasutagus began, then stopped.

"How?" I whispered again, this time praying he had an answer. Maybe he could think of something I could not. Because there was no way. If Prasutagus insulted my father,

Saenunos would finally get his wish. He would be proven right. And I knew what would happen then.

"The druids..." Prasutagus whispered. "I will speak to the druids." Prasutagus cupped my face in his hands. "It is the old love between us," he whispered. "I can see in your eyes that you loved another before me. And I can see that he is lost to you. But *we* are not lost to one another. We are here now, tonight, under the moon and the eyes of the gods. I promise you, Boudica, I will fix this. I will have no other in this world but you. I know you," he said. "I *know* you," he whispered again, then leaned in and kissed me once more.

And while my mind still shrieked protests, I believed Prasutagus's words. He would fix this. He would make it right. We would be together. We had to be.

When Prasutagus moved to lift me, I didn't resist. Moving carefully, he took me to a spot amongst the wildflowers and tall grasses under the watchful eye of the King Stone then lay me down gently. With the light of the moon on him, I reached up and gently undid the straps on his vest, pushing it off, then pulled his shirt over his head, revealing a muscular chest that had been tattooed with a myriad of swirling designs. I pulled off my riding vest and tunic, then slipped out of my trousers and undergarments. Prasutagus did the same. Soon, we were swathed only in the moonlight.

We would find a way to make this right. There had been a mistake. That was all. Prasutagus and I wanted one another. We belonged together. It was the will of the gods. On this night, we were the Forest Lord and the Maiden. We were one. We fell into one another's embrace. I kissed his bare skin, tasting the salty tang of sweat on his skin. I nuzzled his neck as his hands stroked my back then cupped my breasts. My skin prickled, naked under the moonlight. Prasutagus groaned in my ear, awakening a deep longing with me. Our hungry mouths roved each other's bodies. In the fields below, drums played. But the forest also spoke. From the clutch of trees, I heard the call of an owl. The moon shone brightly, and the stars danced.

My arms wrapped around him, our bodies melded together. My mind recalled Gaheris for a fleeting moment. But I let him go. At this moment, there was only Prasutagus. And while this was the first time our flesh had met in this life, a deep sense of the familiar washed over me.

He was right.

We were not strangers.

I had known this man before.

A hundred lifetimes.

Always, him.

A voice whispered from deep within me.

Always.

Him.

CHAPTER 56

It was the grey hour before dawn when I finally woke. My head was aching. I opened my eyes slowly to find myself lying in the tall grass, curled up against Prasutagus. Raven stood dozing nearby.

At some point during the night, Prasutagus must have covered us with his cape. I stared down at his sleeping face. His long, red lashes lay on his cheek, where a smattering of freckles decorated his face. Two emotions gripped me at once: pure joy and despair. I felt filled with love in a way I hadn't since Gaheris. My spirit felt light and happy. As I gazed down on Prasutagus, I saw a future unfurl before me that filled me with hope. And at the same time, grief, despair, and regret gripped me. This man was intended to marry my sister. My sister. What if the wedding could not be undone? What if I had bedded the man who would become my sister's husband? The deep shame and reality of that betrayal filled me with regret. How could I do such a thing to Brenna?

I sat up slowly.

The camp below was still quiet. The others had not yet

woken, but I could sense the sunrise coming. My gaze shifted to the nemeton. There, I saw the druids stirring. They would perform the morning sunrise rites. Even from this distance, I could see them banking up the fires.

It would not do for Prasutagus and me to be found naked in the field.

And yet, the thought of leaving him was unbearable.

What if he was unable to find a way to fix this?

My father would never forgive the insult. Saenunos would use it as the excuse he needed. Everything would go wrong.

And what of Brenna? What would my sister say when I explained there had been a mistake? The shame she would feel... I loved her. I never wanted her to feel pain. But surely Brenna would not want to be married to a man who did not love her, a man who had wanted me?

I cast my gaze to the King Stone. There was an odd shimmer around the stone. And for a moment, I thought I heard the murmur of voices.

"Boudica..." Prasutagus whispered sleepily.

I turned to find him looking at me.

Smiling gently, he reached out and touched my hair, wrapping a curl around his finger.

I looked back toward the stone.

"Do you hear that?" I whispered.

He sat up, his gaze following mine.

After a long moment, he nodded. "The gods are awake. I have been hearing them for days. Soon, it will begin."

"What will begin?"

Prasutagus shook his head. "A change in seasons for our people. I've had many dreams. There are omens and signs."

I nodded. "Yes. I have seen them too. The greenwood whispers to me. And occasionally, knocks me out of trees," I said with a light laugh.

Prasutagus reached out and touched the amulet hanging from my neck. "Is that why you have this?"

"I don't know why I have that. But I trust the one who put it there."

"Let me guess. The wisewoman from your fort?"

"Yes."

Prasutagus's fingers danced from the talisman to the frog pendant. He touched it gently. "A gift?"

I nodded but said nothing more. Gaheris would never be forgotten. No one would ever take the space in my heart that belonged to him alone.

Prasutagus touched my chin. "I promised you last night. I will promise you again. I will make this right. My father had the best heart. He wanted me to be happy, but he was very old and often confused." Prasutagus shook his head. "As I have wed you in the greenwood, I will make you my queen," he said, then leaned in and placed a kiss on my lips.

Hope lodged in my heart. I would have this man. He would be mine.

We would find a way.

❦

ONCE THE SUN HAD RISEN, PRASUTAGUS AND I REDRESSED.

"I must go back to Venta. I will speak to the druids as soon as possible," Prasutagus told me.

"Bran will be wondering where I have gone."

Prasutagus nodded.

"When shall we meet again? Tonight? Here?" I asked.

"Yes," Prasutagus nodded as he fastened his cloak. "In

thunder, lightning, or in rain. When the hurlyburly's done. Your father's druid…"

"Belenus."

"Belenus. What influence does he have on the king?"

I paused for a moment, feeling conflicting loyalties, then said, "Little. He is more of a family friend. It is Dôn to whom my father will listen. Dôn made my father promise not to wed me to anyone until Beltane," I said, then paused as a terrible realization washed over me. "Prasutagus… there has been talk between my family and the Catuvellauni."

Prasutagus grew still. "What kind of talk?"

"That they… My uncle would see me wed to Caratacus."

"By the gods," Prasutagus said gruffly. "Is anything agreed upon?"

"I'm not sure. They planned to talk here."

Prasutagus frowned heavily. "It makes no difference. I will have you as my wife, Boudica. Nothing will stand in my way." He kissed me once more, then turned to mount Raven, but paused. "I don't like leaving you on your own here. I can call up the enchantment—"

"I'm fine. I can see my way," I said, pointing back across the river. "And I have my spear."

He chuckled lightly. "So I noticed. Very well. Tonight, then?"

I nodded.

After a moment, Prasutagus rode off.

I sat in the field, watching the mist rise off the twin rivers.

It had all been a mistake. He hadn't wanted Brenna.

Prasutagus *did* feel for me what I'd felt for him.

It was all a misunderstanding.

But how could he explain that to my father? And to

Brenna? How could he explain it in such a way that Saenunos wouldn't pounce the moment he heard the news?

I wrapped my arms around my stomach. But we had to try. When Gaheris died, I thought I would never love again. I thought there was no future left for me. But now... I didn't care about being Queen of the Greater Iceni. I just wanted Prasutagus.

I was startled when the grass rustled beside me. A moment later, a woman plopped down at my side.

I reached for my spear but paused. Something about this woman was so familiar. She had a foxtail clipped in her wild blonde locks and woad on her face. It seemed impossible, but I swore I recognized her from my visions.

"What's that, then?" she asked, pointing to the camps below.

"The Beltane festival," I replied, eyeing her battered armor. She wore twin swords on her back and had at least three daggers in her boots. But there was something odd about her clothes. The style was unfamiliar, old-fashioned.

"The Beltane festival. Where?"

"You don't know where you are?"

"Sure I do. Ye just told me. The Beltane festival."

"Where did you come from?"

She pointed over her shoulder. When I followed her gesture, I found myself looking at the King Stone—and beyond, to a mound that sat some distance away. Both the stone and the mound had a golden glow.

"Wait, are you saying—"

"What rivers are those?" she asked, pointing.

"The Tas and Yare. You are in the lands of the Greater Iceni."

"All right," she said, then rose, sticking her hand out to me.

"Come on, Boudica. I'm hungry. 'Bout time for the morning meal, isn't it? Feels like I haven't eaten in a hundred years."

"Who are you?" I asked, bewildered.

She paused a moment. "I don't quite remember," she said with a shrug, then laughed. "But they call me Pix the Fox. Let's go."

"Wait, you don't know your own name, but you know *my* name? How?"

Again, she gestured over her shoulder.

"I…" I began, but I didn't know what to say.

Pix strolled down the hill toward the river. "Get off yer arse, Red. Can't expect me to be of much use to ye if I'm half starved."

"Of much use for what?"

"Fighting Romans, of course."

CHAPTER 57

Confused, I hurried after her. "What do you mean, fighting Romans?"

We made our way down the hill, across the plain, and back into the market.

Pix eyed the place with curiosity. "I smell fish. Bit early for fish. Suppose anyone has honey cakes? Even a good porridge would do. My head is aching. Suppose yers is too, by the look and smell of ye."

"Smell?"

Pix laughed. "Ye smell like a bottle of wine...and sex."

"I..."

She laughed louder, her nose crinkling up. "Oh, don't worry. It's the fox nose," she said, tapping the tip of her nose. "No one else will know ye played the role of the Maiden in the green last night—except the fey, of course. But they're a nosey lot. There," she said, pointing. "Porridge with currants and nuts. Just like my mum used to make."

She hurried toward one of the vendor tents. It was still early, the sun barely risen. The merchants had just started opening their shops, but those selling food were already at work stoking their fires or frying breads.

I followed quickly behind Pix—why, I had no idea. I didn't know this woman. And yet...

Pix went to a woman stirring a massive cauldron full of porridge.

"Do ye have currants in there?" Pix called.

"So I do," the woman replied.

"We'll have two bowls," Pix told her, then motioned to me.

I raised an eyebrow at her.

"Come on and pay the woman," she told me impatiently.

I half-laughed-half-sighed, then did as she asked. The woman handed us two bowls and spoons.

"Go on by the fire, girls," the old woman said. "It's early still, and there's a chill in the air."

Taking her advice, we went to the fire and stood eating.

"Mmm," Pix groaned happily. "I'd forgotten the taste. Real food, not fairy dust and sparkles," she told me, then called to the woman, "Just like my mum used to make."

The woman smiled and nodded at her but kept stirring.

Pix looked back at me. "You've got grass in your hair," she said, pointing with her chin.

"Who..." I paused, plucking some clover from my long locks. "What's all this about, then?"

"More grass," Pix said, pointing with her spoon.

Irritated, but also grateful, I plucked the rest of the grass from my hair. "You didn't answer my question."

"Yes, I did. I'm here to help ye. Ula told ye I was coming. At least, that's what they told me."

"Ula..."

Pix nodded. "They said ye'd need a sword at your side. Someone who knows how to fight Romans. That's me. Yesterday, I was chasing Caesar until Caesar chased me into a mound," she said, then laughed loudly.

The old woman stirring the porridge gave Pix a questioning look but turned back to her work.

"Caesar?" It had been a hundred years since Caesar had been on our shores.

"Wasn't really Caesar's fault I got stuck, though," Pix said, then shrugged. "Should have known better than to accept that invitation to stay. My stomach is to blame," she said, then pointed her spoon at me. "Do not accept faerie gifts," she said, punctuating each word with a spoon jab. "They've nearly had ye once or twice thanks to that mouth of yers."

My skin rose in gooseflesh as the mad woman's story began to take shape.

"Banshees be cursed," I whispered under my breath. "Is it true then? You fought Caesar?" I asked.

Pix nodded, then frowned at her empty bowl. "Ye going to finish that?" she asked, looking at my porridge.

I shook my head.

She took my bowl from me, trading me for her empty vessel. "I was on the coast with the druids. I saw the eagle try to come ashore. More ships than bubbles in seafoam. But the gods would not have it. The waves rose up and smashed Caesar's boats. What men did get on land, I killed. At least, as many as I could. I tracked Caesar until he reached the Thames," Pix said, pointing in a westerly direction. "Was a mighty battle then. He brought along so many men—and elephants. Ever see such creatures? Giant things. Can't outfox them. Did what I could, but when it was time to run, that's what I did. I hid in a mound. That's where the real trouble began. I decided to stay in those rose-covered gardens for a bit. But then they told me my sword—and my nose—were needed to protect the queen. So, they sent me out of faerie land to ye, Red."

"I'm no queen."

She smirked. "Not yet."

"Mad talk," the woman stirring the porridge said under her breath.

I gestured for Pix to finish her food then collected her bowl, returning both to the woman.

"Beware of mad things," the vendor told me in a low voice, "especially on Beltane."

"Thank you for the kind warning," I replied, inclining my head to her, then turned to go, Pix falling into step with me.

The narrow streets of the festival were drenched in fog that rolled off the nearby rivers. But at the nemeton above the valley, fires burned. I could hear voices calling in the mist as the others woke for another day of revelry in honor of Bel.

I turned to Pix. "I don't know why you're here, but there are no Romans in Briton now. At least, not the way you mean. There are vendors in the shanty port of Londinium selling wine and oils. And there are a few Romans who live peacefully amongst the Cantiaci and the Regni, but they are of no consequence. There is no threat here now."

"Wrong," Pix said, then pulled her sword. "Ye shall see. Now, I need to get this blade sharpened and my armor repaired if I'm going to be of any use to ye. I'll find ye later, Red," she said, then turned, disappearing down one of the foggy side lanes.

"Pix?" I called.

"Red as strawberry wine," Pix called in singsong in reply. "I'll find ye!" She disappeared into the mist.

I stood still for a moment, trying to understand what in the world had just happened.

As the porridge maker suggested, she was no doubt a madwoman.

But then…

Turning, I made my way back toward our camp. It was Beltane. The greenwood was awake. I fingered the amulet hanging from my neck. I didn't know why Ula had given it to me, but if she'd been trying to keep fey eyes off me, she'd failed.

Or, the amulet was intended to do precisely the opposite, calling up some ancient warrior from the Otherworld to be my protector.

Or…the amulet had brought me to my king.

Only the gods knew what Ula had intended.

As the events of the night before replayed in my mind, a sick feeling rocked my stomach. I loved Brenna. I loved her with all of my heart. I would never want to hurt her…but there had been a mistake. That was all. How in the name of all the gods would I ever be able to fix it?

Andraste.

Dark Lady.

If you are listening, I need your help. Help me find a way to bring me to my love. Please.

In a tree overhead, a raven cawed at me then flew off toward the nemeton.

I hoped it was a sign, because if I had any hope of ever being with Prasutagus, it might take all the gods to make it happen.

CHAPTER 58

By the time I made my way back to the tents, Bec and the other priestesses were gone. I slipped into the tent to redress for the day. Pix—whoever she was—was right. My hair was a mess. It was apparent I had not spent the night in my cot. I dipped into the bag Brenna had prepared for me, feeling a sting of guilt in the process, and pulled out a fresh tunic and other clothes, then redressed. I pulled my long, curly locks into a braid. Once I was properly washed up and hopefully not smelling like *anything* anymore, I made my way back outside.

At the tent beside ours, I spotted Bran talking to a tall, dark-haired stranger. The man was nicely dressed in brown leather trousers and an embossed leather jerkin with a green cloak pinned at the shoulder. He wore a thick neck-ring, and his eyes were darkened with coal. Strapping my spear on my back, I approached.

"Ah, here is my sister," Bran said in a very *correct* voice. "Finally awake, sister? Boudica, come join us."

Something inside me began to panic. My heart started beating faster. Who was this person?

A moment later, Cai and Davin passed leading the horses. When Druda caught sight of me, he whinnied loudly.

"Good morning to you too," I called to him, then joined my brother and the stranger.

The stranger grinned at me. "Your horse gets a 'good morning' before your brother?"

My gaze flicked toward Bran. He was smiling pleasantly, but I could see he was not altogether happy.

"My brother doesn't have to carry my weight across Iceni lands."

The man chuckled.

Bran shook his head then said, "Boudica, may I introduce King Togodumnus of the Catuvellauni."

Banshees be cursed.

I inhaled deeply, collecting myself, then bowed to him. "Merry met this Beltane season, King Togodumnus," I said, inclining my head politely.

"And to you, Princess Boudica," King Togodumnus said.

"The king came to speak with his druids when he happened upon our camp," Bran explained.

"I hadn't known the Northern Iceni had already arrived," Togodumnus said.

"It is only Bran and me. We came as escort to our ladies of the holy grove," I replied.

"So your brother explained," Togodumnus said with a nod. The king's eyes lingered on me, eyeing me up and down. His gaze halted on my breasts. "Your uncle has told us of your beauty, Princess. He was not boastful in his words. Caratacus and I have been in Venta with Prasutagus. We hope your father will arrive soon. I know my brother is eager to talk to King Aesunos," he said, then finally lifted his gaze to meet my eyes.

I said nothing, simply willed the rage inside me to be still. My imagination conjured up images of me poking his unwelcomed gaze out with the sharp end of my spear. Perhaps the king felt something of my sentiment because his eyes went to the weapon.

"Saenunos mentioned your wild beauty, but he didn't mention you were also a warrior woman," he said with a condescending chuckle.

"The spear is just a precaution. At times, men's eyes rove where they have no business. The spear serves as a reminder that I have no patience for such behavior."

King Togodumnus coughed lightly. "I see." He turned to Bran. "I look forward to talking with you further, Prince Bran. Perhaps we can share an ale tonight. My brother and I are setting up camp on the ridge," he said, pointing off in the distance.

"Sounds good. I hope we cross paths again," Bran replied politely.

King Togodumnus turned to me once more. "Princess," he said, inclining his head.

"King Togodumnus," I replied, returning the gesture.

With that, the king left us.

Standing side by side, Bran and I watched him go.

"I hope he got your *point*," Bran said.

I huffed a laugh.

"Should I ask where you were last night?"

"Should I ask where *you* were last night?" I replied.

Bran laughed. "Best no one asks anyone anything, then."

"Agreed."

"Bec is already back at the nemeton. We're going to the horse races. Want to come?"

I shook my head.

Bran looked up at the sun. "Hours are wasting. Once the others arrive, our fun will be done."

"Bran…" I began, but I wasn't sure what to say. In the days to come, my actions may tear my family apart. Perhaps it was better to say nothing. Maybe the matter could be quietly resolved by the druids. I had to have faith. Leaving the issue with Prasutagus aside, instead, I said, "Have fun. Don't wager all your coin."

"Stop worrying about my coin."

I laughed, then waved to my brother, who departed.

I turned my gaze in King Togodumnus's wake. If the king's behavior foreshadowed what I could expect from his brother, I needed to pray to the gods and quickly. Because the truth was, I had given my heart to Prasutagus. I hadn't thought such a thing was even possible after Gaheris's death, but it was. And now that it was given, no one could force me to place it elsewhere.

CHAPTER 59

A fter Bran had gone, I went to find Druda. When he
saw me, he snorted in frustration.

"What's the matter? Lots of pretty mares about,
and we have you tied to a post? Poor young man," I said,
giving him a pat.

I pulled out the horse's bridle and readied him. Leaving the
saddle behind, I slid on. We rode first to the river where I
dismounted and led Druda to drink. I leaned against him,
watching the excitement in the distance. Two tall bonfires had
been lit in the field nearby. The local farmers were herding
their livestock through the flames. Two druids called prayers,
blessing the animals as they passed. Even at Oak Throne,
Belenus performed such rites, blessing the herd animals.

"Come on," I told Druda. "Let's get Bel's and Epona's
blessings on you."

Leading the horse, I joined the others.

"Come along. Come along. Run them between Bel's fires,"
one of the men called, directing the flow of traffic as people

brought their animals for blessings. He motioned to a young man who sent his small flock of sheep between the flames.

On the other side, a druid stood with his arms raised. He had a branch from an apple tree in his hand. He swished it before the animals as they passed, making signs in the air.

Druda eyed the bonfires warily, snorting and stomping his foot nervously.

"What, don't want to produce a brood of offspring this season?" I asked with a laugh, stroking Druda's face to calm him.

"Some animals don't take to the fires," one of the men, who was leading a white heifer, told me. "The flames spook them."

Druda snorted once more.

With a sigh, I grabbed a handful of mane then hoisted myself onto Druda's back. "Fine. We'll go together."

The man with the heifer laughed. "You ride him through, he won't be the only one who gets Bel's fertility blessings. Be careful."

I chuckled. "As long as I don't jump the fires later, I should be all right," I replied, referring to the tradition of maidens removing their undergarments and jumping over an open flame to catch a lightning seed.

The man laughed.

"All right, you big baby. If a sheep can pass through, so can you," I told Druda. "Let's go," I added, coaxing the horse between the roaring bonfires.

On the other side, the druid in his dark robes chanted out his prayers as Druda and I approached.

Epona, bless Druda. Keep him healthy and strong.

Bel, bless Druda. Help him to sire fine offspring.

May you both be praised this Beltane.

"Easy," I whispered to the horse, gently patting his neck as I guided him through.

On the other side, the druid spoke in a language I didn't know and made signs in the air before us. Then, he said, "Merry met, maiden. May Bel's blessings be upon you both," the druid called, gesturing with his branch.

"Thank you, wise one," I said, inclining my head to him, then patted my horse. "You see," I told Druda. "All that prancing and snorting over nothing. Come on," I said, then clicked to him.

We sauntered into the market. As we went, I spotted many vendors and tents, people selling a wide variety of skins, metalworking, and even animals. Another trader was peddling spices, oils, and wine that were distinctly Roman.

"A jar of garum, young lady?" the vendor called. "Something for your kitchens?"

I shook my head then rode on until I reached the horse market. Dismounting, I led Druda behind me until we found a spot along the fence. In the corral, a man was leading a young mare for the audience to take a look. Soon, the bidding would begin.

"What do you think, Father?" the young man beside me asked the man at his side.

"The bid will start at five silvers," the auctioneer called.

"Price is right," the father said.

I shook my head. "She's too thin," I told the pair. "At her age, she should be more robust. Could be underfed. More likely, she has some ailment and doesn't want to eat or can't keep anything in her. I'd wait."

The elder looked to me, eyeing over my clothes, his gaze going briefly to Druda.

"Northern Iceni?" he asked.

I nodded.

"They're good horse folk," the man told his boy, then turned to me. "Obliged."

I eyed the beasts waiting at the other end of the pen. "The white one with the grey mane and tail," I said, gesturing with my chin. "See her prancing, and she's as thick as my belly after Yule meal. That's the one you want."

The young man chuckled. "What do you think, Father?"

"She is a pretty one, and, no doubt, will cost a pretty price."

"Pray to Epona, my friends. She will bring you what you need. But put your silver on that white mare if you can. She'll bring you luck," I said, then inclined my head to them. "Beltane blessings…"

"And to you," the elder of the pair called.

Leading Druda, I went back into the marketplace. As we went, I eyed the goods being sold. There was the usual fare of leather goods, household items, and food. But a vendor selling rare spices, cloths, and stones caught my attention. Everything on his table looked like it had come from afar. Perhaps… I went to the man.

"What can I offer you today, maiden?" the man asked in an unfamiliar accent.

"Maybe the answer to a mystery," I said, pulling the coin Tristan had found from my pocket. "I've come upon a coin from a tribe I don't know. It's an odd hobby, to be sure, but I have an interest in coins. You seem to have traveled the world far and away. Do you recognize it?" I asked, handing the man the coin.

He eyed it carefully, looking it over. He stroked his long, silver beard as he considered. It was then I noticed he had small bells attached to the braids in his beard—curious man, indeed. "I have seen this coin somewhere," he said. "In Gaul. Yes. That is where I have seen it."

"In Gaul?"

He nodded then handed the coin back to me.

"What tribe? Do you recall?"

"Menapii," he said. "I was with them at the harvest fest."

Inhaling slowly, I nodded. "Menapii. Thank you, sir." I looked over his wares, spotting a small polished metal, suitable to catch your reflection, trimmed with glass beads and gemstones. It occurred to me that Melusine might like to make such a thing if she had a model. I lifted the piece. "I'll take this."

"Very good. Two silver," the man said, meeting my gaze.

We both knew he was asking far more than the piece was worth. I was paying, not just for the piece, but also for the information.

I handed the man the coins. "Thank you for your help."

"And for you for your purchase," he said, bowing to me. "Remember, maiden. Coins travel. That is their nature."

I inclined my head to him. Slipping the piece into my pocket, I turned away from the vendor.

Menapii. They were a large tribe in Gaul near the coast. Had they sailed to Northern Iceni territory? Why? What would they want from us? I frowned. Perhaps the vendor was right. Maybe the Menapii coin had come in the pocket of someone not from that tribe at all. I carried Greater Iceni and Catuvellauni coins in my own pouch. The mystery of what had happened to Gaheris always seemed just beyond my reach. But something told me that one day, I would discover the truth.

With a heavy sigh, Druda and I made our way through the fair. Soon, we spotted the horse races.

"Let's go," I told Druda.

Spectators lined up to watch as a pair of racers made ready at the starting line. The sprint was not a long one, no longer than any stretch of beach Druda and I had raced against Gaheris and Mountain. A man came before the two riders. After a moment's pause, he waved a flag. The horses took off, speeding down the field in front of us, mud flying in clumps behind them.

The bay stallion and his rider had easily taken the win. The winner went to the far end of the field to wait alongside what I presumed to be the other winners.

"Come along, come along," the race master called. "Another pair? Let's have it? One more pair willing to race this morning?"

Druda snorted.

"All right," I said with a sigh. "But I'm not even in a saddle."

A cheer from the crowd rang out.

Another rider, a young man with wild, blond hair riding a sorrel stallion, came forward. He was dressed in the fashion of the Catuvellauni, his eyes smudged with kohl.

"Come on, Druda. We can take him," I told the horse, then turned to the game master. "We'll race," I called.

The man laughed. "Very well! Welcome, Red. Welcome. Welcome. Epona's blessings on you. It's a coin to race, young lady."

I dipped into my pocket, fingering out a coin, then took my spot opposite the sorrel.

I smiled at the rider, but he gave me a stern look.

"What's the matter with you?" I asked.

He huffed. "Hardly a race riding against a girl. Fine horse or not."

447

"Then why are you bothering?"

"My sorrel will win me the prize."

"If you're so confident, why complain?"

The man shook his head.

"Complaining about racing a girl," I protested loudly to Druda. "Wonder what Epona thinks of that?"

"Boudica!" I heard a voice call.

I turned to find Grainne, Tatha, and Dôn watching. Grainne waved to me.

Catching Dôn's eye, I gave her a mischievous grin, which she returned in kind, then waved for me to pay attention.

The race master stood before us. "First to cross the finish line is the winner. The winner will join the others, and we'll have one final group race."

Tucking in my knees, I leaned down and braced myself.

"Come on, Druda. Let's show that sorrel what you're made of."

"Three… two… one…" The race master waved the flag.

I was glad I had made ready, because Druda, understanding the game afoot, took off like lightning. Laughing, I held on tight.

Druda raced across the green, his feet barely touching the earth as we covered the stretch of the racetrack in a blink of an eye. Soon, we passed the finish line.

"Red on the dapple-grey is our winner!" the race marshal called.

"Well done, my friend. Well done," I said, clapping Druda on the neck.

Druda pranced in a circle.

I turned back to the man on the sorrel, who looked even grouchier than before. "*Now* I know why you didn't want to race. Not much fun when you know you're going to lose," I said gingerly, making the man scowl harder, then Druda and I joined the other winners.

The race attendants lined the riders up at the start. The horses around me snorted and pranced in anticipation.

Druda, still excited from his last win, was raring to go.

"Now, we shall race to crown our winner," the marshal called to the crowd then turned to us. "May Epona grant your horses speed and surefootedness. On my mark," the marshal called then went to the side. He whistled, capturing all of our attention. "Ready?" he shouted, his voice lingering on the wind.

"Come on, Druda," I whispered. "We can do this." I leaned in.

Druda's withers shivered.

"Three... two... one... Race!"

The horse beside me reared, losing its rider the moment the race began.

Druda set off. Sprinting quickly, he made his way across the green.

Out of the corner of my eye, I saw the others closest to me fall behind, but I kept my focus. I held on tightly, feeling Druda's powerful body pounding across the earth.

Bearing down on the finish line, I tapped his side lightly. "Now. Now!"

Druda blasted forward.

"Winner. Winner! We have our winner. The blue dun takes the win. The dapple-grey takes second!"

I scanned down the line.

There, a young man with short, dark hair pumped his arm in jubilance. The crowd clapped and whistled in cheer. He, too, was Catuvellauni. He was dressed similarly to the man I'd beaten earlier—and King Togodumnus—his eyes smudged with kohl. His men called to him.

Breathing deeply, I gave Druda a pat on the neck. The horse was as breathless as I was. "Well done, my friend. Well done. There is no shame in second."

"Will you ride out to the field, lady?" a boy said, pointing to the race marshal who was gesturing to me. "There is a prize for second place."

I nodded then rode Druda to the front. Dismounting, I came to stand beside the game marshal.

The Catuvellauni winner inclined his head to me. "Well done, maiden," he said politely. "He's a fine horse."

"Yours as well. Fast as lightning," I said with a grin.

He chuckled softly. "I saw a blur of red gaining on me. You had me on the run."

I laughed. "Almost had you. Next time."

The man chuckled.

"Ladies and gentlemen, our winners!"

The crowd cheered.

"For our second-place winner…twenty silver and this fine cup," the gamemaster called, handing me a sack full of coins and a small but finely adorned silver goblet.

The crowd cheered. Among the voices, I heard Grainne.

"And for our first-place winner, fifty silver and this lovely hairpin with the image of the Queen of Horses, Epona, all courtesy of King Prasutagus!" The game marshal handed the prize to the Catuvellauni winner.

The crowd let out a cheer.

I turned to my competitor. "Congratulations," I told him.

He eyed the hairpin in his hand. "It seems only fitting that a likeness of Epona goes to a maiden on Beltane," he said, offering the pin to me.

I hesitated then handed him the cup. "It must be a trade. I insist."

"But..."

"I insist."

"Well, if you *insist*," he said, then chuckled. With that, we swapped our winnings.

"If you'd like to trade sacks of silver, I'm always open to that too," I said with a grin. "For Epona's sake, of course."

The stranger laughed, evoking a pair of delightfully handsome dimples. "I hope Epona will forgive me for declining."

I grinned, then gave his horse a soft pat on the neck. "Your master risks offending the gods. I hope that does not extend to you, Lightning."

"Myrdyn," the man corrected me.

"Well raced, Myrdyn," I told the horse, then turned to the man. "Thank you for the trade. Blessed Beltane to you both," I said, giving him a bow. Then, leading Druda behind me, I turned and went to join Dôn and the others.

Grainne was grinning happily. "Boudica," she said excitedly. "My heart was pounding in my chest. I thought for sure you'd win!"

"That blue dun is very fast, but Druda made me proud."

"All of us," Dôn said. "He is a fine example of our northern horses."

"You hear that, Druda? You are the perfect northern specimen."

"Can I see the pin?" Grainne asked.

I handed it to her.

"It was very kind of the gentleman to trade with you. They should have given you the pin in the first place."

"The cup was worth less," practical Tatha said.

Grainne shrugged. "Perhaps, but this hairpin depicts the

lady of horses. It is a proper gift for a woman and a very beautiful piece. Put it on," Grainne told me, handing the hairpin back to me once more.

I turned to Dôn then eyed the braided bun on the top of her hair, the rest of her long locks hanging long. I gave the priestess a grin, then reached up and affixed the hairpin on her head. "It looks better here," I said.

"A priestess needs no adornments," she told me.

"Of course not. But what about a woman?"

Dôn chuckled lightly. "If you insist, Boudica."

"I'm making a habit of it today."

Dôn smiled at me. "Thank you."

I inclined my head to her.

"If you are done racing, come join us," Dôn told me.

"Where are we going?"

"To the nemeton. There is someone I want you to meet."

My heart beat loudly in my chest.

Had Prasutagus already spoken to the druids? I could only hope.

"Yes, Mother," I said, then turned and followed the priestess. If the matter could be settled between the druids and holy people before my father arrived, we'd all be better off—and I would never have to meet King Caratacus.

CHAPTER 60

We returned to our camp where I left a triumphant Druda and went on with Dôn, Grainne, and Tatha deeper into the valley toward the area where the two rivers converged. We passed the tents of the other druids. I saw pennants from many villages.

Dôn led us to the river where we crossed over a footbridge and made our way up the banks toward the nemeton. Like our home at Oak Throne, the nemeton had a wide dyke on its outer circle, an earthen footpath allowing one to cross into the space. Within the circle was another, smaller ditch cut into the earth in a crescent-moon shape. At its center, tall timbers set in a semi-circle reached into the sky. The bark had been stripped from the wood, making it appear shiny in the sunlight. Within the circle, many druids had gathered.

In the green space before the nemeton, however, many priestesses gathered around a fire. Dindraine, the Catuvellauni priestess who had welcomed Dôn, joined us, another woman alongside her.

The priestess alongside Dindraine was an ancient thing

with long, white hair, which she wore in braids. She wore loose, pale blue robes, and her face had been decorated with woad.

"Boudica," Dôn said, gesturing for me to come forward, "this is Selwyn. She is from the druids of Mona."

"Wise one," I said, bowing deeply.

"Blessings, Princess," the woman replied, then touched a lock of my hair. "Red as fire," she said with a laugh. "As you told me," she added, grinning at Dôn.

Dôn smiled.

"I wanted to see your face," Selwyn told me. "Your mother trained under me. She was a determined, studious girl. Always bright. Always quick to learn. I wanted to set my eyes on her daughter."

"You trained my mother?"

Selwyn nodded. "Dôn tells me that the old blood runs in yours and your sister's veins."

"Brenna has the makings of a bard," Dôn told Selwyn.

"Then she should be with us. It is only fitting that a daughter of the Northern Iceni come to Mona. Given who Damara's mother was…" she said to Dôn then turned to me. "Dôn also tells me that you have visions and an ear for the greenwood, but that you are not as quiet and studious as your mother, and far less patient," she said, then gave me a wink.

"Much like her teacher, who has taught her well," Dôn replied.

"Who? Belenus?" I said, raising an eyebrow at Dôn.

Dôn smirked at me. "Ula."

"Vexing woman," Selwyn said, shaking her head. "I suppose there is no talking to her."

"No more than there ever was," Dôn replied.

Selwyn sighed, then nodded. She turned back to me. "Sadly, I don't think you are fated to come to our island."

"The Dark Lady riddles," Dôn said, a tone of annoyance in her voice.

"When doesn't she?" Selwyn replied with a chuckle, then took my hand. "The very likeness of Damara...and your grandmother, Rian. I am glad to have set eyes on you, Princess."

"As am I to have met you, holy one."

Dôn bowed to Selwyn and gave Dindraine a nod.

The two priestesses left us then, rejoining the others.

Dôn turned to Grainne and Tatha. "Go on," she said, gesturing for them to join Selwyn and Dindraine. "I will speak to Boudica a moment."

The priestesses nodded then went back to the fire.

Taking my arm, Dôn walked with me back to the earthen bridge.

"Boudica," she said, her voice serious. "There was a rider from Venta this morning. Prasutagus's druid, Ansgar, came to speak to me."

I froze.

Dôn met my gaze. "He relayed to me a tale of great misunderstanding and heartbreak."

"I... yes."

"Then you know that the king had wanted to wed you, not Brenna. It was a mistake on the part of ancient Antedios."

I nodded. "Yes. I spoke to Prasutagus yesterday. He was unaware I had a sister, and his father was confused."

Dôn nodded slowly. "The Dark Lady decreed you were not free until Beltane, not even if Gaheris came back from the grave. But, perhaps, now we know her purpose. Nevertheless, this news will cause trouble for your father and pain for your sister."

"I love Brenna. I would never take from her something she wanted. But..."

Dôn raised an eyebrow at me.

"She does not want this marriage. She only agreed out of duty," I told the priestess.

"Are you certain? I don't know your sister as well as I know you. You must not let your words be clouded by your *want*," she said, giving me a knowing look.

She was right to caution me. Right now, my heart was flying, but at what cost to Brenna?

"I am certain. Brenna's heart is with her lyre. She wanted to go to Mona but let the dream die. She accepted her fate but didn't desire it."

"Very well. When the king comes, I will speak with him. Send someone for me at once."

"Thank you, Dôn."

"Do not thank me yet, Boudica. We cannot always understand why the gods plan the things they do. It may not go as you hope. You must rein in your feelings. Think, then act. Do you understand me?"

I was already too late for that, but I understood her meaning. "Yes, Mother."

"Very well. I will return to the others," she said, then turned to go.

"Dôn," I called, stepping toward her once more. "How in the world does Selwyn of Mona know Ula?"

Dôn chuckled. "My girl, Ula was once the high priestess of Avallach. Hasn't she told you?" she asked, giving me a wink, then made her way back to the others.

High priestess of Avallach? The holy isle of apples? Impossible. Yet… Ula knew so much. I would get answers out of her when I got home. But even as I thought it, I shook my head. Ula would tell me only what she wanted to tell me, which was likely nothing at all. Or she would laugh at me, slap me, and call me names—which seemed far more likely.

I touched the amulet hanging from my neck.

"Ula, what have you been up to?"

CHAPTER 61

My mind spinning, I made my way back through the festival tents. If anyone could convince Father, it was Dôn. Even Saenunos would listen to her, wouldn't he? But Dôn was right to caution me about Brenna's heart. I needed to speak to my sister. Already, I felt tied to Prasutagus, but at what cost to Brenna? She would be relieved, wouldn't she? I prayed to the gods it was so.

"Boudica?" a voice called.

My steps halted. I turned to find Caturix riding toward me, Melusine beside him. A contingent of my brother's warriors, along with his standard-bearer, followed along. My gaze went to Melusine. I smiled at my sister-in-law, giving her a wave, then looked back at Caturix. As always, my brother was frowning heavily. He rode his horse alongside me then dismounted.

"Boudica, where are you going? Where is Bran?"

"It's good to see you too, Brother. I was going to drink wine and watch the chariot races," I said, suddenly feeling waspish. "I have no idea where Bran is."

"King Prasutagus said Father is not yet arrived. We've just come from Venta."

"Belenus wanted Father to rest another day or so. His leg… Surely, they will be here tomorrow. Bran and I rode in early with Dôn and the priestesses of the grove."

"Did it not occur to either of you to pay a visit to the king before you ran off drinking wine and watching chariot races?"

I had already seen the king. *All* of him. "We were waiting for Father."

"Where is your camp?"

I motioned behind me. "There. Not far from the river."

Caturix turned back to his men. "Ride ahead. By the river, you will find my father's standard. Make camp nearby," he told them. Leading his horse, he joined me, his brow furrowed. "You are a princess, Boudica. This is not Oak Throne nor Frog's Hollow. What you do here reflects on all of us. You are not free to wander like a drunk about the fair."

"Caturix, should I…" Melusine said nervously, motioning to the men who had ridden on.

Ignoring her, Caturix glared at me. "You will attend Melusine," Caturix told me. "That will be your duty until Father arrives, not this other foolishness. We are here to discuss your match with King Caratacus, and Bran has left you to wander about like a wild thing. We will have words about this when Father gets here," he said, then turned to go.

"And to think, I was looking forward to seeing you," I snapped at him.

Caturix paused, looking over his shoulder at me. His gaze softened for a moment. "I…" he began but said nothing more and walked on.

Melusine dismounted then joined me. Impeccably dressed in a green-and-white gown, her long, golden hair pulled into a neatly braided knot on the top of her head, she embraced me. "It is good to see you, Boudica. Sorry about the wine and the races."

"I certainly will *not* listen to Caturix's grousing. We'll get ourselves a jug after my brother finds somewhere important for himself to be." It was then that I noticed that Melusine was wearing a stunning necklace. "Your handiwork?" I asked as I reached out and touched the amulet hanging on her chest. It had a large yellow gemstone and was trimmed with leaves and vines worked in gold.

She nodded, a genuine smile returning to her pretty features. "My best so far, I think."

"It's beautiful. Come. I have something for you."

Melusine slipped her arm into mine. "I am so glad you're here. I cannot tell you how much. And Brenna will be here too. She is to wed Prasutagus?"

"Well…"

"I liked him. He was very polite, although I could not read him well. Brenna should be happy with him. And you with King Caratacus?"

"Nor will I be marrying King Caratacus. That might come as a surprise to my male kin. In fact, more than one jug of wine may be needed to fortify my tongue on that matter."

Melusine laughed loudly, causing Caturix to glance back at us.

I giggled.

We finally made our way back to the campsite. There, Caturix's men were already working to erect his tent. Caturix directed one of the lads to go fetch some firewood. He eyed Bran's tent, then frowned.

"Boudica, where did you stay last night?"

In the grass under the stars with Prasutagus. "With the priestesses."

Caturix puffed his breath through his lips.

"Caturix," a voice called.

I turned to see Bran, who looked dirty and disheveled, coming our way.

"Brother, merry met this Beltane." Bran clapped our elder brother on the shoulder.

Caturix frowned at the dust Bran left thereon. "Have you been rolling in the mud?"

"Yes. I have. And won third place in the wrestling match and a sack of silver to prove it," Bran said with a laugh, then went to Melusine. "A vision of loveliness, as always. Like Blodeuwedd herself," he said, giving her a kiss on the cheek.

Melusine blushed. "Thank you, Bran."

"Go get yourself cleaned up," Caturix told Bran. "You're coming with me. We will meet King Caratacus at the horse fair."

Bran sighed. "Very well."

"Ector and Divis will stay behind and see that the tent is finished. I will rejoin you later," Caturix told Melusine, then added, "Keep Boudica with you."

"Yes, husband," Melusine replied.

Caturix gave her an assessing look as if he was not sure if she was being docile or impertinent. I wasn't sure either, but the glint in her eye told me it was the latter.

In spite of himself, Caturix gave her a soft smile. "I will be back once I have this business done."

Melusine grinned at him. "Good."

Leading Melusine away, we went to the fire outside Bran's tent and sat down on the log someone had placed there.

"Are you ready?" I asked.

"For?"

"Hold out your hands," I told her, snatching her hands and forming them into a cup shape.

Grinning, she did as I asked.

Reaching into my vest, I removed a pouch and poured the pearls into her hands.

Melusine gasped. "Where did you get these?"

"A ten-minute swim offshore and more than one deep breath to go under."

Melusine laughed lightly. "You gathered them? Of course, Boudica. Of course you did," she said, then played with the pearls. "My mind is spinning. Earrings for these, perhaps," she said, pushing two nearly identical pearls to the side. "And for these, a pendant. This one has a green tinge. Did you see?" she asked, gesturing to one of the pearls.

"I thought it was dirty."

Melusine laughed. "They are beautiful, Boudica. Thank you. I will make good use of them."

"I'm glad to know Caturix hasn't made you give up your jewel crafting."

"He calls it commoner's work," she said with a laugh. "But when he sees what I make, he always has a compliment for my craft." Melusine lifted the sack to her nose. "I smell the sea."

I giggled.

Bran appeared from the tent. He had hastily redressed, buttoning his tunic as he emerged from the tent.

Melusine and I rose to join him.

"Feel free to make a bad impression on King Caratacus," I said, misbuttoning one of his buttons.

Bran laughed then corrected my error. He cast Caturix a side-long glance. Caturix, distracted with criticizing Ector, hadn't noticed him yet. "If you see Bec, will you tell her where I've gone?" he whispered to me.

"Of course," I said, then fixed his hair. "Don't let Caturix promise anything."

Bran frowned at Caturix. "I had my own plans for the day," he said, then shook his head. "When Father comes, I will be done with this performing." He turned to Melusine. "Don't sit here all day. Let Boudica find some mischief for you both," he told her with a wink and then straightened his jerkin.

Melusine grinned at him.

Caturix rejoined us, giving Bran an assessing glance. "I guess that will have to do. Let's go."

"Be well, Sisters," Bran called.

"Caturix..." Melusine said softly.

My elder brother paused, then turned back. He handed Melusine a coin pouch. "On second thought, why don't you go to the market? Buy what you like."

"Another dog?" she asked with a mischievous smile.

Caturix grinned. "No more dogs," he said, then he and Bran set off once more.

Melusine stashed the coins into an unseen pocket. "I'm glad I didn't tell him I brought money of my own. Now, some wine?"

"Yes, please."

"Come on. Let's go enjoy the Maying."

CHAPTER 62

Melusine and I made our way into the market. I kept a wide berth away from the horse fair, instead leading Melusine to the vendors. As promised, I procured us another jug of wine—this time of the dandelion variety—and we made our way perusing the goods.

We marveled over pottery and fabrics, and Melusine spent a very long time talking to the craftsmen who made jewelry. In fact, her discussion grew so lengthy that when she went around the back to try her hand at one of their tools, I wandered off to watch a gaggle of children playing a game. Each child carried a raw egg precariously balanced on a spoon, racing from one end of the green to another.

The laughing parents called out to their children as they ran, encouraging them.

I sipped my wine and chuckled at their antics.

"The blond-haired boy with the braids will win."

I turned to find Pix, the strange woman I'd encountered that morning, beside me. She slugged back some wine then offered the bottle to me. I shook my head, showing her that I had my own.

"How do you know?" I asked.

"Look at his face. All determination. Not speed. Not guile. Determination."

We both watched, Pix grinning as the boy gained on the others who fell due to over-enthusiasm or self-assuredness.

"And we have our winner!" the gamemaster called, lifting the little boy's hand to declare him victorious.

"Ye see?" Pix asked with a grin.

"Boudica," Melusine called, rejoining us. "Look," she said, hoisting up a strange tool.

"What's that?"

"For winding silver. Look at all these," she said, motioning to a basket she was carrying. "All new tools."

I chuckled. "Caturix sent you to buy scarves, baubles, and pretty bits, and you're returning with tools."

Melusine laughed. "I know. I make a terrible princess," she said, then turned to Pix. "And who is this?"

"They call me Pix," the woman answered.

"*Call* you?"

She nodded. "Don't rightly remember my name anymore. But they called me Pix."

"They who?"

"The Seelie."

"I... What?"

"And ye are?"

"Melusine."

"Madelaine?"

"Melusine."

"I see. Melusine," Pix said, then grinned. "All right. Come on, *Melusine*."

"Boudica, who is this?" Melusine whispered to me.

I grinned at her. "They call her Pix."

"Pix the Fox, actually. I'm Boudica's protector," Pix clarified.

"Protector?"

Pix heaved an annoyed sigh. "Don't any of you care that you're about to be invaded?"

"Invaded?" Melusine asked. "By whom?"

Frustrated, Pix shook her head then paused as if to listen. To what, I wasn't sure. "They tell me yer smarter in the next life," Pix told Melusine with a roll of the eyes.

"Hey," Melusine protested.

"Who tells *ye* that?" I asked with a grin.

Pix gestured to the air around her.

Wonderful. As if my world couldn't get any more complicated and confusing, Pix the Fox, a hundred-year-old warrior who talked to the Seelie, creatures of the greenwood, and swore the Romans were coming, had nominated herself as my protector.

What could possibly happen next?

ALONG WITH PIX, MELUSINE AND I WORKED OUR WAY THROUGH the festival, pausing to watch tests of arms, dancing, and chariot races.

"I was ne'er one to bother with all that," Pix told us, gesturing to the chariots. "My way of killing Romans is better."

Melusine, having decided Pix's stories were nothing more than a joke, leaned in and asked, "And what way is that?"

"I get into my fox skin and sneak up on them."

"Your fox skin?" Melusine asked, arching an eyebrow.

She nodded. "Shifting form."

"Let's see," Melusine said.

"Can't do it here and now. Too obvious," Pix replied.

"Uh-huh. I see," Melusine replied skeptically.

"Oh, ye will see," Pix said, crossing her arms on her chest. "Nearly time, it is."

"And how do you know that?"

Again, Pix gestured in the air around us.

Melusine laughed, but I narrowed my gaze and studied the woman. The muscles on her arms told of long days of training. She was every bit as taut as Bran. And the marks on her skin showed she had seen her share of combat. Was she mad? Or was there truth to her tale? Either way, I liked her stories.

The sun was beginning to set when Melusine sighed then said, "We should go back. I'm sure Caturix will return soon."

My stomach was tied into a knot. My brothers had spent the day with King Caratacus. While Bran would never promote a match against my will, Caturix was a different matter. For him, everything was about duty, as Kennocha and Mara knew too well. I only hoped he had not promised anything. There was significant risk now. Not only could tensions rise between my father and Prasutagus over this matter of confusion, but if my family was quick to make a bargain with Caratacus before Prasutagus and I made things right, that risked hostility between the Catuvellauni and the Greater Iceni—and something told me Caratacus didn't need much of an excuse to invade his neighbors.

We made our way back to the tents to find Caturix, Bran, and Bec along with the others at the fire. Food had been prepared, and everyone was eating.

Bran waved when he saw me. "Ector roasted some chickens," he called to me, his mouth full.

I laughed.

Caturix looked over his shoulder at Melusine and me, his eyes going briefly to Pix.

We joined the others.

"With Boudica at your side, I half-expected you to return painted in woad," Caturix told Melusine lightly, making space for her to sit beside him.

Melusine dipped into her bag of tools and pulled out a clamp. "I dare you to say so again," she told him with a grin.

At that, Caturix smiled, which surprised me.

I took a spot beside Bran and Bec, motioning for Pix to join me.

"This is Pix," I told my brother and the priestess.

Pix gave Bec a long look. "Priestess," she said, lifting her hands to her forehead in honor.

Bec raised an eyebrow at her. "Merry met."

"Are you Greater Iceni, Pix?" Bran asked the warrior woman, but I could hear the suspicion in his voice. He assessed her armor.

"I'm nothin' anymore," Pix replied, helping herself to some food.

"How can you be nothing?" Cai asked her.

Pix paused and looked at him. "Aren't ye handsome. I'll find ye tonight by the fires, and ye shall discover what I am," she told him with a naughty wink, then turned to Bran. "I'm here for Boudica."

That was enough to raise Caturix's suspicions. "Here for Boudica? For what?"

"I was sent to be her guardian."

"Sent by whom?" my elder brother asked.

Pix stuffed a massive bite of food in her mouth then said, "Greenwood."

Bran chuckled. "Where did you find her?" he asked me.

"She just told you. She stumbled out of a mound to protect me."

"She's been in the Otherworld for a hundred years, since the time of Caesar. Do I have that right?" Melusine asked.

Pix pointed to her, bobbing her finger to confirm the story.

Caturix frowned at me. "Boudica, it is not wise to bring mad people around."

"Who's mad?" Pix asked him with a wink.

Caturix frowned.

Bran, however, was grinning at Pix. "Who are you here to protect Boudica from?"

"The Romans."

Several group members grew silent, but Bec asked, "Why will Boudica need protection from the Romans? They are not on our shores anymore."

"Waves do not come ashore only once, Priestess," Pix replied, her eyes on the chicken leg she was eating.

The others looked toward Bec.

"Mad," Caturix swore under his breath.

I met Bec's gaze. From her expression, I could see she disagreed with Caturix.

After finishing off her last bite of chicken, Pix tossed the bone into the fire then rose. "All right, handsome. Ready?" she asked Cai.

Cai grinned at her, unabashed. "For?"

"A little dancing. A little wine. A little frolic."

Cai winked at Bran then rose. "What else is Beltane for? Come on *Mad* Pix. Let's frolic."

The others laughed.

"Mad Pix," Pix said with a laugh. "Handsome, ye have no idea…"

CHAPTER 63

Soon, the others departed. Melusine pulled out all the tools she had purchased, explaining to Caturix each item and how they worked. I was glad to see my brother listening intently to her. Caturix's moods were hard to track. While he was clearly annoyed with me—which was hardly unusual—his relationship with Melusine seemed to have improved. I was glad to see it. Kennocha was a good woman and deserved happiness. I was truly sorry she couldn't have that with my brother. And Mara deserved far better. But Melusine was an innocent in their tangle. She also deserved better.

I was about to slip away when Bec set her hand on my arm. She motioned for me to step aside with her. Bran followed us.

"Boudica, this woman who latched herself to you—" Bec began then paused.

"Pix."

Bec nodded. "The things she says… If it is to be believed…"

"Wait, you don't think she's telling the truth, do you?" Bran asked.

"About which part?" Bec replied.

Bran's brow scrunched up. "All of it."

"I sense no malevolence in her, but you know the rule," Bec reminded me. "Beware of faerie gifts—in all forms."

"Is she not just mad?" Bran asked Bec. "I mean, her story is so impossible."

"Is it? She has the sheen of the Otherworld on her, and Boudica is like a flame to that moth."

"I'll be mindful," I told Bec. My eyes went to the distant fields. Under the light of the moon, I could see the silhouette of the King Stone.

Bran studied me. "Your mind has been elsewhere all night. What is it?"

There was no one I trusted more than Bran. Everything was about to implode in my face. Perhaps it wouldn't hurt to have someone on my side.

I met Bran's gaze then said, "I... Bran, you were right about Prasutagus and myself."

"What do you mean?" Bran asked.

I inhaled deeply, letting out a slow breath, then said, "King Antedios made a terrible mistake. He thought he'd arranged for Prasutagus to wed me. They didn't even know Brenna existed. Sadly, the ancient king got confused. The arrangement for Brenna was a mistake."

"Prasutagus thought he'd asked for *you*?" Bran asked.

I nodded.

"Ah," Bec said. "That explains the conversation between Dôn and Prasutagus's druid this morning."

"Have you spoken to Prasutagus?" Bran asked in all seriousness.

I nodded.

Bran frowned. "This confusion will not be easily undone. Saenunos... King Caratacus asked many questions about you today. But he asked even more questions about our people. Our forces. Even Caturix hesitated. This businesses with the Catuvellauni that Saenunos has masterminded will lead us into a disaster."

"Then let's hope it comes to nothing. Prasutagus hopes to clear up the confusion between the druids. But I'm worried about Brenna..."

"Don't be. Brenna will be glad. Don't worry about her," Bran told me. "I knew I was right. Boudica, why didn't you say anything?"

"What was there to say? All these months, I thought Prasutagus had cared nothing for me."

"Ay, Boudica," Bec said, setting her hand on my arm.

"I had the love of my life," I said, my fingers touching the frog amulet on my chest. "I thought myself greedy to want another. But...I do."

"Father will come tomorrow. Hopefully, he can be convinced," Bran said.

"And we don't tear apart our alliances and our family in the process," I said glumly.

"Maybe it's good Pix showed up after all. If the Catuvellauni start a war to claim you..."

"That's not even funny," I said, but laughed lightly regardless. My gaze went to the hilltop. "I need to go."

Bran smiled gently at me. "You can rely on me, Boudica. I am with you."

"As is Dôn," Bec reassured me. "I do not know her mind, but I can read her face. She is with you. As am I, for what it's worth."

"It's worth a lot to me. Thank you, Priestess."

"You're welcome, Princess."

I looked at my brother.

"Everything will come to pass as it's supposed to. Trust in the gods," he told me.

"Let's only hope they're on my side."

"If Pix is any clue," Bec said. "I don't think you need to worry."

AFTER LEAVING BEC AND BRAN, I MADE MY WAY ACROSS THE river and to the King Stone. Prasutagus was not there when I arrived.

Sitting, I pressed my back against the stone and looked out on the valley below. Music wafted through the river valley. The bonfires illuminated the surface of the river. It was a beautiful sight. Playing with the little frog amulet, I stared at the scene.

It had almost been a year since Gaheris died.

Had I let enough time pass?

Would he want this for me?

I hadn't even considered what was on the other side of all of this confusion if things worked out. I would become Queen of the Greater Iceni. Queen. That was not a title I ever wanted —except to be Gaheris's queen of oak. But Gaheris was gone. And as much as I wished he were at my side, he wasn't. But there was Prasutagus. Yet with the man came responsibility. And truth be told, I knew little of Prasutagus's daily life.

No matter which direction I turned, I would wear a crown.

Of the Greater Iceni...

Of the Catuvellauni...

And once upon a time, in a life not lived, of oak...

"Boudica?"

I looked up to find Prasutagus approaching.

I rose. "No Raven?"

He shook his head. "I came on foot."

Prasutagus looked worn, dark rings under his eyes.

"What is it?" I asked, going to him, setting my hand on his cheek.

"I sent a rider to Oak Throne, asking your father to join me as soon as he arrives. There are rumors that you are already given to the Catuvellauni. Besides the disservice and offense to your sister, I fear there may be greater obstacles between us."

I sighed heavily. "My brothers met with Caratacus today. As I understand, both came away skeptical. My elder brother, Caturix, takes everything seriously. Perhaps there is less to be worried about than we think. If Caturix is put off, there must be good reason."

Prasutagus nodded, but I could see his mind was still distressed. "That is not all."

He shook his head. "I've had word from my spies amongst the merchants," he said. "There is movement in Gaul. More legions have come from Rome. More ships. Boudica..."

"An attack? You think there will be an attack?"

"I am almost certain of it now."

"Then the issue of who weds who is nothing. We must rally together before it is too late."

Prasutagus nodded. "I must meet with your father and the Catuvellauni brothers at once. Aedd Mawr of the Trinovantes has been seen in Gaul along with Verica."

A shiver washed over me. Aedd Mawr was the rightful heir of the Trinovantes tribe which had been subdued under Caratacus and Togodumnus's father's reign. The fact that he had been seen with Verica of the Atrebates in Gaul suggested only one thing. The Celtic Kings had come to retake their lands, and with them, they'd brought the might of Rome.

Why was Prasutagus the only one who seemed to be paying attention to the threat across the sea?

"My father…my uncle… They have no fear of Rome. They dismiss it as rumor."

"I must speak to the others, convince the druids…" he said, an anguished look on his face. "Ah, Boudica. I'm sorry. You came here to meet a lover, not a troubled ruler."

"I came here to meet the man I want as my partner—lover and ruler alike."

Prasutagus reached out and gently touched my cheek, his finger stroking my lip. "Boudica," he whispered then leaned in and set a kiss on my lips. He pulled me close, the two of us squeezing one another tightly.

All the fear and pain washed away, and in that moment, there was only him.

In the distance, music played, drums beat, and we could hear the sound of merry-making. But there, in the dim light of the moon, it was only Prasutagus and me. Once more, we laid in the green, touching one another gently until our passions got the better of us. Soon, we were flesh upon flesh again, with only the eyes of the stars upon us.

It was late in the night, the moon high in the sky, when we finished our own frolicking.

Prasutagus kissed me on the top of my head. "I don't know what the future holds," he whispered, gently stroking my bare shoulder, "but whatever comes, I will have you at my side."

"And I, you," I said dreamily then fell into sleep.

THERE WAS A DENSE FOG ON THE FIELD WHEN I OPENED MY EYES IN the grey hour before sunrise the next morning. I wiggled closer to Prasutagus for warmth, only to feel another body squirm close to me. I opened my eyes to find Pix lying on the other side of me.

"Banshees be cursed," I said, sitting up.

Alarmed, Prasutagus also sat up.

Pix yawned tiredly then stretched her long, muscular limbs. Like Prasutagus and myself, she was completely naked.

"Pix," I said, surprised. "What are you…"

"Boudica," she said with a laugh then gave my breast a gentle squeeze. "I was out picking strawberries," she said, her nimble hands dancing from between my legs to Prasutagus's. "Like bright berries in a field," she said then flopped back down, her eyes on Prasutagus's body. "Looks like I have yer attention," she said.

My gaze shifted to Prasutagus whose manhood was erect once more.

"I…" Prasutagus said then looked at me. "Who is this?"

"She calls herself Pix the Fox," I told him. "She befriended me yesterday."

"I was with the Seelie. I came through the King Stone," Pix said, sliding her fingers up my inner thigh. "I came for Boudica. Shall we both make a queen out of her?" Pix asked with a naughty grin.

"Stop," I said, halting her hand, but the expression on her face made me laugh.

"The King Stone…" Prasutagus said, looking back at the carved stone.

"Come now, druid. Ye know the ways of the greenwood," Pix said then leaned in and set a kiss on my lips, giggling lightly. "Sweet," she said then danced her hands across Prasutagus's chest. When she reached for his manhood, he stopped her.

"My heart belongs to only one woman at a time," he told her, his voice serious.

"What about yer cock?" Pix asked.

Prasutagus chuckled. "That too."

"No matter," Pix said then rose. "I left that handsome boy lying around here somewhere," she said then wandered off back into the mist, as naked as the day she was born.

"Boudica... Who... What..."

I chuckled lightly. "You know as much as I do. She is Pix, as she said. According to her, she was sent by the Seelie."

Prasutagus frowned. "These are strange times. I see omens everywhere. And now this?" He looked back at the stone. "We should go."

I nodded then began to redress, Prasutagus doing the same. When we had both made ready, we met one another's gaze.

"The druids will begin the rites today. They will greet the sun. I should join them," Prasutagus said.

I looked off in the distance. "I should go back to the camp. My brothers..."

Prasutagus nodded then pushed a strand of my curly red hair behind my ear. He met my gaze. "We will find a way."

"Yes."

He leaned in, placing a soft kiss on my lips.

When he pulled back, he set his forehead against mine. "Thank you," he whispered.

"For what?"

"For forgiving me. All these months, you must have thought..."

"It is forgotten now. I'm sorry too. When you used your

druid's magic to share with me what you learned of the coin and at Samhain, I was cold to you."

"I am sorry for any heartache you endured and any your sister may face in the days to come. It pains me to think an innocent lady has been pulled into this mess."

"I will see to Brenna. My sister is reasonable."

"But still, I hope she will know how sorry I am for any pain I may cause her."

"You are good to think of her."

"My sweet father," Prasutagus said, then wrapped me in his arms. "His last, good deed...all a mess," he said then kissed me on the top of the head. "I will see you soon."

I nodded.

Prasutagus held my hand, giving it one last squeeze, before he let me go. Then, he, too, disappeared into the mists as he made his way back toward the nemeton.

After he'd gone, I went to the King Stone and set my hand thereon.

"I know you see me," I whispered. "And I know you hear me. Whatever path you are planning for us, I hope it is for the good of us all—not just for you."

"*Boudica...*

"*We are all one.*

"*The human world and the green.*

"*And we are all in danger!*"

CHAPTER 64

S haken, I returned to my camp. By the blessings of the gods, only Melusine was awake to greet the sun.

"Boudica," she said with a grin. "Look what I've been working on," she said, motioning for me to join her.

Melusine had been twisting strands of silver and fashioning the pearls to look like a bunch of grapes on a vine.

"That's... You just made that?"

Melusine laughed. "I couldn't sleep last night after—I just couldn't sleep," she said, her cheeks coloring red.

I sucked in my lips to keep from smiling. Melusine could not know how glad I was to learn she and my brother had found their way together. Although his choice not to fight for Kennocha frustrated me, I also pitied Caturix. To know he had taken to Melusine, and she to him, made my heart glad.

"The Maiden and the Forest Lord dance the whole night long in the hours before Beltane. Few of us are immune to that force," I said finally.

"So I've noticed. And where did you run off to?" Melusine asked as she settled in with her design once more.

"In the direction of drama," I said, looking into the fire.

"Do I dare ask?"

"Ah, sweet sister-in-law, the gods have made a mess of things."

Melusine nodded. "No matter the mess, I'm glad to see you happy. I worried for you over the winter. Brenna told me how much you loved Gaheris."

I nodded slowly. "I never expected to care for anyone again. And yet, here I am…"

Melusine smiled. "I'm happy for you."

I sighed heavily. "We shall see."

On the hilltop not far away, I heard the voices of the druids and the priestesses lift up in prayer. Both Melusine and I looked toward the nemeton. Within, we could see the robed holy people and hear their song as they called upon the gods. The sun broke over the horizon, sending shimmering rays of light onto the nemeton. I scanned the horizon, seeing the beams of sun shining on the King Stone as well. All the hair on the back of my neck rose.

Melusine rose. "Do you feel it?"

I nodded.

"The gods are awake. But there is something else. I feel it just below the surface. It's a terrible sense of…dread. I can't seem to shake it," Melusine said.

"The rumors from Gaul grow darker with each passing day."

"My father whispered of the same, but all he cared about was the Catuvellauni and assuring our alliance with your tribe. No one knows which direction Caratacus and Togo-dumnus will turn next. Whose tribe they will come for. And yet…"

"If the rumors are true, the Catuvellauni are the very least of our problems. That is why Prasutagus has brought everyone together."

Melusine turned and looked at me. "Because of the Romans."

I nodded.

We stared at the shrine in the distance, watching as the priestesses and druids moved in circles.

The sound of a carnyx echoed across the valley, the long trumpet's call beckoning the gods.

A shiver went through my body.

"How do you know why Prasutagus gathered everyone?" Melusine finally asked me.

I turned and looked at her. "He told me."

Melusine held my glance for a long moment. In her eyes, I could see her put the pieces together. Finally, she nodded then smiled gently, setting her arm on mine. "The gods are working. I can feel them. And in the mist and flames," she said, motioning to the festival fields, "I sense them walking amongst us. Something is coming. This is a piece of it. May all our gods—and Pix—protect us."

CHAPTER 65

I t was late in the morning when Bran stumbled out of his tent looking messy and happy and like he'd drunk far too much wine the day before. Even if the disaster unfolding around me was about to explode, I was glad to see my brother in such a state. I loved my siblings, even Caturix. All I wanted was their happiness.

"Boudica," Bran said in greeting, rummaging around the table where the food had been laid out.

"Good morning."

He winced. "Not so loud."

I chuckled.

"Where is Caturix?" Bran asked.

"He and Melusine went to the horse fair. Apparently, he saw something there he liked yesterday. He's planning to try to buy the horse before the auction this morning."

"Ah," Bran said with a nod. "I'm glad he saw something he liked. I, on the other hand, saw things I did not care for yesterday."

I narrowed my gaze. "Such as?"

Bran looked over his shoulder. Cai and the other warriors had gathered around the fire. The pair of us were alone.

"Saenunos is a fool," Bran said. "We must work with Prasutagus. Soon, the Catuvellauni will turn our way. Wedding us off to any of them is a mistake. Already, they have their eyes on our corner of the world."

"How do you know?"

"From the questions they asked. The day started pleasant enough, but once they warmed us up, the questions started. Caturix turned to stone. Togodumnus does not hide his ambitions well, but Caratacus…he is the one to watch. Pleasant. Jovial. He's the kind who smiles as he sticks a knife in your back. Our father has been mistaken to let Saenunos speak to these brothers on his behalf. There is danger there. Caturix and I both agree. We must stay close to Prasutagus."

"I am sure Prasutagus will agree, but for the moment, Prasutagus's eyes are on Gaul."

"Gaul? Why? What has he heard?"

"That Gaul is swarming with Romans."

A moment later, a horn called.

"Ah, banshees be cursed," Bran swore, mimicking me as he winced at the noise.

We both turned to see riders trotting our way. And with them, the green oak standard of our father.

A terrible pain gripped my stomach.

Now, it would all be undone.

Bran turned to the group of men gathered at the fire, spotting a boy amongst Caturix's servants.

"Lad," he called, getting the boy's attention. "Go fetch my brother from the horse fair. Tell him the king and the chieftain have come." Bran met my gaze. "I am with you. Don't forget," he said, taking my hand.

I turned back to the crowd, spotting my father and sister riding in a chariot, Saenunos and Belenus riding behind them.

Brenna smiled when she saw us, giving us a wave.

Epona. Great Mother. Andraste. Help me. Don't let me break Brenna's heart.

AS EXPECTED, SAENUNOS BLUSTERED INTO THE CAMP, CRITICIZING everyone and directing his men to work.

I watched my uncle. He was not a tall man, but he carried himself like he was a giant. His piercing grey eyes took in everything and everyone, looking over the crowd with disdain.

"Bran," he said sharply. "You look like you slept in a ditch. Go get ready to meet with Prasutagus."

Bran did not reply, merely went to Brenna and Father. I joined him, offering my father my hand as he got down from the chariot.

"Father," I said. "How are you?"

"Fine," he said, ignoring my gesture.

Frowning, I turned to Brenna instead. "Sister," I said, helping her down.

"Oh, Boudica. I'm so glad to see you," she said, taking my arm.

"Are you feeling well?" I asked, noticing she looked pale and had dark rings under her eyes.

She nodded. "Yes. I'm all right. It's just... My head is aching from all the worries."

"We must talk," I told her in all seriousness.

Brenna looked at me. "Is something wrong?"

I nodded. "We must speak in private as soon as we can."

One of Saenunos's men, taking over for my uncle, began barking orders to the men to get the camp ready.

"Where is Caturix?" Father asked, looking over our party.

"He and Melusine had business to attend to. I've sent for him," Bran said.

I heard a happy yip, and to my surprise, I saw Bear running to join us.

"There you are," Brenna said, picking him up.

"What is he doing here?" I asked with a laugh.

"We were nearly halfway here when one of the lads spotted him following us. No escaping him, I guess," Brenna said, then smiled, kissing the dog on the head, then set him back down.

Belenus joined us. "Boudica," he said, bowing to me.

"Belenus, I am glad to see you."

The ancient druid smiled at me. "Do you know where Dôn is this morning?"

"At the nemeton, I believe," I said.

Belenus turned to Father. "I will find Dôn and return at once."

Father nodded, and the druid went on his way.

Brenna turned to me. "Something is happening. A messenger came from Prasutagus yesterday. I don't know the matter, but I know we will see the king—along with Dôn—at once. You don't think Prasutagus will push for the wedding to come earlier, do you?" Brenna asked, her voice trembling with anxiety.

I swallowed hard. "No, Sister. It is quite the opposite. We must talk. Brenna—"

"Ah, here is Caturix," Saenunos said loudly. "Let's depart, Aesunos."

My father turned to Caturix. "We will see Prasutagus this morning. Come along."

Caturix turned to Melusine, speaking softly to her.

"I will come," Melusine told him.

Caturix nodded.

Saenunos went to one of his men. "Find King Togodumnus and King Caratacus. Inform them that we are here. We will meet them in the afternoon before the rites."

The man nodded then disappeared into the crowd.

A moment later, Pix appeared. "What's this about then?" she asked.

"My father and uncle," I said, motioning to the men.

Pix eyed them carefully. "Hmm..." was all she said. Given how loquacious she was about everything else, that "hmm" said a lot.

"And this is my sister, Brenna," I added. "This is Pix," I told Brenna.

"Oh. Hello," Brenna said, looking confused as she eyed over the tattooed warrior woman.

Pix eyed Brenna up and down, then chuckled to herself.

"What is it?" I asked.

"Like the rings of a tree—all of us. So, where are we off to?"

"To see King Prasutagus."

"The Strawberry King? I'll get him yet," Pix said with a wink.

"I suspect you had enough fun on your own," I whispered in reply.

Pix let out a whistle, getting Cai's attention.

He turned toward her.

Pix kissed at him, making him laugh.

"You have no idea," she told me, then turned to Melusine. "Merry met, not-Madelaine."

Melusine laughed. "Merry met, Mad Pix."

Turning, I met Bran's gaze.

May the gods be with me.

CHAPTER 66

Once our party was ready, including Dôn and Belenus who joined us, we rode from Arminghall to Venta. Like Oak Throne, the city was completely walled. Three sides of the city had a vast trench dug for fortification; the fourth side was protected by the River Tas. But Venta was enormous, ten times that of our fort. I hardly remembered the place from when I was a child. But now, as I rode across the earthen bridge and through the gates, it was all I could do to keep from gaping.

Everywhere I looked, I saw buildings and people. The city sprawled in every direction, with alehouses, covered marketplaces—one for livestock, one for food, one for textiles—even a temple stood in the middle of a green space. We rode down the main lane toward a massive complex to the north. There, we found another walled fortification. We rode to the gate.

"It's King Aesunos," one of the guards called down from the watchtower above.

A moment later, the gates swung open for us to reveal a massive roundhouse with several smaller buildings and sheds.

Covered walkways connected the smaller buildings to the immense structure at the center of it all. Before the great building stood a stone carving of the goddess Epona.

A moment later, Prasutagus appeared at the door. He was finely dressed in tan leather breeches and a deep green shirt covered by an embossed leather tunic. He wore a woven cape over his shoulder, pinned with a horse brooch. He had braided his hair from his temples, his long, red hair hanging loose. A thick, golden torc sat on his neck.

I could feel Brenna's gaze as she glanced at me for reassurance.

I panicked, not sure what to do, then met her gaze.

The nervous expression on Brenna's face when she looked at me, a confused expression washing the worry away.

I looked away, turning to Prasutagus.

For a brief moment, Prasutagus met my gaze. His eyes sought to reassure me, but it did little to help.

Prasutagus then stepped forward, a black-robed druid and a younger priestess dressed in white joining him.

"King Aesunos," he said, bowing to Father. "You and your family are welcome to Venta," he said, then turned to Belenus. "Wise father," he said, then looked to Dôn, "Lady of the grove, I am very pleased to see you again," he said, lifting his hands to his brow in a gesture I recognized as a gesture of respect between our holy people. "Please, won't you all come inside?"

Father motioned for us to dismount.

"Pretty words," Saenunos, who rode behind me, muttered.

I dismounted, lingering beside Druda, trying to steel myself, then turned to join the others. When I did so, I found Brenna beside me.

"What's wrong?" she whispered.

"Brenna. There has been a terrible mistake," I whispered. "Please, Sister, in the moments to come, please forgive me."

Confused, Brenna shook her head. "What do you mean?"

But there was no time to explain.

"Boudica. Brenna," Father called.

Without a chance to speak further, we joined the others. Our party was ushered into the roundhouse. In its layout, the house reminded me of my own home. It was circular in style, with the main dining hall at the center of the house. Hallways led off from the main entryway to private rooms. Stones lined the floor, and a massive firepit—unlit due to the hot weather—sat in the center. Rather than leaving it cold, someone had arranged greens and flowers therein. The dining hall had three tables along one side of the room. On the other side were benches and couches placed for comfortable, private discussion. Rich fabrics covered the benches, and furs covered the floors.

The servants, ready with trays of wine goblets, gestured for our party to sit.

"Rich as a faerie king," Pix whispered in my ear.

I gave her a look, willing her to be silent. Already, the others would question why I had brought a stranger. "Go join Cai and the others," I whispered to her, gesturing with my chin to the small group of soldiers who'd accompanied us. Prasutagus's servants were settling them in at one of the tables.

Pix shook her head. "Where you go, I go."

"Belenus," Prasutagus's druid said, taking Belenus's hand. "It is good to see you, my friend. It has been too long."

"Ansgar," Belenus said, clapping the man on the shoulder.

"King Aesunos, we were wondering if we may have a

word with you, Dôn, Belenus, and your daughters in the king's meeting chamber for a moment?" Ansgar asked.

Father rose. For a moment, I saw him struggle with his leg. Brenna intervened quickly, taking Father's arm. She was so swift and nonchalant in her manner, hiding Father's ailment from the others in what appeared—on the outside—as a show of affection. Brenna steadied Father then met Prasutagus's gaze.

"Of course, King Prasutagus," Brenna said, a nervous tremor in her voice. She gave Prasutagus a forced smile.

I felt like I might vomit.

Without being invited, Saenunos rose to join us.

Prasutagus signaled to the man I presumed to be his housecarl. Leaving the others behind, we followed Prasutagus, his housecarl, and the druids from the main hall to a meeting room. The small room felt like a family space with a brazier, couches, scrolls, a spinning wheel, and other familial comforts.

My nerves getting the better of me, I went to Dôn.

We all sat.

A servant passed us all goblets of wine then stood by the door.

"To Bel, the Forest Lord, and the Maiden," Prasutagus called, lifting his cup.

We all joined him in the toast.

When I raised my glass, I met his gaze.

Prasutagus gave me a reassuring smile.

"What have you to say, Prasutagus?" Father asked, a tone of suspicion in his voice.

"King Aesunos, I am honored to have you in my home. This room was a favorite of my father's in his later years. He said the light was best here. He would sit with these," he said, gesturing to a wall lined with scrolls, "the whole day long. My father was a good king and a kind father. He knew the death of my wife Esu was hard for me. When I spoke to him of my visit to Oak Throne and of your daughter, my father thought to do me one kindness before he left this world—to arrange a marriage that would wed his son to the only woman who had moved his child's heart these long, dark months. And strengthen our alliance."

Out of the corner of my eye, I saw Brenna's brow furrow in confusion.

My father's gaze, however, darkened. I realized that Father had already worked out the problem, but he said nothing, waiting for Prasutagus to continue.

"When I came to Oak Throne over the matter of the raids, Prince Bran and Princess Boudica treated me with great honor. And I... I rather unexpectedly found a kindred spirit in your daughter, Boudica. And she in me. When I returned to Venta and told my father about her, he did what any loving father would do—he asked for her hand. Except, my father was old, forgetful, and he did not remember the lady's name. When you and my father exchanged messengers, confusion arose," Prasutagus told Aesunos, then turned to Brenna. "Princess Brenna, I swear by all the gods, I did not know you even existed. I thought Boudica was the only daughter of King Aesunos. I believed my father had arranged for me to wed the woman with whom I'd felt an unexpected attachment. Only of late did I learn of the confusion. I never meant any harm to you... please know that. As much as I fret about the damage this confusion may cause to my alliance with the Northern Iceni, I regret the impact on your heart even more. You are an innocent in this mess. But I must be plain. My love has been given to Boudica all this time. And, I think, hers to me."

The room fell silent. From the other side of the house, we could hear Prasutagus's musicians in the great hall.

"I…" Brenna began, then turned and looked at me.

Saenunos rose. "What game are you playing?" he hissed at Prasutagus. "You know, don't you? You know our plan to wed that girl to the Catuvellauni," he said, pointing at me, but his gaze was on Prasutagus. "You do not fool me, boy, with false stories of love. You are no dizzy youth. You are too old for this game, Prasutagus. Come, Aesunos. We're leaving."

"Father," I objected, turning to my father.

"Silence, Saenunos," Father said sternly.

"Aesunos, are you blind? I warned you not to trust him. Look at this game he has concocted," he said, then turned to me. "Pulled you into the snare, didn't he? Well, I'm sure that was easy enough. You always think with your lust before your mind anyway. First that chieftain's son, now this. Did he bed you already?" Saenunos shouted at me.

Dôn rose. "You will silence your tongue in the presence of your betters," she told Saenunos, pulling about her the cloak of power. Dôn suddenly seemed taller, more imposing. The light in the room dimmed, the flames flickering low. Everyone fell silent as it quickly became unclear whether it was Dôn speaking or the Dark Lady Andraste. "All is as the gods will. You are nothing to them, Chieftain. Hold your tongue in the presence of the hands of fate. While dark clouds roll toward our land, the Catuvellauni seek to strangle us all like ivy, creeping gently. No, Saenunos, you do not see as clearly as you think. It is Boudica who is fated to wed Prasutagus, not Brenna. Brenna will go hence from this place with her lyre to Mona. And by nightfall, Boudica will come to the bed of Prasutagus. These are the words of the Dark Lady Andraste."

The room was struck silent.

Furious, Saenunos stormed out of the room.

"Saenunos!" Father called angrily, but my uncle did not turn back.

Dôn exhaled heavily as if a weight had come off her. When she swooned, I grabbed her, helping her to her seat once more.

"Wise Dôn, we hear the words of the Dark Lady and will obey," Ansgar said. The druid looked shaken.

The young priestess beside him stared from Dôn to me.

I turned to my sister. "Brenna," I whispered.

Unshed tears clung to Brenna's eyes. "Is it true?" she whispered.

"We didn't know there had been a confusion until it was too late," I told Brenna. "Sister..."

Brenna swallowed hard, then nodded, tears trailing down her cheeks. And for the first time in a very long time, I could not read my sister's expression. My heart broke when I saw the tears.

"Wise Dôn, we hear great Andraste's words," Prasutagus told her, then turned to my father. "King Aesunos," Prasutagus began, "I mean no disrespect to your house. Quite the opposite. I love Boudica," he said, his gaze going to me. "Your brother is wrong. You and I desperately need one another right now."

"You—" Father began, his voice terse, but Dôn cut him short.

"You will listen, Aesunos, grandson of Saenuvax, son of Egan," Dôn told him, her voice commanding.

"Aesunos, Verica and Aedd Mawr are in Gaul," Prasutagus told him. "The Romans are gathering their forces. At the same time, Caratacus and Togodumnus's eyes are everywhere, including upon us. We *are* surrounded by enemies, but *I* am *not* an enemy. The future of all of our people is at stake. While the Catuvellauni plot to pluck us from our lands, the Romans *are* coming."

"You know this to be certain?" Belenus asked, alarm in his voice.

"I would stake my life on it," Prasutagus said.

Father turned to Dôn. "What says Andraste?"

"Dark clouds," Dôn said with a shake of the head, "rolling like smoke across the water. And at the same time, the noose of ivy on our necks. You must act quickly, but time is not on your side, Aesunos."

"If what you say is true, we must turn the Catuvellauni's eyes to Gaul before it is too late," Father said. "My grandfather, Saenuvax, made many promises to Rome on behalf of the Northern Iceni. If Claudius comes to collect what was promised to Caesar…"

"You must not fear, Your Highness," Belenus said. "The gods and the druids repelled the Romans once before. They will do it again."

"Old friend," Ansgar told Belenus. "It does not matter how often you sing that song, it will not make it entirely true. The Iceni—all of us—must make ready."

"But he's right," Pix interrupted. She turned to Ansgar. "The druids *did* send them away. On the white cliffs, they stood, painted with sigils, arms in the sky, fire in their hands. They called upon the waves, and the gods of the sea smashed Rome's ships. What Romans landed were swallowed up by the greenwood. The druids called upon the forest, and the greenwood rose to fight. We sent them back to where they came from."

"Who are you?" Father asked, then turned to me. "Who is this woman?"

"I'm Pix, Your Highness," Pix told Father, as if it were obvious.

"I hope you and wise Belenus are right," Prasutagus told Pix. "Either way, we must convince Togodumnus and Caratacus to listen."

"Shall I send for them?" Ansgar asked.

Prasutagus nodded.

The druid bowed to Prasutagus then left, the young priestess following along with him.

There was silence in the room for a long time, then my father said, "As for my daughters, I will take you at your word regarding your intentions and feelings toward Boudica. And I shall obey the words of the gods."

I turned to Brenna, but her eyes were on her lap.

"Princess Brenna…" Prasutagus said.

Brenna smiled lightly, collecting herself, then looked up. "I love my sister. I am glad to know you share in that love," she told him, then turned to Dôn. "May the Great Lady be thanked. I am glad to go to Mona."

Dôn inclined her head to Brenna.

"I would speak to Prasutagus alone," Father said, motioning to us. "Belenus will stay with us. Boudica, instruct the others to return to Arminghall."

"Yes, Father," I said.

"Everyone except Caturix. My son Caturix will join us," Father told Prasutagus, who nodded.

"As kings plot, so do druids and priestesses," Dôn said with a light laugh. "I will return to the nemeton," Dôn told Father. Dôn rose then turned to Prasutagus. "The eyes of the gods are upon you, Prasutagus. Now and in the future. You are a father to the Greater Iceni. As a father, you must protect them as *you* see fit, not as others see it. Remember that," she said, then looked to Aesunos once more. "All parents seek to do what is best for their children. It is only natural," she said, then smiled. "But all things are as the gods will, even when their plans are not clear to us. Damara would be glad of this, Aesunos. Your children belong to her and you—*not* to your brother," she said, then turned and left the room.

Brenna kissed Father's hand, curtsied to Prasutagus, then followed Dôn.

I held Prasutagus's gaze for a long moment then turned to my father, but he did not look at me.

Not knowing what else to say, I departed, Pix following along behind me.

I had won my love. But what lay beyond the doors of Prasutagus's stronghold filled me with dread.

CHAPTER 67

We returned to the main hall. There, the others sat drinking wine and speaking to some of Prasutagus's warriors. Prasutagus's housecarl flagged down a servant and asked him to fetch our horses.

I went to my brothers. "We will return to Arminghall," I told Bran, then turned to Caturix. "But Father wishes for you to join him and King Prasutagus."

"Where did Saenunos go?" Bran asked, looking puzzled.

"A storm blusters where it will. There is no helping that," Dôn said.

Caturix gave me a questioning look then turned to Melusine.

She smiled softly at him. "It's fine. I will ride with Boudica and Brenna."

Caturix nodded then went with one of Prasutagus's servants back to the meeting room.

Brenna looked pale and shaken. I tried to catch her eye more than once, but she was lost to her own thoughts.

"I am Galvyn, Prasutagus's housecarl," Prasutagus's man

499

said, introducing himself. "I've sent for your horses. Is there anything else you need?" he asked, directing the question at me.

Me.

But of course he did. Very soon, I would be queen here.

Beside me, Pix chuckled lightly.

"No. Thank you."

"Princess," he said, inclining his head to me. "If you will…"

Galvyn led us back down the halls of the roundhouse to the square outside. There, the horses waited.

Feeling like I was in a daze, I mounted once more. With two of Prasutagus's men riding as guards at the front, Bran just behind them, we left Venta. Pix rode beside me. Behind us followed Dôn and Brenna, who looked lost to her thoughts. She wouldn't meet my eye.

"She isn't mad," Pix told me.

"You don't even know my sister," I replied more tartly than I had intended, my worries getting the better of me.

"I have known her for a hundred lifetimes. She loves ye, and she will not be mad. Ye shall see."

I turned and looked at Pix, eyeing her sword and armor. They truly were in a style dated a hundred years back. And the way she spoke, her tone and manner, smacked of another time. Was she really telling the truth?

"If the druids really fought back the Romans all those years ago, how did you end up here?"

"Like I told you, through the mound."

"I don't think I like the idea of having a guardian who hid from the Romans in a mound."

Pix grinned at me. "There were twenty of them and one of me. And, I was already bleeding," she said, then lifted her tunic to show a massive sword wound on her side. "So I shimmied into my other self and hid."

"Your other self."

"My fox form, of course."

"So, you're a shapeshifter."

"And you're not?"

"What? No. Of course I'm not."

"You just shifted form from a second daughter to a future queen," Pix said with a grin.

"That's different."

"Is it? Shifting into your animal form isn't even *that* hard. I can teach you."

I rolled my eyes and shook my head.

Pix laughed. "What? Have the druids become so weak they don't know their other forms anymore? The fey warned me that the magic in the land was dying. But they think you're special. You are fire."

"You're giving me a headache."

"Oh. Don't worry. Something tells me that before this is done, you will have far worse than a headache."

"When what is done?"

Pix grinned. "You'll see."

WHEN WE RETURNED TO THE CAMP, DÔN SPOKE BRIEFLY TO Brenna, then the priestess set off down the path toward the nemeton. There was some flurry of excitement happening at Saenunos's camp. Bran went to investigate.

I followed Brenna into our tent.

"Sister," I said gently, entering the tent behind her.

Brenna froze, her back to me, then asked, "Why didn't you just tell me?"

"Tell you the man I cared about didn't want me? Tell you the only man I had felt anything for since Gaheris died asked for you instead of me?"

Brenna turned and looked at me.

"I wanted you to be happy. I knew that if I said anything, it would take from your happiness. I... I liked Prasutagus very much, but I thought he didn't want me. I didn't want to color your thoughts or take anything from you."

Brenna frowned. "When did you find out about this confusion?"

"When Bran and I arrived. Prasutagus and I spoke, and the misunderstanding revealed itself."

Brenna looked down at her lyre case sitting on her cot. She inhaled deeply then exhaled slowly. "You believe him that it was a mistake? That King Antedios misunderstood?"

"With all my heart. He is an honest man. Please, don't listen to Saenunos. I didn't contrive any of this."

Brenna nodded slowly. "Your sadness this winter speaks to your honesty. And I remember what Bran said, that there appeared to be a connection between the two of you. You have never lied to me before."

"I only did it out of love."

My sister smiled weakly at me. "I believe you."

"Brenna, I would never bring shame or pain upon you. I can tell Father—"

"Tell him nothing. I, too, heard Andraste's words on Dôn's lips. In the end, I will go to Mona, and you will go to the man you love. What more can we ask for? I am embarrassed, but I am also deeply relieved. I never wanted to marry a stranger."

I smiled at my sister, then went to her and took her hand. "Am I forgiven?"

Brenna smiled at me. "Yes. You *and* Prasutagus. I know you, Sister. You can read people's intentions before they even think them. If you believe him, I believe him. He was earnest in his words to me."

"He does care. Truly."

Brenna smiled. "I feel like a ton of stones have been lifted off me. I will leave here for Mona, and I will not have to wed. Boudica, you haven't wounded me. You have saved me."

I laughed. "Is he really so ugly?"

Brenna chuckled. "No. Not at all. But what good is a handsome face if you know nothing of a man's heart? And now that I know his heart—and that it belongs to you—there is no other question. The Dark Lady is kind to us today," Brenna said, then pulled me into an embrace.

My sister exhaled heavily, and I could feel the weight leaving her, but her words gave me pause. The Dark Goddess Andraste was many things—shrewd, riddling, merciless—but rarely known for spreading insipid kindness. Everything the Dark Lady did had a purpose.

"May the gods be with us all—now and in the future," I said.

Brenna nodded. "Now, and in the future."

CHAPTER 68

Bran, returning from Saenunos's camp, joined Brenna and me. He looked confused and upset.

"What is it?" I asked.

"Saenunos told his men to break camp. He's leaving. He said he would not sit and watch while Prasutagus stuck a knife into the back of the Northern Iceni."

"Where is he now?" I asked.

Bran shook his head. "He stormed off somewhere. What happened?"

"Nothing that should matter to Saenunos," I said angrily. "Prasutagus and I will wed, and Brenna will go to Mona."

"Father agreed?"

"Yes."

"Wait... You knew? About Prasutagus and Boudica?" Brenna asked Bran.

"Only of late," Bran replied.

Brenna nodded.

"Why would Saenunos be so angry about it? What is it to him?" Bran asked.

I paused a moment. "Caratacus… Saenunos has been talking to Caratacus."

"Yes, but that was on behalf of us all—" Bran began.

"But what if it wasn't?" I said, cutting him off. "What if this bargain with Caratacus had implications we know nothing about? What if Saenunos promised more than any of us understand? Father is sick…"

"You suspect Saenunos of plotting? Against Father?" Brenna asked.

"Father. Or Caturix after him. Or Prasutagus. Or the gods know who and for what purpose," I replied. I turned to my brother. "We need to find out where Saenunos went." I turned to Brenna. "So much for the gods being kind."

My sister chewed her bottom lip.

Motioning to my siblings, we stepped back outside. Down the lane from us, Saenunos's men were busily working tearing down the tents they had just erected.

"Did his druids come with him from Holk Fort?" I asked Brenna.

She shook her head.

Melusine and Pix joined us.

"What's happening?" Melusine asked.

"Chieftain Saenunos is leaving," I replied, then turned to Pix. "The chieftain left his camp. We need to know where he went."

Pix nodded to me, then left. She made her way into the crowded thoroughfare, then a moment later, disappeared.

"Pix told me what happened with Prasutagus," Melusine said carefully. "Is all—" She turned to Brenna. "—Is all well?"

Brenna nodded. "My sister and I understand one another. The matter is resolved."

Melusine exhaled heavily. "I'm so glad. Family should not

quarrel," she said, her eyes going to Saenunos's men once more. "My father once said the chieftain was slipperier than an eel."

"Yet he wed you to Caturix all the same," Bran said.

"He trusted King Aesunos."

"Let us hope that trust is shared. Something tells me, soon, we may need all the allies we can get."

AN HOUR LATER, PIX RETURNED.

"Found him," she said, sitting down at the campfire beside us. "He's coming along now."

"Where was he?" Bran asked.

"With those brother kings."

Bran and I looked at one another.

"Where are they now, Caratacus and Togodumnus?"

"The brother kings went to see Prasutagus," Pix told us, uncorking a jug of wine and taking a swig.

"Did you hear anything? See anything?" Bran asked Pix.

"Arguing. A lot of arguing. I couldn't get close enough to hear much," she said, then handed the wine jug to me. "Heard yer name," she told me. "And yer father's. And that of yer elder brother, Caturix."

A moment later, Saenunos returned to camp.

"Boudica," Brenna said, a nervous tremor in her voice.

"Stay with Brenna and Melusine," I told Pix, then motioned for Bran to come with me. I grabbed my spear, and the two of us made our way down the lane as Saenunos barked orders at his men, then called for his horse.

"Uncle," Bran said firmly.

Saenunos turned toward us. His face was a thundercloud.

"Where are you going?" Bran asked.

"Back to Holk Fort and away from all of this duplicity," he snarled, then turned to me. "You, girl… You have no idea what you have done."

"I have done nothing that has not met with my father's approval and that of the gods. You are not king. You have no say over me."

Saenunos clenched his jaw hard, the muscles under his eye trembling. His face and neck burned red. "You will learn better in the end," he said, then called to his men who brought his horse. He mounted then turned and rode off, his people hurrying to follow along behind him.

"Bran, Father must know."

"Going to get my horse now," Bran replied.

I stood watching as my uncle disappeared into the crowd.

Now, I understood Prasutagus's impatience with all of this back-biting.

The Romans were coming.

And no one seemed to care.

Except for the greenwood.

My gaze went back to Pix.

Except for the greenwood.

"Boudica.

"Queen of Oak.

"Protect the trees.

"Protect the rivers.

"Protect the stones.

"They are coming."

CHAPTER 69

I t was several hours later when Father, Caturix, Bran, and Prasutagus returned. Along with Prasutagus came his druids and much of his household. It was late afternoon. Soon, the sun would set, and the rites would come to fruition. Already, bonfires lit the hillside. The sound of drums and music filled the air. The druids chanted at the nemeton. From where we were, I could see them with their arms lifted in the air as they performed their ceremonies.

Not far from our camp, a rite was being held where the rivers Tas and Yare met. The priestesses gathered there. Standing on the river banks, they sent flaming votives along the waves, the votives joining where the rivers met. Bel's eyes were upon us—as were those of all the gods.

Aesunos wore a look of unworried detachment. But under that placid exterior, he was a torrent of emotions. In that single moment, I understood my father far better than I ever had before. By now, he would have known Saenunos had left. By now, he would have explained to Caratacus that there could be no alliance between our tribes—in fact, I would wed Prasutagus this very night. By now, Prasutagus would have explained to the brother kings the more significant threat from Rome.

But had they listened?

And still, my father looked unfazed.

The look on Caturix's face, however, was less cloaked. Things had not gone well.

We rose to join them, Brenna and I going to my father to help him dismount.

"Father," I said gently.

My father gave me such a dark look, I said nothing more and simply held his horse's reins while Brenna offered him her arm.

"Shall we walk to the henge, King Aesunos?" Prasutagus asked him.

"I'll join you in a moment," Father told him. He whispered to Brenna then left us, going into his tent, Belenus behind him.

I handed off the reins to one of the lads then went to Prasutagus.

"Prasutagus, how were the talks?" I asked him quietly.

Prasutagus met my gaze and held it. "Depends on the subject," he said, then smiled lightly. "Caratacus and Togodumnus will join us for the rites," he said, then looked toward the nemeton.

"And the matter of the Romans?"

"They were less willing to listen."

"And the news of our marriage?"

Grinning, Prasutagus shook his head. "Met with humor."

"Humor?"

"The brothers found the confusion amusing, not insulting. I don't know. A game has been played here. I cannot see all the pieces. Nor, I think, does your father. They wish us well—at least, those were the words on their lips."

"And in their hearts?"

Prasutagus tilted his head, showing he had his doubts.

"Do you know Saenunos has gone?"

He nodded.

I sighed then looked toward the nemeton once more.

"I am sorry, Boudica," Prasutagus said.

"For?" I asked, confused.

"For any tensions between you and your family, particularly between you and your sister."

"Brenna is amenable. And while I couldn't care less what he thinks, it's what Saenunos does next that concerns me."

"And me."

"That said, my uncle is usually more bluster than action."

"Let's hope he remains so. I must make one more apology."

"For?"

"Tonight, you will be a bride. And you haven't had a moment to make ready."

"By the gods," I said, looking down at my leather trousers and jerkin. For a brief moment, my dream of a perfect wedding gown made of deep purple fabric and embroidered with orange, yellow, and red flowers—as I had planned to wear when I wed Gaheris—danced through my mind. "With everything happening, I never had a moment to give it a thought. I'll become your wife smelling like strawberry wine and campfire smoke."

Prasutagus touched my cheek. "We made our marriage in the greenwood already. This is for the others."

I smiled at him, moved by his caring.

"King Prasutagus," the druid Ansgar said, joining us. "Princess Boudica."

"Ansgar, is it not?" I asked.

"Yes, Princess. May I introduce Ardra? She is a novice of my order," he said, turning to the young woman I had seen shadowing him.

"Princess," Ardra said, bowing deeply. The woman had pale blonde hair pulled back into a light braid, a smattering of freckles on her nose, and light blue eyes.

I smiled at her. "Merry met."

"And you, Princess, soon to become our queen."

"I… thank you." *Queen.* I turned to Prasutagus. He was what I wanted. But queen?

"We should join the others at the nemeton, my king," Ansgar told us.

"My father…" I said, turning to the tent only to see Aesunos return once more. He looked paler than he should, and he was walking with a staff.

I frowned.

Prasutagus took in the situation then said, "King Aesunos, perhaps your charioteer can drive you to the—"

Father lifted his hand. "I am well, Prasutagus. This day belongs to Bel. I will not dishonor him or the gods any further this day with my mortal complaints."

Prasutagus nodded, then said nothing more.

"Come," Father called to Caturix and Bran, motioning for the others to join us.

Belenus, Ansgar, and Ardra leading us, we left the camp and began our trek to the nemeton.

"Now, that is familiar," Pix said, popping up beside me once more.

I followed her gaze to the shrine. "The rites?"

She nodded. "In a world where much seems different, at least that's the same."

"What else is different?" I asked, playing into her game.

Pix eyes twinkled. "Clothing style. The way ye talk. And, there are more people now. Is everyone fornicating more than they used to?"

I giggled. "I guess so."

"At least that's one good change."

I laughed.

"Laugh now, Red. I'll get ye and yer Strawberry King yet."

I rolled my eyes. "Something tells me we have far more important things to worry about."

"More important than fornicating?"

I laughed. "Yes."

"Killing Romans and picking strawberries in the greenwood... two of my greatest pleasures."

"Be careful not to get lost in the Otherworld this time."

"Oh, Boudica. No chance of that. This time, I am with you 'til the end."

CHAPTER 70

As the sun dipped toward the horizon, the people crowded near the nemeton. The tall wooden henges glimmered in the fading sunlight, the orange and pink rays picking up the hue on the barkless timbers of the henge.

Singing softly, the priestesses left the riverside and joined the druids at the nemeton. It was a beautiful sight to see all of the priestesses from sacred stone rings, groves, glens, waterfalls, and other holy spots in one place. Their colorful veils and adornments made them look like spring flowers. In the crowd, I saw Dôn, Grainne, Bec, and Tatha in their midnight-blue gowns. Unlike the druids who served all the gods, each sect of priestesses served only one goddess. At seahenge near Holk Fort where Saenunos ruled, there was a seaside temple in honor of the sacred spring and its goddess whose waters fed the Wash—though I didn't see them here. The holy people stood in rings around the bonfire at the center of the henge. In the crowd, I spotted Einion, the druid of Stonea.

A man I had not seen before stood on a stump before the great bonfire.

"Who is that?" Brenna whispered.

"Caoilfhionn," Prasutagus answered. "He is the Arch Druid of all the Britons."

The High Priestess Selwyn stood at his side. On his other side stood a woman in a pale, lavender dress wearing a veil. Amongst the priestesses, I also spotted a group of women similarly dressed, their faces veiled.

"The Maids of Avallach," Pix whispered, pointing with her chin.

"The priestesses of Avallach have come?" Melusine whispered in amazement.

"Ansgar sent word to all of our holy people," Prasutagus told us. "The veiled woman beside the Arch Druid is their high priestess, Venetia. While it may take more than talk to convince my fellow kings of the dangers off our shores, the druids are another matter. If I can get them on my side—"

"Then they can convince the people," I finished for him.

Prasutagus nodded.

My eyes drifted across those gathered there, pausing as I caught Bec's gaze. She looked dazed, her eyes glossy. Her hair was unbound, and her feet bare. The gods had her.

"Gather. Gather," Caoilfhionn called. "Britons. Iceni. Catuvellauni. Trinovantes. Coritani. All the people of this sacred island. Gather before the fires of Bel. Gather before the eyes of the gods," the druid called, his arms upraised.

"Your Highnesses," Ansgar said to Prasutagus and Aesunos. "Come. Princess Boudica, you as well," the druid said, then motioned for us to follow him to the center of the circle.

I cast a glance at Brenna, who motioned for me to go on.

Father would not look my way but followed behind Ansgar.

Prasutagus took my hand and led me through the crowd until Prasutagus, Father, and I stood before the bonfire. My siblings gathered behind me.

A moment later, King Togodumnus joined us, and at his side...

"Blue dun," I said as the stranger—and not a stranger—joined us.

"Dapple-grey," he replied with a smirk. "Princess Boudica?"

I inclined my head to him. "King Caratacus?"

He nodded, then chuckled. "The gods work in mysterious ways, Princess. Yesterday, your wild beauty and excellent riding skills inspired me to make the trade for the pin. This morning, you were supposed to be my wife. Now, you will become queen of the Greater Iceni," he said, then laughed.

Prasutagus listened to our exchange, a confused expression on his face.

"I thank you for your acquiescence in all subjects," I told him.

Caratacus chuckled then turned to Prasutagus. "Had I known the princess was the red-haired horsewoman who'd given me such a good race yesterday, I might not have so easily let her go," he said, then turned to me. "And you're not even wearing my pin, Princess."

I chuckled. "It's been put to good use."

Caratacus smiled at me, giving me that same flirtatious gaze he had at the race. At that moment, I recognized his game. Whereas Togodumnus did not hide his crudeness, Caratacus was a stealthy operator. His game was one of hunter and prey. And while he seemed far more charming of the pair, that only made him more dangerous.

I turned my attention back to the druids.

Once the crowd had gathered and the sun dipped toward the horizon, a hush fell over all of us. The roar of the bonfire was the only sound to be heard.

Caoilfhionn raised his hands once more. "Britons! We have gathered here this night to honor our gods. As the sun falls this Beltane, let Bel's fires light up the night's sky. May the Horned Lord and the Maiden be honored as we move into the summer season. Great ones," he called in a loud voice, "we honor you!"

Selwyn stepped forward. "May the Lord and Lady grant fertility to our land. May our animals be blessed. May our crops be blessed. May our wombs be blessed. As the Maiden becomes the Mother, so too do we all come to fullness. May the Forest Lord offer his seed to the land, to us all, coaxing new life."

The high priestess, Venetia, stepped forward.

She nodded to a woad-painted man behind her who lifted his carnyx. The long trumpet let out a deep, sorrowful sound that echoed across the river valley.

The high priestess raised her arms. Her long sleeves fell back to reveal the silver bracelets that adorned her wrists. A moment later, she began singing in a language I did not recognize. The hair on my arms rose, and I shuddered lightly, feeling magic stir in the very air. Whatever language she was singing, it was ancient. The greenwood around me seemed to shiver.

When the song was finished, the player blew the carnyx once more. The sound hallowed the space around us.

"May Bel's fires burn," Caoilfhionn called, "warding off the darkness. But even as the summer fires burn across our land, crowns of flame on every sacred hilltop, darkness rolls toward us. My honorable kings," he said, looking toward our party. "We must keep one eye on the horizon, for even in the brightest days, darkness comes."

"But for this night, we honor Bel," Selwyn called. "We will leave aside the darkness and embrace the light. My people, tonight the Stag King and the Maiden walk amongst us. As a sign that the gods are with us, we shall see a great union of our people. And under the eyes of the gods, we shall see King Prasutagus of the Greater Iceni wed Princess Boudica of the Northern Iceni."

At that, the crowd cheered.

Selwyn gestured to the priestesses, and soon their voices lit up in song. They sang of the May Queen, Cernunnos, and all the greenwood.

The priestesses of Avallach came forward carrying branches covered with apple blossoms. They approached me.

"Princess Boudica," one of the women said, "we are your attendants this night. As you are the maiden queen, we are your handmaids," she said, then set a ring of flowers on my head. "Come," she said, motioning for me to follow her.

Singing sweetly, the maidens led me to the other side of the fire before Caoilfhionn.

The nemeton sat on a slight slant. The entrance to the holy place faced the river. When I came to stand at the feet of the Arch Druid, I looked back to see my family—and the hundreds of people gathered there—watching.

I wasn't just becoming Prasutagus's wife; I was becoming queen.

These people would rely upon me to shelter them, care for them.

And if the Romans were indeed coming…

I would need to lead.

I would need to do so much more than be a wife.

Suddenly, a sense of terror washed over me. Was I strong enough for this? Panic gripped me.

Gaheris, be with me.

Gaheris, help me.

Gaheris, it was supposed to be you. As I stand here, I see a future before me so different from what we dreamed. Be with me. Please, be with me.

"*I am always in your heart…*" a soft voice whispered in reply. "*You are strong enough for this. For this and so much more. There is no one stronger.*"

Ansgar went to Prasutagus, placing on his head a crown made of oak leaves wound around the horns of a stag. He spoke in low tones to the king then led Prasutagus around the other side of the fire to join me.

We stood across from one another—me crowned with apple blossoms, Prasutagus the picture of Cernunnos himself. We turned to the Arch Druid Caoilfhionn.

Caoilfhionn cleared his throat then said, "Tonight, King Prasutagus and Princess Boudica embody the Maiden and the Forest Lord. This night, for the first time in the history of our people, the Northern and Greater Iceni unite. Let this joining of our people strengthen our already-firm alliances. With the kings of the great Catuvellauni as our allies, none can come to these shores to harm what we hold sacred.

"Prasutagus, son of Antedios and Enid, Princess Boudica of the Northern Iceni comes to you this night as the May Queen. Will you take this woman as your wife?" the druid asked.

"I shall."

Caoilfhionn turned to me. "Princess Boudica, daughter of

King Aesunos and Damara, King Prasutagus comes to you this night as the Forest Lord. Will you take this man as your husband?"

"I shall."

Caoilfhionn motioned to the high priestess of Avallach, who stepped forward, a length of ivy in her hands.

She locked our hands then twisted the vine around them. When she was done, she lifted our joined hands. "Handfasted. Promised. From one life to the next, may you be bound together," she said, her soft voice carrying on the wind. "Two halves of one whole. You are now one. Man and woman. King and queen. Northern Iceni and Greater Iceni. Earth and fire. Together, rule this land. Protect your people. And protect one another," she said. "May the Great Mother and the Forest Lord hear us. Not only do they unite as man and wife, but they unite our lands. By the fire, as the flames as a witness to your oaths, kiss and be wed."

At that, Prasutagus and I leaned forward, meeting one another for a soft kiss.

The crowd erupted in cheers.

"This Beltane night," Caoilfhionn called, "we are doubly blessed. Our alliances strengthen. Our friends are with us. And the blessings of the gods are upon us. Drink. Cheer. And honor the gods."

The druid sounded the carnyx once more. Afterward, the massive crowd fell into revelry.

I gazed up at Prasutagus. Everything was happening so quickly. So much confusion and pain were washed away in what felt like a single moment. In the end, there was only him... my husband.

"Boudica," he whispered, leaning in to kiss me once more. When he pulled back, he set his forehead against mine.

"May all the gods be praised," I whispered.

"Especially Andraste, who made this night come."

"Praise Andraste."

"Praise Andraste."

"And may the greenwood watch over us."

CHAPTER 71

When the rites were done, Father retreated without speaking to anyone. I watched as he disappeared into the throng of people back to our tents. Was he angry or ill? Belenus paused a moment, watching him go, then turned to Prasutagus and me.

"King Prasutagus, Queen Boudica, may the gods bless you both. Your mother would be very happy for you, my dear," he told me, pulling me into an embrace.

"Thank you, Belenus."

The old druid turned to Prasutagus. "King Prasutagus, many blessings."

"Thank you, wise Belenus."

Bran and Brenna crowded in next.

"I am happy for you," Brenna told me, kissing me on the cheek then whispered, "He doesn't seem so bad after all—but you can keep him."

I chuckled. "Thank you, Sister."

"When Riona hears you wed in trousers, she will never forgive any of us," Brenna added with a laugh which I joined.

She turned to Prasutagus. "King Prasutagus, I give you my blessings."

Prasutagus smiled softly at Brenna. "Of all the well-wishes here, I am most grateful for those, Princess Brenna."

"I'm not one to be wounded over small confusions."

"I suspect not. No one of your family is made of such fragile stuff."

Brenna smiled.

Bran then pulled me into an embrace. "Queen of the Greater Iceni."

"Brother... let's hope you are next to come before the gods in matrimony."

"We shall see."

I turned to find Melusine, who moved Bran aside to hug me. "Congratulations, Boudica. I have nothing in my hand for you. I'm so sorry."

"You are here. What more can I ask for?"

When she let me go, I met Caturix's gaze.

"It has been a strange day for you," he said finally.

I nodded.

He mustered up a light smile—the best Caturix could ever do—then embraced me. "I am glad to see you have found happiness again," he whispered in my ear.

"As have you, I think?"

"Yes. Despite all odds," he said then turned to Prasutagus. "You are welcome to our family."

Prasutagus inclined his head to Caturix. "Thank you, Brother."

Caturix turned to me. "I will see to Father now."

I nodded.

Belenus along with him, Caturix retreated.

Togodumnus and Caratacus joined us.

"We wish you well, Prasutagus. You and your new queen," Togodumnus said. "My brother and I will leave in the morning. You have given us much to consider. But I still say that one shouldn't put stock in rumors."

Prasutagus nodded slowly. "Let's hope that's all they are."

Togodumnus turned to his brother. "Since Caratacus will not be wed," he said, then gave me a sly grin, "we will ride south to the Regnenses. If there is any word of Verica attempting to return, we will find it there."

"Besides, they also have a princess," Caratacus said with a laugh.

"I thought you would try for Cartimandua instead," Togodumnus told his brother, a confused expression on his face.

"Let's see how the Regnenses princess looks first."

"I'm starting to feel less guilty over the turn of events," I told Caratacus.

"Don't," he told me. "You must swim in guilt forever. I prefer redheaded horsewomen above all. And they tell me your sister is for Mona. I am twice denied the house of Aesunos," he told me with a wink.

I laughed.

"But all the same, I wish you well, Queen Boudica."

"I am grateful, King Caratacus."

With that, the brother kings bowed then left us.

"King Prasutagus, Queen Boudica," Arch Druid Caoilfhionn said, joining us. "I am honored to oversee your wedding this night."

"We thank you, wise father," Prasutagus told him.

"I still say I am sorry to see you king, Prasutagus. Many hoped to see you in my place one day."

"I am flattered by such words," Prasutagus replied.

Caoilfhionn turned to me. "Prasutagus was a novice under

me," he said, then nodded. "A most skilled one at that. And your mother, Boudica, was once a priestess. Let us see what children the gods give the pair of you. Many blessings," he said, clapping Prasutagus on the shoulder, then left.

It was then that Selwyn approached to speak to Prasutagus, but out of the corner of my eye, I saw the High Priestess of Avallach making her way toward me.

"Sacred Lady," I said, turning to her.

"Queen Boudica," Venetia said, her voice light and silvery. "The sisters of Avallach are honored to be with you on this day."

"I am the one who is honored."

"Hmm," Venetia mused. "Queen Boudica... I have heard your name whispered amongst the oaks, in the breath of the stones, in the small voices of the good neighbors, and in the dark places. Prasutagus is right to keep his gaze south. We see. We know. And so does the greenwood. Please know that you are always welcome on our island. It is a place of refuge. Remember that."

"That is... That is an honor without compare."

"I shall see you again, I think," she said, then turned and rejoined her group, the veiled priestesses disappearing once more into the crowd.

I scanned the horizon. The crowd had dispersed back into the fields. The festival was in full swing. Music came from every direction. Fires burned. I heard laughing and cheering. The fire-spinners worked at the side of the river. Everywhere I looked, I saw revelry.

"Boudica," Prasutagus said, taking my hand.

I turned back to him, greeting him with a smile.

"Come, my wife. It is Beltane, and we are wed."

CHAPTER 72

After saying goodbye to the others for the night, I collected Druda, and Prasutagus and I prepared to ride back to Venta.

I had just mounted Druda when I spotted Pix slipping onto Cai's horse. She clicked to the beast then joined Prasutagus and me.

"And what are you doing?" I asked.

"Coming with ye to Venta."

"On Cai's horse?"

Pix grinned. "I'll have the beastie back in the morning."

I sighed. "All right. But it is *my* wedding night. Remember that."

Pix laughed. "No strawberry picking? Understood."

Prasutagus smirked at Pix then turned to me. "Do the others want to come to the roundhouse? Your brothers…"

"I offered, but they will stay for the festival."

"And your father?" he asked, looking toward the tent.

The truth be told, I hadn't tried to see Aesunos. My father

had consented to the marriage, but clearly, his mind was troubled. "I didn't ask him."

Prasutagus nodded slowly, thoughtfully. He was right to hesitate.

With a sigh, I looked back toward my father's tent. "I will bid him goodnight."

Prasutagus nodded.

I slipped off Druda and went to the tent.

"Father," I called. I waited for a long moment, but there was no answer.

Feeling annoyed, I moved the tent flap aside and went in. There, I found my father sitting before a fire. He stared into the flames.

"Father," I said again.

This time, he looked up. He studied me for a long time then said, "Queen now."

I wasn't sure what to say, so after a moment, I simply said, "I will return with Prasutagus to Venta. Would you like to come? You would be more comfortab—"

He laughed loudly, halting my speech, then looked back at the fire. "You always get what you want. Even as a child. It made no difference what we told you, if we told you no, if we forbid it. You would do as you wished anyway. Your mother always said to let you be, that it was good that you were forthright about your desires. But I could see the trouble ahead. You wanted things the way you wanted them. You have the wit to convince anyone of anything. But you never pause to look around you. In the end, you get what you want—may anyone between you and your desires burn."

I stood still for a long moment, then said, "I did not create this confusion. And Andraste—"

"Even the gods bow to Boudica's will," he said with a hard laugh.

"Why do you begrudge me? What difference does it make to you if one daughter over the other weds Prasutagus?"

My father stared into the fire. "You will learn. You will learn why it mattered."

"Brenna has forgiven the confusion and—"

"Of course she has," he said testily. "What more can you expect of her? Now, she will leave as well. She will ride with the druids to Mona in the morning. Everything is as Boudica wanted."

"You cannot decide if you are friend or enemy to me, your mood changing like the tide," I said waspishly. "What kind of father does not congratulate his daughter on her wedding day? What kind of father curses his child? I wanted Prasutagus. That is true. But when I thought he'd asked for Brenna, I said nothing. I gave up the man I wanted for my sister's sake. I suffered the sting of that. But when the truth was revealed... It was the gods—it was Andraste—who has slighted your will here, not me."

"Then a curse upon you both!" my father said, rising.

The fire beside him flashed up, making a terrible pop and crackle, the flames flickering blue for a moment.

My father and I both stared, recognizing the bad omen.

"May the Dark Lady forgive your rash tongue," I told him.

But my father said nothing.

Frustrated, I turned and went back outside. Without saying another word, I slipped back onto Druda and rejoined the others.

"Boudica?" Prasutagus asked.

I forced a smile. "Let's go."

He nodded to me, then our small party set off for Venta. As

we passed through the crowd, the people called to us, show-ering us with well-wishes and calls of happiness. I got from strangers the blessings I could not wring from my own father.

But as much as he hurt me, it was not the rift between us he should be worried about.

The Dark Lady Andraste was not forgiving.

And she had marked his words.

WHEN WE RETURNED TO VENTA, I DISCOVERED THE SERVANTS working hastily to prepare for my sudden and unexpected arrival.

"Queen Boudica," an older lady said, bowing to me. "You are welcome to Venta. We are endeavoring to get everything ready for you. Please forgive us for the delay."

"Boudica, this is Nella," Prasutagus said, introducing the woman. "She will tend you."

I studied the woman. Nella had pale brown hair streaked with silver. The hair all around the frame of her face was white. She wore her long locks pulled back in a long braid and wore a simple dark green gown pinned at the shoulders. "I am glad to meet you, Nella," I told her. "Please, don't trouble yourselves. All I need is a bed and a round of bread."

She gave me a tight smile then turned to Prasutagus. "Your Highness, we have moved everything to the east chamber as you asked. I sent some of the lads there now with hot water to prepare a bath for the queen," she said, then turned to me. "Do you have a maid with you? Your belongings…"

I patted the bag strung on my back. "Only this," I said with a laugh. "I will return to Oak Throne for the rest. I don't have a maid, but my companion"—I gestured to Pix—"will need lodging."

Pix stood studying the display of arms on the wall. She reached out to touch one of the spears hanging there when the latch on it broke, and the spear clattered onto the floor.

"That wasn't me," she said with a grin, then winked at Prasutagus, who chuckled.

"This is Pix. Can you see that she has her own accommodations and anything else she might need?"

Nella eyed Pix carefully. "Very well," she said, then turned to Prasutagus. "Shall I see the queen to your chamber?"

Prasutagus shook his head. "I shall escort her."

Nella smiled stiffly. "Very well."

Leaving Prasutagus a moment, I went to Pix, who was trying to fix the display.

"The maid will see you settled," I said, then lowered my voice. "No stories with the servants. From today onward, at least here in Venta, you are my old friend from Frog's Hollow in the lands of the Northern Iceni. Understood?"

"Frog's Hollow. Sound's like a muddy place."

"Pix."

"Understood. No stories about Caesar. From now on, I'm from the mud hollow."

I rolled my eyes at her. "I'll find you in the morning."

"I hope not."

"No?"

"I hope you wear yourself out and don't wake until midday meal. Otherwise, you aren't doing it right."

I laughed. "Good night, Pix."

"Good night, *Queen* Boudica."

I rejoined Prasutagus.

He grinned at me. "All right, my queen," he said, then

scooped me up, carrying me. "Let me see you to your chamber."

Two young servants who stood not far away chuckled, then Prasutagus carried me down the hall to a chamber that sat at the very back of the house.

When we entered, I found a brazier burning. Two colorful lanterns also hung from the beams, sending a rainbow of colors all over the room. A reddish-colored blanket covered the large bed on which lay rich furs. Chests and wardrobes outfitted the rest of the room, the space larger than three of my own chambers at home. A basin with steaming water sprinkled with wildflowers and herbs sat ready beside the fireplace. Candles sat all around the room, drenching the place in a soft, orange glow.

Prasutagus set me down.

"How lovely," I said. "This is your room?"

Prasutagus crossed his arms on his chest then surveyed the space. "It is now. I asked for a new chamber to be prepared for us."

A new chamber…one he had not shared with his first wife. While he didn't say so, I knew that was his meaning. His thoughtfulness on the matter touched me—both his honor of her memory and any sensitivity I might have to sleeping in the bed he once shared with her.

I gently touched one of the colorful lanterns hanging from the beam. "Such fine glasswork."

"There is an artisan here in Venta."

I nodded then set my bag on one of the trunks. I turned to Prasutagus.

"Is it all right?" he asked, gesturing to the room.

"More than."

Prasutagus crossed the room and took my face into his

hands, kissing me. When he was done, he leaned back and whispered, "Can I help my queen with her bath?"

Grinning, I nodded.

Prasutagus smiled gently at me then began unlacing the ties on my jerkin. His movements were careful and slow. When he was done, he gently pulled the piece off then set it aside. He moved on then to the laces on my breeches, untying those then helping me slip them off. He then gently slid his hands under my tunic, setting them on my bare waist, then lifted the clothing off. Then, he gently pulled off my under-breeches.

Prasutagus sucked in his bottom lip as his eyes roved over my body. Setting his hands on my waist, he pulled me close, then leaned in and placed kisses on my neck and shoulder.

"You told my father you love me," I whispered in his ear, my whole body tingling in response to his touch.

"From the first moment I saw you."

"They say such a thing isn't possible."

"Who are they?" he asked. I could hear a smile in his voice.

I chuckled. "I don't know."

Prasutagus met my eyes once more. "I feel like I have known you a thousand lifetimes. The moment I saw you, my heart was yours."

I swallowed hard, feeling tears well in my eyes. "And mine was yours…"

Prasutagus leaned in and kissed me then, his hand gently touching my breast. I groaned lightly. His other hand trailed down my back to my bottom, where he squeezed me.

Unable to resist him, I reached out and began working the ties on his clothes, undressing him as he had done to me. Between kisses, we moved closer to the bed. Before I knew it, we found one another there. Our mouths roved over each other's skin, Prasutagus lingering on my nipples before drizzling kisses down my chest, stomach, and between my legs. I grabbed the coverlet in ecstasy, my mind reeling. Everything happening in a blur of flesh and feeling, we moved together as one—man and woman, Maiden and Forest Lord, husband and wife, king and queen. When we had both found release, we lay in one another's arms, both of us sweaty from the exertion.

"Your bath is growing cold," Prasutagus said.

I chuckled. "It's still beautiful to look at," I said, gazing at the purple, yellow, blue, and white flowers floating on the surface of the water.

"Like a flower soup," Prasutagus said, making me giggle.

I sat up then unbound my tangled braid. When I was done, my hair made a massive plume about me.

"Like fire," Prasutagus said, running his hands down my locks.

"Your red locks curl and wave and are as smooth as rabbit fur," I said, twisting one of his curls around my finger. "Mine is like a tangled inferno."

"Perhaps you have more fire inside than me," he said with a grin.

We both chuckled.

I rose and went to the washing tub, sticking my toe in. It was still warm. "Want to join me?"

He shook his head. "I'm content to sit here and watch my flower maiden."

"In my soup."

"In your soup," he agreed.

Laughing, I slipped into the tub, letting the water envelop me. On a stool nearby, the maid had set out several perfume vials. I opened them, giving each a sniff. The scents were so pungent, they made me sneeze.

Prasutagus laughed. "You've no need of those. The wild-flowers are perfume enough for you."

I winked at him, then holding my breath, I slipped underwater. The warm liquid enveloped me, caressing my body, reminding me of warm days at the Wash under the sun—with Gaheris.

Gaheris...

Gaheris, forgive me for loving another...

Gaheris...

I slipped out of the water only to find Prasutagus there, ready with a piece of linen. I dried my face. My husband, still undressed, took a seat behind me.

"I will wash your hair," he said, then got to work.

I was wed.

I was a bride.

I was the wife of King Prasutagus.

And I was queen...

Prasutagus tended to my long locks, then dressed them with oil.

"You are as good as my maid," I told him.

He laughed.

When I was done, he helped me out of the tub, taking me back to the bed once more. There, we curled up together, lying in each other's arms.

"Boudica," Prasutagus whispered in my ear. "The days before us will not be easy, but I swear by all the gods, I will do everything in my power to keep you safe."

I smiled softly. "Good. I shall do the same for you."

Prasutagus chuckled lightly. "Warrior woman."

"Would you rather have a soft, perfumed thing?"

"Never," he said, then kissed my shoulder. "There is no one

else in this world for me besides Boudica," he said, then kissed me again. And again. And again.

Soon, we were lost to one another once more. When we were done, I lay half-awake, half-asleep in Prasutagus's arms.

Great Andraste…

Dark Lady…

Thank you…

And in the darkness, I heard quiet laughter in reply.

CHAPTER 73

It was late in the morning when I woke the next day. I could hear Prasutagus moving about the room. I opened my eyes to see him washing his face from a basin of hot water. The scents of rosemary and verbena filled the air. The bathing tub was missing, the candles extinguished.

"Prasutagus?" I whispered.

He turned and smiled at me, crossing the room to kiss me. "I've had a messenger from Arminghall. The druids of Mona are leaving this morning. I was about to wake you. I thought you would want to say goodbye to your sister."

I nodded. "Thank you."

"I hung your things. I'm sure Nella will do a better job, but it's a start," he said, pointing to a wardrobe.

I opened it to find the items Brenna and Riona had packed for me hanging there. Suddenly, I was sorry I hadn't remembered to redress last night. My favorite lavender-colored gown was there. The last time I had worn the frock was the day my father had agreed to let me wed Gaheris.

The two of us redressed then made our way to the dining

hall where I found Pix talking to the servants as she ate a round of bread—the bread in one hand, an apple in the other. Everyone was red-faced from laughing at some story she'd told.

Galvyn, Prasutagus's housecarl, was also there. Prasutagus joined him while I went to Pix.

"This is your kitchen staff," Pix told me, her mouth half full. "Betha, her daughter Ronat, and little Newt," she said, tousling the kitchen boy's curly brown hair.

"Newt?" I asked.

The boy, his eyes twinkling mischievously, nodded. "On account of my spots," he said, pointing to his cheeks.

I bent to look him in the eye. "Hmm," I said, studying him. "I see," I said seriously.

"And on account of you always scurrying about so quickly," Betha said. She was a reed-thin woman, who had a broad smile and a mountain of curly blonde hair.

I smiled at her. "I am pleased to meet you all," I said, turning my attention to Ronat, a mirror of her mother, but her manner far shyer. "Please, call me Boudica."

Betha inclined her head to me.

I turned to Pix. "We need to return to Arminghall."

Pix nodded. "I'll get my things."

Prasutagus joined us. "I've sent a boy to fetch the horses," he told me.

"I can only imagine Druda's mood after being in a strange stable all night. I'll need to meet your horsemaster later. My boy is particular."

"Let's hope Raven kept him good company."

"Here you go, Ginerva," I heard Nella say as she guided an elderly woman into the room. She took her to the table and settled her into a seat. The woman was an ancient creature, frail as glass, with snow-white hair she wore pulled up under a cap that laced at the neck. She had a pinched expression, her eyes squinting as she tried to take in the room. "There is currant bread today. You'll like that. Betha purchased many new goods and spices from the fair."

"What fair?" the woman demanded angrily.

"It is Beltane, remember?" Nella said gently.

"Where is Esu? She went to get me new boots from the fair."

Prasutagus turned to me. "I... There was no time to mention it. This is Ginerva, Esu's mother. There was no one to look after her, so I kept her here with me after Esu—"

"Say nothing more," I told him.

Prasutagus gazed sadly at the woman. "Many times, she does not remember Esu is dead. She and my father often had the maddest conversations," he said then laughed lightly. "Please, don't take offense to anything she says."

"I am sorry for her."

Prasutagus nodded. While he had not meant to, he exhaled heavily—in relief, I realized. The truth was, I knew very little about Prasutagus's daily life. There was a whole house full of people here whose names and faces I didn't know—not to mention the many chieftains of the Greater Iceni. I had much to learn in the days to come.

"Ginerva," Prasutagus said. "Good morrow to you."

"And you, and you," she said, bobbing her hand at him dismissively as she filled her plate.

"I want you to meet someone," he said. The pair of us went to the side of the table.

Nella stepped back, but I could see she watched us closely —me, in particular—a firm expression on her face.

"Ginerva, this is Boudica," Prasutagus said, introducing me.

The old woman paused then looked at me. "Your sister," she told Prasutagus matter-of-factly.

"No," Prasutagus said. "She is my wife."

"Esu is your wife," Ginerva said with a laugh. "What jokes you make, Prasutagus." The old woman eyed me closely. "You have red hair."

"I do."

"And a temper to match?"

"Not when I can help it. But I confess, I can't always help it."

The old woman laughed. "My hair used to be red, just like yours. Now I look like I have a pile of snow on my head. Where is the clotted cream?"

"Here you are," I said, shifting the pot toward her.

"Ah. Good. Thank you, girl."

"Won't you welcome Boudica?" Nella asked her.

"Who?"

I smiled, then set a gentle hand on the old woman's frail shoulder. "I am pleased to meet you, Ginerva," I told her.

The woman looked up at me. "Esu's new maid has red hair," she said absently, then turned back to her meal. "Where is the orange jam? Why is there never orange jam?"

"It is hard to get such items here," Nella told her. "But there is honey."

Ginerva sighed heavily. "Very well."

Pix appeared once more, fully armored, my spear in her hand.

I turned to Prasutagus, who nodded.

"We'll return later," he told Nella, who inclined her head to him. "Can I bring you anything from the fair, Ginerva?" Prasutagus asked her.

"No. My father will bring me something."

Prasutagus gave her a sad smile, then motioned for us to go.

Prasutagus, Pix, and I left the roundhouse. There, we found Raven, Druda, and Cai's horse, Brandywine, waiting. Along with them was a small band of guards.

"Does Cai know you have his horse?" I asked Pix.

"I'm sure he's figured it out by now," Pix replied with a grin.

I shook my head. "Sorry, Brandywine," I said, stroking the horse's nose. "We'll get you back to your owner."

Pix chuckled.

The three of us mounted, then rode out, Prasutagus's guards following.

As we made our way through the city, people called out to Prasutagus and me.

Prasutagus turned to me. "I am sorry I didn't have time to apprise you of the situation in my home."

"Make no apologies for having lived a life before me."

"Esu was a commoner," he told me. "After she died, there was no one to care for Esu's mother, so I kept Ginerva with me."

"I am sure Esu is comforted in the Otherworld to see her mother looked after."

Prasutagus shifted slightly then said, "And... her son."

"Her son?"

Prasutagus nodded. "Esu was barely sixteen years old when her father wed her off in a marriage of monetary convenience. A son was born of that marriage—but both Esu's father and husband died of fever. The boy, Artur, is also in my care."

"Artur… I didn't see the child."

"He's hiding in protest, I am told."

"How old is he?"

"Ten."

I frowned.

"It's too much," Prasutagus said, misreading my expression. "I should have told you before you agreed—"

"No. Not at all. I am only sorry the boy is upset." It saddened me to no end to know the boy was upset over my arrival. No doubt, my presence in his home undid everything he knew to be true about life just a slim year after losing his mother, followed by the death of King Antedios. Poor child. I would do my best to make it right by him. "I'm sure we'll be fast friends before long."

Prasutagus gave me a grateful smile. "It *is* too much to ask of you, but I cannot express my great relief to hear you say so."

I reached out and took his hand. "Our worlds are one now."

"Our worlds are one now."

CHAPTER 74

We made our way through the fair. While the vendors were still busy selling their wares, getting the last sales they could, most people had started packing up to leave. The fields were quiet now. The sounds of the flutes and drums had faded, the bonfires put out. Many of the camps had already been struck.

When we approached the campsite of the Northern Iceni, I noticed some commotion. Caturix's men were preparing to depart.

"Boudica," Bran called, joining us. "King Prasutagus," he said, bowing to him. "Good morrow. Ah, here is Brandywine. Cai thought you'd run off with him," Bran told Pix.

Pix simply grinned.

"Where is Cai?" I asked as I scanned the camp. A number of warriors were missing.

"Father set off for Oak Throne this morning. Belenus and some of the warriors went with them, including Cai—on my horse, thanks to Pix. Dôn will leave tomorrow. Father told me to ride with her. This band stayed with me," he said, gesturing to his warriors.

"King Aesunos has left?" Prasutagus asked.

Bran nodded. "A messenger came from Oak Throne in the night. I don't know the matter, but he left in haste before the sun rose.

"Perhaps Caturix knows..." I said, my gaze going to my elder brother.

Bran shrugged. "No one tells me anything."

Prasutagus dismounted then went and spoke to one of his men. A moment later, the man rode off. From the look in Prasutagus's eyes, I could see this news unnerved him.

"Prasutagus?"

"I have sent my men to check on the Catuvellauni."

A terrible feeling washed over me. "We should speak to Caturix."

Bran, Prasutagus, and I went to Caturix's tent. Melusine rose when we entered.

"Ah, here is the happy bride and groom," she said, reaching out for me. She gave me a quick embrace then turned to Prasutagus. "I am Princess Melusine, daughter of King Volisios of the Coritani, wife of Caturix."

"I am glad to meet you, Princess."

Caturix joined us. "King Prasutagus. Boudica," he said.

"Father has gone back to Oak Throne?" I said to my brother, waiting to see the expression on his face.

"He rode out at first light," Caturix replied.

"Why?"

Caturix frowned, then said, "I don't know the full matter." Caturix's lips twisted as he warred within himself, unsure of how much to say. "Before he left, Father woke me and told me to ride back to Stonea in the morning and wait for word from him."

"Word of what?" I asked.

"He would not say. He told me to go back, that's all."

I turned to Prasutagus who crossed his arms, a dark expression on his face.

"Did Father say anything about Prasutagus? Or...or the Catuvellauni?"

Caturix's gaze flicked from Prasutagus to me. "No."

A moment later, the flap of the tent opened to reveal Brenna. "Here you all are," she said. Her cheeks were flushed, and she had an excited expression on her face. "The party from Mona will leave any moment now. I hoped you'd come back in time to say farewell."

Bear rushed in behind her, the small dog barking at us in welcome.

I looked to Caturix, who gestured for me to say nothing more for the moment.

"Brenna," I said with a smile, turning to her.

Brenna studied my face. "Is anything the matter? I feel like I've caught you all in the middle of something important."

"No. Nothing is the matter," Caturix reassured her.

"It is a long way to Mona," Prasutagus told Brenna. "Is there anything you need? I can have someone fetch you food, drink—anything you may want."

Brenna shook her head. "Thank you, King Prasutagus. No. I have this little ruffian," she said, lifting Bear and putting a kiss on his head. "And my lyre. What else could I possibly need? I should get back, but I didn't want to leave without saying goodbye. Where is Father?"

Caturix stiffened, then said, "He returned to Oak Throne."

"Already? Was he feeling all right?"

Caturix gave her a curt nod.

"Oh," Brenna said, a hurt and confused expression on her face. "I...I'm sorry I was not able to say goodbye," she said, then paused, mastering her feelings. "You will wish him well for me," she told Bran, who nodded.

"Safe riding, Sister," Bran said, pulling Brenna into an embrace. "I wish you good fortune in your studies and hope we see you again soon."

"Thank you, Brother."

"I can't wait to hear your music when we see you next," Melusine said, embracing Brenna. "Be well, Brenna. May the Maiden keep you safe."

"And you, Sister."

Brenna reached out for Caturix's hand.

"I wish you well, Sister," he told her, kissing her hand.

Brenna nodded to him.

"I'll walk with you back to the druids," I told Brenna, then turned to Prasutagus. "I'll rejoin you shortly."

He nodded.

Brenna and I made our way back outside. Overhead, dark clouds had started rolling in. I could smell rain in the air.

"I'm glad Riona insisted on a cloak and cap," Brenna said, eyeing the skyline.

"It is a long ride to Mona."

Brenna nodded. "Riv is waiting with the druids. We will ride the countryside then take a barge to the island. I can't wait to see it. There has been such a strange turn of events. I can barely get my mind to accept it. How unlikely."

"Andraste moved us where she wanted."

Brenna nodded. "Then may we both serve her well."

The party of druids waited on the other side of the Yare. Brenna and I crossed the bridge, joining them. There were half a dozen wagons between them and many riders on horseback.

"Boudica, is everything all right?" Brenna asked, looking behind us toward the tents. "It's strange that Father left already, and Caturix looked upset."

"When isn't Caturix upset?"

"I know. It's just…"

I struggled with whether or not to tell Brenna the truth. The last time I'd lied to her, we'd both suffered as a result. Remembering that, I said, "The truth is, we don't know why Father returned home in haste. He ordered Caturix to return to Stonea."

"Do you think… You don't think Father is planning something, do you? Or maybe something has happened?"

"He wouldn't tell Caturix. I don't know what's happened."

"Why didn't Caturix just tell me that?"

"He didn't want you to worry. You should focus on your new life now. The druids are beyond tribal squabbles and petty arguments. You are part of their world now."

"But you are my family."

I took Brenna's hand. "The gods have called you, Sister. Take your opportunity. We are your family, but a new life is waiting for you."

Brenna kissed me on my cheek. "That may be, but you are still my family. If there is anything the matter, send a rider. Promise me."

"I promise. There will be no more secrets between us ever again."

Brenna smiled. "Good. May the gods keep you, Boudica. And Prasutagus."

"And may Epona see that Riv is sure of foot on the long ride, and you safe."

"Brenna?" Selwyn called, gesturing for my sister to come.

I waved to the druidess, who inclined her head to me.

"I love you," I told Brenna.

"I love you too." Giving my hand one last squeeze, Brenna departed, Bear rushing off behind her.

I stood on the rise, watching as the druids loaded into their carts to depart for their island once more.

"Just like before," a voice said from beside me. I turned to find Pix there chewing on a lamb chop. Where did she find that?

"How so?"

"The druids..." she said, her mouth full. "They are this land's best weapon."

I ruminated on her words as I watched Brenna mount Riv then depart with the others. While I should be happy for my sister, a terrible sense of foreboding held me.

Overhead, the sky rumbled.

"Bel is done. Now, Taranus rules the skies. His wheel is turning. His chariot rolls across the sky, getting into place once more."

"In place for what?"

Pix shrugged. "War."

CHAPTER 75

After seeing Brenna off, Pix and I rejoined the others. As we approached Prasutagus, I was surprised to see another party riding toward us—King Caratacus and King Togodumnus. With them was the messenger Prasutagus had sent into the crowd. The kings spoke briefly to one another then everyone stepped into Caturix's tent.

Caturix met my gaze.

Pix and I picked up our step then hurried behind them.

Bran and Melusine followed us.

When I entered, King Caratacus was speaking, "For months now, the chieftain has been campaigning war against you," he told Prasutagus. "We've known you a long time, Prasutagus. You are a good friend and ally to those around you. The Greater Iceni have never had a reason to fear my brother or me."

"He visited you yesterday?"

Togodumnus nodded. "He told us he disapproved of your marriage," he said, his eyes flicking to me for a moment. "The chieftain had promised Boudica to my brother."

"Who promised? Chieftain Saenunos or our father?" Caturix asked.

"The chieftain," Togodumnus replied. "And even after the confusion was revealed, the chieftain guaranteed Caratacus that the marriage would happen no matter what transpired—as long as we were with him."

"With him in what?" I asked.

King Caratacus turned to me. "That is the question, isn't it, dapple-grey? Your uncle left here in quite a hurry yesterday. He insisted he'd send word soon."

I turned to Caturix. "Father said nothing more about why he left?"

My brother shook his head.

"We need to ride north," I told Prasutagus.

I turned to Caturix, who nodded then said, "I'll gather my men." He turned to go, but then his gaze went to Melusine. He paused a moment.

"Princess Melusine, I will have my men escort you to Venta if you don't mind staying with us," Prasutagus said.

Melusine inclined her head to him. "Yes. Thank you."

"Thank you, King Prasutagus," Caturix said, then left.

"Boudica," Bran said, uncertainty in his voice.

"Stay with Dôn," I advised.

King Caratacus chuckled. "I see now what in-law troubles I escaped. Prasutagus, I assure you, we only sought an alliance with the Northern Iceni. Nothing more. Anything else the chieftain dreamed up was entirely from his own imagination. Our ambitions lie elsewhere."

Prasutagus nodded, but I didn't feel so sure about Caratacus's honesty.

"We should go," Togodumnus told his brother, then turned to Prasutagus. "I'm sorry we can't be of more help. We just struck camp and are preparing to ride south in search of your rumors. But if you need us…"

"No. We will see this matter settled. May the gods be with you. And may you find *nothing* in the south," Prasutagus said.

"May Cernunnos hear your words," Caratacus agreed, then turned to me. "Dapple-grey," he said, inclining his head.

"Blue dun," I replied.

And with that, the kings departed.

"I don't like this," Prasutagus told us. "I'll send for my warband. We'll ride north at once."

I nodded, but his words did little to ease me. Something told me I needed to get to Oak Throne as quickly as possible.

WITHIN THE HOUR, WE WERE READY TO GO.

"I should come," Bran told me.

I shook my head. "Keep Dôn safe until we can find out what is happening."

"Do you trust those Catuvellauni kings? They could be lying. For all you know, they are trying to get you to leave Venta unguarded."

"Then it's a good thing you're here."

Bran frowned.

"No, I don't trust them. But something is amiss here. I don't know what to think."

We were just preparing to ride out when we saw a rider thundering through the crowd toward us. I recognized the horse first, then the bloodied man upon it.

"Cai… it's Cai," I said, turning to Caturix.

Cai pulled Bran's horse to a stop. The beast was lathered and breathing hard, his eyes wide.

"Cai. What's happened?" Caturix asked.

"Saenunos's men attacked us on the road. The king..."

"The king what?" Caturix asked.

Bran joined us, looking up at his friend.

"Prince Caturix... the king, your father, was killed, and the druid, Belenus. We were outnumbered five to one. We fought to protect the king, but we were overwhelmed. I only managed to escape because Bran's horse is so swift," he said, then turned to Bran and me. "I'm so sorry. I...I couldn't get to him in time."

It felt like someone had punched me in the stomach. "You're sure it was Saenunos's men?"

Cai nodded.

"As I feared," Prasutagus said, then turned to the warrior beside him. "We'll ride north with the warband. Return to Venta. Rally the rest of the men. Tell them to make haste and meet us on the road to Oak Throne. We will wait for them at the river."

The man nodded then hurried off.

I turned to my elder brother. "Saenunos has taken Oak Throne," I said, my voice shaking.

"For now," Caturix replied, then mounted his horse.

Bran spoke a few words to Cai, then grabbed another horse, joining us. "Cai will carry the news to Dôn and watch over the priestesses. Our father is dead. I will not sit here waiting idly while our uncle takes everything from us."

I nodded to him. "May Andraste have mercy on Saenunos, because I will not."

CHAPTER 76

W e rode out at once, Caturix and Bran at the head, Prasutagus and I riding behind them.

How had it come to this?

Saenunos's ambition had never been a secret, but to kill his own brother? What did he think would happen next?

The answer was clear.

He thought Caratacus and Togodumnus were behind him. With the powerful Catuvellauni brothers as his allies, his plans became clear: kill father, attack Prasutagus, force me into a marriage with Caratacus to firm the alliance—or worse, force Brenna to return to do so. Become king of the Northern Iceni.

As we rode away from Venta, worry nagged at me. Caratacus and Togodumnus had vast armies. If they were lying about riding south...

It was a day's ride from Oak Throne to Venta. If Father had been ambushed and defeated on the road, that meant Saenunos's forces had likely already taken Oak Throne. He would have been able to ride into the fort without any resistance, only to slaughter anyone who stood in the way.

I gripped my reins more tightly. How many people would die? The household staff? The guards? The warriors? The common people? The children? Ula?

And my father…

I couldn't think about it now. I couldn't let myself feel. Father and Belenus were dead. The druid had been like family to us. Now…

No.

I would not let this happen.

Andraste.

Dark Lady.

Help me. Help me make him pay.

A short time later, we arrived at the banks of the Stiffkey.

"Water the horses," Caturix called to the others. "But watch your backs."

I clicked to Druda, coaxing him toward the river, but he resisted. Instead, his ears were turned toward the forest. His nostrils were flaring as he watched.

"Prasutagus," I said, following the horse's gaze.

Prasutagus took in the situation then followed my glance.

A moment later, a party appeared at the edge of the woods.

"There!" one of Prasutagus's men called. "At the edge of the forest."

Prasutagus's men turned toward the party. Prasutagus turned to ride out. I went to join him, but then, Druda whined.

A moment later, I heard a familiar whinny in reply.

"Mountain," I whispered. "Prasutagus. Hold! You men, hold!" I called then reined Druda in to join the others.

"Who is it?" Prasutagus asked.

"Lynet, the chieftain of Frog's Hollow and her people."

We rode on to meet them.

"Boudica," Lynet called, trotting to meet me.

Mountain called to Druda once more, my horse responding in kind.

"Lynet, are you all right? Frog's Hollow…"

"We're fine. We're all fine. The news came from Oak Throne," she said, her gaze shifting from me to my brothers to King Prasutagus. "Saenunos has taken the fort. The gates are closed. We don't know what is happening inside."

"My father was killed on the road."

Lynet nodded. "So we learned. I've had people watching the roads to the south, waiting for you," she told us. "We've come to help. You cannot follow the road north. Spies are waiting."

"We'll pass through the forest," Caturix said.

Lynet nodded. "Very well."

"My men are coming to reinforce us. They should be here any moment," Prasutagus told her.

"Lynet, this is King Prasutagus. Prasutagus, this is Chieftain Lynet," I said.

Prasutagus lifted his hands to his forehead in honor. "You are a sister of the isle of mist."

Lynet returned the gesture. "The druid king. I am honored to meet you. I am only sorry it is under such difficult circumstances."

Prasutagus gave her a soft smile.

My stomach felt ill. Too much was happening. And in the middle of it, how could I explain to Lynet I had wed this man?

We returned to the river to water the horses while we waited for Prasutagus's men. It wasn't long before the thunder of hooves could be heard on the road behind us.

"King Prasutagus," the lead warrior said, joining us.

"Water the horses. Quickly," Prasutagus told him, then turned to Caturix and me. "We'll be ready soon."

"Boudica," Bran said, joining us. "If Saenunos has taken Oak Throne… The people…"

I nodded, a sick feeling in my stomach.

My gaze went to Caturix.

My elder brother met my glance. He said nothing, but I knew where his mind was: Kennocha and Mara.

Bran frowned. "We have no idea what allies Saenunos has. He has always been close with the Coritani. Do you think they have played into this? Your marriage," he said, turning to Caturix. "What if this was all part of his plan to grab power? Perhaps the raiders who killed Gaheris and the others were Coritani after all. We could be walking into a trap."

Prasutagus nodded. "Bran is right to be cautious."

"Whatever plans our uncle was making, he did not expect Boudica to suddenly be wed to you," Caturix told Prasutagus. "His departure was hasty. He was in a panic. Let's hope the Catuvellauni told us the truth. Otherwise, we have no idea what has been unleashed upon us all."

I felt Lynet's eyes on me.

Prasutagus surveyed his men. "I think we are ready, Prince Caturix."

Caturix left to collect the others, Bran following him.

I turned to Lynet.

We held one another's gaze.

Reading the moment, Prasutagus clicked to his horse. "I will rouse the men," he said, then rode off.

"You have wed the king of the Greater Iceni," Lynet said.

I swallowed hard then nodded. "Against all odds, my heart was moved again."

Lynet reached out and took my hand. "He's an old soul—just like you. I can see it is a good match."

"Lynet—"

"Say nothing more, Boudica. Gaheris would not want you to mourn him forever. I wish all the happiness this world can offer. Now, come. Wicked deeds are afoot. It is up to us to set things right again."

CHAPTER 77

Caturix and Lynet leading the way, we disappeared into the forest, following one of the old paths back to Oak Throne. I had taken this way myself many times. It was good for hunting—animals and herbs—if a person had the inclination. More than once, I had followed Ula this way.

I cast my gaze in the direction of the fort.

My father was dead.

Belenus was dead.

If anything had happened to Ula, I would rip Saenunos's eyes from their sockets and wear them for earrings.

It was dusk as we neared the fort. Two great plumes of smoke appeared on the horizon. Something was burning. Caturix, Bran, Lynet, Prasutagus, and I dismounted, Pix following along behind us. Leaving our horses behind, we worked our way to the edge of the forest.

The gate to the fort was closed, and some guards were milling about on palisades, but they were not our guards. They were Saenunos's men.

"We need a closer look," Lynet said, then moved to go, but Pix set her hand on Lynet's arm.

"I'll go."

Lynet looked at Pix, a curious expression on her face. "Who…" she began to ask, then uttered a soft gasp.

Pix winked at her.

But before Pix could leave, an unlikely feathered creature appeared on the horizon, making its way to us. I watched as the bird flew straight toward us.

"Morfran," I said, then held out my arm. "Morfran." The raven flew to me, settling in on my arm. He was holding a bit of moss in his beak. He dropped it into my hand.

"Boudica, come. Boudica, come," the raven chatted at me.

I stroked his head, smoothing his feathers. "Morfran."

"Boudica, come. Boudica, come."

I turned and looked back at the fort.

"There is no easy way to take the fort, not with the gate closed. We need to get inside and get that gate open," I said.

"What if Lynet takes a small party," Bran suggested. "Saenunos may not suspect her. He may open the gate to her."

"Boudica, come. Boudica, come," Morfran said, hopping up and down on my arm.

"Too risky," Caturix said. "There has to be another way."

"Boudica, come. Boudica, come."

I studied the bird, reflecting on its words. "There is… There is another way."

"What do you mean?" Caturix asked.

I eyed my brother hesitantly, then said. "There is a secret entrance into the fort."

Everyone turned to look at me. "What? Where?" Bran asked.

"The old, dry well just behind Ula's cottage. You can travel from the well to the mossy forest. There is a small network of caves below Oak Throne. We can take a party. We'll enter through the secret entrance, subdue the guards, and then open the gates."

"Why didn't you ever tell us about the secret entrance?" Caturix asked, looking annoyed.

"I just learned of it myself," I replied tartly, then turned back to the fort once more.

"Boudica, come. Boudica, come."

I snatched an oak leaf from one of the nearby trees and gave it to Morfran. "To Ula. Take this to Ula. To Ula."

With the leaf in its beak, the bird flew back to the fort.

"All right," Caturix said. "Boudica and Bran can lead a party through the mossy forest. Prasutagus, Lynet, and I will wait for your signal. Agreed?"

I nodded then turned to Prasutagus, who was grinning at me. "What is it?"

"You are full of surprises."

"I'm just getting started."

He chuckled lightly.

Bran went back to his warriors and gathered a dozen men. After a moment, they rejoined us.

"Boudica, are you sure?" Bran asked nervously. "The mossy forest…"

Bran's gaze and the looks on the faces of the others told me the problem. Everyone knew the stories about the place.

"What's the worst that can happen?" I asked.

"You disappear into the Otherworld for a hundred years. Don't eat or drink anything. That was my mistake," Pix said with a grin.

I frowned at her. "You're not helping." I turned back to the others. "It will be all right. It's just a narrow cave, nothing more. All right. Let's go."

"Boudica," Prasutagus said, leaving the rest of his words unspoken.

I winked at him, then turned and made my way into the woods, the others, including Bran and Pix, following along behind me.

"If I get kidnapped by the little people of the hollow hills, I'll never forgive you," Bran told me.

"Brother, if this doesn't work, I'll never forgive myself."

Pix turned to us. When she did so, her eyes cast a mirror-like reflection. "I'll scout ahead," she told me.

"You don't even know where you're going."

"Ah, greenwood queen, how little you still understand of magic," she said, then headed off, disappearing into the darkness.

"Where did she go?" Bran asked.

Ahead of us, I heard the light yip of a fox.

Bran looked at me.

I shrugged.

"Only you would make a friend out of someone from the Otherworld."

"She's not from the Otherworld. She's from the past, remember?"

"So she told me. Either way…"

With that, I laughed lightly as we continued into the darkness and the mossy wood.

CHAPTER 78

Padding through the darkness, we made our way to the mossy wood.

"Fey place," one of Bran's men whispered. "We'll all disappear in here."

He wasn't wrong to be cautious. Even Ula had warned me against going into the mossy wood at night—although she never hesitated to come here for night-growing mushrooms, herbs, or flowers. Under the light of the moon, we made our way over the blanket of moss and under the broad limbs of the oak and ash trees.

Every rustle and snapping twig in the forest sent my nerves on edge.

I couldn't hear what was happening in the fort, but I could feel the waves of despair. And more, I felt rage. When I got my hands on Saenunos, that would be the end of him.

I nearly fainted when Pix appeared once more, stepping out from behind the trees. "The forest is clear. There is nothing human here."

"Nothing human?" Bran asked her.

Pix shrugged.

Bran gave a nervous laugh.

Winding around the trees, we made our way to the hidden, narrow glen that concealed the cave entrance. I paused before it.

"Make no turns into the smaller tunnels. Stay left the whole way. When we reach the bottom of the well, you have to climb up. It's as good as any ladder. If old Ula can make it, so can you."

I looked at Bran.

"I'll take the rear," he told me.

I nodded then moved to enter the cave.

"It's an inauspicious time to travel through such a place," Pix said in warning.

"Good thing I have my protector with me," I told her.

"I'm here to fight Romans, not the little people of the hollow hills."

I pushed aside the cascade of ivy and entered the darkness, pausing at the entrance to grab the torch and tinder box. Pix sparked the fire, lighting the torch for me. We lit two others, passing them down the line. I wound through the narrow rocks. The flecks of silver in the stones shimmered under the torchlight. Once more, I got the strange, uneasy feeling of eyes upon me. As I made my way, passing the small off-shoots from the main tunnel, I could feel the eyes of the Otherworld upon me.

I touched the amulet hanging from my neck. Pix was right to warn us against coming in here. As it was, we were still in the hours just past Beltane. The hair on the back of my neck rose.

A soft, feminine voice called to me, the sound of my name echoing almost like trickling water somewhere in one of the smaller caves.

"Boudica…

"Boudica…"

"The greenwood is calling you," Pix whispered to me.

"You hear it too?"

"Yes. Pay it no heed. They will distract you from your task."

"Queen of the greenwood…

"Champion of the greenwood…

"Boudica…"

Intent on getting into the fort, I made my way forward. The deep, rich smell of the cavern, smelling like mud, minerals, and earth, filled my nose. I kept my gaze ahead into the darkness. The voices of the greenwood fell away. But from the darkness of the smaller cracks and crevices in the cave, I sensed something darker, something older, something different…

"The little people of the hollow hills are watching," I told Pix.

"Yes," she told me. "No doubt they wonder what we are about."

"Just passing through," I said, directing my voice ahead. "Just passing through."

Ahead of me in the darkness, I sensed movement. My torchlight spotted a small figure darting into a side tunnel, seeing only the slightest of glimpses for a scant moment.

"Did you see that?" I whispered to Pix.

"I did. You must leave them a gift. You must show them you mean no harm, or we will never reach the end of this place."

When we reached the section of the cave where I'd seen

movement, I slowed. There was a narrow gap in the wall close to my feet, a crack running from my knee downward.

I stopped.

For a brief moment, I touched the frog necklace on my chest, but I couldn't part with it. Instead, I pulled out the bag of silver I'd won at the horse race. Kneeling, I left it at the entrance to the offshoot cave. "A thanks for our passage," I said, then looked up at Pix and the men following her.

I nodded to Pix, who dug into her boot, pulling out a small knife.

"Thank you for allowing us passage," she said, adding the knife to my pouch of silver.

Behind us, the others watched. Understanding our meaning, they began pulling off charms, digging for coins or other goods, and prepared to do the same. Apparently, I wasn't the only one feeling the eyes of the little people on me.

I met Pix's gaze, and we continued on.

Soon, I caught the scent of fresh air.

Winding around the rocks, we finally came to the bottom of the well. Beams of moonlight shimmered down, casting a blue hue on everything. I listened for a moment but heard nothing.

"Wait for me here," I told them then turned, grabbing a handful of rock, and climbed up.

CHAPTER 79

I slipped out of the well, landing on the soft ground at the side. The fort was quiet. Something near the roundhouse was on fire, as well as something deeper in the village closer to the gate. Creeping low, I slipped through the darkness to Ula's door.

It was unlocked.

Opening it slowly, I went inside.

"Boudica, come. Boudica, come," Morfran called the moment he saw me.

Ula was sitting on the ground before her firepit. Bones, roots, feathers, and stones were cast before her. She looked up. "Boudica," she said, a deep sense of relief in her voice.

The sound surprised me.

She rose. "You alone?"

I shook my head. "We came by way of the well. The others are waiting below. King Prasutagus's forces and the warriors of Frog's Hollow are waiting in the woods with Caturix. I need to get the gate open."

"Saenunos has taken the place. They say your father is

dead."

I nodded, feeling a lump in my throat. "I have heard but have not seen. He and Belenus…"

Ula clenched her jaw hard, and the muscles under her eyes trembled. "Many good men died today, including the men of Oak Throne who died defending this fort—some of whom I brought into this world. I told you that you should have poisoned him."

"You weren't wrong."

"If you hadn't gotten here by morning, I would have done so anyway," Ula said then clicked her tongue as she thought. "He has men on the wall and at the gate, but only a handful of people patrolling the village. The rest are at the fort eating your father's stores and harrying Cidna to a fright."

I felt a terrible rage wash up in me. "I'll get the others. We'll get the gates open."

Slipping outside her small hut, Ula and I went to the well. I whistled to the others, letting them know it was safe to come out.

Standing with my spear at the ready, I kept watch, but no one came to this tiny, forgotten corner of Oak Throne.

After a few moments, everyone climbed out.

I scanned over our party—all persons accounted for. We hadn't lost anyone to the fey or the little people of the hollow hills. Yet.

"Half of us can go around Bodyn's roundhouse and up the west stairs," Bran whispered. "The palisade walls are higher there, easier to go undetected. The other half will have to work their way to the gates."

"Wait," Ula said then stepped forward. "It's a clear night. The moon will reveal you, and you'll all be dead before you can get those gates open."

"What should we—" I started to asked when Ula looked back and shushed me, a scolding expression on her face.

Behind me, some of the warriors chuckled—it seemed we all knew Ula well.

Ula stepped toward the edge of her property and faced the wall. She raised her hands into the air and began speaking in a language I didn't understand.

My skin rose in gooseflesh. The air seemed to shiver, and that strange sense of magic filled the air. It felt charged, like the shuddering discontent you felt when lightning struck too close. A soft wind blew, shaking the talismans hanging on the front eve of Ula's small house.

Then, the mist began to roll in.

Moving like a living thing, it rolled over the walls like a wave of water and began to cover the entire fort in fog.

"The old magic," Pix whispered.

We stood watching until the bank of mist covered the entire fort.

Ula lowered her arms then staggered a little.

I hurried to her, taking her arm.

"Used to be easier," she said with a soft chuckle.

"Back on Avallach?" I asked, raising an eyebrow at her.

"Nosey girl," she said. "Mind your own business," she told me then pinched my cheek—hard.

She laughed then righted herself. "Now go on. The fog doesn't have all night to wait on your beck and call."

I turned back to Bran. "Pix and I can lead a group to the gate."

"I'll clear the wall. Watch yourself, Sister."

"And you," I said then turned back to the men.

A handful of warriors joined me, the rest going with Bran.

I turned back to Ula.

"May the gods go with you, girl," she said then gestured for me to go on.

At that, I turned and headed into the night.

WORKING OUR WAY THROUGH THE MIST, WE WOVE BETWEEN roundhouses, grain stands, and animal pens to the gate. We turned down a lane only to catch the sound of voices farther down the row.

"It rose up off the river just like that. Such a strange mist," one of the men said.

I pointed to the others to go the other direction, slipping around the leatherworker's shed.

The back door of the place opened, revealing little Phelan. The boy looked startled.

I lifted my finger to my lips, silencing him, then motioned for him to go back inside.

The boy nodded to me then slipped back inside.

His father was one of the strongest men in the village.

I knew from Phelan's red, puffy eyes, the man had not survived the day.

Gripping my spear hard, I willed my rage to be still. But my heart pounded in my chest. Ula was right. Good, innocent people had died today—not just my father, Belenus, or the warriors who'd ridden with him, but the people of Oak Throne. Saenunos had killed his own—the Northern Iceni—to seize power.

Fury washed over me, and I quickened my step.

When we arrived at the gate, we found it guarded by a dozen men. The fog was dense, but their torchlights revealed their numbers. They stood in a crowd, laughing, joking, and talking about the strange mist.

Crouching behind a shed, we watched.

I turned back to the men with me, faces I knew well.

"Archers first. We will take them unaware," I said, gesturing to Davin and Gwri. "Make ready."

The two men got into position. They nocked their arrows, nodded to one another, then began.

The arrows flew silently through the misty air, the first striking one of Saenunos's men in the back, the other in the throat.

The guards paused, shaken by the sudden assault, then realization washed over them.

"We're under attack," of the men said loudly then moved to grab a horn.

"Gwri," I called.

The archer took aim, stopping the man before he could call for reinforcements.

"Now," I called to the others, and we rushed the party. Spinning my spear, I entered the fray. Saenunos's warriors, taken by surprise, reacted clumsily.

One of Saenunos's men, a warrior twice my size, pulled his sword and rushed at me. I firmed my stance and thrust my spear at him, jabbing him through the throat.

The man stopped cold, then his eyes rolled back.

I pulled my spear back, blood gushing as I did so.

The warrior fell.

Gripping my spear hard, I turned once more to engage another warrior. And then another. And then another. The skirmish became a blur as I simply moved, my spear firm in my grip. Pix, fighting with dual blades, cut her way through the warriors.

Additional soldiers streamed down from the palisades, but there were few and the archers worked quickly picking them off.

A moment later, I saw Bran and the others on the wall.

"We have them," Bran called to me. "Open the gates!"

We rushed forward, darting around the final fighting pairs and stepping over bodies. Working with the others, we moved the heavy brace from the gates. Another pair of warriors turned the crank, swinging the gates wide open.

On the rampart above the gate, Bran grabbed a torch and began swaying it back and forth, signaling to Prasutagus and the others.

But from the roundhouse, the sound of alarm rang out.

Someone had gotten the news to Saenunos.

But it didn't matter. The sound of horse hooves pounding across the land echoed in the mist.

"Clear the way," I said, motioning for the others to step aside.

Bran rushed down the stairs, joining me.

I grabbed his arm. "Saenunos is a coward. He will not leave the safety of the roundhouse."

My brother nodded.

Motioning to the men around us, we retreated back into the village. Hiding between the buildings, we watched as Saenunos's men rushed toward the gate. But they would be too few and too late.

We were halfway there when I heard someone shout. "It's Prasutagus! It's King Prasutagus!"

A smirk lit up my face. It was not Prasutagus they had to fear. Given the rage in Caturix's eyes, my brother was going to take great pleasure in punishing those who had killed Belenus and our father—as would I.

We passed the great oak and rushed toward the hall. When we arrived, we found half a dozen warriors guarding the door. Not waiting, we rushed them.

Pix screamed loudly then attacked, her blades working like whirlwinds. A dagger in one hand, a sword in the other, Bran launched at the men.

Seeing the others had the matter well in hand, I dodged around the back of the roundhouse toward the kitchens. There, I found Nini sitting outside. The dog whimpered nervously when she saw me.

"It's all right, Nini. It's okay," I whispered to her then slipped into the kitchen.

Inside, I found Cidna standing at her workbench. She stood frozen, her gaze toward the dining hall.

"Cidna," I whispered.

"Boudica," she said in a gasp, turning to me.

I suppressed a gasp when I saw her blackened eye and reddened cheek.

"Where is he?" I whispered.

"Dining hall," she said, pointing. "Two men with him."

"Bran's at the door. Caturix is coming with a warband."

Cidna grabbed the biggest knife she had sitting on her bench. "That's good enough for me."

I nodded to her, and then the two of us worked our way quietly toward the dining hall.

"Let them try to get in," Saenunos called with a laugh. "They will see! They will all see!"

I pointed to the man standing closest to the kitchens. His back was turned. I gestured from him to Cidna.

She nodded.

Lifting my spear, I took aim at the man across the room then nodded to Cidna. "Now," I whispered.

I sent my spear flying across the small space. The impact knocked Saenunos's warrior off his feet. He slammed against the wall, the spear piercing his heart.

Cidna grabbed the other warrior by his hair then slid her kitchen knife across the man's throat, dropping him to the floor.

Saenunos rose just as another warrior burst into the hall.

"Chieftain! It's Prasutagus and Aesunos's sons!" the man yelled.

Saenunos looked around wildly. "Prasutagus? How? How!"

The warrior stopped mid-step. Before he could say another word, blood gurgled from his mouth. He fell to reveal Bran behind him.

His eyes bulging, Saenunos looked from Bran to me.

"You red-haired strumpet," he said, pointing. His finger shook as he spoke. "This was your doing. You are a curse upon your family!"

Bran rushed across the room and grabbed Saenunos by the neck. "You will pay for what you have done. Why? Why would you do this? Your own brother... You would be king soon enough."

Saenunos sneered. "Because of her," he said, looking at me. "She has ruined everything!"

Caturix and Prasutagus rushed into the room.

"You," Saenunos hissed at Prasutagus. "What are you doing here?"

"Explain yourself. What do you mean?" Bran asked, giving our uncle a hard shake.

"Caratacus. Togodumnus. They said..."

I looked from Saenunos to Prasutagus.

Prasutagus studied my uncle for a moment then said,

"They said what? That they were your allies? That they would attack the Greater Iceni, crushing my people, then hand the throne of all of the Iceni to you?"

"You…they…"

"You killed your own brother—our father—in this sloppy, half-baked plan to make yourself king of all the Iceni?" Caturix asked, his voice dark. "Did you not think I would come for you?"

"Togodumnus and Caratacus rode south to the Regnenses," Prasutagus told Saenunos. "Whatever you thought was going to happen isn't going to occur."

"You killed our father for this? You killed the good people of Oak Throne for nothing?" I spat at Saenunos.

I turned to Caturix.

The rage on my brother's face was unmistakable. His brow deeply furrowed, his eyes dark, he pulled his dagger from his belt and crossed the room.

Bran let Saenunos go and stepped out of the way.

"Caturix… I made you a strong ally to the Coritani. You will be king after me. I have no son. You are like a son to me. I settled everything so that we both have strong alliances in the future and—"

But Saenunos didn't get to speak another word. Striking like lightning, Caturix slid his blade across Saenunos's throat.

Saenunos's eyes went wide, then blood dripped down his neck. A moment later, he toppled over.

Caturix stood motionless for a long moment, then let out a long, slow breath.

"May the gods be praised. The chieftain is dead. Long live the king," Cidna said in a shaky breath.

"Long live the king," we called in reply.

CHAPTER 80

We left the roundhouse, joining the other warriors out front. Lynet, a smear of blood on her cheek, stood cleaning her blade.

"It's done," I told her.

She nodded. "Good. It is as the gods will, Boudica."

I set my hand on her arm, smiling at her with gratitude. Even though she had not become my mother-in-law, I was eternally thankful for her presence.

"Where is our father's body?" Bran asked the others.

Those who had gathered shook their heads. They didn't know.

Cidna stepped forward. "We put him around back in the storage shed," she told us. "Saenunos's men dumped him and Belenus with the other bodies to be burned in the morning. People have been collecting their kin all night. We servants brought Belenus and Aesunos back to be readied for the pyre."

"Oh, Cidna," I said, sorrow and gratitude swelling in tandem in my stomach.

"I'll collect them," Bran said, a pinch of pain in his voice.

Caturix turned to the crowd. Alongside Prasutagus's and Lynet's warriors, others from Oak Throne had come. After a moment's hesitation, Caturix stepped forward. "The fort is safe now," he called in a loud voice. "We shall ready the pyres ourselves and send our dead to the Otherworld in a manner befitting of our people—my father and Belenus included."

"May the gods bless you, Prince Caturix," someone called.

"Thank you, Prince Caturix."

"Our prince—our king."

"Thanks belongs to Chieftain Lynet and King Prasutagus as well," Caturix said, turning to them.

Murmurs of thanks went through the crowd.

Caturix left us to join Bran.

I turned to Prasutagus. "Saenunos... He was an overly ambitious and foolish man, but his words about the Catuvellauni have me worried. Riding here, we have left Venta exposed."

Prasutagus frowned. "The thought also occurred to me."

"Could this be a trap? Do you trust the word of Caratacus and Togodumnus?"

"Not entirely."

"Nor I. My family, my people, they need us here, but I don't know... Either Saenunos bungled all of this himself, or there was some half-truth to what he said."

Prasutagus nodded. "My men need some rest, then we should ride back to Venta. A half-truth is still a dangerous thing. Something tells me that if Caratacus and Togodumnus saw an easy way to take all of the Iceni territories, they would. There may have been some truth to the chieftain's words after all."

I nodded.

I turned then, seeing Bran and Caturix returning with two small carts. On them were Belenus and my father.

Prasutagus and I joined my brothers.

"We washed the bodies, tried to prepare them as best we could," Cidna said, joining us.

I went first to my father. He had been redressed in his robes, his hair combed. His skin had an odd shade of blue all about the edges.

As I stared down at him, a sad realization washed over me. Our last words had been harsh. My father had cursed me—and the Dark Lady Andraste.

Now, he was dead.

"Oh, Father," I whispered. "How rash."

I set my hand on his for a moment, then went to Belenus.

The druid had a nasty wound on his throat, but it had been sewn closed. I smelled the scents of rosemary and lemon balm on him. As with my father, he had been nicely redressed.

Ula appeared beside me, looking down at him.

"It's a sorry thing," she said. "Old as he was, he still had more to do."

"He was always there for us. For as long as I can remember…"

"Of course he was. He was your grandfather," Ula said matter-of-factly.

Bran and Caturix, who had been standing nearby, turned and looked at her.

"What did you just say?" Caturix asked.

"Don't scowl at me, boy. King or not, I'll not have it," Ula told him waspishly.

Caturix softened his gaze.

"Ula, what do you mean?" I asked.

"Damara was the daughter of Rian and Belenus. Belenus was your grandfather."

"How do you—Belenus said Damara was the child of a greenwood marriage."

"So she was, between the Arch Druidess Rian and Belenus. A man and woman still know each other, even skyclad by the light of the bonfires," Ula said with a chuckle. "Belenus could not claim Damara, but he knew."

"Why didn't he tell us?" Bran asked.

"Young people don't need to know everything."

I set my hand on Belenus's shoulder. "I am so sorry I didn't know," I whispered. "You will be missed." Tears welled in my eyes. After a long moment, I turned to Ula. "How did *you* know?"

Ula grinned at me then tapped the side of her nose.

Behind us, Pix chuckled.

Ula turned and looked at her. "You're in the wrong place," she told Pix.

"So are you."

At that, Ula laughed. Pix joined her, pointing knowingly at Ula. But neither said another word.

Turning back, I looked at Bran, who had a sorrowful expression on his face. My gaze went from him to Caturix. My brother stared glassy-eyed at Belenus for a long moment, then looked beyond me, back into the crowd. His eyes searched the party gathered there.

I looked back.

She wasn't there.

Not saying another word, Caturix left us then went into the village.

I turned to Prasutagus.

"It is a sorrowful day when such wise men leave this world," he said, looking down at Belenus.

"Let me go and get some ale for the others. It has been a hard day."

I had just turned to go when I spotted a rider rushing down the main thoroughfare toward us. The horse's hooves were flying. I didn't recognize the man, but from the color of his cape, I understood him to be from the Greater Iceni.

I turned to Prasutagus, whose gaze hardened. He stepped toward the rider.

Had the Catuvellauni attacked Venta?

One of the warriors of Oak Thone met the man, taking the reins of the rider's exhausted horse.

Prasutagus and I hurried across the square to meet the rider.

"King Prasutagus," the man said, bowing.

Prasutagus nodded. "What is it?"

"My king. An attack," the breathless man said.

"On Venta? Caratacus and Togodumnus—"

"No, my king. No. A messenger came from the south. Word is spreading all across our land. They've come. They've landed. Hundreds of ships. Thousands of soldiers… They've come."

"Who has come?" I asked.

The man's eyes went wide. "Rome."

To be continued in *Queen of Stone: A Novel of Boudica, The Celtic Rebels Series* book 2. Available on Amazon.

As a special thank you for purchasing a copy of *Queen of Oak: A Novel of Boudica*, please stop by this webpage for your free, bonus downloads: https://www.subscribepage.com/queenofoakpreorders

ABOUT THE AUTHOR

New York Times and *USA Today* bestselling author Melanie Karsak is the author of *The Harvesting Series, The Celtic Blood Series, Steampunk Red Riding Hood,* and *Steampunk Fairy Tales.* The author currently lives in Florida with her husband and two children.

amazon.com/author/melaniekarsak

facebook.com/authormelaniekarsak

instagram.com/karsakmelanie

pinterest.com/melaniekarsak

ALSO BY MELANIE KARSAK

THE CELTIC BLOOD SERIES:

Highland Raven

Highland Blood

Highland Vengeance

Highland Queen

THE CELTIC REBELS SERIES:

Queen of Oak: A Novel of Boudica

Queen of Stone: A Novel of Boudica

THE ROAD TO VALHALLA SERIES:

Shield-Maiden: Under the Howling Moon

Shield-Maiden: Under the Hunter's Moon

Shield-Maiden: Under the Thunder Moon

Shield-Maiden: Under the Blood Moon

Shield-Maiden: Under the Dark Moon

THE SHADOWS OF VALHALLA SERIES:

Shield-Maiden: Gambit of Blood

THE HARVESTING SERIES:

The Harvesting

Midway

The Shadow Aspect

Witch Wood

The Torn World

STEAMPUNK FAIRY TALES:

Curiouser and Curiouser: Steampunk Alice in Wonderland

Ice and Embers: Steampunk Snow Queen

Beauty and Beastly: Steampunk Beauty and the Beast

Golden Braids and Dragon Blades: Steampunk Rapunzel

STEAMPUNK RED RIDING HOOD:

Wolves and Daggers

Alphas and Airships

Peppermint and Pentacles

Bitches and Brawlers

Howls and Hallows

Lycans and Legends

THE AIRSHIP RACING CHRONICLES:

Chasing the Star Garden

Chasing the Green Fairy

Chasing Christmas Past

THE CHANCELLOR FAIRY TALES:

The Glass Mermaid

The Cupcake Witch

The Fairy Godfather

Find these books and more on Amazon!

Made in the USA
Monee, IL
24 February 2023

28616701R00350